THE BLACK MASK LIBRARY

THE EARLY YEARS (1920–26)

The Man in the Shadows: The Complete Black Mask
Cases of Terry Mack *by Carroll John Daly*

THE SHAW YEARS (1926–36)

Blood on the Curb *by Joseph T. Shaw*

Black Harvest: The Complete Black Mask
Cases of Jules Tremaine *by Norvell W. Page*

Boomerang Dice: The Complete Black Mask
Cases of Johnny Hi Gear *by Stewart Sterling*

Dead Evidence: The Complete Black Mask
Cases of Harrigan *by Ed Lybeck*

Laughing Death *by Raoul Whitfield*

Luck: The Complete Black Mask Cases of
Oscar Sail *by Lester Dent*

Murder Maze: The Complete Black Mask Cases of
Jerry Tracy, Volume 2 *by Theodore A. Tinsley*

The Price of a Dime: The Complete Black Mask
Cases of Ben Shaley *by Norbert Davis*

Somewhere in Mexico: The Complete Black Mask
Cases of Jerry Frost, Volume 1 *by Horace McCoy*

South Wind: The Complete Black Mask Cases of
Jerry Tracy, Volume 1 *by Theodore A. Tinsley*

THE LATER YEARS (1936–51)

Dead and Done For: The Complete Black Mask Cases
of Cellini Smith, Volume 1 *by Robert Reeves*

Dog Eat Dog: The Complete Black Mask Cases
of Cellini Smith, Volume 2 *by Robert Reeves*

It Happened at the Lake *by Joseph T. Shaw*

Let the Dead Alone: The Complete Black Mask Cases
of Luther McGavock, Volume 1 *by Merle Constiner*

Murder Costs Money: The Complete Black Mask
Cases of Rex Sackler, Volume 1 *by D.L. Champion*

Murder on the Midway: The Complete Black Mask Cases
of the Human Encyclopedia, Volume 1 *by Frank Gruber*

MURDER MAZE

The Complete

BLACK MASK

Cases of Jerry Tracy

1935–37

THEODORE A. TINSLEY

---

introduction by Will Murray

illustrations by Arthur Rodman Bowker

cover by John Drew

BLACK MASK

2022

Table of Contents

Introduction

THE FULL SIGNIFICANCE and influence of author Theodore Adrian Tinsley (1894–1979) has only emerged in the last decade or so.

Tinsley was one of that legion of writers who entered the pulp magazine field in the Roaring Twenties, when the industry started booming, pay was handsome, and cheap fiction magazines were proliferating at such a rate that writers were being recruited in great numbers.

Tinsley first broke into print in 1925 with a Western story for Fiction House, a powerhouse of a publisher that started up in 1921 and swiftly became one of the titans of the field. During this period Tinsley wrote Westerns, Mounted Police, and Aviation stories, not necessarily full-time because his output was steady but rather desultory during the 1920s.

He doesn't seem to have bothered with recurring characters until Fiction House launched their 1932 rival to *Black Mask*, entitled *Black Aces*. For this new title, Tinsley created the Amusement, Inc., series which featured Major John Lacy and his ex-Marine buddies. Formed in the aftermath of their World War I service, they took on the growing menace of prohibition-fueled organized crime with military tactics. Every issue of *Black Aces* contained an Amusement, Inc., story, the only series regularly featured during the magazine's short run.

Some critics have seen in Lacy and his battling veterans a template that suggests Doc Savage and his crew of World War I veterans turned civilian crime crushers, but on a more modest scale. Both groups were headquartered in one of New York City's tallest skyscrapers, had access to tremendous wealth and a fleet of bulletproof vehicles.

A few years later, writing for Street & Smith, Tinsley began ghostwriting for *The Shadow Magazine,* writing four novels a year under the house name of Maxwell Grant. No one realized it at the time, but Tinsley's first Shadow novel, *Partners of Peril,* was used as the template for the first Batman story in 1939, with writer Bill finger essentially purloining the plot, while artist Bob Kane copied liberally from the interior illustrations for his drawings.

A year later, Tinsley launched the Carrie Cashin series for Street & Smith's *Crime Busters* magazine. It was an inversion of the typical private detective and his girl Friday. The supposed secretary was in fact the actual detective, while the male sidekick who presented himself as the head of the agency, was simply hired muscle. This series, both hard-boiled and screwball at the same time, ran in nearly every issue for six years.

Decades later, the popular television series *Remington Steele* would be built upon precisely this premise. While it may be a coincidence, between 1937 and 1943, Carrie Cashin was a very popular series and one extremely early television broadcast featured her in a one-shot telecast circa 1940.

A few months after Black Aces folded in 1932, Tinsley broke into *Black Mask* with the first installment of his long-running Jerry Tracy stories.

One of the challenges an editor like *Black Mask's* Joe Shaw had was the monthly problem of assembling an issue of a single-genre magazine while ensuring a variety of contents.

In the Western magazines, the editor struggled with balancing cowtown stories, ranch stories, range stories and frontier stories, as well as other considerations of that genre, such as whether the protagonist was a lawman, a cowboy, or a range detective.

With *Black Mask*, the problems ran roughly parallel. Private detectives were the most popular characters, but you can't fill a magazine with five or six different private detectives without running into the story-limiting problem that private detectives can only tackle certain kinds of cases. Police detectives made for a perfect counterpoint to that because they had both authority that went beyond the private detective's remit, but they also had the lawful restrictions of their profession—although they might exceed them based on personal willingness to take risks. Ordinary beat cops were good for variety, but they were less glamorous. Occasionally stories were built around Underworld characters of all types. And when the F.B.I. attained prominence in the mid-1930s, G-Men were added to the mix.

There was also the vexing problem of the crimes to be solved. Bank robberies, kidnappings, murders, extortion, gambling, and so on. An editor would, in selecting stories for an upcoming issue, need to balance not only the type of protagonist, but the kind of crime being investigated. You just couldn't have an issue overpopulated with multiple kidnapping plots or jewel-theft capers.

For a while, during the period when Westerns were wildly popular, Joe Shaw often included one Western story per issue. Typically it would be a modern-day Western with a hard-boiled slant, such as a Texas Ranger or Mexican border story, but it would be unmistakably a Western. The odd Royal Canadian Mounted Police yarn popped upon from time to time.

Shaw phased out these outdoor stories in 1934, further limiting his choices. This left him with private detectives and official lawman, although some interesting variations surfaced in both categories, such as W.T. Ballard's Bill Lennox, the Hollywood troubleshooter and Red Drake, Ballard's race track sleuth.

In the private detective category, the limitations were greater. Once Carroll John Daly and Dashiell Hammett had established the template, the struggle was to maintain individuality of characterization and avoid the inevitable stereotype. On a month by month basis, the need for diversity was relentless— and Joe Shaw was exacting.

"Most fiction characters," he once observed, "are just puppets pushed around the stage by the author who seems to hold them on wires."

Enter Jerry Tracy, the wisecracking Broadway columnist for the *Daily Planet*. Tough as nails, but possessing a heart of gold which he carefully concealed from public view.

Today, no one recalls how this character came into existence, but he was almost certainly modeled after Walter Winchell, the Broadway gossip columnist for the New York *Daily Mirror* between 1929 and 1963. Winchill was also a syndicated radio personality whose staccato machine-gun-style delivery of celebrity anecdotes and innuendo made him one of the outstanding—and feared—media personalities of his era. Having millions of readers and listeners, he could make or break stars with his carefully-crafted bulletins.

Winchell's punchy delivery was filled with neologisms and catchy turns-of-phrase. The fast-talking radio commentator became celebrated for his inventive portmanteau descriptives such as "welded" for wedded and "infanticiptation" to describe an expectant couple. He pioneered the concept of news as entertainment—or "infotainment," to use a modern term Winchell himself might have coined.

Holding court at Table 50 of the Stork Club, Winchell evolved into a celebrity in his own right, and a magnet for press agents, politicians, bootleggers and other such human flotsam and jetsam of the Main Stem. His quips and sayings, like "Nothing recedes like success" and "Broadway is the main artery of New York life—the hardened artery" are still quoted today.

So symbolic was he of the Great Depression that when *The Untouchables* was made into a television show in 1959, Winchell was hired to narrate it, delivering clipped commentary that was perfectly attuned to the times being dramatized.

Walter Winchell's Sunday broadcast was only two years old when Theodore Tinsley distilled his radio commentator persona into *Black Mask's* newest hard-boiled protagonist.

As a newspaperman, Jerry Tracy was a perfect alternative to the revolving door of cops, private dicks, and sundry others. Since his beat was Broadway, he could investigate situations other gumshoes might not encounter. Additionally, he possessed personal contacts and had an inside track to work cases based on existing relationships. His column was also a powerful weapon for exposing criminality and corruption to the public.

Unlike the often ruthless Winchell, Tracy was a hard-boiled sentimentalist. He didn't always print the dirt that came his way. And he was in the grand tradition, a champion of the underdog. He made a great snappy-speaking protagonist for gritty Manhattan stories.

I imagine the success of Fred Nebel's stories of Captain Steve McBride, which had been running since 1928, might have encouraged Shaw to entertain the feasibility of a Walter Winchell-like hard-nosed nose-for-news character. The perpetually drunken newspaperman Kennedy of the *Free Press* had been a minor character in the early McBride stories. As a series progressed, Kennedy emerged as its costar. Readers loved the character. In the absence of Dashiell Hammett, who had moved on to Hollywood and hardcover books, Nebel became one of *Black Mask's* mainstay writers.

But Nebel couldn't carry the magazine. No one writer could.

It's clear that from the beginning, Shaw and Tinsley conceived Jerry Tracy as a series character. The first six stories ran in six consecutive issues, beginning with "Party from Detroit" in the October 1932 issue through "Somebody Stole My Pal" in the July, 1933 issue.

Yet a year passed before Tracy returned for his first novelette appearance, a story called "Smoke." This was in the July 1934 issue. Nearly another year came and went before he returned for "Keep on Asking" in *Black Mask,* May 1935. Thereafter, Tracy appeared regularly but sporadically to the end of the Joe Shaw era, and into the Fanny Ellsworth interregnum, concluding with "My Candle Burns" in the April 1940 issue, published two issues before Popular Publications took over the magazine and replaced Ellsworth with Ken White, Jr.

The inexplicable absence of Jerry Tracy stories for nearly two years on the face of it is mysterious. Fortunately, we have an explanation, courtesy of one of the writers magazines of that era.

In a gossip column published *Writer's Review* December,

1934, it was revealed that Tinsley "has temporarily abandoned writing his 'Jerry Tracy' yarns for *Black Mask* to do radio scripts for *The Shadow* programs..." This was for CBS, during the period when The Shadow narrated his show and had not yet evolved into its protagonist. This gig presumably led to Tinsley ghost writing the Shadow novels, starting in 1936. Consequently, there were exactly 25 published Jerry Tracy stories, when the number probably would have been closer to twice that.

During that sabbatical, Tinsley contributed his only *Mask* tale that didn't belong to the Tracy series. But he didn't travel far from Tracy's busy stamping grounds. "Murder by Arrangement," March 1935, featured a Broadway ticket broker named Max Ward.

The temporary absence of Jerry Tracy may have, directly or indirectly, led to George Harmon Coxe's extremely popular series about a newspaper photographer who investigated crimes as a adjunct to his regular work. Jack "Flashgun" Casey first appeared in the May 1934 *Black Mask* and ran well into the 40s, as well as finding his way to radio, film, and later television.

Jerry Tracy might seem to have been a natural for radio as well, but he never made the transition. Probably because the character would come across in radio as a Walter Winchell knockoff. Yet four of his adventures were adapted for B pictures between 1936-37.

While many of Joe Shaw's loyal writers abandoned *Black Mask* after his departure in 1936, Tinsley was one of the few who did not. Evidently, Fanny Ellsworth thought his stories fit into her thinking of what a post-Shaw *Black Mask* should be. Ellsworth was actively recruiting fresh blood for her pages, which were now aimed at female as well as the traditional male readers, leaving some of the Shaw-era regulars to fall by the wayside. It must be noted, however, that Tinsley only wrote two Jerry Tracy stories after the last burst in 1938, one the following year and the final entry ten months later in 1940.

While not as famous as other *Black Mask* characters, the Jerry Tracy stories were highly regarded by readers, as well as by Tinsley's contemporaries.

In 1936, author Arthur J Burks singled out "South Wind" and especially "Beyond All Light" as "two of the swellest yarns *Black Mask* ever published, which means they were tops!" Joe Shaw selected "South Wind" for reprinting when he put together his *Hard-Boiled Omnibus* in 1946.

Beyond that, Jerry Tracy has rarely been reprinted. Possibly because he is too much of a celebrity-status figure of his time and not a hard-boiled archetype like Carroll John Daly's Race Williams or Dashiell Hammett's Sam Spade.

Most remarkable, perhaps, was that Ted Tinsley, a third-generation native-born New Yorker, was not a habitué of the Broadway night clubs his character inhabited. The story is told that for years he had never seen the smoky inside of one. Later in the 1930s, after most of his Jerry Tracy stories had been published, some of his pulp-writing colleagues dragged him to a night club—and only then did he finally realize what he had been missing.

Theodore Tinsley's career ran nearly twenty years, ending after World War II broke out and the resultant paper shortage squeezed all pulp publishers, forcing many of the regular magazine markets to fold. He followed his fellow *Black*

Mask contributor Norvell W. Page to Washington and worked for the Office of War Information, later migrating to other government agencies.

Page was a former newspaperman and one wonders if Tinsley based any part of Tracy on Page, whose reporting experience covered several states before ending in New York City in 1933 when Page's fiction sales far outpaced his reporter's salary. The two were close friends.

Tinsley never commented publicly on his influences. But Joe Shaw had this to say:

> Ted enlivened *Black Mask* pages first with "Jerry Tracy", the impeccable little columnist who scorned the emotion he was unable to repress and never forgave a trickster. Many readers have sought to identify "Jerry"; but Ted maintains he is entirely a personage of his own creation. Possibly, "Jerry" reflected Ted's wholesome philosophy of life, for Ted at heart is a fun-loving and not a sad-faced humorist.

Of course, no one would state publicly that Walter Winchell—or any other living person—served as the inspiration-model for Jerry Tracy, for fear of litigation, so the above must be taken with an appropriate modicum of salt.

As far as anyone knows, after his last story was published an *Argosy* in 1944, Tinsley stopped writing fiction, and never looked back.

This volume of Jerry Tracy exploits consists of the middle group of stories, all of novelette length. As with the first volume, the reader finds that Tinsley's gift is deft exploitation of then-contemporary 1930s slang, much of it now lost but exquisitely realized in tightly-plotted tales evoking The Great White Way as it was then as few writers ever did. Damon Runyon had nothing on Ted Tinsley. Walter Winchell, might want a word, however.

More importantly, these stories posses a rare quality not often seen in hard-boiled fiction—heart. This was from a writer whose pulp efforts are otherwise characterized by an uncompromising brutality and violence. As such, these often humorous tales represent the flip side—and doubtless the genuine—side of Theodore Tinsley.

Three of these efforts—"Five Spot," "Body Snatcher" and "Manhattan Whirligig"—were adapted for the screen in 1936 and 1937 as *Panic on the Air, Alibi for Murder* and *Manhattan Shakedown,* respectively. *Panic on the Air* starred Lew Ayers as radio commentator Jerry Franklyn, while *Alibi for Murder* featured William Gargan as broadcaster Perry Travis. John Gallaudet played Jerry Tracy in *Manhattan Shakedown* and *Murder is News,* which was based on the 1937 novelette of the same name. George McKay co-starred as "Brains" McGili- cuddy in both Gallaudet entries. Brains stood in for Tracy's hulking valet-bodyguard, Butch. Coincidentally, Gallaudet had a minor role in *Alibi for Murder.*

The Jerry Tracy stories remain among Tinsley's most success- ful pulp efforts, even though the character's trademark greet- ing, "'Lo, Bum," never seemed to catch on with the general public.

—Will Murray

Behind the Column

Jerry Tracy noses into a Numbers Racket blot-out

JERRY TRACY STRODE BRISKLY along through the incoming bustle of Grand Central. The distant tooting of taxis brought a sparkle to his eye, curved his thin lips into a dreamy smile. Monday morning became suddenly bearable. That weekend at Scarsdale had been swell, but… His stride lengthened. He bumped heedlessly into a fat woman and caromed off her bosom.

"Why don'tcha look where you're walking?" She glared.

"Thank you, lady. And how have you been?"

Hotcha! Back in town! Honed and stropped, ready to slash expertly at the fat jowls of complacent Manhattan.

He shoved his expensive leather bag through a half-caged window. His fingers made eager, snapping music.

"Check, my lad, and don't spare the horses."

Something in the staccato enunciation of the *Daily Planet's* star columnist made the attendant's eyes bug suddenly with recognition. Few people off Broadway knew what Jerry Tracy looked like, but a lot of people had heard him galloping briskly through their loud speakers.

"Hey! For gosh sake— Ain't you—"

"Fine, sweetheart. And you?"

Tracy pocketed his check and walked up the long concrete ramp to Forty-second. There was a brisk breeze winging from the west, but the morning was balmy and warm. Grand old burg, Jerry chuckled. He ignored the soft, cooing call of a gyp taximan and strolled towards Fifth. A morning like this called

for a bus ride. Maybe grab a snootful of copy from the hurricane deck. Gangway for a little guy back on the job!

Fifth Avenue was jammed as usual, he discovered. Traffic
lights red and a flock of stalled buses at Forty-first. He toed
the curb and reached for a cigarette. Before he could light
his butt an automobile horn blared an imperious ocean-liner

contralto and heads craned curiously all along the curb. A sleek-looking police sedan was coming northward past the red lights. Jerry caught a glimpse of the uniformed cop behind the wheel. Barney Callahan—Fitz' screwy young driver. Where in the heck was Inspector Fitzgerald going so early on a Monday morning? Tracy could see Fitz hunched forward on the edge of the back seat; same conservative old derby, same double-breasted gray suit.

The columnist of the *Daily Planet* skipped monkey-like into the gutter, made rapid windmill motions with his arms.

"Hey, Barney! Barney!"

The chauffeur's slitted eyes veered briefly and he grinned. Fitzgerald nodded and beckoned. The police sedan braked with a harsh wail halfway up the block. Tracy trotted up the asphalt and climbed in.

"Hello, Jerry," Fitz growled. The police sedan began again insulting red lights. "Where have you been? I tried to raise you on the phone a little while ago."

"Scarsdale. A classy golf community up in Westchester County. If I ever do it again, Fitz, kill me with much agony.... Where are we going, sweetheart?"

"Uptown." The keen blue eyes stared at the newspaper columnist with a searching expression. "I tried to get you at your office. Thought maybe you might disgorge something useful."

"Such as?"

"A tip, Jerry. On a dark horse I'm interested in."

"You mean a dead horse, Fitz?"

"Yeah. A feller named Sam Ritter."

"Who made him dead?"

"Dunno. That's what we're gonna find out. Wholesale cloak-and-suit. At least, that's how he's been filing his tax reports. In business up to now with a feller name of Morris Fink. Somebody stabbed Ritter to death last night in a Spig tenement up in Harlem. Discovered it this morning. Sergeant Killan's up there now."

"How come you're on it, Fitz? Big time?"

"Big enough. From what Killan says, this guy Ritter—and maybe Fink—have been running that million-dollar numbers business up in Harlem."

"Uh-huh.... You're not kidding a little columnist, are you?"

Fitz' blue eyes glared wrathfully.

"Would I pick you up to pass the time of day, nut? I tell you that numbers mystery has had me stewing for the last year. Huge profits—wholesale killings. A murder a week for the last six months. No leads, no clues. I tell you, Jerry, the whole set-up has had me worried as hell. Killan say that this dead Sam Ritter is the answer—and I hope to God that he's right!

If I'd been sure about it yesterday, I'd have knifed Ritter myself! Boy, I've suffered lately and I'm not fooling."

Again that peculiar searching glint came into Fitzgerald's blue eyes.

"CARDS ON THE table, Jerry! You know what I mean. Have you got one of those special tips of yours—on Sam Ritter?"

Tracy coughed, looked somewhat embarrassed. He laid a friendly hand on the inspector's gray trouser knee.

"If I had, Fitz, you'd get it—right off the bat, without any 'ifs' or 'buts,' Trouble is—" He sighed faintly, "Maybe I'd better tell you the whole truth about those tips. I mean, those special red-hots I've been running in the column lately. Every one of them as accurate as hell. Every one of 'em based obviously on some underworld source as trustworthy as a supreme court judge. I give you my word of honor, Fitz, that I don't know any more than you what the source is, who the mysterious tipster is—what it's all about. All I know is that I get 'em, I use 'em—and they've never been wrong once."

The inspector nodded.

"Okey, Jerry. I merely thought you might have some kind of dope that we could use."

"Sorry. If I did—wait a second! Whoa, baby!"

"S'matter?"

"It's just barely possible.... I've been away over the week-end—just got in town this minute. It's barely possible that one of those tips—maybe if I hopped into a booth somewhere and gave Butch a quick call at the office—"

"Do that, will you, Jerry?" Fitzgerald howled suddenly at

the back of his chauffeur's head, "Hey, Barney! Pull up first telephone sign you see. There's one up at the next corner! Whoa…." Tracy was off the running-board before the police sedan stopped. He banged into the drug-store and was gone forty-seven seconds. Fitzgerald timed him.

"Well?"

"No dice. Nothing doing. Sorry."

Barney Callahan took the inspector's disappointed nod and broad-jumped the sedan into motion.

"How do those tips come to you, Jerry?" Fitz asked with a slow persistence. "Through the mail?"

"All ways. Through the mail. Delivered by bums who can't tell you a thing. Stuck under the office door. No way of tracing 'em. Don't you think I've tried?"

"You mean the stuff is anonymous?" the inspector asked stubbornly. "A free gift? You don't put out dough for those tips?"

"Not a nickel."

"Man or woman?"

"No way of telling. I've often wondered."

"Fingerprints?"

"Pull-eze," Jerry said softly. "You think I'm that kind of a heel?" His soft smile made the inspector flush.

"Well, of course… I didn't mean—I thought that maybe from the handwriting—"

"Typed," Jerry said. "Plain cream note paper. Plain cream envelopes. The stuff you buy in any five-and-dime. Always the same. And I never save 'em for police inspectors. And I never, never look for fingerprints." His soft smile deepened. "Maybe it's the signature that makes me funny that way. Always the same on every message. *God bless you, Jerry. You're a good guy.*'"

"Might be a woman," Fitz suggested.

"Yeah?" Jerry's bright eyes mocked him.

Ahead of them, at St. Nicholas Avenue laid a gaunt, dusty diagonal across upper Harlem towards the dizzy spider-work of the Eighth Avenue Elevated. Barney braked expertly and pulled in alongside the curb. A crowd of loiterers, delivery boys, housewives were spilling aimlessly back and forth on the side-walk, attracted like flies by the police uniforms. Bluebottles, Tracy thought, buzzing morbidly in the clear sunshine.

Patrolmen kept a channel open through the eddying crowd. The channel led straight towards crumbling stone steps, a vesti-bule door with a latch that didn't work, ragged stair carpet that made Tracy's throat tickle with dust.

A respectful voice said: "Fourth floor, Inspector. Rear apart-ment."

A voice utterly lacking in respect said: "Hi, Jerry! What are you doing way up in Harlem, you big old prima donna, you? Another red-hot tip?"

Tracy shoved the fresh *Globe* man back on his heels with a deftly applied palm.

"This concludes the morning broadcast," he said dryly. "For further details, read your favorite small-size newspaper, the *Daily Planet.*"

The chubby little medical examiner was putting on his hat and coat when Tracy inched into the fourth-floor apartment behind Fitzgerald.

"Straight homicide," Goldfarb told Fitz in his pleasant, enthusiastic voice. "Single knife-wound, inflicted at a slight downward angle. *Smacko* into the heart. Fellow that did it knew his business. Probably a bit taller and heavier than the deceased.

Quick job. Dead since—oh, about one o'clock this morning...."

THE BODY WAS in the dinette, a small boxlike cubicle that opened off a long, gangling kitchen. Tracy gazed down with mild curiosity as Inspector Fitzgerald twitched back the soiled sheet. Moon-faced, well-fed, swarthy—the type you're never quite certain is either Jewish or Italian. A well-built, husky-looking corpse. Eyes wide open and faintly surprised.

Sergeant Killan bustled into the dinette, said, "Hi, Jerry!" with a friendly smile, whispered respectfully to the frowning inspector.

"I'd like to show you something pretty interesting in the front living-room, sir."

Their feet slopped on the kitchen floor. The linoleum was wet and oozy with spilled water.

"Where'd all this water come from?" Fitzgerald growled.

Tracy's eye lifted to the wall beside the electric refrigerator, noted the empty socket, the dangling electric cord further along.

"Somebody's pulled out the plug," Jerry murmured. "Probably last night. That icebox has been defrosting all night.... Can't be any tray under the freezing unit—or am I wrong?"

Sergeant Killan grinned. "Not a bad guess. Unit tray is missing, all right. Not a speck of food in that icebox, Inspector. Every shelf was loaded with bottles—rye, bourbon and a whole slew of club soda."

Fitzgerald frowned. "You opened that refrigerator?"

"Yes, sir. Er—that is, the door was ajar when we got here. That's how all that water dripped out, I guess."

"Prints?" Fitzgerald snapped.

"No, sir. No prints anywhere. Gibson and Kominsky left a coupla minutes ago. Everything clean—or wiped. Knife as clean as a whistle. Murderer must have used those rubber gloves over there in the sink."

"Yeah?" Fitzgerald's frown got deeper. "Suppose you let me do all the guessing about this. What's in the front room?"

He clumped solidly away, behind the nimbler feet of Killan.

Tracy lingered in the kitchen for a while, staring aimlessly here and there. The soaked linoleum of the kitchen floor seemed to fascinate him. He kept staring alternately at the floor and the empty electric outlet in the wall; rubbing his nose gently with the tip of his long forefinger, a favorite habit of his when he found something simmering faintly inside his inquisitive skull.

Fitzgerald had let the swinging kitchen door bang shut behind him. For the moment, Tracy was alone. The body of Sam Ritter lay, sheeted and quiet, in the tiny dinette; but Tracy didn't bother with the corpse. With a mildly stealthy expression on his lean countenance, the *Daily Planet's* columnist poked quietly about the empty kitchen.

He stared into dish-closets, looked over a small array of canned goods and packaged cheese; opened the cupboard doors down below. His lips remained pursed in a steady, soundless tune. He pried among pots and pans, examined carefully an electric iron, a toaster, an electric fan. An idea seemed to strike him and he walked slowly up and down the narrow length of the kitchen, sniffing the air with quiet deliberation. The result of his sniffing was a disappointed frown and a low, "Nuts!" to the refrigerator.

Finally, he walked out, padded along the dim hallway to the front of the apartment.

Inspector Fitzgerald was in the living-room, seated at a battered oak desk, talking in a low voice to Sergeant Killan. The *Globe* man had beat it, apparently. So had the rest of the legmen, including the guy from Tracy's own rag.

Tracy knew why as he listened to the dry, satisfied murmur of the burly inspector at the desk. The newspaper lads were all hopping for phones and rewrite men. Headline stuff in that shabbily furnished living-room! Fitz was grinning like a hyena; so was Killan. Both of them had the air of sleek tabby-cats brought unexpectedly face to face with a saucer of fresh cream.

Sam Ritter's murder had unexpectedly removed the covering from a discreet and well-padded rathole. The battered oaken desk, the drawers of a rickety old bureau were crammed with indisputable evidence that here in a shabby St. Nicholas Avenue tenement, was the prize rathole whose existence had long bothered Fitzgerald. Expense slips, account books, tickets, memoranda.... The stuff spilled out of every drawer in the desk. Another pile—currency and silver—was scattered on the floor in front of a small dark recess in the wall where Killan's stubby fingers had pried out a panel whose fitting had looked slightly phoney to the sergeant's experienced eye.

Tracy fingered some of the documents, listened to Fitzgerald's dryly jubilant murmur.

"The numbers racket, Jerry. Biggest and most profitable gold mine in the city for years. I'll bet that at least twenty murders have stemmed from this private little counting-house. And figure how much hush-hush money has been spread among the occasional crooked cops or plain-clothesmen—and how many small-fry politicians, and big ones too, must have had a finger underneath the piecrust! This is one murder, Jerry, that positively makes me gloat with pleasure. It's going to end my biggest headache—along with Harlem's biggest racket."

"You figure that the broad-shouldered gent with the knife in his heart is the head gink in this thing?"

"He has to be or there's no sense to it."

"What do you mean he has to be?" Tracy's arm gestured towards the littered floor. "Aren't you sure? Doesn't this stuff here pin it on him?"

"Not so you'd notice it," Fitz admitted. "The whole layout seems to have been run on a code basis. Agents, district managers, collectors, go-betweens—all represented by alphabetical or numerical designations. No check books, no bank deposit slips. I'm hoping we'll run across the code book before we get through with all this heap of junk. If we do, the patrol wagons are going to be *very* busy. And even if we don't, this charming industry is in for a bad time of it. Customers will start squawking, dirty hints of double-cross and fraud will start dropping all over Lenox Avenue....Oh, we'll get evidence, all right!" Fitzgerald chuckled.

"Take it from me, Jerry, the old man is happy."

"What do you know about this bird, Ritter? Ever had him under surveillance?"

"Never. Not once. Wouldn't know him from Adam if it weren't for the card in his pocket. He had a very pretty front down on Seventh Avenue among the cloak-and-suiters. Sam Ritter and Morris Fink, wholesale clothiers. Morris Fink is the partner. I've sent Delehanty to pick up Fink. I want to hear what he has to say on the subject of partnership and—alibi."

The inspector conferred briefly again with the sergeant. Together they began poking systematically among the disordered papers. There was a mild hubbub out in the hallway and Sergeant Killan popped to his feet and went outside. In a moment his head poked back again.

"Delehanty is here with Ritter's partner," he said tersely. "Wanna see this Fink guy right away?"

"Yeah."

MORRIS FINK SIDLED into the room in the grasp of the massive Delehanty like a reluctant small dog on a leash. His round, greasy face was gray with poorly concealed apprehension. Fat and jowly he was, like the dead Ritter; but smaller, flabbier, gelatinous-looking. His eyes bobbed timorously about. When he spoke he didn't talk to anyone in particular.

"Gentlemen, I swear I had nothing to do with—this. I don't know what it's all about. This police gentleman will tell you that I came willingly, gladly. I'm a respectable business man."

"That's swell," Fitzgerald said. "What's your name?"

"Morris Fink."

"Where do you live?"

"5724 Central P-Park West. Apartment 12-B."

"Has he looked at the body, Delehanty?"

"Yes, sir."

"Do you know that guy in the dinette, Fink?"

"Sure, sure. Yessir."

"Who is he?"

"*Mein*—my partner. Sam Ritter."

Fitzgerald nodded and made a note on the pad in front of him. Tracy lit a cigarette and the little cloak-and-suiter jumped spasmodically as the match sputtered.

"Any idea what Sam Ritter was doing way up here in Harlem in a cheap tenement?" Fitzgerald asked softly.

"No, sir."

"Or why he was killed?"

"Well—" Fink hesitated, licked his thick lips, leered suddenly in an indecently confidential manner. "I couldn't exactly be knowing. Maybe—"

"Maybe, what?"

"Sam was a funny guy about—about goils, see? Always went kinda heavy for Cubans and—and brown goils. I figure that in this neighborhood—well, maybe some dame lured poor Sam up here and some boy friend of the goil was waiting with a knife, hah?"

"Did *you* kill him, Fink?" Fitzgerald asked curtly.

The pudgy little man turned white as chalk.

"No! *Mein Gott*, no! For why I should do such a—"

"Ever been in this apartment yourself, Fink?" Fitzgerald asked him.

"Not never. Positively, no. Never even knew such a place existed even!"

The inspector's hand waved languidly towards the litter of records on the floor.

"Any idea, Fink, what this stuff might be?"

"Absolutely, I couldn't say." He scanned with a lackluster eye the numbers slip that Fitzgerald thrust at him. "It might be a business maybe," he conceded cautiously.

"Yeah. It might.... Where were you around midnight last night?"

"I was home," Fink cried eagerly. "I can prove it, yet. A alibi, I got. You can ask my wife, you can ask—"

"What kind of an alibi?" Jerry Tracy inquired curtly. It was the first question he had asked.

"*Mit* cards, I play; *mein* wife *und* I. From nine o'clock, maybe nine-thirty, We play rummy. Till eleven. Then I go to bed. The whole evening yet, I am at home. I never leave the building even. You can ask *mein* wife; you can ask the elevator man; you can ask the night hallman. Positively, I demand you should ask them!"

"I'd rather ask you something," Tracy murmured.

"You should go right ahead." Morris Fink beamed shakily at the famous little columnist of the *Daily Planet*.

"Did you, by any chance," Jerry inquired, "get up after you went to bed? Get dressed? Walk softly down the staircase that houses your service elevator? Pass quietly through the basement and out by the delivery entrance? Return the same way—perhaps around one-thirty or two o'clock this morning?"

"No. I didn't. I'm telling you before already what I—"

"Do you have a service elevator, such as I have described, in your apartment building?" Jerry persisted.

"I—I think so. Maybe. I would have to look, y'understand."

"One more question, Mr. Fink, if you don't mind?" Tracy eyed the clothier with the air of a man pumping rifle shots at a distant target. "Are you interested in electric irons? Toasters? Or maybe electric fans?"

Fink's eyes looked first blank, then cunning.

"Suits and dresses, I sell," he said warily. "Hardware is merchandise I positively don't touch."

"Okey," Jerry said. "Skip it."

Inspector Fitzgerald's blue eyes were boring into Tracy. "Something, Jerry?"

"Nope. Just horsing around.… What are you going to do with Monsieur Fink here—if anything?"

"Lock him up," the inspector snapped. "Material witness, till I have a look at his service stairs and talk to the people at his apartment house and go through some more of these papers here."

"Don't," Tracy murmured.

"Huh?"

"Don't lock him up. I'd keep an eye on him, if I were you, Fitz—but I wouldn't lock him up. That is, not yet."

"You think he's a fall guy in this thing?"

"Yes and no," Tracy said. His smile was dubious and peculiar. "This whole set-up hath a peculiar stink, milord. It will bear looking into and much pondering. In the meantime I don't think that jail for Monsieur Fink would help us any. At least, not yet."

"I wish to God," Fitzgerald growled, "that tipster of yours would come through for you with the real McCoy on this!"

"You and me both," Jerry sighed. He squirmed suddenly into his featherweight topcoat, made his face suddenly good-looking with a careless snap of his hat-brim.

Morris Fink backed up against Delehanty's long legs as Tracy gave him a granite-eyed once-over.

"I think you're a rat, Morris, my lad," the columnist said at last. "I think you could double-cross with ease and agility. I think you know a lot. Maybe you might even know something about electrical appliances. Or a knife in an annoying partner's gizzard.... S'long, Fitz!"

He flapped jauntily out of the living-room, started for the door—then changed his mind. He went back to the kitchen. This time he got down on his hands and knees to look at the linoleum. He examined particularly the edge of it along the wall. When he got up, he was smiling. He picked a tiny sliver of glass from his cut forefinger, sucked the small cut clean and dusted off his smeared trouser knees with his good hand.

He murmured, cryptically, to himself: " 'No' is a bum word; but sometimes it's almost as good as 'yes.'"

He let himself out of the apartment, grinned cheerily at the familiar face of the bluecoat on duty outside.

"Hello, Tom. You're looking more like meat and potatoes every day. Did you ever get rid of the wife's mother from Bridgeport?"

"Did I?" The patrolman beamed all over his face with a happy recollection.

"How did you do it?"

"Ye'll never find out from me, Mr. Tracy," he guffawed. "The wife would moider me if she knew the trick I pulled. But if ever ye git caught wid a mother-in-law on your hands, call me up. My method is a darb!"

He was still chuckling windily as Tracy vanished nimbly into a taxi.

THE COLUMNIST MADE a beeline for his own shabby little hideaway in the Times Square sector. Resolutely he dismissed the pudgy figure of Morris Fink from his mind. He forgot about leaky refrigerators and stabbed bodies with startled eyes. Long time, no work!

He leaned back in the jouncing taxi-cab, drawing material from recesses of his memory for his next column set-up, framing wisecracks to fit each separate item while the cab droned through Central Park.

He was in high good humor when he reached his dusty

office. Even the fact that Butch had on the rumpled pink shirt that he persisted in wearing, in spite of all arguments to the contrary, failed to ruffle Tracy's spirits.

" 'Lo, Boss," Butch mumbled.

Tracy sailed his hat at a peg—missed it—laid a losers quarter in Butch's palm. Pink sleeve-garters, too! Damn the guy!

"Scram, sweetheart," he said briskly. "We gotta work."

Butch didn't move. He hovered uneasily in the inner office like a tethered dirigible.

"I'm good and sore," Butch mumbled. "On account of I couldn't do nothin' about it. No kiddin', I am sore."

"Sore about what?"

"Aw, nuts. You know. About what you told me."

He laid a square cream-colored envelope in Tracy's palm and the columnist stiffened and got very quiet around the eyes.

"When, Butch?"

"Jist about ten minutes ago."

"How?"

"Right here, Boss. Jeeze, it makes me so mad, on account of I promised yuh that I'd—"

"Phooie! I oughta smack you on the skull, you ape! Where did you find this thing?" Tracy kept staring at the square envelope in his palm, his slow words trickling upward at Butch. "Didn't you see anything? Didn't you hear anything?"

"I'm tellin' yuh I hoid nuttin'. Just plain nuttin'. I was readin' something, see?—and when I looked up, there's the dam' thing on the floor stickin' inside the door. Somebuddy musta shoved it under, I figure. I mean, that's what I figure, see?"

Tracy was still looking vacantly at that envelope in his palm. The echo of Inspector Fitzgerald's voice made sudden sound in his mind: *"I wish to God that tipster of yours would come through again with the real McCoy!"*

"Outside, helpmate!" Tracy snapped.

He inserted a lean forefinger inside the flap and burst the envelope with a quick jerk. Cream notepaper inside. Same old cheap stuff. Five-and-dime. No sense trying *that* angle!

A typed message. Underwood portable, as usual. Same two letters out of alignment. 'R' and 'Y.' Always so glaringly noticeable because of the combination of letters that formed his own name, Jerry Tracy.

He had already read the note while his mind bubbled foolishly with these stale old guesses and surmises. Now he read it again:

> *Morris Fink was at the St. Nicholas Avenue apartment last night. Both Fink and Sam Ritter had keys to the joint. They met there once a week regularly. Maybe you know why. That's all I know now. God bless you, Jerry. You're a good guy.*

Tracy nodded over the message for a while like a wrinkled little gnome. Finally, he went to the telephone and called Inspector Fitzgerald.

"I'm playing fair, Fitz. As fair as I can. Fink was at the St. Nicholas Avenue apartment last night.... Yeah. No doubt about it.... Uh-huh. As deeply involved as Ritter in that numbers thing, apparently. Has a key to the joint—or maybe he got rid of it by this time. And I *still* say—don't throw him in the can. How can you trap a guy when you've got him locked in a cell, dope?"

"What did you do with the tip? Tip, wasn't it?"

"I burned it up, sweetheart. Are you mad?"

"You're a liar," the inspector said very softly over the wire. "But let that pass. We're both playing fair, Jerry. The tip angle is your own exclusive. But I still think you're an awful sucker not to try and trace your informant. If it was me, Jerry, I'd regard that person as a pretty good friend of mine. Or look at the thing this way: that informant of yours is going to get into one hell of a jam about these tips, sooner or later. If you knew exactly who the person is—well, you might be able to step in some time and stop a killing that I, personally, would sure hate to see happen. So much so, that any time you need cops to save your informant from a mess—I'll turn out the whole damn' homicide squad! And, remember, I'm just thinking about the police angle—and nothing else...."

"Too late," Jerry said steadily into the transmitter. "I burned the thing right after I read it."

He hung up with a wooden face. Scratched a match and held the flame near a corner of the cream-colored paper. He watched the slow, sooty smoke curl upward from the flame of the poised match. Suddenly, the stubbornly wooden look went out of his eyes. He threw the match on the floor, ground it under his heel. Carefully he folded the notepaper and locked it away in a drawer of his desk.

His soft black pencil made a hurried crayon-scrawl on a desk pad:

Who killed Sam Ritter, suave undercover czar of the city's biggest racket? Who had a key to the murder apartment on St. Nicholas Avenue? Who was there before or during the time that Ritter was stabbed through the heart? Who has an alibi that won't hold water?

Who is going to be arrested and convicted and burned to death for a planned murder committed last night?

"Nice," Tracy said softly.

Again he scooped up his telephone. He called the office of the *Daily Planet*. He talked with a very important personage, gave him the item slowly, word by word.

"Cut anything you like," he said. "I don't care apples for what you cut. Run it spaced, with wide margins. Top of the column."

The very important personage on the other end of the wire said something that made Jerry Tracy laugh suddenly. For a moment the tired lines about his mouth relaxed.

"How would you like to go to hell?" he said, and hung up.

At that precise moment the world-famous columnist might have sat for the portrait of a pleased eight-year-old boy. His eyes puckered impishly at the frayed old calendar on his wall.

"I'll bet," he whispered gleefully to the calendar, "that I'm the only guy in the world that can tell him that—and get away with it!"

LONG HOURS LATER, the electric light in Tracy's untidy little office seemed suddenly hard and yellow and intolerable. He leaned back in his chair with a tired grunt, closed his eyes, relaxed gratefully. He had been working at top speed for a busy afternoon and evening, cleaning up a hundred little details of fact and rumor with staccato efficiency. That brain of his was like the sharp flick at the end of a slave-driver's lash; a perpetual goad to his own easygoing inclinations. He didn't *like* to work, but somehow—if he laid off the column, even for a dull week-end party—*aw, nuts.* . . .

Butch had long since donned his oversize derby and left the office. Below Tracy's window, Broadway was a bright, glittering slash of raw color. A bedlam of beating noise that, to Tracy, wasn't noise at all but a kind of magnificent symphony; taxi horns, traffic whistles, crosstown gongs, the drone of movie barkers, an occasional siren, a *brrrrp-brrrrp* of a police motorcycle.... Point and counterpoint in that music, Tracy thought behind his tired eyelids; an intricate symphony that never grew stale. The challenge of stone and cement and car-tracks to seven million pretty smart humans, clustered together like flies at a pie-counter: *"How old are you, Big Boy? Too tough for you, Girlie? What d'yuh say? Can you take it?"*

Jerry Tracy opened his eyes, glanced at his watch, knew suddenly that he was hungry. Ten after nine! Hadn't eaten a morsel since that alleged breakfast up in Scarsdale! He slammed his desk shut, clicked out the lights and dozed downward to the street in the night elevator.

To the taxi-driver he snarled irritably: "How do I know where? Wait a minute and lemme think."

"Okey, Mr. Tracy," the hackman replied. That pleased the little guy. He liked people to know him, liked to be recognized wherever he went.

"Better make it *Calligans*," he grinned, his irritation gone.

Calligan's joint was a nice place for a little guy with a lot on his mind. Soft Irish music from a five-piece orchestra, hard Irish waiters who were apt to be pleasantly familiar and palsie-walsie in their manner—but that was all right, too! After two *Bacardi* cocktails Jerry felt a lot more human. He asked for a scow-load of corned beef and cabbage—and pretty near got it. Faces began to focus; people nodded to him and smiled from nearby tables.

A big dark guy's lips said, inaudibly: "How's tricks, keedo?" The girl sitting with him mouthed: "Hello, Jerry!"

Tracy waved a hospitable fork at them and the dark guy got up. The girl's hair was henna now; it used to be black. She followed her husband's broad shoulders to the columnist's table.

"Hello, Ralph. Alma, you're looking swell.... Some more chairs, waiter! And make it three on the B & S. I've had enough corned beef to last me till next groundhog day.... Well, well!"

He grinned at the pair, but mostly at Alma.

"S'matter, kids? What do you mean by eating out? Afraid of the menu in your own garbage emporium?"

Alma giggled. "Where's the fun in owning a restaurant—if you can't eat somewhere else?"

The brandy was swell. They sipped it and Tracy said: "How's married life, Alma?"

Alma giggled again. "You ask me—and you keep looking at Ralph. Is that nice?"

It was sure great to be married, Ralph admitted. A full year, keedo, and Alma hadn't thrown a dishpan at him yet! Big, nicely modeled head; strong, meaty shoulders; a laugh like a bass clarinet. Good-looking guy, for a Greek! But then, Tracy thought, what was so funny about that—weren't people always talking about guys like Greek gods?

Alma looked fondly at Ralph and giggled some more. She hadn't used to giggle like that. The henna hair wasn't doing her any good, either. Made him kind of sorry. Alma was a sweet little scout.

"How's the hash biz?" he asked.

"Grand," Ralph boomed. "Pretty good, keedo."

"It's okey," said Alma. "Why don't you come over some time and sample? You'll like the ketchup."

"It's a date. Maybe later tonight, huh?" Tracy waved his hand like an emperor. "I wouldn't care a bit, kids, if you passed the word around that I was dropping in for a snifter or two. I mean, if it'll help in any way to move some of that bum hash off your shelves."

"Well, Jeeze, that's sure nice of you, keedo," Ralph said.

Alma's eyes misted suddenly. Nice eyes. And that henna hair wasn't so bad—not when Alma smiled and went soft around the mouth.

"You're sweet, Jerry," she whispered.

"Ssssh.... Keep it under the hat or you'll lose me all my column customers." He grinned wanly. "When you call me sweet in public, always spell it r-a-t! See you later—and folks— that ketchup had better be good!" He paid the check and spilled aimlessly alone up Broadway. Not so crowded at this hour. Last movie showing well under way. Nut shoppes and pineapple juiceries waiting stolidly for the brisk midnight pickup. The big billion-watt toothpaste ad a little gloomy-looking.

At 49th a taxi-driver was arguing shrilly with a disgruntled fare.

"Why don't the bums mix it, for Gawd's sake," a voice muttered at Tracy's elbow. "Just a bunch of woids!"

"Words, my friend, properly bunched, have their value," Tracy murmured.

"I don't getcha."

"No?" The columnist shrugged and—stood suddenly quite still.

"Yeah," said the voice.

The steady pressure of something invisible was hurting Jerry's ribs. He became conscious of a lot of things. Two guys, both of them damned casual. The worst kind—youngsters. The fella with the concealed gun got Jerry walking westward without any fuss. The other guy dropped back as they came abreast of him and sauntered along behind. He had straw-colored eyebrows and a long chin like a spade.

Jerry Tracy's mouth felt dryish and cottony.

"A couple of Morris Fink's boys," he thought. "Fink saw that tip in the column, figures I know too much—and gets busy. Am I a dope! That soft-butter little partner of Sam Ritter is just scared enough to have my top blown! And I'm the dope who advised Fitzgerald not to have that fake little cloak-and-suiter tossed into the tank!"

THE CAR WAS at the curb, halfway up the block. Engine idling smoothly. The spadechinned kid took the wheel. Tracy preceded the gunner to the rear seat. His light topcoat was unbuttoned, flapping wide open. He stuck out his legs and relaxed—or pretended to, for the kid's benefit. With the most natural air in the world he slid his hands deeply into his side trousers pockets.

The gunner tautened like a coiled spring. "Be nice, buddy—or take it right now!"

"I am nice." His hands stayed put.

"What's in them pants pockets?"

"A handkerchief and a small gold-plated penknife. Scared?"

"Yeah. Scared to death, Mister." He laughed with a brief, sneering wheeze. "A little dude like you wouldn't carry a gun—but I made sure about it when I slapped you on the sidewalk."

"The knife," Tracy said in a humorous, mincing voice, "is gold-plated. A gift from a dear old aunt, whose money I hope to inherit some day. I wouldn't want to lose it. It has one blade, an inch and a quarter long, but I promise I won't try to stab you. No kidding, that's a promise."

"You're a darb," the kid chuckled.

"You mean I'm a dub, don't you?"

They laughed about that, too. Tracy kept his hands in his pockets and worked up a nice chummy atmosphere. He said nothing at all about Morris Fink, nothing about the speeding car's destination. Just a screwy wiseguy, kidding aimlessly in a tired drawl, making those dull, ratty eyes beside him crinkle with a sneer of stupid amusement.

His abductors made no effort to hide the route they were taking. Straight southward, then across town. West. Through the dark, somnolent Thirties, past the black carcasses of department stores and furniture warehouses. Over towards the Hudson, towards the strings of rickety and condemned tenements that only a cycle of depression years had saved from the pickaxes and rubbish-chutes of the house-wreckers. Tracy knew the section well, knew what his fate would probably be. A sordid and very quiet assassination, followed by a leisurely disposal of his damaged remains in the clammy Hudson....

The car halted suddenly. The gunner's voice got businesslike and practical. "Out, buddy. Me first, this time. And don't get noisy. I want this thing to look good."

A slatternly brick tenement. Yellow light flickering through torn window-shades. Kids who should have been in bed hours before, playing a vicious whispering game on a crumbling stone stoop. A dingy grocery store, with a few apathetic loafers leaning against the greasy plate-glass.

None of the loafers said anything to either of Tracy's companions; just stared. Were the two killers strangers in this very clannish old neighborhood? Tracy's forehead beaded with sweat as he hoped fiercely that they were. He had only two slim chances to rely on; intelligent co-operation and the magic of his name.

He walked slowly past the loafers, a companion hedging him on either side. He didn't mind it when the fellow with the spade chin growled in his ear: "Make it snappy, buddy. Think we got all night?" He loved these two dumb killers for their alert watching of his face. While they watched his face they couldn't see anything else.

They shoved him along faster, but it didn't make any difference now! Through a shabby vestibule door—*boooomp!* Up uncarpeted wooden stairs—*crick, crack, crick!* A key making quick, nervous rustlings in a lock. Door open, door shut. *Squueeeeee;* from a long purplish flame on a gas bracket.

"Sit down, stupid!" one of them snarled.

"On that sofa!" Spade Chin ordered. His fist helped Tracy sit down and made his nose bleed. Jerry made no effort to quench the crimson trickle.

In the gaslight they looked wolfish, without a shred of humanity. No chummy stuff, now. No grins and chuckles. Two youthful chillers on a paid job. Nothing in their eyes, now, but the dregs of a dull, unclean joy for the imminent kill. A kill, Jerry thought with a frightened shudder, that could bring them nothing better than the few greasy dollars they needed to buy dope—and disease.

"What are you boys going to do?" Jerry asked them unevenly.

The one over at the window pulled the shade down across the glass before he answered.

"What do *you* think, Mister?"

"How about listening to a little reason?"

"How about keeping your wise trap shut? Or would you like another bump on the schnozzle?"

"Let me go and I'll hand you more dough than you ever had before in your lives."

"You like to talk, don't you?" He walked deliberately across and drove Tracy's head back against the wall with a right swing. He grinned at Spade Chin. "How am I doing, Steve?"

"Not bad."

Tracy came dizzily to a sitting position on the sofa. Sat there, swaying.

"I'm not kidding you about the dough, boys," he whispered. "I mean a real payoff. You know me, exactly who I am. Five grand—right on the line. No kickbacks. Five grand—and you don't have to play with a murder rap. Is it a deal, boys?"

"Run a little water in the bathtub," Steve told his partner.

He padded swiftly into a small, closetlike recess and Tracy heard the noisy splatter of water.

"What do you say?" the *Daily Planet* man pleaded.

"Jeeze, are you a persistent guy!"

"You can't get away with it. Really, you can't. I'm a pretty prominent gazabo. And besides, that rod of yours will make things too tough to handle—the minute it goes off."

"Who says we're usin' a gun?" Steve grinned. He raised his voice. "Ready with that bathtub, Harry?"

"Yeah." The water stopped running and Harry came back. "What's the little punk beefing about now?"

"Dough."

"Yeah? What's he good for?"

"Five grand, he says."

"No kidding. Can yuh beat that? A lousy five grand." Harry smashed his fist against the columnist's jaw. He seemed to like hitting Tracy. Tracy fell off the sofa and got up again.

"I'll double it, boys. Five grand apiece; and no tail on you after you cash in. No double-cross."

"You wouldn't fool us, would you?" Harry croaked. He winked at Steve, nodded meaningly at their captive.

"Sure," Steve said. "Hand him one for me. In the belly."

They waited with enjoyment until the paralyzed stomach muscles quivered and let an agonized gasp of air suck back into Tracy's lungs.

"Wanna know a little secret?" Steve said. "You ain't got enough dough in the bank to spoil this party, Mister. We're gonna *like* doin' this job. Am I right, Harry?"

"I'll say. Jeeze, don't this guy bounce when he's socked! I'm gettin' tired."

"Me, too. Let's lug him inside and git through."

"Wait!" Tracy gasped. He could hardly recognize the hoarse quaver of his own voice.

"Huh?" Harry said. "Whaddye mean, wait?"

"Sock him in the puss," Steve said. "This guy gits on my noives."

"Who hired this kill?" Tracy whispered from the floor. "Was it—Morris Fink?"

He had to keep his aching head alert—and stall, stall, stall! Drag it along, play for time! Still a chance, a slim hope…. If the cops came, they'd come softly, without bell or siren….

"Morris Fink, wasn't it?" he groaned, his lips twisted in an aching counterfeit of a smile.

They let go of him and his head thumped hollowly on the floor.

"Sure, it was Fink," Steve said. "So what?"

"I—I thought all along that Fink was a wrong guy," Tracy mumbled. "He ran the numbers racket fifty-fifty with Sam Ritter, didn't he? That innocent cloak-and-suit stuff was the bunk, huh?"

"Sure it was the bunk," Steve said.

"Shut up!" Harry growled warningly. "We ain't paid to gab."

"What's the diff? If it'll make the guy die any happier in that bathtub, wise him up, I say."

"Why did Fink sic you boys onto me?" Tracy begged.

"You got him sore with that stuff of yours in today's column," Steve said. "He figgers with you out of the way—let the dumb coppers go ahead and pinch him. They ain't got a thing on him. But Fink kinda thinks that *you have.*"

"Did Fink kill Sam Ritter last night?"

"He thinks you got him lined up for the rap," Steve grinned. "Anyhow, there's one—"

THE WINDOW BEHIND Steve smashed suddenly into a thousand jangling fragments. The taut windowshade bellied out grotesquely, ripped down from its roller in a flapping tangle around the arms and shoulders of a uniformed policeman. He came diving head-first into the room. The flame of his gun burned a hole through the crumpled shade and dropped Steve a scant second before the killer's startled finger could press his own trigger.

Almost in the same instant, it seemed to Tracy, the front door of the apartment crashed flat on the floor. Cops spilled helter-skelter into the room, raced over the flattened door like a gangplank. The trapped Harry squealed shrilly and tried to run. He hurdled the prone body of Steve and made for the bathroom alcove.

Twice his shaking gun flared scarlet. Then he dropped to one knee and crumpled on his side, wriggling spasmodically like a hooked fish. A broadsoled police boot kicked the gun away from his feebly groping fingers. He was hauled feet-first out of the alcove and flopped alongside the motionless Steve.

Jerry Tracy struggled dazedly to his feet.

He was conscious of an arm about his waist and, bending his head upward, saw that it was Inspector Fitzgerald. He could see other things—the beam of a police flashlight on the grating of the fire-escape outside; the thick sole of a cop's shoe, stamping methodically on the smoldering sparks that ringed a bullet-hole in a crumpled window-shade on the floor. He recognized some of the faces that swam so queerly in his vision—Hindermann, Joe Caldwell, Rice, Sinnott, Mojeskie. A fat cop, whose name he couldn't recall, was sucking calmly at a bloody gash on his left hand....

"Feel all right?" Fitzgerald was asking him.

"Oh, sure, sure. I—I guess so."

There was a dull pain in his ribs where somebody had kicked him. He said, "Ouch," when Fitz touched him. But it developed that the ribs were all right. "No fracture," Fitz beamed. "Just a hickey. The boys hadda come in a little too fast to be careful."

A drink appeared magically from nowhere and Tracy gulped, blinked once or twice, came out of his trance.

He stared at the two quiet killers on the floor and shuddered. "Dead?"

"Kinda," Fitz said mildly. "Know 'em?"

"The fella with the chin is Steve. The other lad's name is Harry."

"It was Harry," Fitz corrected calmly. "What goes on, anyway? Where did they pick you up?"

"Broadway and 49th. Neat, too. Scooped me up like a pancake."

"Working for little Morris Fink."

Jerry nodded. "That squib of mine in the column did me no good, Fitz."

"I'll say it didn't. When you feel a bit stronger, you might take a squint in that bathroom. Might interest you."

"What's in there?"

"Oh—just a tub half-full of water and the biggest butcher knife I've seen in a year of Sundays. Wouldn't surprise me if we turned up a couple of nice gunny-sacks somewhere. The two boy friends seem to have had a swell old-fashioned idea about how to get rid of a prominent guy."

"Quit it, Fitz!" Jerry shuddered and set his jaw. "How did Fink arrange this thing? Didn't you cover his phone?"

"Sure did, Jerry. I'll swear he never did it over a wire."

"Where is he now?"

"On his way to a steel one-room apartment," Fitzgerald said grimly. "From now on, we quit playing. Incidentally"—his blue eyes narrowed quizzically at the columnist of the *Daily Planet*—"does this thing happen to be yours?"

He held out a handkerchief, held it spread wide open so that the embroidered name in the corner was vividly apparent. It was large enough to be vivid without much displaying of it: *Jerry Tracy.*

"How did you lose this—er—little affair without those muggs seeing you?" Fitzgerald asked.

For some unaccountable reason Tracy's ears began to get pink. He talked rapidly as though to hide a growing embarrassment.

"I figured the scheme out in the automobile. Felt the handkerchief and the gold-plated penknife when I shoved my hands in my pants pockets. Gave me an idea. I balled up the handkerchief, got that and the knife into my topcoat pocket. Kidded the lad with the gun, told him exactly what I was carrying. Fed him a line of comedy; kept working gently with one hand until I had the blade of the penknife open. I slit the pocket while they were walking me along the sidewalk outside the tenement. Held on to the penknife, poked the handkerchief out. The two muggs were too busy telling me to get a move on to notice anything. I took a chance that one of those sidewalk bums would notice the name on the handkerchief, think there was something phoney going on—and do things."

"Yeah," Fitzgerald said dryly. "They did. One of those grocery store lizards was a stool, sonny—and damned lucky for you. Damned lucky, too, that we were near enough to make a quick run of it." His smile widened. "What is this handkerchief—a souvenir, or something?"

"You mean the name on it?"

"Yeah. Do you always carry these flags—or was it just luck tonight?"

"Not exactly luck," Jerry muttered.

Fitz whooped with delighted laughter. "You mean you *always* carry one of these things?"

The face of the *Daily Planet's* famous columnist became a deep, unhappy red. The circle of grinning cops turned discreetly away from his belligerent glare. He didn't glare at Fitzgerald; just smiled rather foolishly.

"So that's it," the police inspector said softly.

"That's it, sweetheart. Shall we change the subject?"

"Right…. I doubt like the devil if I'm going to be able to tie up a foxy guy like Morris Fink with these two dead palookas. But I *can* tie him up with Sam Ritter. I *can* tie him up with that well-oiled numbers racket that he claims he doesn't know a thing about."

"You're going to need a lot of evidence."

"That's no worry. What does worry me is the murder of Sam Ritter."

Jerry Tracy didn't say anything.

"What was that crack you made about hardware this morning, Jerry?"

"Hardware?"

"Sure. You asked Fink about electric fans, toasters and a couple of other gadgets."

"Oh, that." Tracy grinned. "I was off on the wrong foot. Made a bum guess."

"Did it have anything to do with that defrosting refrigerator?"

"Not directly. I was more interested in the electric outlet in the wall."

"Yeah? What about it? Did you spot anything positive about the killer?"

Tracy hesitated. "Not exactly," he said slowly. "The conclusion I drew was negative."

"What's that mean in English?"

"If you don't mind, Fitz, I'd like to play with it alone for a while."

"And get yourself killed for good, huh?"

Tracy shook his head. Smiled faintly. "With Fink in jail, I think I'll make a fair risk for any insurance company. Don't worry, Fitz, I'll be all right."

He picked up his light topcoat, shrugged his arms into the sleeves with a tender slowness. He walked over to a far corner of the room and picked up his trampled hat.

"Hey, where are you going now?" Fitzgerald growled.

"Just remembered I've got a date. You forget things like dates when guys are trying to murder you. I promised a couple of people I'd drop into their restaurant tonight."

He stepped across the ruined door, pushed through a small knot of murmuring loiterers and walked east till he found a nighthawk taxi.

THE FRESH AIR was good for that dull, throbbing ache in his head. He was a little more like his flashy, imperturbable self when he walked into Ralph's and Alma's restaurant.

Alma was smiling at him, pretty as hell tonight, more flustered than there seemed any reason for her to be. She gave him a table in the middle. A waiter was standing beside it, apparently ready for him, grinning amicably at the honored guest.

First time the columnist had ever been inside the joint.

"How's the liquor, Emil?"

"George, Mister Tracy. Liquor is swell. Like something to eat, too?"

"Mmmmm…. Maybe. Let's see a menu. Anything here I can use ketchup with?"

Alma giggled. She hadn't used to giggle like that. They chatted together for a minute; then a party of four came in and she excused herself and hurried away.

The waiter's soiled finger came across Tracy's arm and began hovering down the menu card.

"For Gawd's sake, don't tell me hash!" Tracy growled. "Bring me the best rye highball you can find. Try across the street. And leave my menu alone. Maybe I can find a natural all by myself."

The highball was rotten but he finished it and ordered another. The thought of food made him mildly sick. He eyed the menu languidly. The usual soups—a grand choice of two. The usual fish—only this time they called it Brook Trout. *Beef à la Creole with creamed gravy.* His eye came back to that again. He didn't want the damned stuff! Creamed gravy!

Suddenly the menu card moved between his slim fingers. He glanced up, looked across the room.

His waiter had his thumb in a bowl of soup at another table. Tracy picked up his card again. His eyes seemed to be playing him a queer optical trick. Instead of *creamed gravy,* the cheap mimeographed card seemed to be saying *Jerry Tracy.* The "R" and the "Y" did it. Out of alignment. A hair's-breadth jump downward in the reproduced typing.

The *Daily Planet's* columnist caught his waiter's eye, jerked an imperious finger.

"Another highball, Emil."

"George, sir."

"Sure. George is swell, too. Another highball. And will you tell—er—Alma, if she has a minute to spare, to come over?"

Alma refused a drink with a murmured apology and that new giggle of hers. Tracy knew the answer to her nervousness at last.

She must have had reason a-plenty to worry in the last eight months or so. He tried to cast swiftly back in his mind and date that first typewritten tip that he had frowned over, checked—and found oke. Yeah—just about eight months ago. An additional fact joined with it in his mind and did things to his lips.

"What are you scowling about, Jerry?" Alma asked.

"Was I scowling, sweet? How's that? Better now?"

"Much better."

"I guess I never knew how much you really like me, Alma," he said.

"I ought to like you, Jerry." Her voice was tremulous, barely audible. "You did something for me once, something I'll never forget."

"I think you're a dope," he said harshly.

"Not now. But I was then. A little dope fresh from Schenectady. Green as canned spinach. And you were a bigshot then—just like you are now. But that didn't stop you from doing something for me that was so utterly decent and unselfish, so *damned* sweet—"

She started hurriedly to rise from her chair. "So long, Jerry. I—I gotta beat it."

His hand dropped momentarily on hers. Under its brief, feathery pressure Alma seemed to wilt suddenly, to go soft in the legs.

"You should have stayed in show business, Alma. You had a future. I could have helped you a lot."

"It's okey. I'm satisfied."

"How long you been married, keed? You sent me a cute announcement, I remember."

"Ten months. Not quite a year."

"Gosh. Time sure flies, doesn't it? Ralph's a swell guy, eh?"

"Yeah. Ralph is swell."

Tracy fumbled with the menu card. He felt very sorry for this poor little kid with the tired mouth and the henna hair. Leveling all the time! Not a crooked bone in her whole decent little body. And loyal to him for that favor he had done for her. What more loyalty could a guy want! Playing a desperately dangerous game, shooting him valuable, dynamite-loaded tips. He should have guessed her identity months ago. That signature of hers: "God bless you, Jerry. You're a good guy." Who else, but Alma?

"I'm going to make a little guess," he told her gently. "This menu here—you typed it for the mimeograph, didn't you?"

"Why—why sure."

"On an Underwood portable?"

He could see her body tensing. "Why do you ask that?"

"I'm still the same old Jerry you've always known. Cards on the table. Square as hell with square people.... Did you type that menu on an Underwood portable?"

"Yes."

The color was draining slowly out of her face. She could sense now what was coming. Frightened. Cold with terror.

"Take it easy, Alma," Jerry said. "People may be watching. Laugh at me a little. Get a bit coy as though I was trying to make you.... Good girl! You're a trouper."

"How did I give myself away?" she breathed.

"The menu, sweet. That typing hit me right in the eye. So you sent me every one of those tips, didn't you?"

"Yes, Jerry. I did."

Silence. Tracy's fingers idly caressed a highball glass half-filled with lousy rye and soda.

"I've only known about six grand people in this town," he said to his glass. "You're one of 'em."

"Don't, Jerry! I—I gotta keep on smiling."

"You on the inside of something? In with a wrong crowd, Alma?"

"Maybe. What's the diff?"

"You'd have to be, I guess, to keep sending me that brand of true-talk."

He handed her a cigarette, leaned intimately across the table to light it for her.

"Did Morris Fink kill Ritter?"

"Please, Jerry."

He stared at her. "Tell me you're involved and I'll drop it and forget it. You clean about this thing yourself?"

"What do you think?" She was trying; pitifully, to be jaunty about it.

"We can't talk here, Alma. That's a cinch."

"No. We can't."

"Where? My place?"

"Too dangerous," Alma breathed. "You don't realize, Jerry, how really tough and ticklish this whole mess is. Beat it—please. People are beginning to look over here. We're causing comment."

"Nuts to that. Where do I see you?"

"My apartment. Tomorrow morning. I'll be free then. The restaurant here doesn't open until noon. Say about—ten?"

"Check on ten.... How about Ralph? Will he think I'm getting funny about you?"

"Ralph won't be there. He'll be down at the market. He attends to all the ordering. Ring a long and two shorts on the bell and I'll know it's you."

"Swell." Tracy laughed with a sudden jovial noisiness, patted her arm, glanced at his watch ostentatiously. "Check, waiter!"

Alma rustled demurely away.

A few minutes later Tracy was jouncing homeward in a well-dented taxicab towards the swanky penthouse that hadn't seen him since the preceding Friday.

RAIN SLANTED BRISKLY on Manhattan from ragged, gray clouds that drove steadily from the East River. Jerry Tracy sloshed pleasantly along in a belted raincoat and a not-so-good hat. He hadn't far to go; and besides, on a puffy, wet morning like this he disdained taxis.

He went plodding along through the wetness—a little guy in his own home town, a guy who asked directions from nobody.

He turned and let the gusty breeze push him around a corner. Halfway down a short, sedate block, he stopped under a striped and dripping canopy and a fat man dressed like an admiral opened the door.

"Is she expecting you, sir?" a second man said.

The third man was a boy. He said, languidly: "Fourth floor. Apartment Three B."

"Just enough of you guys for indoor polo," Tracy grinned. "Why don't you try it some time?"

"Beg your pardon, sir?"

"What's the difference, so long as you're healthy? Ever listen to Jack Benny?"

He watched the ornate doors of the elevator close and depart. As he turned towards 3-B a slight frown chased the smile from his shrewd eyes.

"Capital D for this dump," he said pensively to himself. "Now I know why Greeks go into the restaurant business."

There was a small bronze knocker on the door, carved like a wreath of metal holly; but Tracy paid no attention to it. He lit a dry cigarette, shot the paper match end over end and pushed his fingertip against the bell button. A long and two shorts.

Instantly—as though Tracy himself had caused it—a woman screamed shrilly inside the apartment. A muffled explosion, unmistakably a pistol shot, cut across the scream and stopped it.

Tracy's lips let go of his cigarette. He skipped nimbly backward from the closed door, coughing a little from the smoke he had inhaled the wrong way.

No further sound came from the apartment. The columnist stood where he was, crouching, hardly knowing exactly what to do next. The thing going on behind that closed apartment door had built up on him without a second of warning. Just a long and two shorts on the bell and—*whango!* Did that shrill scream of terror come from Alma? And if so, who was in there with her? Who had boldly cut her down with a quick chunk of lead?

Tracy's eyes flicked across his shoulder towards the elevator panel. The signal arrow was moving upward. The rattling of a door-knob whirled him around to face Alma's apartment again. He saw the apartment door fling open.

A woman in a black silk negligée—swaying blindly, half fainting—a pistol in her slack right hand.... Alma!

"Jerry," she moaned. "Is that you, Jerry?"

"Are you all right, sweet?" He sprang at her, braced her under an arm-pit, slipped the gun out of her relaxing fingers. "What's wrong in there? What happened?"

"Come inside," she gasped. "Quick! Shut the door."

He slammed it shut. Sniffed the burned powder smell in the air and stared toward the dim living-room. "Who did you plug, Alma? Where's the guy?"

The body was just inside the living-room. On his back and stone dead, apparently. One leg doubled up, the other leg flat; with a ridge of rug bunched under his left hand where he had clawed briefly. Alma's Greek husband. The big, good-looking, curly-haired Ralph, with a great big gun in his dead right hand.

Tracy looked downward at him, nodded his head "yes" for some peculiar reason. He didn't seem so surprised, after all.

He stared at the deadly little gun, still warm in his own hand—the gun he had just taken from Alma's slack fingers. She had killed this mugg husband of hers, all right. Tracy still didn't now the how or the why of it yet—and didn't give a damn! All he was conscious of was that this loyal little dame had saved the life of Jerry Tracy and was up to her neck in trouble if he didn't do something lightning fast to clear her of the murder rap. That elevator operator would be pounding on the door in about 'steen seconds!

Tracy bent downward and pried Ralph's gun out of his dead hand, thankful of his own gloved fingers. The gun was fully loaded. None of the cartridges had been exploded.

Jerry leveled the weapon, calmly pulled the trigger. The bullet smashed through a glazed pottery bowl on the table and lodged in the wall. In a moment the columnist forced the exploded gun back into Ralph's right hand, made quietly sure that the dead fingers were molded properly around the weapon. Only a few swift seconds had intervened between Alma's shot and

Jerry's. He'd try and kid the police with a phoney story of self-defense on his part—take the rap for the whole thing....

The front doorbell began to ring. The reedy voice of the elevator boy echoed shrilly through the closed door. "Are you folks all right in there? Anything wrong?"

"Tell that sap it's okey," Jerry whispered. "Tell him it's all right, Alma."

But Alma wasn't talking. She was hanging halfway off the couch, halfway on it. Fainted.

The doorbell kept on ringing. Long idiotic toots.

"Beat it, sonny!" Tracy bawled. "Everything's all right."

"Is—is it all right for the Super to unlock the—the door and come in?"

"No. Wait a minute...." Jerry's eyes swept haggardly about. "Tell you what you do! Listen, can you hear me?"

"Yessir."

"Go downstairs. Walk up to the corner—Madison Avenue. See if you can find a cop—a traffic cop will do fine. Bring him back here. And don't make any fuss about all this when you talk to him. If you do, I'll—I'll sue the landlord for heavy damages. Get me?"

"Yessir."

ALMA WAS BEGINNING to snap out of her fainting spell. She swayed unsteadily to her feet, her eyes wide with a sick terror, her face white.

"What did you do, Jerry?"

"You know damned well what I did, baby," he said steadily. "I shot that tramp husband of yours."

"No, no.... Jerry—no!"

"In self-defense. He let go one at me and missed—the big overgrown dope! You can see, I did much better."

"You can't do it, Jerry. I won't let you."

"Ssssh! Let's not waste time wrangling. Did that last crime tip that you sent me come from him—from Ralph?"

"Yes."

"Just what I thought. And if something else I'm fairly sure about is true—we're both sitting pretty.... Don't cry, sweet, for the luva mud! There'll be a cop banging on our door in about a minute and I want to squeeze in a quick phone call to Inspector Fitzgerald."

He ran across to the telephone like a brisk little ferret. He jerked up the instrument and dialed fiercely....

"Hello, Fitz? Jerry.... Yeah—Jerry Tracy; right! Listen—hop it up here fast, will you?" He gave Fitz the address and apartment number. "A guy just got dead up here. A tie-up with the numbers racket and that Ritter murder or I'm very wet.... What? Oh—I forgot—*I* killed him. Yeah, *me*."

He could hear the voice of Fitzgerald sputtering incoherently on the other end of the wire.

"Will you quit burping and get under way?" Jerry snarled. "Bring Killan along with you. And keep this news temporarily under the hat like a good guy."

He banged down the instrument and swung impatiently back towards Alma. She was staring at him with her lips still open.

"How did you do it, sweet?" he asked her gently. "How were you able to get the drop on Ralph?"

"When Ralph first came in, he did something so—so horrible to me that I knew he was determined to kill you without mercy the moment you rang the bell. I went to the bedroom, palmed the gun and had it behind me in the chair. I let him have it the moment he got up and sneaked towards the door to let you in."

She began to weep suddenly, to lose some of that dreadful rigidity from her throat....

"He—he was going to kill you. The minute you came in the door."

"Why me?" Tracy sounded like a man who already knew the answer.

"Ralph said," Alma whispered brokenly, "that you knew too damned much, that you were nosing too close to him."

"How did he know I was coming here to see you this morning?"

"I told him," Alma moaned. "He suspected something and beat it out of me. I—I couldn't help it. He—he made me tell. Then he sat there, grinning, with a gun ready, waiting for you, to ring the bell." Her voice cracked. "Said if I opened my—my trap, tried to warn you—he'd hand it to us both as a betrayed husband."

She gestured hopelessly and a corner of the black negligée slipped from one shoulder. Tracy, eying her, grunted savagely and took a swift step towards her.

"So Ralph made you tell him, eh?"

He yanked the frail lacy stuff away from both her shoulders. The sight of her naked back made him wince and curse faintly.

"What did he use on you, sweet? A whip?"

"A dog whip. Said a dog whip would be swell for a —— like me. He—he locked the bedroom door and—"

"Just a nice guy." Tracy stood over the dead man with smoldering eyes.

Then he dropped to one knee, went through Ralph's pockets. A little croon of satisfaction escaped him.

"Greedy man," he whispered and re-placed the object carefully.

The doorbell began to ring. Urgently. No letup to it. Tracy opened the door and smiled mildly at the drawn gun of a traffic cop.

"It's okey. Battle's over. Come on in."

The cop's gun stayed menacing. He was looking fixedly at Tracy's belted raincoat, the damp hat that was still on his head.

"You live here?"

"Nope. Just a friend of the bride and groom. Come on in."

The cop gave Ralph's stiffening body a quick professional glance.

"Who done this?"

"I did, Officer," Jerry said.

"Yeah?" He eyed Alma, the lacy negligée she had hurriedly bunched over her breast. "You the dead guy's wife?"

"Yes. I—I—"

"You were out like a light when it happened," Tracy warned her swiftly. "You wouldn't remember a thing."

"A wise guy, eh?" the cop snapped. "That'll be about enough outa you. I'll do all the talking. And keep them hands right where they are, or I'll make things tough. Who are you? What's your name?"

"The name, my businesslike friend, is Tracy. Jerry Tracy."

"Huh?" The cop's eyes studied the wizen-faced little fashion-plate with a new and more lively interest. "Jerry Tracy? You mean that you're the—"

"Yeah. I mean. Of the *Daily Planet*. And if I were a bright young officer, I'd stick around and take things easy—before I got too smart and pulled a boner."

The traffic man grunted doubtfully. Then, with his eyes on the columnist, he began to back slowly towards the small table in the corner of the room.

"I've already phoned," Jerry smiled. "If you'll wait for about two more minutes—"

The front doorbell rang again. Jerry was beginning to feel almost fond of that bell. He chuckled with relief.

"Shall I let Inspector Fitzgerald in, or will you?"

The cop let him in. Sergeant Killan came in with him. Fitz' blue eyes looked at the traffic man and the cop became at once inconspicuous.

"Mmmm…" Fitz said thoughtfully. "Who is he, Jerry?"

"A Greek by the name of Ralph. Let's see if I can remember his last name—Koulopolis.…That hole in the wall came from Ralph. That hole in Ralph's belly came from me."

Fitz blinked. "What's the story, Jerry?"

"Ralph runs a restaurant. A very phoney one, it seems. This sweet little lady here—" His eyes burned suddenly but the gesture he threw towards her was polite and mechanical. "—had the very tough luck to be married to this rat. Alma, meet Fitz, a square cop. Sergeant Killan, ditto."

The *Daily Planet's* little columnist smiled.

"Alma put me wise to something I was just a little vague about. I came over here to see her about it. Our Greek friend was waiting for me with a gun. He got tough and I deaded him.…Alma, by the way, is that sweet little tipster you've been so worried about, gentlemen."

"Uh-huh," Sergeant Killan muttered.

The inspector said: "Mmmm…. Am I getting this thing right? This fellow Ralph was in on the numbers thing? A tie-up with Ritter and Fink?"

"In way up to his Grecian neck—and over, sweetheart. Listen, has Morris Fink done any talking since you—"

"Plenty," Fitz snapped triumphantly. "His cloak-and-suit business was strictly a cover-up—a phoney. Fink and Ritter split fifty-fifty on the numbers graft. They met regularly every Sunday night at that St. Nicholas Avenue dive. Fink caved in, finally, with a little help from Killan here, and admitted he was at the St. Nicholas Avenue place Sunday night. But he swears that Ritter was still alive when he left. Says he didn't kill him."

"He didn't," Tracy said. "This guy did."

"Are you sure?"

"Take a look at his pockets," Tracy suggested. "He was greedy enough to steal something. A Greek, bearing a gift. Vest pocket, Fitz."

The inspector grunted as he studied the watch. A diamond-studded little masterpiece. On the inside of the paper-thin case, a couple of lines of microscopic engraving: "To Sam, my woolly old woof-woof, from Belle."

"ALL GREEKS ARE art lovers," Tracy suggested mildly. "Ralph couldn't resist swiping the ticker after he had stabbed the guy."

"How did you know he stabbed Ritter in the first place?"

"I didn't, Fitz. Remember how I told you I had reached a conclusion; but that it was negative? All I knew until recently was that Morris Fink *didn't* kill Ritter."

"How come?"

"Fink was too small, too soft—too weak. The whole thing hinged on that sloppy wet floor in the kitchen. Some one had pulled the electric plug out of the wall and the refrigerator had been defrosting all night. The door had been left partly open and there was no tray under the freezing unit—hence, sloppy floor. It looked as if someone had been cleaning something off the floor, and that made me curious, got me to looking around, and let me discover where the killing had been done."

Killan said slowly: "You mean Ritter was killed in the kitchen?"

"Correct. I'm afraid you didn't notice the tiny smear of blood between the ragged edges of the linoleum and the wall. The murderer thought he had wiped it all away, but he overlooked the crack at the edge of the linoleum. There was also a tiny sliver of broken glass, sharp enough to cut my dirty finger and make me worry till I slapped some iodine on it later.... What I think—the guy stabbed Ritter while they were having a sociable drink at the icebox. Ritter went down like an ox and his hooked arm caught the wire and dragged it down with him. The murderer heaved him up and carried him into the dinette where we found him. Now, we know that Ritter was a heavy man, husky as hell in the shoulders. His partner, Fink, couldn't possibly have carried him. Too weak, just a buttery-fleshed little runt."

Tracy shrugged.

"Ergo, don't bother with Fink for the murder rap but look for a guy as big, or bigger, than Ritter. As a matter of fact, a guy who turns out to be none other than our good-looking and oversize friend here."

"How did he get in the apartment?" the inspector wondered.

"I'll tell you," Alma said. Her voice sounded weak and very tired. "Ralph told me about that. Kept boasting to me while he was sitting here with a gun in his hand waiting for—for Mr. Tracy. Ritter let Ralph into the apartment right after Fink left. They had arranged a private conference beforehand. Sam Ritter was planning to freeze Fink out of the profits and tie up with Ralph instead."

Her breast heaved.

"The murder happened exactly the way you said, Jerry. Ritter didn't suspect a thing. He died while they were drinking a toast to each other. Ralph killed him because he wanted to get the racket for nothing. He took Ritter first because Ritter was the tougher of the two partners—and because he figured that any hurried alibi Fink was forced to dig up wouldn't hold water. With Ritter dead and Fink accused of the crime, the numbers racket wouldn't have to be bought out. It'll be ripe to pick up out of the gutter. Ralph was all set to grab it for nothing."

Alma's eyes blinked the tears away.

"He made me send you that last tip, Jerry. That tip was deliberate. He was using you and your column in the *Daily Planet*. Using you to hand him a fortune for nothing."

Tracy gave Inspector Fitzgerald a hard look. "You've got what you wanted, Fitz. Call in the mob whenever you like. But let me handle the newspaper slant on this thing. Alma is out of all this. Maybe I'm in it. I dunno yet. But whatever I tell the boys will be as plausible as hell. Satisfied?"

"Your dice, Jerry," Fitzgerald said. "Roll 'em as neat as you can!"

Ticketed for Death

Jerry Tracy's hunch of crime or adventure
is not always a safe one to follow

THERE WAS SOMETHING about the man in the brown suit that Jerry Tracy didn't like. He first saw the fellow loitering over near the ornate cigar stand in the *Diplomat's* swanky lobby. His eyes were beady; he looked like a shabby brown fox.

Tracy happened to be behind the theater ticket desk by a mere fluke. With a few minutes to kill he had wandered into the *Diplomat,* and wound up talking to Peterson at the agency desk. Peterson had promptly seized the opportunity to buzz off for a quick cup of coffee; and Tracy, bored and lazy, nodded and said, sure, he'd watch things for a while. It was barely three o'clock in the afternoon and Tracy was in no hurry.

He had tabbed this shabby guy with the first shrewd glance. The man seemed mildly uneasy as he stared out of the corner of his eye. Tracy catalogued him swiftly as he walked across to the ticket desk.

Crafty brown eyes, long nose, thick brownish eyebrows that needed a mite of scissor trimming. Brown mustache, ditto. Bum teeth. The whole summed up to something out of the ordinary, to Tracy's supersensitive alertness to things that were not exactly on the up and up.

Tracy felt the sharp inner excitement that always came to him at the beginning of a bizarre adventure. He had a strong feeling that this shabby stranger was going to provide either the material for Jerry's famous *Daily Planet* column or perhaps another of those brisk crime tangles that Tracy loved to jump

into with both feet. Jerry grinned faintly as he thought of
Inspector Fitzgerald: maybe he could hand Fitz a crime and
solution all on the same platter. He knew he could count on
plenty of cooperation from the police; they had profited from
Jerry's detective ability on many an occasion. The arrangement
was very simple—Tracy enjoyed the thrills; Inspector Fitzgerald got the credit.

"I want an orchestra single for tonight," the man muttered.
"It's gotta be D-101. I positively can't use anything else."

Tracy grinned. "If there was no trouble digging up tickets, who would ever bother paying an extra premium? Am I right, mister?"

"I'll pay the freight," the man grunted. "All I'm interested in is the ticket."

Peterson came striding back at this precise instant. Tracy frowned meaningly at him, said coolly; "I'm busy with a customer, Fred. Stick around a minute, like a good fella."

Peterson grinned and took the hint. "Sure thing. I got lots of time."

He eyed the stranger and so did Tracy. About 160 pounds, the *Daily Planet's* columnist thought swiftly. Wiry looking, well muscled; about Tracy's own build. Bad breath, disguised poorly with spearmint flavor. A cheap watch ticking loudly somewhere in the guy's vest. No visible lump from the gun tucked out of sight in a shoulder-holster, but the gun sag in the ready-made coat was unmistakable.

"What show did you want the ticket for, mister?" Tracy asked.

"Alabama Moon. At the *Parkhurst Theater."*

"Mmmm…. Musical, eh? Smash hit. Right away you start making it hard…. For tonight, you said?"

"Yeah. You see, I'm a traveling man. Just in town for one day. The wife has D-103 for tonight—bought the damned thing weeks ago. I've gotta leave for Chi tomorrow and I'd like to take in *Alabama Moon* with her before I pull out. We could exchange her ticket for something else, but the wife happens to be as deaf as the dickens—and all I can find around town is stuff in the balcony, which is no good for us at all."

He said the whole thing almost in one breath. His complete

lack of hesitation underlined the falsehood in Jerry Tracy's attentive mind. People with long-winded explanations and odd requests usually simpered, hesitated, looked faintly embarrassed. This brown-mustache guy with the gun was entirely too glib.

"Mmmm.... Try any of the other ticket agencies?"

The man grinned. "I tried 'em all."

"That's a large statement, mister," Tracy murmured. "Maybe I know a few spots to dig a single at the last minute—that the public never heard of. If I do, it won't cost you no four-forty. It'll cost you about—" purposely, he made the price steep "—about twenty-two bucks for that single ork."

"Okey," the man said instantly. "The wife's pleasure is worth a lot more to me than the dough, on account of I only see her every—"

"Sure. Naturally.... Where do you want the ticket delivered? To your wife's address?"

"No, no. Send it to the *Hotel Cantwell.*"

Tracy didn't comment but his puzzled eyebrows made the customer talk some more.

"It's much simpler to stay at the Cantwell than to go over to my apartment for the one day," the man explained. "You know how it is with salesmen—I have my sample case handy—dealers know where to find me. So being just the one day in town, I don't usually bother to—"

"Sure, sure," Tracy said soothingly. "What was the name, please?"

"Davidson. Harry Davidson. Room 729 at the *Cantwell.* Can you get it there by six?"

"Six it'll be there," Tracy nodded. He lurched awkwardly

forward, said, "Excuse me," and bowed the visitor away with a respectful smile.

Peterson said in a discreet undertone: "He had a gun, Jerry."

"Yeah. So I noticed."

"He sounded pretty phoney to me. That yarn of his about his deaf wife smells like last year's herring."

"Herrings fool you sometimes," Tracy said.

"You think he's a phoney?"

"I'm not telling you what I think, boy friend. Mmm.... *Alabama Moon*. Ticket must be D-101 and no substitute will do at all. Willing to blow twenty-two bucks for the thing without a squawk. And he loves his home but prefers the *Hotel Cantwell*.... Be a good guy and forget about all this, will you, Fred?"

Peterson shrugged and nodded.

"I'll take a walk to the *Parkhurst Theater*," Tracy said. "There's a bookie on Forty-fifth owes me an even hundred on *Flying Fiddler* to show. Maybe I can scratch his ear for it."

A HALF-DOZEN PEOPLE were waiting in line at the *Parkhurst* box-office. Tracy said, "Hiyuh, Joe?" to the guy behind the window, went around to the side and let himself in. In a couple of minutes the treasurer swiveled around and grinned.

"You're looking fine, Jerry. What's new?"

"Oh, nothing much. How's for a little favor, Joe?"

"Sure. Anything special?"

"Ork single. For tonight." He got casual. "D-101."

"Huh?" The box-office man grinned suddenly. "You in on that thing, too, Jerry? I'll bet I know who your friend is."

"Tell me, sweetheart."

Joe described the man in the brown mustache and Tracy nodded.

"He was around here this morning," Joe said. "He looked kinda crumby for one of those 'must have it right away' people. I got leery right off the bat. Besides, there's something screwy going on behind that D-101 business. Do you know the guy?"

"Maybe," Jerry said. "What's the matter with D-101?"

Joe hesitated. "It's been puzzling me like hell. Sounds sorta crazy; no sense to it."

"Shoot!" Tracy said curtly.

"Well, this particular ticket—just the one single—has been reserved every Thursday night since the show opened. The week before the show opened I got a cash remittance, ordering that seat for the first two Thursdays. The following week more cash came, reordering in advance. And so on. Ever since."

"What's funny about that?" Tracy inquired.

"Listen," Joe said. "The seat has never been used. Not once! I know because I checked on it, see? And then, last week, the money stops coming. And the minute that happens up walks this crumby guy in the brown mustache and must have the seat at any price—for the same old Thursday performance— which is tonight."

He spread exasperated hands.

"Look, Jerry! When it's paid for—nobody wants it. When it's not paid for—*somebody* wants it. Queer, or not?"

"Who signed those advance orders you received?" Tracy asked.

"They were unsigned. Just a typewritten note, with the currency folded inside. Postmarked Grand Central. All alike."

"And whom were you asked to mail the ticket to? A man named Davidson—Harry Davidson?"

"No. A woman. Mrs. Claudia Shale. 225 Clayborn Avenue."

"Where's that? Bronx?"

Joe grinned tolerantly. "You Broadway guys are the nuts! Nope, it's in Manhattan, believe it or not. Between Riverside Drive and upper Broadway—over near Columbia.... I even remember the apartment number; it's 1-C. Had half a mind to drop in on that dame some time and ask her how come."

"Don't," Tracy advised him softly. "You might get that snub nose of yours bitten off.... Where's the ticket now? For tonight's show, I mean."

"I gave it to Dave day before yesterday."

"Dave, eh?" Tracy chuckled wryly. "That makes it tough. What did you charge the fat robber?"

"I only tilted it two bucks. Six-sixty—with a return privilege if Dave can't make the thing gallop at his own price."

"Gimme that Mrs. Shale's address again," Tracy muttered. He wrote it down and squeezed out the tiny doorway.

"Hey," Joe called. "Where you going now? Over to Dave's?"

"Down to the zoo to see a fat elephant," the columnist said with a slow smile. "Elephants are supposed to remember favors for years and years? S'long, Joe."

It wasn't much of a walk to Dave's joint. Tracy trudged south for a couple of blocks and then went west through the dusty sunshine. Two doors from the corner of Seventh Avenue, wedged in between a chain drug-store and a restaurant notorious for its male clientele, was Dave Lipmann's stationery-and-cigar store.

A thin-faced kid who looked like an old man was leaning

on the battered counter with both elbows, poring sleepily over a racing form.

"Gimme a half-pack of Camels," Tracy murmured lazily.

"Huh?" The kid looked up and grinned. "Oh—hello, Mr. Tracy!"

"Dave around?"

"He's in the back. Grabbing a little shut-eye. Want me to wake him up?"

"Don't bother. He's an easy guy to wake."

Jerry Tracy lifted a greasy red curtain and passed into the tiny cubicle back of the store. An exceedingly fat man was fast asleep on a shabby auction-room sofa. He lay there utterly relaxed; one plump hand trailing on the floor, the other flattened limply on his capacious stomach.

If Dave's nose was just a little bit longer, Tracy thought, he *would* look like an elephant! He reached down and laid a fingertip softly against the fat jowl.

Dave's eyes blinked open instantly. They were blue, intelligent, alert. "Hello, Jerry." He sat up and let his inquiring eyes save wear and tear on his voice.

"I want to dig a ticket, Dave. *Alabama Moon*. Ork. D-101."

"Why not?" Dave grinned. His fingernail made slow sandpaper noises on his enormous chin. "Twelve-twenty okey?"

"It's okey for the public," Tracy said slowly. "How much for me?

"Okey, no profit. Take it for eight-eighty."

The *Daily Planet's* columnist handed him very gravely a five-spot and a single. He fished in his pocket and added a half-dollar and a dime. Dave's admiring guffaw made his huge chin waggle.

"What a guy! You been over to the *Parkhurst* and checked on the price with Joe, huh?"

"Wouldn't you?" He waited while Dave dug around in an ancient card index box and found the pasteboard.

"Why all the interest in *Alabama Moon?*" Dave asked him curiously.

"I love its balmy air, 'cause my mammy comes from there," Tracy told him with dead-pan gravity.

He stopped on the sidewalk and glanced at his watch. Twenty after three. He walked back to Seventh Avenue and hooked a cab to the curb with a gentle but persuasive forefinger.

A FEW MINUTES later Jerry Tracy rode vertically for nineteen floors in an elevator operated by a good-looking brunette in a short uniformed skirt. She smiled pertly as he gave her the double-O. Not bad at all; her legs rated a second look.

The glassed door on the nineteenth floor said in small, well-bred block: *Dill C. Haig, Private Consultant.*

Haig was sitting in his private office. His round, dimpled cheeks made him look like a chubby, not overbright little fellow. He nodded pleasantly, didn't say anything.

Tracy grinned at him. "You won't do at all. Is Pat around?"

"Outside somewhere. Want him in a hurry?"

"Yeah."

His desk phone brought long, skinny legs and a thin inquisitive face into the room.

"Hello, Pat," Tracy said. "Got a little job for you."

"Am I in on this thing?" Haig asked plaintively.

Tracy said, "No," and rose to his feet. Pat led the way to a smaller room, hardly big enough to contain its two chairs, a table and a water-cooler.

Tracy told him about Mr. Harry Davidson and added: "I want you to dig me up a fuzzy brown mustache. Understand me—I don't want to disguise myself as Davidson; I just want to look different enough that anyone who bumps into me won't recognize me as Jerry Tracy. Can do?"

Pat grunted briefly, "Sure, why not?"

He bustled out for a minute or two and returned with a theatrical make-up box and a weird assortment of brown mustaches.

Jerry picked one. Then Pat did a slow, careful job. Jerry eyed his altered appearance with a little grin of satisfaction. He borrowed the scissors from Pat and trimmed the ragged brown mustache a shade more on the left side.

"How about it," he asked Pat, "will the mustache stay on?"

Pat grinned. "It'll hurt plenty when it comes off. Say—what's this all about, Jerry?"

"I don't know. Maybe nothing to it at all. This is the easiest way to case a hotel room that I know of. You don't have to bribe hungry desk clerks and house dicks—or swing down from cornices like you sleuths are supposed to do in the movies."

He pushed a sudden forefinger into Pat's vest.

"Stick around here tonight just in case. I'll tell Haig on the way out that it's a paid assignment."

He walked over to the phone and called the *Hotel Cantwell* in a shrill, whining voice.

"Has Mr. Davidson come in yet? Mr. Harry Davidson? Room seven-two-nine?"

He could hear the switchboard operator buzzing patiently.

"Never mind. I'll call him again tonight."

He grabbed a taxi and rode uptown to a roaring Sixth Avenue corner. He walked the extra half-block to the *Cantwell.* It was one of those narrow-doorway places, with a long rectangular lobby. Warty-looking palm trees in glazed pots. Huge white urns, filled with a messy mixture of gray sand and cigarette butts.

The brown-mustached, fox-like Mr. Tracy slid inconspicuously through the lobby behind an evening paper.

He rode up to the seventh floor, walked along a moldy gray-plush carpet to Room 729, and tried the clever little skeleton keys Pat had given him. After a while the door swung open.

For a moment Tracy stood tense and watchful, breathing a little faster than usual. The room was empty. Shades neatly drawn, bed made up, waste basket and ash tray emptied and clean.

The bathroom door was partly open. He stuck his head in, took a cautious peek—and stiffened with frozen horror.

STARING DOWN AT the dead man, Jerry Tracy had a sickening feeling that he had not handled this thing just right.

The real Davidson was dead, all right. Not peacefully dead, either. Flat on his back, with a tiny bullet-hole in his waxen forehead. There was terror in the contorted mouth, stark amazement in the glazed eyeballs.

Jerry Tracy snapped out of his trance. He turned swiftly back into the bedroom. He stood on tiptoe near the bed, watching, listening, sniffing; trying with every acute sense he possessed to rip some intelligent meaning out of his surroundings. As far as Tracy could discover from his swift, lightning survey not a single thing in the room had been moved or tampered with. There was no gun in sight. He had a hunch, having seen the dead man's wound, that if he found the gun, it might be a .32. Tracy walked softly across to the walnut dresser and picked up the room phone. He called the desk and spoke carefully.

"This is Mr. Davidson calling. Room Seven-two-nine. I've been expecting someone to get in touch with me all afternoon. Are you sure that no one has called or left a message?"

"Just a moment, Mr. Davidson. I'll check."

The voice returned in a few seconds. "There was a phone call for you a little while ago. Just before you came in. No message. Man said he'd call back later this evening."

Tracy pretended mild surprise. "Are you sure no one asked at the desk for me this afternoon?"

"No, sir. Just that one phone call."

"Okey. Thanks."

Damned funny, the columnist thought. A dead guy—and, according to the clerk, no one had called on him.

Frowning, Tracy went through the pockets of the dead man. He found something he hadn't expected: a metal shield. The fellow wasn't a crook, after all. Somehow, the discovery didn't surprise Jerry so much. A private dick, eh? Mmmm....

He looked at the shield. Whalen Detective Agency. Tracy had never heard of the outfit; probably some cheap, furtive, two-bit affair. He'd have to check on it with Dill Haig. He shoved the shield in his own pocket and concentrated on a more interesting find—a slip of paper with the pencilled name and address of Mrs. Claudia Shale. It was in a tiny ball, rolled up with shreds of tobacco in a corner of Davidson's vest pocket.

Tracy thought things over for a swift instant. Was Mrs. Shale a client of the Whalen Agency? A frightened woman, trying to buy protection for herself from some threatened danger by hiring a private dick? Oh was the dick after the Shale dame for some reason?

A sudden clicking sound roused the Broadway columnist from his puzzled reverie. His eyes jerked towards the mirror of the dresser. He became very still. He was staring at the reflected image of a man with a gun. The muzzle of the weapon was trained on the exact center of Jerry Tracy's cold back.

"Stick 'em up, Davidson!" a low voice snapped.

Tracy lifted both hands obediently above his head. He turned stiffly. The connecting door between the dead man's room and the room adjoining it was partly open. That was where the sly gunman had come from. Inwardly, Tracy cursed himself for his stupidity. His absorption in the dead detective's shield and the crumpled shred of paper with the pencilled memorandum had made him a ridiculously easy victim.

The man with the gun was a young fellow. About twenty-two or so. His hand wavered slightly but there was no tremble in the set of his chin or the sound of his menacing voice.

"Thought I didn't know about you—eh, Davidson? You're not as wise as you thought you were."

Evidently the gunman didn't know Davidson by sight. This was Davidson's room and that the man in it should be Davidson seemed obvious to him.

The gun in his hand looked a lot like a 32.

"Take it easy," Tracy whispered. "Don't shoot. I don't know who you are, but I'm not fixing to make any fuss."

"Never mind who I am."

The guy looked dangerous. Coldly alert blue eyes, a muddy

pallor on his strained face. Keyed up to killer's tension. As vibrant as piano wire.

Jerry had shut the door of the bathroom before he telephoned. The gunman stared at the closed door and back again at his captive.

"Come on! Fork over that theater ticket!"

"I don't get you, buddy. What theater ticket?"

"Turn around!" the gunman growled. "Get that back of yours towards me. Try any wise stuff—and I'll let you have it in the spine."

He was no amateur at a stick-up; he knew his search business. He frisked the columnist carefully from the rear, one knee bent forward to protect his groin from a treacherous kick.

"Dunno what it's all about, huh?" His laugh was as cold as an ice cube. "Never heard of the Whalen Detective Agency, huh? And who told you about Mrs. Shale—a mind reader?"

Tracy didn't say anything. He was trying to stow away in his brain every rememberable detail of the man's face and figure.

The man chuckled as he found the theater ticket Jerry had bought from Dave Lipmann. He didn't bother taking the shield; just grunted scornfully and dropped it back in Tracy's pocket.

"Are you planning to take in *Alabama Moon* tonight?" Jerry inquired politely.

"Ask Mrs. Shale—if you think you can get away from me!"

He whirled Tracy with a brutal shove of his left palm.

"Get going! Into that bedroom. And don't try any cop stuff, if you want to keep on living."

There were three lengths of clothesline lying on the bed in the adjoining room. Under stern necessity Tracy clasped hands behind his back and the gunman tightened the first rope across the joined wrists.

The fellow wasn't taking a single chance. He made the pseudo Davidson lie down crossways on the bed; on his belly, with his head hanging over the edge. He leaned over Jerry's helpless wrists and bound his thighs and ankles in a tight squeeze. With a quick gesture, he wadded a handkerchief and stuffed it into Jerry's mouth. Made the gag immovable with a couple of strips of adhesive tape.

In five minutes he had the whole job done, the connecting door between the two rooms locked—and was gone.

JERRY TRACY ROLLED stiffly over on his back. His mouth and throat ached like the very devil. He had to get out of this hotel room in a hurry and find out who this Mrs. Claudia Shale was. What kind of a murderous mess had he stuck his nose into, he wondered? A lot of people seemed to be desperately anxious to get hold of that D-101 pasteboard!

In the meantime, here he was, tied up on a hotel bed! As helpless as a trussed chicken—or so the boob with the gun thought.

The *Daily Planet's* columnist grinned at the shabby ceiling. He began gently manipulating his overlapped hands. He was slow, methodical, not in the least jittery. That was the beauty of being a Broadway personage! You met everybody worth meeting—and all of 'em knew things. Tracy had never spent much time with the late Henry Houdini, but he did know Joe Dengler. He had spent a whole rainy week-end once with Joe and had discovered with a delighted interest just why God had put thumbs on people's hands.

In eleven minutes the disguised columnist's trussed wrists were free. His ankles and thighs took about a minute and a half.

He rode down in the elevator with a gentle and ruminative smile. He could count on a delay of—say—till ten o'clock the next morning before the chambermaid let herself into 729 with a pass-key and discovered the body of the unfortunate Davidson. By the time the chambermaid was rushing out of 729 with a shrill Hibernian yelp of terror, Jerry ought to know a lot more about this theater ticket mystery.

He didn't walk past the desk on his way out. Instead, he descended three steps in the rear of the long lobby, sauntered inconspicuously through a noisy restaurant and stepped out on the cool sidewalk in the hotel's rear.

He drove straight home to his comfortably luxurious penthouse up near the sky. He glanced at his watch. Ten after six. A lot to do tonight and no telling how much inconvenience he might run into later on. Might as well freshen up and enjoy the quiet interim.

He removed his clothes and with considerable difficulty got rid of the mustache. The sound of gurgling water sloshing into his expensive bathtub made him hum *Alabama Moon* cheerfully. He wondered if the long-legged Pat was obeying his orders and hanging around the agency office awaiting a possible phone call. He dawdled in his bathtub, slid without haste into clean silk underclothes, dug a light-weight suit out of his extensive wardrobe.

It was past eight when the *Daily Planet's* fastidious columnist departed. He strolled across 52nd and down Broadway. *Alabama Moon* was an 8:40 musical and Jerry made the crowded lobby of the *Parkhurst* with almost five minutes to spare.

"Nice gross last week, Paul," he told the gray-haired veteran at the door.

Paul chuckled, nodded with a friendly grin. "Capacity business, Mr. Tracy. Coming back for another peek at that smash opening number?"

"Yeah."

He squeezed in with the mob and hunted up a harried-looking girl in a crinoline costume. She handled Center Orchestra and she looked as busy as a colony of ants.

Tracy touched her arm and she smiled at him and listened attentively.

"Do me a little favor, Edith. Is D-101 still empty?"

"Just a second, Jerry…. Yeah."

"Listen," he whispered. "I want to squat in D-101 for just a minute or two of the opening number."

The theater orchestra was blaring the overture blend of *Alabama Moon, I'd like to cotton to you,* and *Howja get so Southern?*

Tracy leaned closer to the usherette and talked fast:

"If the seat-holder arrives right away, stall for a minute. I don't want to be discovered, see? I'll beat it the minute you show up with your flashlight. It'll be a cinch on account of the blackout opening. Can do, honey?"

"Okey. If it doesn't get me in a jam."

"It won't. And thanks a lot. I'll remember the favor, sweet."

He hurried up the aisle. The overture ceased. Footlights and house lights faded and plunged the theater into total darkness. The curtain rose. On a jet-black stage the magnificent Cotton Boll Number began getting slowly luminous.

Tracy was already in D-101. He paid no attention to the

stage, was entirely oblivious to the gasps of admiration that ran through the invisible audience at the gorgeous spectacle of faintly luminous nudity poised against a black sky under nodding head-dresses of fluffy white cotton. The music from a pit flowed warmly, like a caress. A wave of handclapping swept like a sudden rainstorm through the darkened theater.

With a flickering match cupped under his palm, Jerry Tracy was examining D-101 in lightning detail. He looked swiftly at the seat, at the wire hat-rest underneath. He fingered the brass number plate, tested the screws, tried to lift it. He examined the opera glass contrivance on the seat in front. Nothing—not a damned thing.... He even felt the floor carpet, fingered it swiftly for a cunning slit, a pouch underneath, the telltale bump of something hidden. Still nothing....

His match went out and, feverishly, he struck another. People all about him were tapping impatient feet, "shushing" at him with sibilant irritation. A voice growled in a harsh undertone: "Why don'tcha look for it in the intermission, dope!"

He blew out the second match and glanced backward down the dark tunnel of the center aisle. The tiny yellow oval from the usher's flashlight was racing up the carpet toward him. Coming straight toward D-101. Tracy squirmed out of his seat like an eel and, dropping his face slightly, but not his eyes, walked swiftly towards the rear of the theater.

He passed the two of them, taking care to go by on the usher's side. The guy with her was a young man. Jerry perceived, without any astonishment, that it was the same young fellow with the pallid face, who had stuck him up with a gun in the Hotel Cantwell an hour or two earlier.

THE MUGG WAS blinking like an owl. He didn't tab Jerry's face. Wouldn't have helped him if he had! The only time he had ever seen Tracy, the columnist was wearing a ragged brown mustache and carrying a tin shield from the Whalen Detective Agency.

Jerry Tracy didn't hang around the back of the auditorium. He sidled toward the red light where late-comers were still trickling in. He pushed past Paul into the glare of the lighted lobby.

Paul gave him a puzzled stare. " 'Smatter, Jerry? Had enough already?"

"Yeah. Just wanted to take another look at that opener of yours. It's still a wow, Paul."

"I'll say it is. Greatest smacko opener a musical's had since poor Ziggy died!"

Jerry Tracy went out to the sidewalk and hesitated a moment. A short distance away a mounted traffic cop was sitting idly on his horse talking to a couple of cute wrens on the curb. Jerry drifted over and rubbed the animal's sensitive muzzle.

"How are things shaping up, Herman?"

"Pretty good, Mr. Tracy." The cop smiled down at the two shapely wrens. "I can't complain."

"Glad to hear it."

He kept hanging around. Finally, the wrens pouted and beat it. Tracy kept chatting idly with the mounted cop, his careless eye on the entrance of the *Parkhurst Theater.* He wondered keenly whether the guy in D-101 would stick for the whole performance—or would he show up pretty soon?

The guy showed.

He came out in a brisk hurry, took a quick, nervous look up

and down the crowded sidewalk. Then he turned on his heel and hurried east toward Broadway.

Tracy said, idly. "S'long, Herman. Remember me to the missus."

He drifted east in the wake of the guy he was interested in. He wondered, moodily, whether the guy had gone into *Alabama Moon* to pick up something—or whether, like Tracy himself, he had gone in on a pure hunch. There was no indication that the gunman had gathered any prize package during his brief stay in the theater—unless the swift streak he was making for Broadway was a hint that he had located what he was after and was about to go places.

The *Daily Planet* columnist stepped along a bit faster himself. He was still some distance behind, however, when the guy reached the corner and went *fffwt* out of sight.

Tracy frowned, broke into a little trot and went *fffwt* himself. He rounded the corner just in time to see his quarry race out into the gutter and climb into a miraculously empty rolling cab.

At this hour on Broadway no roller had a right to be empty, Jerry thought savagely. He hooked his eyes up and down for another. No dice.

A voice roared: "Hey, wanna lose all your toes, Stupid!" and Tracy skipped nimbly back to the curb. By the time his nervously shrill yelp had got him a Checker, it was too late. The mysterious gunman in that damned Yellow had scooted through a honking maelstrom of traffic into invisibility. The columnist swore grimly and changed his mind about following him.

"Beat it," he told the Checker driver irritably. "I don't want you now."

Tracy walked a slow half block to get the disgust out of his system. By that time he came to the Liggett's drug-store on the next corner he had all the useless anger out of him—and an absolute honey of an idea in.

He was tagging the wrong end of this thing, anyway! The logical stunt was to stick his curious nose in on this Mrs.— what the devil was her name?—this Mrs. Claudia Shale, of 225 Clayborn Avenue. Up around Columbia, the box-office man had said; just off Riverside Drive. The stunt was to find a cockeyed excuse for dropping in on the dame.

Jerry grinned: His scheme was plenty cockeyed.

He shouldered into Liggett's and raced a fat guy to the only empty phone booth. He won, only to remember with a silly grin that he didn't know the phone number. He came out and the fat guy snorted victoriously and went in.

Jerry turned over a flock of dog-ears in a chained Manhattan book and concentrated on the S's. Monument 1-0902. He crowded the end booth and grimly saw to it that he was next.

In a few seconds a middle-aged female voice said faintly: "Hello?"

"Is this Mrs. Claudia Shale?"

"Why, yes.... Who is this, please?"

Tracy put ripe Southern culture into his voice.

"I hope you'll pardon me, Mrs. Shale, for calling you up to tell you of an almost unbelievable coincidence that has just occurred to me. You see, I'm a stranger in town. I just bought a theater ticket for *Alabama Moon*."

He heard a faint, smothered gasp but he kept right on.

"The seat was for the orchestra. D-101. And here's the amazing part of it. Your name and address was written in pencil on the back of the ticket."

"Impossible. I've bought no ticket for that show."

"It's written on the ticket, I assure you," Tracy insisted courteously. "And the coincidence was so—well, so absolutely astounding—that I didn't go to the show. I decided to call you up and tell you about it."

Mrs. Shale sounded puzzled, confused. "That's all very interesting but I don't quite understand what you mean by coincidence. Just what coincidence are you referring to?"

"Oh, yes." Tracy chuckled. "I beg your pardon. I forgot to tell you in my excitement. You won't believe it—it's really too silly for words—but my name happens to be Shale, too. Mr. Edwin J. Shale."

"I—I see. That's—that's certainly quite unusual, isn't it?"

"As I say, I'm a stranger in New York. My home is in Alabama. Just a few miles outside of Montgomery. Is your family—er—Southern, Mrs. Shale?"

She was hesitating again. Scared sick about something or Jerry was all wrong. That D-101 had hit her right in the kitchen sink!

"My people," the faraway voice murmured slowly, "come originally from Tennessee, I believe."

"In that case," Tracy said drawlingly, "there's a good chance that we are actually related. My uncle Albert has lived for years in Nashville. Mrs. Shale, I hesitate to ask it, but you can do me a very gracious favor if you will. May I come and see you for just a few minutes? I wouldn't bother you if it were not for the fact that I'm here in New York for only a day or so. May I present myself as a namesake from Alabama, a very homesick Shale asking a few minutes indulgence to talk with you?"

He lied persuasively. "There is only one other Shale in the New York book—and I've already called him. He's a news agent in the Times Building and no relation at all. May I come and talk with you? Please!"

Her voice was very low and very tremulous.

"I'm—quite busy. However—that D-101 theater ticket puzzles me. If you care to call, I'll—I'll see you."

"Thank you," Tracy said softly and hung up. There was a film of sweat on his imaginative forehead. He frowned.

He said in a shaky whisper to the black-rubber transmitter: "We-uns are sho' nuff makin' headway, Masser Shale!"

The inevitable taxicab hauled Jerry Tracy swiftly northward along the diagonal trail of Broadway. There was a temptation to close his eyes and wonder what this Mrs. Shale looked like, to speculate why she seemed so frightened over the wire about this D-101 business. But Jerry was not the guy to go wool gathering unless there was something to be gained thereby. His main difficulty, of course, was the fact that he couldn't produce the D-101 pasteboard with the old gal's name written in pencil on the back. Half of the damned thing was in the ticket box at the *Parkhurst;* the other half in the pocket of the tough young guy with the gun. However, the lack of Exhibit A didn't worry Jerry too much. He'd hand this Shale dame a line of malarkey. Jerry never had much trouble soaping people, particularly females.

He got out of his cab at 116th and Broadway and walked down the steep hill to Clayborn Avenue. It was a short residential street, the last thoroughfare before you hit Riverside Drive. Two-Twenty-five was a tall, gray-faced elevator building of the old style, drowsing quietly in the darkness across the street from the huge dormitories of Barnard College. Looked like a stodgy and sedate joint, the kind apt to be inhabited by professors and the more successful of the neighborhood retailers.

Apartment 1-C was on the ground floor directly in the rear of an imitation-marble lobby. It adjoined the elevator shaft. The elevator door was open and a sleepy, gray-thatched negro rolled smoky eyeballs inquiringly at the visitor; but Tracy shook his head and punched the bell button of 1-C.

He punched it three times before he frowned and snapped over his shoulder: "Come here a minute, Alfred!"

The negro laughed as though at a marvelous joke. "Ah ain't no Alfred, boss. I'se Phillip." He frowned helpfully at the closed apartment door. "Don't she answer, boss? Maybe she ain't home."

"She is home," the columnist contradicted sharply. "I was talking with her on the telephone not more than ten minutes ago. Did she go out during the last ten minutes or so?"

"No, sah. She sho' didn't."

"How do you know?"

"Cause Ah ain't rode but one pusson up in de last half hour. Dass how Ah knows. I been right here all de time, sorta cogitatin' 'bout things." He laughed with a rich chuckle. "Ah's a great feller for cogitatin'."

With a queerly sober face Tracy rang the bell again, held his finger against the button for a long fifteen seconds. No answer.

"Yo' done think they's somethin' wrong, boss?"

"I don't know. Looks damn funny to me. You people got a master key to these apartment doors?"

"Yassuh. Sho' has. But—But—"

"Go get it!" Tracy had a flash of inspiration and remembered something in his pocket. He gave the negro a half-second glimpse of the dead Davidson's detective shield. "Don't give the Super any story about me. Tell him a tenant forgot his key and wants to get in. Make it sound ordinary. Understand?"

"Yassuh. But I sho' wish—"

He departed rather unwillingly. When he reappeared his black face was wrinkled with worry.

"Miz Shale is a nice, quiet tenant, sah. We ain't nevveh had no police gemmen here befo'. Ah hope yawl ain't fixin' to make no—"

"Unlock it," Tracy snapped. "And keep your mouth shut. If you open your trap to anyone but me, I'll slap you in a precinct cell."

He closed the door of 1-C softly behind him. Motionless, he waited in the darkened foyer of the apartment, watching, listening. Directly in front of him were glassed double doors, closing off what was probably a living-room. A dim light inside yellowed the panes of the closed doors.

The columnist tiptoed closer and glanced, right and left, along a high-ceilinged hall. Kitchen at one end, a bedroom at the other.

Someone was groaning very faintly. The sound was so low that only a man with Tracy's supersensitive ears would have been aware of it. A church bell began to toll somewhere in the neighborhood and Tracy waited till the bell stopped. The groaning was louder now. It came from the closed living-room.

He turned the knob slowly, made an infinitesimal crack. Suddenly he gasped and stepped swiftly inside the room.

A GRAY-HAIRED WOMAN was lying on the floor

near an opened window. The window curtain was blowing and billowing across her crumpled, motionless figure. Her eyes were closed. Her head was bleeding from a small gash in her scalp just above her right temple.

Tracy sprang forward and lifted her from the floor. He got her into a high-backed chair and her head rolled weakly against the blue-striped slip-cover. She was not unconscious but groggy as the devil. Jerry popped out into the hallway, found the bathroom and filled a blue unbreakable cup with cold water.

Her eyes fluttered open presently and she moaned. Terror was in her eyes but it faded as she saw the face of the columnist.

"Is—Is he—gone?"

"Yeah," Tracy said gently. He glanced at the open window. "Take it easy, madam. You'll be okey in a couple of minutes."

He picked up the thing that had slammed her. A wooden rolling-pin, lying incongruously on the living-room rug, near the small bookcase directly under the window-sill. He glanced at the smear of blood on it, laid the thing down again where he had found it. He poked his head out the window. He was looking across the concrete paving of a backyard towards the brick rear of a Riverside Drive building. The drop from the open window was probably ten or eleven feet. An easy jump for anyone. He craned up and down the concrete length of the adjoining backyards. Towards 116th the yards ended smack against a tall brick wall; but up the other way, Jerry could see a dark cross street and beyond it a tall church tower with a red light burning steadily at its gloomy peak. That must be where the infernal bell had been booming, Tracy thought sourly. No sense climbing over the back fences after the vanished housebreaker; by this time the guy must have long since reached the side street, beat it swiftly over to the Drive and handed a dime to a bus conductor. He'd be well on his way now past Grant's Tomb—or maybe the other way, through Cathedral Parkway for a quick fade later in midtown Manhattan. The oldish dame with the gray hair was showing signs of snapping back to normal.

"Who—Who are you?" she gasped.

"I'm the gentleman who called you on the telephone," Jerry told her gently. "My name is Shale. Edwin J. Shale. If you'll remember—"

"Yes.... Oh, yes.... You are the man who—" Her dulled eyes began to look frightened again. "You had a theater ticket—with my name written on it. How—How did you get the ticket? May I see it?"

Jerry Tracy blandly ignored the question.

"I was afraid there was something wrong," he murmured, "when you didn't answer my ring at the bell. I got the hallman to unlock your door.... What happened? A sneak thief?"

"He—He must have been."

She hesitated, eying her visitor with that same indefinable suggestion of bewilderment and terror.

"I was in the living-room here, looking over the *New Yorker*—when I thought I heard a stealthy noise in the kitchen. I—I didn't pay any attention at first; sometimes the gas-oven door makes a funny bumping sound like that when it's heated. But I heard it again, and it scared me because I was all alone. I got up and walked cautiously to the door and—"

She shuddered and Tracy said: "You're all right now, Madam. Take it nice and easy. What happened then?"

"He—He was sneaking along the hall from the kitchen. He—had the rolling-pin in his hand like a—a club. I tried to scream—to run—but he sprang into the living-room after me and struck me over the head. I—I— He must have gotten in by climbing up from the backyard somehow—got in through the dinette window and sneaked through the kitchen."

"What did he look like? Get much of a look at the man?"

"He seemed—well, young. A young man. It's—It's hard to remember when you—"

"Naturally," Jerry said soothingly. "How about his face?"

"That's the most horrible part of it," Mrs. Shale shuddered. "He wore a mask; a black, shiny thing with slits in it. It made him look inhuman—like a—a—beast."

The columnist nodded thoughtfully. "Excuse me," he said suddenly, and left the living-room. He hurried back to the kitchen, snapped on the light, put his bright, beady eyes to work. He, popped into the dinette and did the same in there. He was gone only a minute or so and apologized when he returned for his abrupt action.

"Thought maybe the burglar might have left some trace," he murmured. "I think we ought to call in the police at once."

"No!" she gasped quickly. "No, no! Not the police. I'm—all right. I wouldn't want any—any newspaper notoriety over my—my mishap."

Tracy said, slowly: "It sounds silly, but do you suppose there could be any possible connection between this attempt at burglary and—and that theater ticket with your name on it?"

"I don't see how—" She was very pale. "What possible connection could a ticket for *Alabama Moon*—an orchestra ticket, you said, for D-101—"

"I beg your pardon, Mrs. Shale," Tracy said quickly. "It wasn't."

"Wasn't? I don't understand." Her hand flew to her breast. "Aren't you Mr. Edwin Shale? Didn't you call me on the telephone and tell me that—"

"I'm Shale, all right. Edwin J. Shale, of Montgomery, Alabama. But I didn't say D-101." He lied coolly. "The ticket I bought was D-201."

"Oh!"

She looked at him blankly. He was able to detect no relief in her scared eyes. What the devil was behind all this? Sneak thieves didn't wear masks; they only cased joints where they figured the coast was clear for a quick finger-grab and a quicker getaway. Was that mask stuff just a bit of baloney to cover up a recognition that Mrs. Shale was afraid to talk about? Her whole demeanor was a plain statement to Tracy that she *had* recognized the burglar's face and was afraid to admit it. Why?

He knew that Mrs. Shale was going to pin him down in a minute about that damned theater ticket he was supposed to have. He was thinking up a suave stall to explain its absence when abruptly the front doorbell rang.

MS. SHALE JUMPED nervously. So did Tracy. This cock-eyed running around in circles was beginning to get his goat.

"Shall I answer it?" she whispered, her voice quavering.

"Yes. Go ahead."

He rose noiselessly from his chair and stood just inside the living-room door, listening.

He heard Mrs. Shale sigh audibly. She said, faintly, to someone: "Oh, hello. Where have you been?"

"Out," a voice sneered.

"Whereabouts?"

"Just plain out. Do I have to give an itemized account of every street corner I stop on?"

It was a man's voice. Petulant. Hard.

"It's a wonder you wouldn't stay at home once in a while," Mrs. Shale said faintly. "I might have been killed."

"Huh?" The man followed her into the living-room and stopped abruptly as he saw a stranger there.

Tracy smiled blandly at the young man and said, "How do?" very politely.

It was the guy who had held Jerry up with the .32 in the *Hotel Cantwell*. The same elusive lad who had sat in D-101 at the *Parkhurst Theater*, whom Tracy had last seen vanishing south-ward in Broadway's traffic in an elusive Yellow taxicab.

The recognition was not mutual. The Jerry Tracy that this fellow had tied up wore a brown mustache and looked anything but like the Jerry Tracy of the moment.

The young man ignored the columnist's politely extended hand.

"Who's this fellow, Auntie?"

His face swung suspiciously towards Mrs. Shale and for the first time, apparently, he became aware that she was hurt.

"Hey.... What happened to your head? What's the matter?"

She told him, with eyes averted, about the burglar's visit. He listened, watching Tracy out of one corner of his eye. Panic flowed into his face as his aunt told him about the fortunate visit of the nice Mr. Edwin Shale, who had come up to see her about a theater ticket.

"This is my nephew, Leo," Mrs. Shale told Jerry. "I'm so glad he's home just now; I'll feel so much safer." Her face gave the lie to her tremulous words. If anything, she looked twice as scared as she had before.

"Please to meet you," Leo mumbled. "Certainly is some coincidence, huh?" His scowl added, unmistakably: "How long are *you* gonna hang around here, mister?"

Tracy noticed that the nephew was breathing a little faster than normal, as though he had arrived in a hurry.

"Been running, Leo?" he asked gently.

"Who, me? I've been climbing that blasted hill from Riverside Drive." A flush came into the pallor of his cheeks.

"What of it?"

"Nothing," Tracy murmured. "If you'll excuse me, I'll be going."

"Don't linger on my account," Leo sneered.

"Leo!" Mrs. Shale murmured reprovingly. "Is that any way to talk to—"

"Aw, let him beat it!" Leo stalked over to a corner table, picked up the *New Yorker,* and pretended to read it.

Mrs. Shale escorted her mythical namesake to the door.

"Leo's a little tired, I expect," she said faintly. "I'm sorry he was so rude. Thank you for your—your very welcome help. I'm sure I'll be all right now."

She said it wistfully, almost beseechingly. The *Daily Planet's* columnist had a strong feeling that her worried eyes were mutely begging him to stay, not to leave her alone with Leo. Tracy smiled at her, however, showed his teeth in the usual insincere grin of farewell and walked out through the dim marble, lobby into Clayborn Avenue.

He did some rapid and heavy thinking as he hurried back

towards 116th. The affair seemed to get phonier by the minute! All the threads seemed to tie up, not with the theater, but with that apartment he had just left. Had the dead Harry Davidson been working under cover for Mrs. Shale? Had she become panicky and lugged in a private dick on the case? If so, where did the sullen Leo fit in? The old lady seemed plenty afraid of her sallow-faced nephew.

And what about the burglar who had swatted Mrs. Shale on the dome—the guy she didn't seem anxious to identify? Tracy smiled dimly as he considered the sneak-thief angle. His mind went back to Leo and played with him all the way to the drugstore on the corner of 116th and Broadway.

He called up Dill Haig's agency and, after a brief wait, heard the voice of Pat. The operative sounded froggy.

"Huh? Oh—hell, Jerry.... Been asleep, I guess. Reading a dopy magazine here all by myself. Guess I musta dozed off.... Anything new?"

"Plenty. Grab your hat and come on uptown. One-sixteenth and the Drive. I'll be on a park bench, waiting for you."

"Gunplay?" asked the practical Pat, with no sleep left in his voice.

"How do I know?" Tracy chuckled. "Of all the bloodthirsty guys I ever met, you're the worst. Yeah—better bring old Sally Ann along. And make it snappy, sweetheart!"

He hung up, and walked down the steep hill to the Drive. He found a bench near the bicycle path and sat there in a mild reverie.

He was glad when the gaunt figure of the practical Pat finally showed up in the darkness. He gave Pat the crisp details of what had happened since he had donned his makeup and gone to the *Hotel Cantwell.*

Pat whistled softly. "So what do we do about it?"

"We're going back to Clayborn Avenue and flash shields on 'em," Tracy said. "Two guys from the homicide squad. Very official and hard-boiled. You may need Sally Ann; I think Leo is heeled.... You flash your own tin and I'll show 'em the thing I took from Davidson."

"Okey." Pat considered things briefly. "What about this Davidson? He still nice and quiet in his bathroom?"

"Yeah. He won't bother anyone till the chambermaid lets herself in tomorrow morning. How come you don't know about Davidson and the Whalen Agency?"

"It's a cheap and very rackety outfit. We never got chummy with that particular agency."

They climbed the steep hill and went back to 225 Clayborn Avenue. Tracy rang the doorbell of 1-C but it was Pat who crowded close to the doorknob.

The minute the door opened Pat had the startled Leo backed helplessly against the wall of the apartment's foyer.

"Hands away from that hip, son," he whispered grimly, "Or poppa blow nice hole through belly!"

JERRY TRACY SHUT the door and smiled at the fuming Leo. Mrs. Shale's sullen nephew recognized their recent visitor and made an ugly sound in his throat. Jerry grinned amiably.

"Who is it, Leo?" a pleasantly youthful voice called from the living-room. It was a girl's voice; Tracy had never heard it before.

"Walk!" he ordered softly and Pat's businesslike Sally Ann dug into their captive's back and prodded him forward.

The young woman in the living-room jumped to her feet

and squealed faintly as the procession appeared. She was dark-haired, dark-eyed, creamy skin, full red lips. Nice figure, too.

"She's in show business," Tracy thought, swiftly. "I'll bet *salami* on that!"

Quickly he jerked out Davidson's shield, flashed it in his cupped palm with a brisk, businesslike gesture. Mrs. Shale had risen to terrified feet from her easy chair over in the corner. She stared at the young woman and Leo. She seemed desperately to be trying to read their faces. Leo, too, was staring fixedly at his aunt.

It was Leo who spoke first.

"Your fake relative seems to have come back again—with a pal," he said bitterly to his aunt.

His eyes swung quickly towards the younger woman.

"I told you this visit of his wasn't on the level, Ruth. Didn't I tell you that Edwin Shale stuff was a bluff?"

"Shut up!" Pat snapped at him. The agency man's lean fingers located and extracted from Leo's hip a squat-looking .32.

"Where'd you get this toy, son?"

"None of your damned business."

"You got a permit for it?"

"I sure have."

"What is the meaning of this—intrusion?" Mrs. Shale wanted to know in a shaky voice. "Am I to understand that you were deceiving me when you—"

"Yeah," Tracy said. "But I'm not deceiving you now. City detectives, ma'am. We're here to find out something about a homicide."

"Homicide? You mean—somebody has been murdered?"

"Correct. A man named Harry Davidson. Ever hear of him?"

"Davidson—dead?" She found it hard, suddenly, to talk. She looked at Leo and if ever Jerry Tracy saw an unspoken accusation of murder, he saw it then as she stared in fright at her sullen nephew.

"My God, Leo," she faltered. "Did you—"

"Cut it out, Auntie," Leo snarled. "Don't be a sap."

The dark-haired girl was still silent. She had clear gray eyes and a nice mouth; Tracy liked her looks.

"Who are you?" Tracy asked her.

"My name is Ruth Glennon," she replied evenly. "This is my brother, Leo Glennon. Mrs. Shale is our aunt."

"Yeah," Leo said thickly, "and if you ask me—"

"Be quiet, Leo," Ruth Glennon said.

"Well, they're not going to hang no Davidson killing on me!"

"You weren't in his room at the *Hotel Cantwell* late this afternoon, by any chance?" Jerry suggested silkily.

"Huh? What do you mean?"

"Are you quite sure you didn't sneak into room 729 with that gun of yours?"

Leo's mouth clamped shut like a steel trap.

"I've got nothing to say," he muttered through clenched teeth.

"It's still your party, Jerry," Pat told the columnist calmly. "What's next on the program?"

"Take Leo and his sister into the next room," Tracy said. "Keep an eye on 'em till I call you back."

"Right."

Mrs. Shale averted her eyes from the venom of Leo's glance. Tracy closed the living-room door softly behind the nephew and niece.

"I'd like to ask you a few questions," he said to Mrs. Shale. "Don't be afraid to talk candidly. No one can hurt you now."

She nodded, her fingers twisting nervously together.

"Was this man Davidson in your employ?" Tracy asked her.

"Yes. I hired him."

"Why?"

She cleared her throat, glanced nervously at the closed door. "Each week, for the past six weeks, I've received through the mail two sealed envelopes. One contained an orchestra ticket for *Alabama Moon*—D-101. The other contained an unsigned typewritten note, threatening me with immediate death unless I used the ticket. I telephoned the box-office of the *Parkhurst Theater* and the man there told me that all he knew was that the money for the seat came regularly to him in cash from some anonymous friend who said he wanted to surprise me. I was terribly frightened about it, but I thanked the box-office man and said it was very thoughtful of my unknown friend."

"Did you tell your nephew and niece about the tickets and the threats?"

"Yes. Leo just laughed. Said it was a practical joke of some kind. Ruth didn't say anything at all, but she looked very queer and uneasy."

"So you went down to the Whalen Agency and hired Davidson?"

"Yes. That was last week. Mr. Davidson came up and looked around my apartment here and—and he told me almost immediately that every one of the notes had been written on—on Leo's portable typewriter."

"Did you tell that to Leo?"

"No. Leo asked me several times to show him the notes, but I refused."

"Mmmm.... Did Davidson accuse Leo of writing them?"

"Leo never saw Davidson. Davidson took the notes with him and said I was to do nothing and wait for the next threat. No more came. Leo seemed awfully curious about the whole matter. He asked me if any more messages had come, and when I told him no, he chuckled and said maybe the joker was getting cold feet.... I was more than ever uneasy on account of something else. Leo—well, Leo suddenly ceased his demands for the money."

"What money?"

"He wanted $10,000," Mrs. Shale faltered. "I'm almost sure he's gotten himself into some kind of a blackmail mix-up. He owes some man $10,000 and he and his sister, Ruth, have been worried and quite bitter about it. They both said I had no right to—to refuse them the money. But I can't give them a penny more than their regular allowance, which is fixed by the court. They both wanted to borrow $5,000 on their inheritance and I—I refused to sign my name to the paper. Either Leo or Ruth is being blackmailed—I am sure of it. They wouldn't discuss it with me."

"What does Leo work at?" Tracy asked curiously.

"He works for an importing house downtown."

"And his sister, Ruth?"

"She's on the stage. A specialty dancer, I think you call it. That's the added suspicious circumstance that made me call in Mr. Davidson. You see, Ruth is employed at the *Parkhurst Theater*. She dances a specialty in the first act of *Alabama Moon*."

"I SEE." TRACY'S voice was low, expressionless. "So Ruth Glennon is actually *in the show*, eh? Tell me—when were you last in touch with Davidson, Mrs. Shale?"

"He called on the telephone early this afternoon. He said he was following up a promising lead and would probably have some interesting news for me tomorrow morning."

"Did he say what he was planning to do?"

"No. He merely told me to sit tight, to be sure to say nothing to either Leo or Ruth. He said he'd get in touch with me tomorrow."

For a moment Jerry Tracy was silent. Then he said, very quietly: "Mrs. Shale, why did you lie to me about the identity of the burglar who struck you on the head tonight?"

Her lips began to tremble. "I didn't lie," she gasped.

"You recognized that burglar," Tracy said slowly. "He wore no mask. Who was it—Leo?"

"I—I don't know. I couldn't be sure."

"But it might have been Leo, eh? I know you don't like to accuse your own nephew of striking you down, but I can't get to the bottom of this unless you're absolutely fair with me. You think it was Leo, don't you?"

"It—It might have been. I won't swear to it."

She looked suddenly, pitifully old.

"He's my—my dead brother's son. I—I tried to bring him up properly. I don't really believe that either Leo or Ruth would ever dream of—" Her jaw tautened. "I'm positive that the man who struck me was not Leo."

"Let's hope not," Tracy said gently. "Suppose you go into your bedroom for a few minutes and lie down. I may want to ask you a question or two later. In the meantime I'd like to talk to your nephew and niece."

He waited till the door of her bedroom closed, then he raised his voice and called Pat.

"Okey," a faint voice replied cheerfully. "Shake a leg, folks. The boss wants to see you."

Leo strode in with a vicious scowl.

"Where do you get this third degree stuff, Mister Detective? If you think you're going to get Ruth and me mixed up in this theater ticket mess, you've got another think coming. Go ahead and arrest us. See how far you'll get."

"Please, Leo," Ruth said tremulously. There was terror and bewilderment in her gray eyes.

"I'll do the talking," Tracy said. His eyes swung to Leo. "You know your aunt has been getting a free theater ticket sent to her every week for the past six weeks or so. Do you happen to know why she *didn't* get one this week? She hired a detective named Davidson a couple of days ago. Do you suppose the arrival of Davidson on the scene had anything to do with the sudden stopping of the tickets—and the murder notes?"

Leo's laugh was bitter, ugly.

"If you really want to know, Sherlocko, I think the whole thing is a pipe-dream. I don't believe Auntie ever got any typewritten notes."

"Who told you that the notes were typewritten, Leo?"

"Why—my aunt," he growled hesitantly.

Jerry Tracy smiled slowly and let that pass.

"Why did you kill Harry Davidson this afternoon in the *Hotel Cantwell?*" he asked Leo.

"He didn't!" Ruth Glennon cried swiftly. "Leo wasn't there. Why don't you let him alone?"

"Where were you, Leo?"

His eyes looked hunted, worried. "I was at the movies."

"Any particular movie—or just the movies?" Tracy purred. No answer.

"I understand that you're in a financial jam right now. You could use a little ready cash in a hurry, no?" No answer. There was sweat on Leo's forehead, a taut bulge at his jaw muscle. Ruth looked as though she were about to faint.

Tracy tried an entirely new tack with the sullen nephew.

"I'd like to play a little game with you, Leo. If you're really innocent, you won't mind playing."

"Game? What do you mean?"

"Oh, just a little word game. For instance, what does the word lead-pencil make you think of? Quick!"

"Eraser," Leo grinned.

"Detective," Tracy said next.

Leo's grin broadened. "Flat feet," he said promptly.

"Corpse," Tracy shot at him with a second's pause.

Leo hesitated. "Undertaker," he muttered uneasily.

"Hotel bathroom. Come on!" This time Leo floundered badly. After a long wait, he said in a low tone: "Cake of soap."

"That's enough!" Tracy said sharply. "You were in that room at the *Cantwell*. And you killed Davidson!"

"You're a liar. I told you I was at the movies."

A shrill scream of terror cut across the murmur of Leo's words. A woman's frightened scream. It came from the closed bedroom of Mrs. Shale.

THE *PLANET'S* COLUMNIST swung towards his thin-faced companion.

"Get in there, Pat!"

"Right!" the agency man snapped.

He sprang through the doorway and ran down the long hall. Jerry kept narrowed eyes on his two prisoners. Neither of them made a move to get away. A subtle look passed swiftly between them. Ruth was white-faced and trembling; Leo seemed to be smiling inwardly.

"I s'pose you'll be blaming Ruth and me for *that*, too," Leo sneered. "Maybe I'm in the bedroom right now, socking dear old Auntie on the dome."

"Shut up!" Tracy ordered. He stood quite still, listening for further sound. The bedroom was as silent as a tomb.

"Pat!" he called out.

No reply.

"Pat! Mrs. Shale! Are you all right in there?"

Still no reply.

Ruth Glennon's scared gray eyes stared at the Broadway columnist. Leo fished a cigarette out of his pocket and struck a match with a show of elaborate unconcern.

"Both of you stay right here," Jerry grunted harshly.

He ran out into the hall and sped swiftly to Mrs. Shale's bedroom. Mrs. Shale was lying on the bed, her eyes bulging with fear. Her finger pointed shakingly towards the opened window. There was no sign of Pat.

In two jumps Jerry Tracy was over at the window and had his head out.

The concrete backyard was empty and dark under the black night sky. Directly below the bedroom window were two motionless objects. One of them was Pat's hat. The other was a cat.

The cat was a coal-black Tom. It was eying the motionless fedora with slitted green eyes that seemed to flame in the darkness. The green eyes lifted and surveyed Tracy lazily. Slowly, the bored Tom cat began methodically licking its paws.

Tracy swore, drew in his head and stepped back to the frightened woman on the bed.

"Quick!" he cried. "Where did he go?"

Mrs. Shale was the color of paper. She could barely talk.

"He went out the—the window," she gasped. "It all happened so quickly that I—I—"

"Did you see anyone? Who did he jump out after?"

"I was here in bed," Mrs. Shale quavered. "I happened to turn my head on the pillow, I looked towards the window. I saw a—a face…. A man…. He was hanging from the sill by his hands—staring in at me…. I screamed and the—the face dropped out of sight. The detective came rushing in, and I pointed—and the detective went out the window after him."

"Did you recognize that face you saw?"

Mrs. Shale shook her head weakly. "It wasn't Leo," she muttered. "It looked more like—like the other man."

"What other man?"

"The man that Leo's been seeing so often lately. The man that Leo has been trying to get the—the money for."

Her eyes closed.

Jerry Tracy turned away with a sibilant oath and ran back towards the living-room. As he stepped through the doorway a muscular hand closed on his throat with a grip of steel. The blade of a large jack-knife made an ugly, prickling dimple in the soft flesh of Tracy's neck.

"Stand still, dick, or I'll rip your jugular in half!"

Leo Glennon's eyes were burning into Jerry's with a glare of desperation and savage satisfaction.

The trapped columnist made no effort to struggle. He was facing the living-room doorway. Looking over Leo's back he could see no sign of the frightened Ruth Glennon.

Leo kept the cold point of the knife steadily against the columnist's neck.

"Hurry it up, Ruth!" he shouted hoarsely. "Don't waste any time. Grab our hats and coats!"

Tracy could hear Ruth's panting breath, her footsteps in the next room.

The floor creaked faintly beyond the doorway of the living-room and a woman tottered into view. It was Mrs. Shale, white-faced, staring. Leo's back was to the doorway. He couldn't see who it was.

"Okey, Ruth?" he snapped. "All set?"

The *Daily Planet's* columnist shot an agonized and appealing look towards the staring aunt. She screamed.

Leo jumped at the sound as though he had been shot. For a split second the point of the jack-knife blade left Tracy's throat.

Instantly, Tracy's knees bent and dropped his alert body a full six inches. With one hand he caught and clamped hard on his assailant's right wrist. His other clutched at Leo's thigh. With a swift shove of his glossy-toed foot, he tripped the fellow and fell on top of him.

They rolled over and over in a desperate embrace. The knife flew through the air and bounced with a faint thud on the rug. Jerry had a dizzily blurred vision of Mrs. Shale, still standing like a gaunt corpse in the doorway of the living-room. Behind her, a shadowy face moved along the hall—Ruth Glennon, fully dressed for the street, a man's hat in her hand....

The thump of Jerry's head against a low bookcase spilled books helter-skelter over the two struggling men. Leo's knee dug viciously at Tracy's abdomen, but the columnist saw it coming and managed to squirm away. He clutched at Leo's shirt and the fabric ripped free from his hooked fingers. Leo swayed upright on his knees, staggered to his feet.

He tried to run but Tracy's grip on his ankle toppled him again. The columnist managed to climb astride the thrashing body of his foe and he dazed him with a clumsy blow alongside the temple. He got one hand on Leo's throat and pinned him immovable for the second it took him to aim a more accurate punch. This time Tracy's hard fist landed squarely on the button and Leo groaned and got like jelly.

THE *DAILY PLANET'S* columnist was on his feet like a flash. He didn't bother trying for the fallen jack-knife on the rug. He hurdled Leo's twitching body and dove past the frozen figure of Mrs. Shale in the doorway.

Ruth Glennon was out in the apartment foyer, her hand fumbling desperately with the catch of the front door. Tracy pulled her gently back, walked her into the living-room, sat her into a chair.

She stared at him like a bloodless ghost.

"Leo didn't do it," she gasped. "Leo had nothing to do with the theater tickets. It was I!"

"You're just a little bit too late with your information," Tracy said mildly. "I know all the answers, myself."

The girl began to weep suddenly, her face staring hopelessly at the groggy figure of her brother. Leo was rising unsteadily from the floor, one hand bracing himself against the overturned bookcase. Jerry Tracy picked up the fallen jack-knife.

"Better be good, Leo," he said.

He nodded reassuringly to the aunt in the living-room doorway.

"Don't worry about Leo, Mrs. Shale. I'll guarantee that he'll behave himself. I'm going to settle this whole mystery right now.... I'd have settled it a lot sooner, only I wanted definite proof."

Tracy's eyes flashed somberly. "Mrs. Shale, was Leo the man who struck you on the temple tonight?"

Leo glared vindictively at her. She shuddered and turned away.

"Yes," she admitted in a whisper that was almost inaudible.

"And the fellow who tried to climb in your bedroom window—the man that Pat jumped out after? Who was he?"

"He was the man Leo wanted the $10,000 for—the man who has some sort of blackmail hold on Leo and Ruth."

"Thanks."

Jerry Tracy nodded. He reached suddenly for the telephone, called police headquarters. He murmured an official's name, got his party after a short delay.

"I want," he said, "a detective over here in a hurry from the West 123rd Street Precinct. With a pair of handcuffs. The address is 225 Clayborn Avenue. Apartment 1-C. And send someone over to the *Hotel Cantwell*. There's a private op. on the bathroom floor of room 729. His name is Harry Davidson and he works for the Whalen Agency. He's been murdered."

The voice in the earpiece buzzed with startled distinctness. "For God's sake, Jerry! What's going on?"

"Tell you later, Inspector."

He hung up with a little click. None of the other three moved. They were like wax figures in a museum, all of them.

After a while the doorbell rang and Jerry Tracy got up and admitted a stocky, ruddy-faced Irishman in a blue serge suit.

"My name's Walsh," the visitor said dryly. "West 123rd Street Station. You Mister Tracy?"

"Yeah. Let me have your cuffs, please."

Walsh blinked. He took his own slow time fishing out the steel bracelets. He eyed the tremulous Mrs. Shale, the damaged Leo. He looked at the weeping Ruth Glennon, took stock of her dark good looks. His eyes drifted back to the Broadway columnist and there were wrinkles of puzzlement on his ruddy forehead.

He handed Jerry the steel cuffs without another word.

Leo's puffy face paled as the columnist walked slowly towards him. He squirmed towards his weeping sister as Tracy's hand reached out.

THERE WAS A grim, menacing tautness on Jerry's lips. His hand shot out suddenly—and went past Leo's slumped shoulder. *Click* went a steel handcuff on a relaxed wrist—and suddenly hell seemed to break loose in the quiet room.

Mrs. Claudia Shale screamed shrilly like a trapped animal. She tore her fettered hand loose from Tracy's grasp and struck viciously at his face with the dangling cuff. He dodged with a grunt, clutched at her again and missed her as white teeth sank into his flesh.

The woman was like a raging tigress, snarling, kicking, flailing at the columnist with a dangling steel cuff that crashed, hammerlike, against his bleeding forehead.

Walsh, the precinct man, leaped to Tracy's aid. There was a fierce, straining flurry of arms and legs, then—*click*—went the second cuff, and with the sound all the demoniac rage left Mrs. Claudia Shale as swiftly as it had possessed her. She stood there, panting, a man on either side of her, and suddenly she laughed. A cold, eerie chuckle, deep in her throat.

"You seem to be a rather shrewd detective, after all," she told Tracy very calmly. "You were clever enough to give me no warning. I think, with a second or two of warning, I still might have outwitted you, my friend."

"Hang on to her, Walsh!" Jerry panted. "Don't let her fool you. Don't let go of this hellcat for one minute."

He turned and ran out into the hall.

"Hey!" Walsh bellowed. "Where are you going?"

"Going to find a friend of mine named Pat. And hoping to God that this she-devil hasn't killed him."

They heard his feet returning in a minute or two, shuffling heavily. He came slowly through the living-room doorway, with the unconscious figure of the agency sleuth in his arms. Pat's scalp was torn and bleeding. He hung dazed and limp in his friend's encircling grip.

Jerry laid him gently down on a sofa.

"May I help?" Ruth Glennon whispered in a small voice.

"Get me some cold water."

In a few moments the battered Pat stirred and began to groan faintly. His eyelids fluttered open and he tried to rise. Jerry's palm held him gently quiet.

The voice of Mrs. Shale—sneering, hard as ice—purred a slow question:

"How did you guess the fool was hidden in my bedroom closet?"

"I didn't guess. I knew!" Tracy replied softly.

The columnist's smile was like granite.

"Pat was unfortunate. You expected *me* into that bedroom, didn't you? Poor Pat took the rap for me—a rap right on the skull. You were waiting just inside your door with a lifted sash weight. You struck him unconscious, heaved him swiftly into your closet, tossed his hat out your window to the backyard—and you were flat on the bed in a fake state of terror when I came running in to investigate. You must have been frantic with rage when you realized I was still on the job."

Tracy's grim smile deepened.

"But you didn't notice the cat below your window, did you, Mrs. Shale? Had Pat's body come hurtling to the ground in pursuit of a fleeing criminal, the startled cat would most certainly have scurried over the fence like a black streak. But when I looked out the window, the cat was lazily dozing down there, watching Pat's hat. Ergo, only the hat had gone out the window—and Pat hadn't left the room. The only place he could possibly be was in the closet."

Jerry's eyes watched the woman like a hawk.

"You see, you had to work entirely too fast, Mrs. Shale. When I called you up on the phone originally, you realized that the Edwin J. Shale story of mine was a fake. But my reference to the D-101 ticket scared you. Maybe you thought I was another detective from poor Davidson's agency. You decided you'd have to look damned innocent in a hurry. So you invented a mysterious burglar, struck yourself on the temple, stretched out on the living-room floor—and waited for me to break in and find you."

Leo Glennon's haggard face lifted slowly from his clasped

hands. He stared at his aunt with incredulous amazement. "And she deliberately tried to—to—"

"To pin it on you, Leo? Exactly. However, I had proof, before you blundered in, breathing so heavily, that the whole assault story was a cooked-up lie."

Tracy nodded and smiled faintly at Mrs. Shale.

"In the first place, madam, a rolling-pin is a weapon no man would think of using as a club—but a woman would! In the second place the yarn you told me brought your burglar through the dinette window and the kitchen. I walked back, you will remember, and I discovered a curious fact. The dinette window *was locked*."

Tracy turned to Leo. "Let's have the truth about your presence in Davidson's room this afternoon. You were there, weren't you?"

"Yes. I—I was there."

"You hired the room next door. Sneaked in with a skeleton key, held up the man you thought was Davidson, tied him up—and stole that fool D-101 ticket from him. Right?"

"Right," Leo muttered dazedly.

"Why did you go to the hotel? How did you know Davidson was there with the theater ticket?"

Leo hesitated, wet his lips. He looked forlornly at his lovely sister.

"Ruth called me up and told me."

RUTH GLENNON'S HEAD jerked up in startled wonder.

"Why, Leo! That's not true. I never telephoned you. I knew nothing of Davidson's being at the *Cantwell*."

"I thought it was Ruth on the phone," Leo mumbled. "She said she had just found out that Auntie and Davidson, between them, were planning to railroad me to jail on account of that— that jam about money I'm in. She begged me to get my gun, rush over to Room 729 in a hurry and get the theater ticket from the private detective. She said the evidence we were so worried about was concealed in the seat D-101."

"And you went, of course."

"Yes. I stole the ticket. I went to the theater."

"And you found—what?"

Leo spread his trembling hands in a gesture of dulled wonder.

"I found nothing at all," he admitted. "I searched every inch of that seat and the carpet under the seat. Wherever the stuff was, it was hidden too cleverly for me."

Tracy smiled grimly at the handcuffed aunt.

"You found nothing, Leo, because there was *nothing there*. Your aunt seems to be a positive genius at the art of suggesting the invisible. Nobody struck her on the head tonight. Nobody startled her in her bedroom. There was *nothing hidden* in D-101 at the *Parkhurst*."

"But—"

"The whole thing was a really devilish piece of cunningly built up psychology. The whole purpose of Mrs. Shale's plot hinged on the murder of an innocent fall guy. Any victim would have done, but she picked a private detective as the goat in order to make her lying story sound all the more convincing. She hired Harry Davidson of the Whalen Agency—and she killed him!"

"You lie!" Mrs. Shale screamed.

"She killed him, Leo, for the sole purpose of sending you to the electric chair as his murderer."

"You mean," Ruth Glennon faltered, "that Auntie paid for all those theater tickets, and typed all those threatening notes—herself?"

"I do. Who would be a more plausible victim than the man she had ostensibly hired to protect her from death? So she killed Davidson and persuaded Leo to go to the *Cantwell* with his own gun. Observe how neatly all the threads of the scheme tied together. It even implicated Ruth Glennon as a suspicious person, because Ruth actually works as a specialty dancer in *Alabama Moon!*"

The frowning Tracy walked across to the sofa.

"Let's see Leo's gun for a minute, Pat. A .32, wasn't it?"

He took the weapon, broke it, smiled. One chamber had been fired recently.

"You see what you were up against?" he told Leo gently. "Your beloved aunt killed Davidson with a bullet from your own gun. The slug in his body bears the individual rifling marks from your weapon and no other gun in the world could match those microscopic scratches. Then your aunt sneaks away, puts the gun back in your bureau or wherever you're in the habit of keeping it. She leaves the house, calls you on the phone—and begs you in your sister's voice to *take that same gun* and visit the scene of an unsuspected murder."

The columnist's voice was like the rasp of a file.

"And I'll guarantee that, in addition to the fingerprints or other traces you left there, Leo, there is at least one damning bit of carefully chosen evidence hidden in Davidson's room to connect you definitely with the killing. To make it easier to slide you right into the electric chair.... Do you care to tell us what you planted there, Mrs. Shale?"

She laughed jeeringly. "If you were to move one of the dead man's hands, my inquisitive friend, you would find one of Leo's cuff-links. I thought it might make an amusing clue."

The woman spat at Jerry Tracy like a cat. The stolid Walsh nodded wisely at Jerry Tracy. "That makes it complete, all right. She admits it, and after all the things she cooked up on the lad, I'm thinkin' he needed just that."

"The only thing I'm not sure of," Tracy admitted, "is the motive back of it all."

Ruth Glennon smiled wanly. "Perhaps I can answer that. Both Leo and myself have thought for a long time that Auntie was worried about our inheritance. She was evasive and uncommunicative whenever we tried to pin her down about details. You see, when Father died, he left over $100,000 in trust for Leo and myself. He named Auntie, his sister, as executrix and administrator. We inherit the principal on our twenty-fifth birthdays—Leo's is next February, mine is a year later. But if Leo and I should die before then, the whole amount would revert legally to the only surviving heir, who is—is—"

"Your dearly beloved aunt," Jerry purred. "Tell me something Leo; why did you put up such a scrap with me, if you were innocent?"

"I was scared—and desperate," Leo mumbled, his face suddenly sickish. "Ruth and I are really in an awful jam and—and I need $10,000 so badly that I—I guess I lost my head. Do I have to tell you about the mess we're in?"

"It would help," Jerry said somberly. "You've been framed so devilishly well by your aunt that it will be hard for me to convince the police of your absolute innocence—unless I have all the facts."

"I stole ten thousand dollars," Leo muttered. "I falsified the books of the importing company where I work, to cover it until I could put it back. It was discovered—and I was given two weeks to make good, or go to jail."

"A thief, eh?" Jerry stared at him. "Why?"

Leo's pretty sister sprang to his side, her clear eyes ablaze with pride and love.

"He's no thief," she said steadily. "He took the money for me. If anyone is the thief, I am." She put a tremulous arm about her brother's slack shoulder.

"I needed that ten thousand dollars for my—my own selfish happiness. I'm engaged to a fine, decent man. Another man, of another kind, got hold of something very foolish that I had written and asked ten thousand dollars for not showing it to—to my fiancé. He's a headstrong man and might have—misunderstood. I love him and couldn't bear to lose him. Leo knew, and—borrowed that money for me. He couldn't get it in time in any other way, and our aunt wouldn't let either of us have it."

"You know the name of the blackmailer, of course?"

"Yes."

Tracy glanced at Walsh and Pat. "Don't tell me now, sweet. We'll straighten that out later," His jaw hardened. "I'll guarantee to get that money back in time for Leo to return it where it belongs."

The agency man was still staring fixedly at Mrs. Shale.

"I still can't figure," Pat muttered, "why this strong-armed old witch banged me on the dome and stuck me in her closet. What was the idea, Jerry?"

"She probably guessed that I was beginning to nose too close to the real truth of this case. I think she lost her nerve when she found herself alone in her bedroom, wondering uneasily how much of her scheme I had tumbled to. So she invented a second fake burglar and put you out of the way. That left me all alone—and if I hadn't wound up this thing quickly, I have a hunch that a ton of bricks would have crashed on my skull, too.... I had to let you stay in the closet because I wanted to keep Mrs. Shale off her guard to the last. I was afraid of her. As it turned out, even with Walsh here, she damned near cracked my skull with one of her hands locked in a cuff!"

Walsh grinned, wagged his head. "Some wimmen are sure hell on wheels when they—"

HE FLEW BACKWARDS with a startled yelp and tripped over the bookcase.

Mrs. Shale, taking advantage of Walsh's brief lapse of attention, had ripped away from his loose grasp and struck at his forehead with her trussed hands.

"Get her!" Tracy yelled. "Watch that window!"

He sprang forward. Pat bounced up from his sofa. Walsh caromed off the bookcase and dove headlong forward for the desperate murderess. He collided with Pat and missed her completely. Tracy got a hand on her clothing and lost her as the thin material of her dress ripped.

Before he could clutch at her again, Mrs. Shale was on her knees on the broad wooden sill of the opened window.

She uttered no sound. She dived headlong into darkness, arms stiffly out-flung like a swimmer. They heard her body strike the concrete pavement below.

"God!" Jerry muttered.

He saw Ruth Glennon swaying, her eyes closed in horror. He caught her as she fainted.

Pat's back and shoulders blocked the open window. He was staring silently down at the courtyard below. When he turned, the gaze he gave Tracy was veiled, expressionless.

"Only about a twelve-foot drop," Pat said. "She took no chances and dove. Landed on her head and—broke something."

Pat shut up abruptly and lit a fumbling cigarette.

Tracy was nodding slowly. "Funny how the one thing that queered Mrs. Shale was pure accident. I mean, my discovery of Davidson's body, merely because I thought there was something fishy about his search for the D-101 ticket. Poor devil, Davidson.... I wonder what lying tale she told him about the ticket?"

He shrugged.

"Okey, Walsh. You'd better phone Headquarters right away...."

He walked to the sofa where Ruth Glennon lay. Slowly he began chafing her cold hands. His eyes were very gentle.

Five Spot

Jerry Tracy takes a long chance on a solo chase

JERRY TRACY WAS flooding the mouthpiece of his dictaphone with swift, nasal comments for his *Daily Planet* column when he heard the ponderous, elephantine tread of Butch's size elevens.

"Hey, Jerry—yuh know what?"

Tracy halted the machine for an instant and snapped over his shoulder: "Get the hell out, Butch. I'm busy."

"Listen, Jerry, I—I feel kinda sick."

Tracy's head jerked around at that and the hard grin bounced out of his eyes. "S'matter, Big Fellow?"

Butch's platter face was pale; there were lines of pain at the corners of his thick lips. He was trying to grin unconcernedly and he wasn't doing so well.

"Remember that accident yesterday? You know—about the flower-pot?"

"Yeah."

"It wasn't no accident."

"What do you mean?"

Butch lifted his right arm away from his body and the columnist grunted as he saw the slash in the cloth and the wet smear of crimson. He kicked a chair forward, but Butch shook his oversize head with a tremulous grimace.

"It ain't so bad, Boss. Really it ain't. It—it just kinda hoits."

Tracy scowled affectionately at him. "Sit down, dope, or I'll knock you down." Swiftly he unbuttoned the coat and the pink shirt, lifted the cloth gently away from the sticky wound. A knife had gone into Butch's ribs about four inches below the right armpit. The lips of the cut were still oozing blood, but the wound, Tracy saw with a sigh of relief, was shallow; more a gouge than a stab.

The tension went out of his eyes and he patted Butch's shoulder with an unsteady hand. He was fonder of Butch than he cared to admit to himself.

"Who gave it to you, Big Boy?"

"I dunno. I got it down in a doorway on Forty-ninth just a few minutes ago." There was blind puzzlement in his eyes, rather than anger. "I'm tellin' yuh, that flower-pot that just missed my dome yesterday was no accident, Jerry. It didn't fall off no fire-escape or roof; someone dropped it."

"Tell me about the knife."

"Well, I'm walkin' along Forty-ninth, past that row o' crumby lookin' actors' boarding houses, when I see this blonde smilin' at me from a doorway an' tippin' me the friendly come-on sign."

"Dope!"

"But listen, Jerry—I think right away that she knows me, see? Because she hollers: 'Hey, Butch!'"

"What did she look like?"

"The hardest faced blonde I ever seen in me life," Butch said slowly. "One of them bony, thin pans—middle-aged an' lots of makeup. Small red lips and the narrowest eyes I ever seen on a dame. So I walks in the doorway an' she's half cryin' an' tells me she's an old friend of yours, an' she's in a nasty jam. She says she's Dolly Crane."

"Never heard of her," Tracy said quietly. "Did she give you the knife cut?"

"No. The guy done that. He comes hoppin' out from behind

the stairs, an' the dame grabs me arms and holds me. But I seen the flash of the knife an' pulls away, and the point just digs me open like you see. While I'm uncorkin' a right swing, the blonde lets me have something hard on the back of the skull, an' the two of them scram up the stairs after givin' me pockets the quick once-over, leavin' me staggerin' around like a drunk on ice-skates."

"You didn't try to go after them, huh?"

Butch scowled. "I sure did.

Chased 'em up to the roof an' lost 'em there. There was about four roof doors open along the line an' I made a bum guess. No sign of them upstairs or down on the street."

"What did the guy look like?"

"Tell you the truth, Boss, I don't know," Butch said shakily. He sat down suddenly and Tracy poured out a quick Bourbon for him.

"Flower-pot yesterday and knife today," the *Daily Planet's* columnist said in a softly meditative tone.

"Ain't it the damnedest thing? No sense to it."

"There's sense to anything that happens outside of an insane asylum," Tracy snapped. "Have you done anything in the last couple of days than might make someone sore at you?"

"Nope." He said it slowly; and Tracy, eying him narrowly, saw that he was embarrassed, holding back.

"Don't try to kid me, Butch. You didn't make a pass at the blonde did you?"

"Whew! I should say not. She ain't the kind you make passes at." He grinned weakly and said, in a diffident manner: "It might be about the five bucks."

"What five bucks?"

"Well, it was a sort of a dirty trick. I didn't really mean to gyp the guy—but you know how you do things sometimes. This sandwich-man stops me on Broadway yesterday mornin' an' shows me a five spot. He tells me a sporty lookin' guy walked up to him and handed him the fin—just like that. The bum with the sign thinks it's a rib an he asts me if the thing was any good."

"Well?"

Butch grinned and looked penitent. "There wasn't a damn'

thing wrong with it, except the mustache on Lincoln—so I told him it was just a phoney and gave him a buck for it as a souvenir."

"Wait a minute! A dropped flowerpot, a knife thrust—and now, a mustache on Lincoln!"

"Let's see that fin," he snapped, his eyes eager.

"I ain't got it. I spent it this mornin'."

"Where?"

"At Higson's *Tavern*. I went in an' busted it to buy a couple o' beers. Jeeze, I didn't think that—"

"Come on! Grab your hat!" Tracy tugged at his arm, and Butch winced and turned white. "I forgot—I'm sorry," the columnist said contritely. "Think you can make it to Higson's before we stop at a doctor's?"

"Aw, sure. I'm okey."

BUTCH STUCK ON his derby with his left hand and swaggered towards the door. Tracy wasn't too worried about him; he knew that the big fellow had a stomach as weak as a kitten's. The sight of the blood had upset him more than the gash in his ribs.

They grabbed a cab and burned up the avenue to Higson's *Tavern*. Billy Higson was curious but obliging. He opened the cash register and handed a thick sheaf of fives to the *Daily Planet's* columnist. Tracy pulled out one, showed it to Butch, and Butch muttered: "Check."

Nothing counterfeit about it, Tracy decided swiftly. An ordinary silver certificate, crinkled and rumpled from long wear, with Lincoln's head engraved in the usual oval. The only queer thing about it was the mustache drawn with indelible pencil on Lincoln's upper lip. It was a scrolled affair, like the curled mustache affected by top-hatted movie villains of the Desperate Desmond type. Looking closely at it, Tracy saw that the scrolled effect came from a blurred series of numbers separated by dashes. 15—10—6—15.

He gave Billy Higson a crisp new five and put the peculiar bill in his pocket.

"What goes on, Jerry?" Higson asked him pleasantly.

"Keepsake. I gave it to Butch by mistake and the boob spends it on beer. Thanks a lot, Billy."

"Keepsake?"

"Yeah. My grandfather once saved Hitler's life on the roller-coaster. Come on, Butch."

Higson eyed Butch's stiff right arm, but he didn't say anything. Higson had built up a million-dollar restaurant trade from a cheap hole in the wall by the simple expedient of serving good food and ferociously minding his own business.

There was no taxi in sight outside, so Tracy and Butch walked a block or two up the avenue, watching for a roller. They were crossing a side street when Butch grunted: "Here comes one now."

A second later Tracy yelled shrilly and jumped. The left wheel of the speeding taxi missed the columnist by a scant inch. The reckless cab-driver roared away with increased speed.

Tracy was up on his feet in an instant, staring at Butch. Butch got up more slowly, his face twisted with pain. There was a smudge of blood on the asphalt where he had dived.

"I'm okey," he muttered thickly. "Damn cut's beginning to bleed again. Did you get that ——'s number?"

Jerry's eye glanced eastward towards Sixth where the speeding cab had already rocketed out of sight. "The guy must have been drunk. Too late now. Let him go."

"But hey—" Butch glared incredulously at his very calm employer. "That bum tried to *kill* us! He aimed deliberately at us."

"Forget it, keed."

There was no cop in sight, Jerry was thankfully aware; but there'd be one along any minute. He didn't want any police curiosity about Butch's wound. He pushed Butch through the growing crowd, elbowed the nosey gawkers aside.

"Come on, dope," he whispered. He hustled Butch along the avenue to the parked cab that he had noticed while the crowd was forming.

"Two-eighty-four Central Park West, and make it snappy!"

The hacker pushed down his flag and peered curiously at his two disheveled fares. "What happened back there? That mugg in the Yellow drunk or somepin?"

"It was our fault," Jerry said mildly. "The lights were against us and we were slow getting across."

He silenced the indignant Butch with a warning grimace. They rode the rest of the way in silence. There was a faint ruminative smile on Tracy's taut lips. He knew that the guy who was driving that bullet-like Yellow cab had done his best to commit murder....

Tracy had managed to get a quick glimpse before he had dived headlong away from those crunching front tires of the roaring taxi. The driver had a long nose and a thin, hawk-like face. It wasn't anyone that Tracy knew. Ditto for the fare in the back seat. Tracy didn't know the woman either—but he had heard about her. Very recently!

His smile deepened as he recalled Butch's description of the dame who had lured him into the doorway. "The hardest faced blonde I ever seen in my life!"

THE WOUND IN Butch's side turned out to be painful but not too serious. Tracy waited in the discreet medical office on Central Park West and watched Doc Collander cauterize it and tape it. He took the big fellow back in his penthouse and shoved him into bed. Ten minutes later Tracy was idling along Broadway, his sharp eyes alert. He was looking for a gray-whiskered sandwich-man with two fingers missing from his left hand. Butch had remembered that detail. He had also remembered miraculously, that the guy was carrying a sign for Madame Blanche's Beauty Shoppe.

To anyone but Tracy the task of finding a wandering sandwich-man along Broadway might be something of a sticker. But Tracy was familiar with the lazy habits of the breed and knew where to look. He found his bum lounging at the curb, staring vacuously at the wreckers tearing down the historic remains of the old Criterion Theater.

The sandwich bum remembered the episode of the five-dollar bill but he was inclined to be surly, till Jerry slipped him a buck, and then he loosened up.

He was standing on the curb, he remembered in a thin, whiskey-quaver. It was windy as hell and he was rubbing the dust out of his eyes, when this guy in the brown suit stopped short, grinned, handed him the five bucks—and beat it without a word. A fat kinda guy, big, good looking, no hat. The guy's gray hair stuck up in a pompadour, and he was wearing a diamond ring like a lighthouse. The sandwich-man was staring at the bill, wondering what the gag was—and then Butch came along—a big fat slob in a derby and—

Tracy stopped the rambling recollections with a curt question. "You didn't happen to *wink* at this mope in the brown suit, just before he handed you the dough?"

"Huh?" He looked puzzled. "I dunno. I—I might have. You see, like I told you, the dust was blowin' to beat the band and—"

"Who else came around to ask you about that five spot?" Tracy cut in. "Someone did; am I right?"

"Sure. How—how did you know that, Mister?"

Jerry chuckled. There was a spot of color in his lean cheeks. "Someone came along looking for it yesterday. You told him the thing was a phoney. You said you had sold it for a buck to a big fat slob in a derby hat."

"Yeah. Only it wasn't a man who come lookin'. It was a dame."

"A big fat woman with black hair?"

"Nope. She was thin. A tough lookin' blonde with mean little eyes. She hung around wit' me a long time, hopin' the guy in the derby would go passin' by. He did, all right, and I pointed him out to her in the crowd."

Tracy's faint smile flickered like a subway light. "Thanks a lot, Pop."

He gave the bum an extra buck and legged it across the street to a taxi.

"*Corinthian Hotel,*" he told the hacker.

He knew now exactly how the sandwich-man had happened to come into the picture. Fin Harrigan was the answer. Fin must have been out to the race track that day and made a lucky cleanup. But where did Fin fit in? Of all the gamblers in the big town, Fin was probably the squarest and most likable. To

Tracy's personal knowledge, Fin had never been mixed up in a phoney deal in his life. He didn't see him very often, but they were good friends.

The description fitted him. So did the five-dollar gift. Fin was always scattering them broadside: that was how he had earned his nickname. He was as superstitious as hell—and tarred with the inevitable generosity of the professional gambler. Whenever he was riding high after a lucky plunge, he had a habit of placating his luck by handing out a fiver to the first man, woman or child whom he caught winking as he passed. The dust in the sandwich-man's bleary eye explained the sudden gift. But it didn't explain the numerical mustache on Lincoln— or the hard-faced blonde and her chauffeur pal who was ready to kill to get hold of it.

Fin was in bed when Tracy dropped in on him at the *Corinthian*. He came into his tiny sitting-room, yawning, dressed sketchily in a green pajama top. His legs were hairy and well muscled. His broad, good looking face seemed curiously young under his stiff mane of gray hair. Fin spent plenty of money in barber shops and gymnasiums.

They shook hands and Tracy chuckled. He looked the gambler squarely in the eye and winked very deliberately. Instantly Fin Harrigan roared with appreciative laughter. He walked across to where his trousers lay humped over a chair, peeled a five dollar bill from a thick roll and handed it to the *Daily Planet's* columnist.

"What is this, Jerry?" he grinned. "A brand-new way to make a quick touch from a superstitious pal?"

He stopped short suddenly. Tracy saw an idea hit him and widen his eyes.

"Hey—I'll bet it's about that blonde! She is a friend of yours, Jerry?"

"So she came to see you, eh?"

"Sure. She was after a five-spot she seemed to think I had. I asked her how come, and she said we were both standing together at the pari-mutuel window when they paid off on *Soapsuds* in the third race. It was as windy as hell and her handbag was open and the wind scattered some of her dough. I remembered it perfectly when she reminded me. I had dived like a gentleman for her dough and gave it back to her—but she seemed to think I had mixed one of her five spots with my own. It was a lucky number, she said, one she didn't want to lose. Naturally, I could see her point."

"Naturally," Tracy said.

"Well, to make a long story short, I showed her every five I had. But none of 'em was hers. She said there was a mustache on the engraving of Lincoln; that was how she could tell it."

Jerry nodded. "Did she try to get you to remember where you might have spent fives the day before?"

"Yeah." Fin chuckled. "Can you imagine that? Me trying to check on all the fives I spend! However, I remembered some of them. The restaurant downstairs, the newsreel theater—"

"And a whiskered old sandwich-man who gave you the first lucky wink after you got back to town from the race-track," Tracy suggested softly.

"Correct. I told her that, too." He frowned at the colum-nist. "How come you know all this, Jerry? Is the blonde on the crooked? They tell me you work for the cops sometimes."

"Sometimes, Fin. But not now. This is a purely personal slant. A boy friend of that lousy blonde stuck a knife into Butch's ribs.

Luck was all that saved him from the morgue. Butch is one guy I don't let people stab, Fin—not without doing things about it!"

"I'll be damned. Butch is one swell guy." Harrigan looked serious. "If I'd known it at the time, I'd have smacked that blonde right in the kisser." He found his green silk pajama pants and hoisted them on his hairy legs. "What's it all about, Jerry?"

"Search me."

Harrigan lit a cigarette. He was obviously in a lazy mood, anxious for company, but Tracy had no time to waste discussing pros and cons. He had a column to turn out, and chewing the rag with the affable Fin wouldn't help a bit. The *Daily Planet* didn't pay Tracy a princely salary in order for him to indulge his fancy in private murder investigations; the *Planet* wanted crisp, sparkling dirt for a couple of million customers all over the country who'd stop buying the sheet if the column skipped an issue.

"I'll let you know if the blonde turns up again," Tracy promised as he shoved off.

"Thanks. I'll appreciate it."

Jerry went back to his Times Square office and got to work. When he was hot on a column, time went by swiftly on greased rollers. It was four-thirty before he leaned back with a tired grunt. The phone rang and he cupped it against his ear.

"Yeah?"

"Is this Mr. Tracy? I wanna talk to Mr. Tracy."

The voice was feminine; but hard, metallic. There was a sharp insistent edge to it that scraped the inside of his ear unpleasantly.

"Right here, lady. What do you want?"

"I want that five-dollar bill you mooched, and I want it no later than tonight—or it will be just too bad for you, wise guy!"

A grim sparkle of interest made Tracy's narrowed eyes glitter. "I'll bet you the five bucks you're a blonde."

"Don't try to kid, Mister. You're too smart a guy to get yourself killed for five bucks."

"Do you mind telling me who you are?"

"Not at all." Her laugh sounded like a file rubbing across a pipe. "I'm the babe who dusted your pants with a taxi this morning, when I seen you were foxy enough to get that dough back over in Billy Higson's *Tavern*. I also handed a knife to that fat slob of a Butch…. Well, what do you say?"

There was a short pause.

"Do I mail it to you?" Tracy asked dryly. "Or do I drop it in a tin can behind an oak tree in Central Park?"

"You hand it to me," the voice snapped. "Here's the schedule. Bring the five bucks over to the *Carteret Hotel* tonight. Come alone. Get there in the lobby at exactly nine o'clock."

"How will I know you?"

"Shut up and listen, punk! When you get there, wait fifteen minutes so I can look you over; and then have yourself paged. If everything suits me I'll come along and hold out my hand and you drop the fin in it. Is that simple enough?"

"It's swell for you, sister. But what do I get out of it?"

"You keep on living," the voice rasped.

"Not afraid I'll come with cops?"

"What are you gonna prove? You think I'm the first dame that took five bucks from a gentleman friend in a hotel lobby?"

The line clicked dead and Tracy put down the instrument. He noticed with a wry smile that his fingers quivered slightly as he lit a cigarette. He had run into plenty of hard dames up and down the Main Stem but this babe sounded as if she wore pants and shaved twice a day. Her voice sounded exactly like the flat whine of Willie Prisk—and Willie had killed two cops before he was rounded up with tear gas and burned to death in Sing Sing.

Tracy took three deep puffs and mashed out his cigarette. He wasn't exactly scared; but he didn't feel any too happy about this thing. He took out the five spot and studied it. As far as he could see, it was a normal run-of-the-mint bill, except for that odd numerical mustache on the face of Lincoln, drawn with indelible pencil. 15—10—6—15....

After a while he put on his hat and walked a few blocks north to a shabby building on Longacre Square. He waited while the five spot was phostated. He took the duplicate and the original back with him to his breezy, sky-high penthouse.

Butch was out of bed, sitting in his underwear in a club chair in the living-room.

"How do the ribs feel, keed?"

Butch laid down his copy of *Variety*. "Stiff as hell."

He watched Tracy take a shave, a leisurely bath and change into his favorite dinner coat—the one with the tricky lapels. The coat was cut to accommodate a flat automatic without bulging. Butch eyed his employer hopefully as the weapon patted into place, but he didn't say anything.

He knew that if Tracy wanted him to go along, he'd have said so.

THE *CARTERET HOTEL* was one of those popular secondclass places that are perennially crowded. Tracy arrived there on the dot of nine after a pleasant dinner. He sauntered without haste through the long rectangular lobby. Plenty of blondes coming and going, but no sign of the vinegar-visaged dame whose bloodless face had glared at him for one stark instant from the rear seat of a speeding Yellow taxi cab.

He walked to a sofa opposite the desk where he could keep his eye on the clock. There was a girl sitting there and she moved a little and made room.

Tracy thought, with a sidelong glance of approval: "I could bear it a lot better, if my date for tonight was with you, baby."

She was tall, slim; nice, rather than beautiful. A perky little hat on her chestnut hair; grey eyes with a glint in them like the play of sunlight on water. Tracy liked her eyes and mouth particularly; they carried out the motif of sunlight and fresh air. It didn't take much imagination to put a golf club in her slim brown hands, or curl her fingers around the wheel of a light roadster. Tracy remembered, with sudden disgust: "I haven't been outside this lousy town for weeks!"

She was reading a magazine, her dark lashes curled attentively above the opened pages. A faint pink crept into her cheeks and her fingers fumbled as she turned the next page. It was the first blush Tracy had seen in a long time. She's wondering, he guessed, if she has on too much makeup, and whether she ought to get up and move or just pretend that she's not aware that I'm staring at her.

He let his eyes wander back to the clock. He didn't want her to move and take away the faint, clean scent of lilac. When the clock showed nine-fifteen he got up and walked towards the tiny L-shaped foyer where the elevator was housed. He conferred briefly with a bellboy and returned to his favorite sofa.

Almost instantly a droning voice began calling his name. "Mister Tracy! Call for Mister Tracy!"

He let the solemn bellboy pull the rigmarole for a moment, then crooked his finger. He took the empty telegram envelope, stuck it in his pocket. There was a blonde over near a potted palm, talking to a hard-faced Italian in a light blue shirt; but her voice sounded sugary and her eyes were coy with a sex-call. Tracy frowned. Where in heck was his nasty blonde?

A hand touched him and he turned. The girl with the chestnut hair was looking at him gravely, her open palm extended.

"Let me have it, please," she said in a low voice.

There was a faint flicker of fear in her eyes. The hand she held out was trembling. Tracy stared at her, uncertain what to do. He would have known how to handle the blonde, but this was a new type of extortioner to the wise little Broadway columnist.

"Let you have what?" he said in a whisper that matched hers.

"The five dollars."

"Will any five dollars do—or did you have something particular in mind?"

"The five-dollar bill you were told about over the telephone," she replied steadily.

Without a word Tracy took out his billfold and laid the marked five spot in her hand. She looked at it, crumpled it swiftly, and crammed it into her bag. The bag was open only for an instant, but Tracy noted the dull glint of a small automatic.

"I'm going to ask you not to try to follow me, Mr. Tracy."

"Any other small requests?"

She started to rise, but his hand closed instantly on hers and anchored her to the sofa.

"I could yell and have you taken in for extortion," he suggested.

"You really couldn't," she said. "It may be indiscreet to accept five dollars from a man, but it certainly isn't criminal."

"It's a marked bill."

"Is it?" she smiled.

It enraged Tracy to realize that she was no longer trembling, but thoroughly mistress of the situation.

"I never knew they had gray eyes and an outdoor complexion," he said deliberately, with a hard smile.

"To what are you referring?"

"Rats."

Her eyes blazed at him but she didn't reply. She got up and walked rapidly through the lobby. Tracy, right behind her, held the door open politely, his glance twisting behind him for an instant to note whether anyone else had joined the procession. No one had. Nor was there any sign of trouble on the dimly lit sidewalk.

The girl walked to the curb and got into the foremost taxi. Tracy took the second in line.

"Follow that cab and earn yourself ten bucks," he told his driver.

"Sure thing, Chief." The hacker wasted ten seconds in a slow scrutiny of his fare, and then made it up going round the corner.

At Tracy's curt order he didn't crowd the fleeing cab too closely. The *Daily Planet's* puzzled columnist didn't quite know what to expect from the self-possessed girl with the chestnut hair; but he wasn't taking any fool chances on a sudden spatter of lead from another car lying in wait somewhere along the route.

THE CHASE LED downtown by zigzag stages all the way to 34th. A wild swing crosstown and up again. At Fifth and 36th a red light brought a curse from Tracy's driver and a swift slithering of braked wheels. A block ahead, the fleeing cab broke through the light with a swift left turn. That left Tracy holding the bag on a wrong-way street. He slipped an extra ten to his chauffeur; and the latter, after a swift glance up and down the avenue for cops, swung his wheel and sped west against the east-bound arrow.

He turned into Sixth after a pause and a brief grunt of satisfaction. At 50th the fugitive cab slid round the corner in front of an east-bound bus. Down Broadway again, pocketed behind a string of intervening cars—and suddenly Tracy's chauffeur grunted in alarm: "Hey—you're gonna lose her! She's just gone into the Paramount Theatre!"

"Get up as close as you can," Tracy snapped.

By the time he was out on the curb the girl had vanished inside the theatre. Grimly he added some more to the hacker's pay.

"Stick in front. If she comes out again, beat it around to the side entrances. I'll be watching there."

"Oke."

Tracy hurried to the corner with eager strides—and stopped instantly. The shrewd girl had already left the theatre by one of the side exits and was crossing the street. Hunched in an orangeade doorway, he watched her come boldly back to Broadway along the opposite side of the street.

She melted into the swirling crowd and Tracy tailed her cautiously to 42nd and down the corner entrance into the subway. She took a northbound express and so did Tracy. At

72nd she got out and walked up Amsterdam to 75th. The chase ended just west of Columbus Avenue, when she disappeared into the entrance of a shabby walk-up apartment.

Tracy thanked his lucky stars for the ill-lighted hallways of the dilapidated old dump. He went up the stairs like a noiseless shadow, listening at each dim landing for the faint rustle of her feet on the staircase above. She went straight to the top floor.

Peering through dusty banisters, his body slanted flat on the stair carpet, Tracy saw her walk to the rear apartment, unlock the door and let herself in.

He hesitated. There was no telling whether the girl was alone inside, or whether she was dutifully handing over the mysterious five spot to the blonde and the sharp-nosed taxi driver who had tried to kill Tracy. It angered Jerry to realize how the girl's clear gray eyes and the elusive scent of lilac perfume had made a sap out of him. All through the taxi chase he had been trying to figure some innocent explanation for her, a harmless out of some kind.

As he tiptoed towards the closed door of the apartment, his mind whispered stubbornly: "Maybe she's a private dick." The thought made him grin sourly. If she was a dick, he was a subway motorman! Tracy had met dozens of lady "ropes" and they were all maternal looking dames of the dowager type, with large bosoms and placid, confession-eliciting faces.

He waited outside the door, listening for some sound from within. Suddenly he heard a key grating on the inside of the lock. He stepped noiselessly backward, his hand darting towards the butt of his hidden automatic.

The door opened slightly and he saw the bloodless face of the girl staring cautiously out. Their eyes met for a clashing instant and he sprang forward. But quick as he was, the girl was quicker. She slammed and locked the door as he threw himself against it. He could hear the receding rustle of her feet; then an L train roared past on Columbus Avenue, and all he could hear was the pound and rumble of its passage.

Tracy rubbed his nose thoughtfully. The situation was ticklish. If the tough blonde was in there too, it meant gunplay sure as hell. It meant butting in on something damned nasty, concerning which he still had no real knowledge whatever beyond the shrewd suspicion of crime, either already committed or impending. He thought of Butch's stab wound and that decided him. Nobody on earth was going to stick a knife into Butch and get away with it! It would make too bad a precedent for later work against crooks!

With his coat loose and his gun handy, Tracy opened a jack-knife he always carried, and went quietly to work with something that looked like an elongated bottle opener of the "anchor" type. Five minutes' careful work took care of the old-fashioned lock. He was convinced that the girl was no longer in the apartment. He pushed the door gently open till it touched flat against the inner wall.

The lights were all on. Nobody in sight. A cheap railroad flat, one room opening into another.

Tracy's eyes widened as he stepped into the bedroom and saw the tough blonde staring at him with expressionless face. She was on the floor, looking up. Very dead. A bullet in her neck. Her heavily rouged face pale, and not so tough after all.

Her flesh was still warm to Tracy's probing fingers. Over near a dresser there was a reflection of something blue on the carpet. He saw the same blue glint under a chair. He bent and picked up two turquoise beads. He sniffed them with a hard smile and it seemed to him he could detect the faint odor of lilac.

Over near the window his foot crushed on something and he picked up another bead. The window was wide open. Rusted fire-escapes led to a small fenced yard below. Tracy didn't bother going down; the smart Lilac Kid had too good a start. She also had the five-dollar bill. And the dangerous blonde was dead. No wonder she hadn't kept the appointment. There was an ugly bruise on her forehead; Lilac must have knocked her out and hurried over to meet Tracy herself. Came back again and killed the blonde under cover of the roar of the Elevated while he, Tracy, had waited like a dope in the hall outside. He remembered the ugly little gat he had seen in Lilac's bag when he had turned over the five spot to her in the *Carteret*.

"It still might have been that razor-nosed taxi driver," a stubborn whisper insisted in Tracy's mind.

Yeah! It might! But in any event, it still left the taxi driver and Lilac to reckon with. And a full-sized mystery to tear apart. There must be oodles of dough behind all this nonsense of a five-dollar bill. Nobody took a chance on murder for five bucks—not in Manhattan, anyway! Greed and murder....

Tracy made a discreet exit from the flat and the building. He didn't want cops adding his own name to the cast of characters.

But before he grabbed a cab home to his expensive penthouse he walked into a Columbus Avenue drug-store and telephoned an anonymous tip to Police Headquarters. He wanted that dead blonde identified in a hurry. It might help.

BUTCH WAS IN bed when Tracy got back but McNulty, the suave and imperturbable Chinese butler who had long since forgotten his real name was Mei-No-Lee, was pottering around with a vacuum sweeper, looking virtuous and indignant.

"Where hell you hang alound allee time?" he hissed. "Man call up, say mebbe important and where is good fliend Tlacy? I make sad usual answer—how hell I know when Mister Tlacy not any time take tlouble tell nothing. No time. Never."

Tracy grinned. "Who was it, Keed?" His eyes narrowed when McNulty told him. "Fin Harrigan, eh? I wonder what he wants?"

"No find out if no call up," McNulty said grumpily.

Tracy looked up Harrigan's number and gave him a buzz.

"Maybe it's not important," Fin said, "but I thought I'd let you know anyway. It's about that five-dollar bill. I remembered something else."

"Shoot."

On his way home from the track, Fin explained, a pickpocket had made a try for his leather. The guy had been clumsy and Fin had whirled in the crowded train shed and made a grab for him. A sneaky-looking dip with bright eyes and a long, thin nose. He was as spry as an eel and made a complete getaway, because a dopey dame chose that exact instant to bump into Fin and throw him off balance. Fin didn't connect it with the blonde at that time, because he was still unaware that he had picked up her five by mistake. Did Tracy think the thin-nosed guy had been after the Lincoln fin?

"Maybe," Jerry said. "Who was the dame that bumped you? The blonde who showed up afterwards?"

"No. If it was her, I'd have remembered and been leery. This other dame was a hell of a nice looker. Tall, willowy, a kind of a cute little hat over one eye—"

"I'll bet it was Lilac," Jerry muttered.

"Huh? How the devil did you know that?" Fin asked in a mystified voice. "Come to think of it, she did smell faintly of lilac perfume. Hey, what the hell is this all about?"

"You got me, brother," Jerry said.

"Well, anyway, I thought I'd tell you."

"Thanks a lot."

Tracy hung up and considered things. After a while he got out his photostatic copy of the bill and examined again the queer numerical mustache on the face of Lincoln. 15-10-6-15—and Lincoln. Could it be a clue to an address somewhere? If there was a lot of dough behind this funny business, it might be hidden dough.

Tracy went into his library and pulled down the big city directory. He found a Lincoln Place in Manhattan, a Lincoln Avenue in the Bronx and—yep, a Lincoln Street over in Brooklyn. Thinking about it didn't do him a bit of good. The hyphenated numbers were no help, either.

He slammed the whole thing out of his mind with a stiff hooker of Canadian rye and went to bed.

The next morning Butch pulled him right back into the thick of things. Butch was yanking at the leg of Tracy's pajamas, waving an inky *Daily Planet* in front of him. A glance at the photograph and the headline brought Jerry leaping out of bed. The hard-looking blonde he had last seen on the bedroom floor had the whole front page of the, tabloid to herself. The headline said with black brevity:

Widow of Jess Spencer Slain!

Tracy read every line of the murder story with grim attentiveness. The details of the finding of the body of blond Dora Spencer didn't interest him worth a damn. But the resume of the life and works of her dead convict husband did! Tracy's memory was pretty vague about Jess Spencer and the notorious Harry Connor kidnaping. It had happened eighteen years before, one of those forgotten *causes célèbres* of crime—like Pat Crowe and the Cudahy snatch.

It all came back to Tracy as he read. It was one of those things the Sunday Edition raked up occasionally for a human-interest yarn: "Prison Walls Still Guard Secret of Missing Two Hundred Thousand Dollars."

After a humdrum career of petty crimes, Jess Spencer had electrified the country by kidnaping little Harry Connor, four-year-old son of a wealthy building contractor, from his father's huge estate in Westchester. It was a one-man job but it worked. The ransom was paid—$250,000—and the boy returned unharmed; but he was a frail child and he died later on. Egged on by the tremendous hue and cry of the press, the police nabbed Spencer. He was tried, convicted and given a twenty-five-year stretch.

But the ransom money had disappeared; that was the big puzzle. Spencer had fifty thousand with him when he was caught, but he stoutly denied any knowledge of the two hundred grand. He named a mysterious pal called "Joe" as the recipient of the missing fortune, but nobody believed that for a minute. Spencer went to prison with a grin. The police arrested Dora—she wasn't a blonde in those days—and they grilled her without result. She was not implicated in the kidnaping and claimed she knew nothing at all of any missing $200,000. The whole thing died away in the cynical laughter of the public. Vaudeville comedians joked about the shadowy "Joe" and even the kids in the street had a chanting catch-word: *"Who got the dough? A guy named Joe!"*

Spencer himself never got out of jail. Another convict had stabbed him to death with a pair of garden shears after an altercation in the prison grounds. Tracy remembered Spencer's death well enough; it had happened three months ago. The wife had dropped out of sight and didn't claim the body. And that was the end of the celebrated Connor case and the end of $200,000.

Abruptly Jerry Tracy threw the *Daily Planet* to the floor. He began pacing up and down, concentrating on the implication of the thing.

Suppose the cunning Jess Spencer had coolly buried the loot somewhere, planning to dig it up again after he had earned a commutation of sentence or a parole from an easy-going system that got sentimental and forgiving as the years rolled by. Pat Crowe had gotten out—why not Jess Spencer? He might have trouble remembering the location of the treasure over so long a period of time. He'd need a written clue of some sort—and whom would he dare to trust, even with the cipher, except his wife? His wife would be damned sure to save the five spot carefully. Not knowing what the symbols meant, she'd be under no temptation to betray the hiding place to some smart lover who might bob up while Jess himself was rotting quietly away in prison.

Jerry Tracy lit a cigarette with unsteady fingers and made the air of his bedroom blue with quick, nervous exhalations of smoke.

Could the thin-nosed taxi chauffeur be the mysterious "Joe" of song and story? Nerts—too young! He was undoubtedly some wise guy who had gotten hep to the importance of the Lincoln note, and had been working hand in glove with Jess Spencer's widow. If he and the blonde had been lovers, as Tracy suspected, the death of the convict and the utter loss of her last hope to find out from Jess what the penciled clue really meant, must have driven them both to greedy desperation.

In that case, where did Lilac fit in? Was she working in cahoots with the taxi guy, trying to rook Dora Spencer? How come Dora had allowed Lilac to muscle in? And why the devil should Lilac murder the blonde after she had grabbed the five spot from Tracy?

Fin Harrigan! Tracy considered that angle. It might be that Fin and this Lilac dame… The columnist bit off an oath of disgust. Fin, he knew damned well, was as honest as the day was long. Might as well suspect Butch or the sandwich-man. Jerry had actually begun to canvass the possibilities of the sandwich-man as a suspect, when he saw the image of his own screwed-up face in the mirror. He burst into a roar of laughter and came back to common sense.

He strode to the bedroom door and threw it open.

"Hey, McNulty! Where the hell are you?"

A shadow moved meekly out of the kitchen. "Hey, hey, Marster! You hungly, mebbe?"

"No. Me thirsty. Bring me a pot of coffee as high as your vest buttons. I need stimulation. It seems I'm a damn' fool, McNulty."

The almond eyes blinked innocently. "When the Marster speaks, let no servant contladict."

Tracy chuckled. "Is that from Confucius?"

"No. That come stlaight from McNulty."

Tracy drank three cups of the black stimulating stuff before he bothered to crawl out of his pajamas. Then he shaved and let the stinging needles of his shower-stall redden his lean torso for a while. A complete change of raiment from the skin out made him feel lots better.

"Goin' out, Boss?" Butch asked him, with a hopeful sidelong glance.

"Yep."

"Kin I come, too?"

"Nope."

"Aw, chee!" Butch's lower lip pouted like a child's. "Anyone would t'ink I was a—a invalid or somepin. Look!" He lifted his right arm swiftly, gasped a little and lowered it with painful care.

"Yeah. I see." Tracy turned and looked at McNulty. "I don't want this dope to sneak out, savvy? If he tries a sneak, you stop him quick like hell."

McNulty went padding into the kitchen and came out again with an agile-looking vegetable knife. "Me savvy."

He took a forward step and Butch, who had had dealings with the literal-minded Chinaman before, backed up hastily and sat down. "Okey, okey! Cut out the foolin'. I ain't goin' out."

Tracy closed the door of the penthouse with a grin.

HE DROVE STRAIGHT to his Times Square office and buckled down to work for two whizbang hours. Then he had an egg sandwich and some more coffee and went spinning downtown, all the way to Worth Street. He walked into the

Bureau of Motor Vehicles and kept annoying people till he got into an office with a high ceiling and a grand view of the river.

"Hello, Brady. Why don't you call off your army once in a while, so taxpayers can get in?"

"Hiyuh, Jerry! Why don't you let a man know you're comin?"

They shook hands and Brady rolled a cigar across the polished desk. He was a pudgy, prosperous-looking Irishman with a nest of shrewd wrinkles around his blue eyes. He played a grand game of golf and had seven children, all boys.

"Last time you were here," he said, with a slow, friendly smile, "you were interested in a headless corpse in a row-boat under the Cunard pier. What is it this time?"

"Just routine."

"Sure. The rowboat corpse was routine, too, as I remember."

"I want to get some dope on a hacker."

"What's his name?"

"I don't know."

"That helps," Brady said dryly. "Do you know who he works for and what he looks like?"

"Long nose. Long and thin and shiny as if he rubbed it every morning on a grindstone. Light eyes, very bright; sort of a piercing glare when he looks at you; you know, feverish, like a consumptive."

Tracy smiled and shrugged.

"I only saw the guy once—and I was damned near under his front wheels when I took my look."

Brady seemed disappointed. "Just a hit-and-run, eh?"

"Yeah."

"Was he a company driver?"

"No. Independent. A yellow cab with a small checker border around it. Not a Checker, though. Am I helpful?"

"Not very much. You've narrowed the possibilities some, but it'll take plenty of looking. You got plenty of time?"

"All day," Tracy said grimly.

Brady took him to the record room and showed him where to look. Even with the big companies and the associations eliminated, it seemed like a hopeless job; but Jerry peeled off his coat and went patiently to work. Brady assigned a clerk to assist him and that helped, but the morning went by without result. Tracy gulped a rotten lunch in a bang-and-clatter joint around the corner from Worth Street, and came back for more punishment. It was past four o'clock when the clerk, who was getting grumpier by the minute, held out a photo and asked indifferently: "How 'bout this?"

The *Daily Planet's* perspiring columnist took one look at the photo and yanked it out of the man's hand. Even in the picture the hackman's eyes looked bright and piercing. And that long, thin beak like a razor was no coincidence.

Jerry took the photo back to Brady's office and Brady pressed a button and collected dope. The fellow's name was Marty Danker. Operating an independent hack for four years. Two traffic violations, but nothing in the way of a criminal record. Home address, 239 Dover Street. Traffic stand at Herald Square, opposite Macy's. Unmarried. Thirty-five years old.

The age part of it made Tracy nod slightly. The guy couldn't have been mixed up with Jess and Dora Spencer in the actual kidnaping of little Harry Connor. Eighteen years ago would make Danker seventeen when the two hundred grand disappeared. It would make Lilac—funny how Tracy's mind kept trying to eliminate her from the thing—about six years old when the snatch took place. If Lilac had killed Dora Spencer and was in a conspiracy with Danker, her knowledge of the hidden treasure must have been recent. Probably since Spencer had died in the prison grounds and left his widow with a valuable and meaningless clue to unravel.

Tracy shook hands with Brady and went up to Herald Square. There were a couple of cabs parked in the triangle but no sign of Marty Danker's battered Yellow. Tracy waited under the striped awning of a snooty men's clothing shop. In twenty minutes or so, Danker drove up from Sixth Avenue, pulled in at the tail of the line and began to read a tabloid.

He hadn't read five minutes when he glanced at the sidewalk and grinned. Under his awning covert Tracy grinned too. The girl on the sidewalk was Lilac, and she seemed to be on excellent terms with the hacker.

Danker got out of his cab and the two began to chat very chummily. He slipped an arm about her waist and she giggled and pretended to slap him. Her clear laugh made Tracy's face darken; he was thinking of her pale face framed in a half-opened door behind which a body lay.

She left Danker and crossed the street. Tracy followed her without hesitation. He could pick up Danker any time he wanted; but he still hadn't the faintest idea who Lilac was or where she hung out.

She went into Macy's big corner entrance and so did Tracy. The place was swarming with shoppers and he closed up the distance between them, fearful that she might pull a sudden sneak into 34th and elude him. The quick rat-tat of her heels took her back to the book section, a quick tour among the perfumes, along the stationery counters and onward towards the crowded elevators.

Tracy was negligently watching the dial on the adjoining shaft, his back to the girl, when a heavy clutch at his shoulder whirled him around. A special officer was glowering at him.

"Is this the man, Miss?"

"Yes." Lilac's gray eyes were clouded with injured innocence as she stared directly at the uncomfortable columnist. "He's been following me for the past half hour. He followed me from Gimbel's, into Saks', and across here. Can't you stop him from annoying me?"

She colored faintly under Tracy's level stare but her eyes never wavered.

"Want him arrested, Miss?" the special cop growled.

"No. I—I just want him to stop bothering me."

"Okey. Come on, you—out! If I catch you in here again, I'll have you run in!"

He walked the silent columnist through a lane of curious faces and twirled him through a revolving door into 34th Street. The cop followed through to make sure he didn't come back.

The roar of traffic drowned out Tracy's quiet murmur and the cop glared at him. "What was that last crack?"

"I said," Tracy repeated softly, "you're a smart girl, Lilac."

He walked to Seventh and took a subway local. Tonight he'd see what he could do down at 229 Dover Street. If Danker kept late hours with his cab, Jerry might be able to get inside the apartment and case the joint.

Up to a certain limit, Jerry Tracy was a privileged person in affairs which were obviously for the police and in which the ordinary citizen would not have dared to venture. In many a baffling crime, to Inspector Fitzgerald in particular he had been a detective without a shield, a minister without a portfolio. His tips, his uncanny knowledge of people and his keen, analytical mind had more than once been of invaluable aid. Jerry knew well enough he had no business to follow this further alone. But he was not ready to call copper yet, and he knew that, short of deliberate murder, he would be forgiven—if in the end he could lead the police to the crime's climax.

IT WAS ALMOST seven o'clock before Tracy called it a day and closed his desk. He didn't bother going back to his penthouse for a bath and a change of clothes, although he felt tired and messy. He dined in a quiet wop joint near the northerly fringe of Greenwich Village and took his time with the meal. It was already dark when he turned into the short three-block diagonal of Dover Street.

The house was a shabby red-brick tenement, tucked alongside a more ornate structure with a canopy and a doorman, in the incongruous architectural clutter of Greenwich Village. Tracy located Danker's apartment by the simple expedient of descending to the tenement cellar and examining the name plates in the dumbwaiter directory. Danker's rooms were on the ground floor in the rear.

The thin wail of a clarinet from a closed door beyond the coal bins told Tracy that the janitor was musically employed for the moment. He walked through a narrow concrete passage to the backyard and surveyed the rear windows of the first floor. The place seemed to be pitch-dark. Tracy eyed the jutting fire-escape and the top of the side fence. It was now or never, he thought.

Two minutes later, he had straddled across to the slatted iron platform and was trying the window of Danker's bedroom. The sash was unlocked and lifted with only a mild squeak.

Tracy saw instantly that his guess about Danker's absence was wrong. There was a faint reflection of light under the bedroom door, and the columnist crouched there for a moment, listening. He could hear the distant buzz of a man's voice and a clink that sounded like a bottle.

He opened the bedroom door. Beyond him were two shadowy rooms and a narrow passage that seemed to lead to the front door. The light came from the kitchen, Tracy decided; that was why he hadn't noticed it from the outside; the kitchen probably fronted on an enclosed shaft.

He froze suddenly as he heard a woman's clear laugh. It was as familiar to him as gray eyes and the odor of lilac. He was as certain she was in the kitchen as though he could actually see the girl.

A man's voice said jovially: "You wouldn't try to kid me, would you?"

"Don't be silly, Marty. Do I look like a gal that kids?"

Tracy moved towards the light with slow care. By dropping to hands and knees and crawling along beside a sofa, the *Daily Planet's* columnist could peer into the kitchen. He could see Danker's shoulder and the left side of his face. Couldn't miss that nose! Danker was pouring whiskey into a small tumbler and grinning at the girl. The girl was Lilac. She was facing the doorway and her eyes were wide and shining.

"I wouldn't fool you the way Dora Spencer did," she giggled.

With a soft oath Danker banged down his tumbler on the table and clutched amorously at her body.

She giggled again as she leaned towards him. "Lemme whisper a big secret in your ear, boy friend."

Danker said, "Yeah?" in a wondering tone. "That's different. That calls for some more liquor! Some more rye—or Scotch?"

HE GOT UP suddenly and lumbered towards the living-room. Tracy rolled noiselessly under the sofa. The sofa went crashing over as Danker's left hand shoved. His gun pointed ominously at the exposed and discomfited columnist.

"Up on your feet, stupid!"

Tracy rose slowly, his face livid with disgust. The girl had seen him—and trapped him with clever cunning. With Danker's gun at his back, he was walked into the kitchen and slapped brutally into a chair. The girl's hand came out of her bag with a tiny automatic.

While the smiling Lilac held Tracy helpless with her weapon, Danker yanked a length of twine out of a kitchen drawer and looped the columnist's hands and feet to the chair.

"Do you still think I'm okey, Marty?" the girl giggled.

"I sure do, babe. Nice eye work." He leered ferociously at his captive. "The great Jerry Tracy, huh?" His laughter boomed softly. "You can write your next column for the *Planet* from the graveyard."

Jerry, watching the girl, saw her eyes widen with a look of absolute bewilderment.

"Jerry Tracy?" she gasped. "You mean he's the man who writes the column in the *Daily Planet*?"

Danker grinned. "Who did you think the mugg was?"

"I—I knew his name was Tracy, but I—I thought he was a crook. I thought he was after the—the—"

Tracy interrupted her harshly. "Is that why you went to Dora Spencer's flat and killed her?"

"I didn't kill her," the girl whispered. Her face was very pale. "She was dead when I got there."

"Huh?" Danker's bright eyes swung towards Lilac with hard suspicion. "By God, Dora was telling the truth! You were there, huh? Dora swore she had been hijacked by some dame, but I thought she was—" He stopped suddenly.

"You thought Dora was lying," Jerry Tracy said evenly. "So you killed her yourself, eh, Danker?"

"Nerts," he snarled furiously. "Keep your mug shut or I'll beat in your skull!" His gun muzzle moved ominously towards Lilac. "You took that five spot from Dora, didn't you?"

She shrugged and began to laugh. "So what? Two hundred grand is a lot of dough. You never were able to cash in on it with Dora. That's why I decided to ease into the picture. I figured that with your muscle and my brains, we could go places and buy things."

She fumbled in her bag and tossed Danker the crumpled five spot with a negligent gesture. He picked it up, squinted for a second at the engraving of Lincoln and sighed noisily.

"I don't quite get you, babe. What's your angle?"

"Just a little girl trying to get along," she said tonelessly.

"You know where the dough is hidden?"

"Not yet," she admitted. "But I got a lot more brains than Spencer's wife had."

"She was sure dumb," Danker said with a clipped oath. "She had the damned five spot worn out, carrying it around with her. She never could figure out what it meant."

"It might have been an address," Lilac said.

Danker scowled and shook his head. "We been all over that, Dora and me. That's the first thing we thought of. That Lincoln stuff sounded like a tip. Jess Spencer was pinched in a house on Lincoln Avenue, up in the Bronx."

"Yeah?" Lilac answered him indifferently but her eyes were bright.

"Yeah. But it's a short avenue. And them numbers on the fiver ain't a house number anyway."

"He wouldn't hide it in a house, silly," Lilac said.

"Why not?"

"Jess knew when he buried the dough that he was in for a twenty-five-year stretch at least, if the cops nabbed him."

"So what?"

"Twenty-five years is a long time. He'd have to be sure the building wasn't torn down while he was in jail. He wouldn't dare bury it in a vacant lot for the same reason. Might find a new house built over it when he got out."

Danker's hot eyes sparkled. "Hey—I think you got the right idea, babe. But where in hell would he go—a museum or a church or somethin'?"

Lilac's cheeks were pink with excitement. She didn't once look toward the trussed columnist; but Tracy had an odd feeling that she was thinking about him and his predicament all the while she was talking.

"Can't you see?" she told Danker impatiently. "Spencer didn't have time to go roaming the city. He was a marked man. He'd have to work fast."

Her finger pointed unsteadily at her companion.

"Is there anything in that Lincoln Avenue neighborhood that might be safe for twenty-five years?"

"There's a branch public library next to the joint where Jess was pinched," Danker said slowly. "That's out, ain't it? Where in hell could Jess hide two hundred grand in a library?"

"Not inside, certainly. That's crazy. Wait—is there a backyard to the place?"

"Yeah. Dora and me looked through the cellar and backyard of the place where Jess hid out—and we took a peek over the fence, too. The yard behind the library is kind of a fancy joint. Grass and stone paths and little green benches and—hey!" He uttered a choked yelp of jubilation. "That library—it's the *Lincoln Branch!*"

He pounded his fist on the table and the flushed cheeks of the girl went suddenly white.

"Okey, Marty. So what do we do about it?"

Danker's glance flitted towards the helpless figure of Tracy. "We scram up there, babe—as soon as we fix up this mugg. We'll hand it to him nice and quiet. Stuff up all the cracks, turn on the gas in the oven, lock the door and—blooie!"

Lilac seemed to nod.

"One move out of you, and I'll kill you," she told Danker in a grave, quiet whisper.

SHE HAD SCOOPED up Danker's discarded gun and she was pointing it at his heart without a tremor. Tracy, staring unbelievingly at the two of them, saw utter determination in the girl's eyes, and a sick fear in Danker's.

Lilac moved slowly backward, gray eyes alert, until her groping left hand found the kitchen drawer and pulled it open. She took out a bread knife and sidled across to Tracy's chair. The pressure of the sawing blade pulled his trussed hands tight for an instant and then sprung them free. He clutched the knife from her without a word and, squirming, slashed the ropes away from his ankles.

"Take the gun," the girl breathed.

Jerry's hand dived along her shaking forearm and took the weapon.

"Get over to the wall, you heel!" he told Danker. "Turn around. Get your face—"

Danker whirled suddenly, his hand flicking at Tracy's wrist like a whiplash. But Jerry had been watching, and he brought the gun downward in a hard smash against Danker's temple. The crook's knees sagged and he dropped inertly to the linoleum floor.

The girl began to cry suddenly. Tracy laid the gun on the table, helped her gently into a chair.

"Did you kill Dora Spencer?" he asked her. "Tell me no and I'll take your word for it."

"No." She looked at him, tremulous but unflinching.

"Who are you? Why are you in this mess?"

He could barely hear the whispered reply. "I'm—Margaret—Connor."

"You're—Well, I'll be damned!"

He eyed her with an astonished comprehension. The sister of little Harry Connor! Six years old when the kidnaping had occurred—add eighteen more—that would make her about twenty-four now. It checked.

Tears were welling in her gray eyes. "I—I knew the money was hidden somewhere—Father's money. His own—stolen from him—and he needs it so desperately now!" Her voice steadied with fierce earnestness. "I came to New York two weeks ago. I went to the police and appealed to them. They said the case was cold, closed, finished. They could do nothing to help me. So I—I decided to go it alone. I got on the trail of Dora Spencer—and through her I found this horrible Marty Danker. I deliberately picked him up on the street, let him ride me around in his cab and make love to me, to—to try and find the clue to where Father's money was hidden."

"How did you manage to trick Spencer's widow and grab the five spot for yourself at the *Carteret Hotel?*" Tracy asked her.

"I was hidden in Dora's flat when she telephoned you. I—I knocked her out with a gun before she could kill me. She—she was like a raging she-devil. I met you at the hotel. I went back afterwards, determined to force her to tell me all she knew. She was dead when I got there. I don't know who killed her."

"I do," Tracy said grimly, remembering Danker's damaging admission a few moments before. He looked at the gun lying on the table. "When the ballistics experts get hold of that gun, they're going to find rifling marks that will put our friend on the floor here in the electric chair."

He stared at her. "Whom did you see when you went to Police Headquarters?"

"A man named Inspector Fitzgerald."

"Fitz? That makes it very swell."

He dashed into the living-room and picked up the phone he had already noticed. He got Fitz after a little delay in re-routing.

"Anyone call to see you about two weeks ago, Fitz? In reference to reopening the Connor kidnaping case?"

"Yeah. Anything new in that line, Jerry? The Connor kid's sister came to see me—Margaret Connor."

"Listen, Fitz! Grab hold of Sergeant Killan if you can. Get a cab and ride up to Lincoln Avenue in the Bronx. Wait for me there and keep under cover. Next door to the branch public library."

He grunted suddenly.

"Wait! I'm forgetting. Come to Dover Street first. The number is two-twenty-nine. I've got the murderer of Dora Spencer waiting here for you."

"What! Hold him, Jerry, hold him!"

The line clicked and Tracy hustled back to the kitchen. He halted stupidly in the doorway. Danker's gun was a glittering menace and Danker was grinning. He was up on his feet and humorously alert. Margaret Connor, her hands stiffly above her head, said hopelessly: "He wasn't unconscious. He was shamming. He grabbed the gun off the table while you were telephoning."

Tracy said in a cool conversational tone: "I should have been more careful. I don't usually take—"

He sprang, knocked the weapon fiercely aside. There was a stunning report, and a white-hot stab of pain wrenched through Tracy's wrist. Danker whirled in the doorway of the kitchen and a second bullet whizzed above Tracy's ducking head and splintered a pile of saucers into swirling fragments.

Danker's feet raced through the front hall of the apartment. A door slammed.

"Where's your gun?" Tracy shouted at the half-fainting girl. She pointed and he scooped it out of her handbag with his left hand. His right was useless; blood from his shattered wrist dripped down his stiffened fingers.

"Come on!"

Pushing the trembling girl ahead of him, he staggered through the front door and down a short flight of stone steps to the street. A man in overalls came rushing up the stairs from the cellar, his dirty face staring.

"Hey! Stand still, you two! What happened up there?"

Tracy's gun chopped round at him. "Get back down in that cellar, or I'll blow your chin off!"

The janitor screeched and dived headfirst out of sight.

They slowed down as they turned the corner into Pearson Street. A cab was swinging west through the triangle from Seventh Avenue. Tracy stuck his bleeding hand in his trouser pocket and hailed the taxi.

"Up to the Bronx, buddy. Lincoln Avenue. I'll tell you the address when we get there."

He grinned haggardly as he realized that he didn't know the number of the tenement where Jess Spencer had been pinched eighteen long years ago. He slid his right hand out of his pocket and held it close to the taxi floor, so that the steady drip of crimson wouldn't mess his clothes and alarm the chauffeur.

"You're bleeding," Margaret Connor gasped. "We'd better stop at a hospital."

"Not on your life," Tracy whispered grimly. "Do you think I'd trade in a bum wrist for a chance at two hundred grand? Hell, I've been waiting to dig treasure ever since I was a kid. And I'm not letting any dumb cluck like Danker put me out of action."

He was afraid she'd see his pain-twisted face and insist on taking him to the hospital. He caught her arm with his good hand and pinned her close to him on the jouncing seat.

"Tell me about the jam your father is in, sweet."

THERE WAS NO sign of Fitz or Sergeant Killan on the quiet sidewalk. The library was as dark as a tomb. In spite of its two-story front of weathered gray stone, it looked mean and shabby like the neighborhood. Kids had scrawled chalk marks on the steps and along the stone façade below the windows. Tracy saw two things, however, that filled him with cold satisfaction. The date chiseled into the cornerstone was 1912—place was built five years before Jess Spencer had been arrested for the Connor snatch. The second item that interested Tracy was the inscription on the smoky stone above the doorway—Lincoln Branch.

The glow of a street lamp threw a gaunt, elongated shadow of empty ash-cans and piled rubbish in front of the tenement next door. At the head of the cellar steps Tracy transferred Margaret's gun to the pocket of his topcoat, his uninjured hand cradling the butt of the weapon. There was no telling where the ugly figure of Danker might be. Perhaps he was already in the backyard of the library, feverishly searching for the ransom money. Or would he be waiting furtively in the cellar of the tenement to wipe out the only two people who were aware of the hidden fortune?

Tracy threaded a dark labyrinth towards the rear of the cellar, guided by the faint yellowish glow of an unshaded bulb in the whitewashed ceiling. The girl shrank close to him, her frightened eyes veering towards the dark coal bins beyond the furnace. Her hand clutched Tracy suddenly, and they both rooted themselves in silence.

"See anything?" he whispered.

"I—I thought I saw something move—back of those barrels."

A second later Tracy uttered a relieved exclamation. A

gray tomcat skidded like a noiseless streak from the bin and vanished under the shadowy slant of the cellar steps.

The back door opened with a faint squeak under Tracy's even pressure and let them outside into a paved yard. Moonlight bathed pavement and fences with a milky brilliance. Tracy found a broken-backed chair, got up on it and peered over the fence. There was nothing moving in the backyard of the branch library.

His quick eyes photographed the place. Green lawn and winding paths covered with flagstones. Garden chairs. A flower-bed gone to seed. An arbor in the back with a long green bench under the trellis and a dark climbing vine. But the thing that made Tracy grunt with eager excitement was the statue.

It was a small bronze bust of Lincoln, mounted on a square stone pedestal.

"Can you get over?" the girl whispered doubtfully. "Your hand and wrist—"

"Not bleeding much," he clipped. "I can make it."

It took a lot of effort and brought the sweat springing out on his pale forehead, but he managed to straddle awkwardly and get across. The girl followed him swiftly, unmindful of her embarrassingly stretched dress and ripped stocking. A thoroughbred, Tracy thought dully. Pain from his throbbing wrist was making his head swim. He fought against the blind desire to keel over on the soft grass and let his aching eyelids close.

The moonlight was so clear that he didn't have to scratch a match to read the inscription cut into the smooth stone of the pedestal below Lincoln's weathered bust: *"With Malice Toward None."*

Margaret Connor repeated the words with a hysterical

moan. *"Malice toward none*—my brother Harry dead, my father impoverished—ruined and bankrupt if he doesn't get that ransom money back—his own money, enough of it to save him from going mad with worry—"

She swayed against Tracy's wounded arm and he bit off a groan. "See any numbers on the thing? Can you remember the numbers that were on that infernal bill? My head hurts so that I—I can't—"

There was nothing but that ironic phrase from Lincoln, cut in worn letters on the stone.

"Substitution," Jerry muttered weakly. "It couldn't be anything else. Jess Spencer wouldn't have time to figure out an elaborate code. All he wanted was a guide to anyone he might have to send over here to get the stuff for him.... What was that first number on the five spot?"

"Fifteen," Margaret Connor whispered.

Tracy's finger moved from left to right along the chiseled quotation. "That makes the first letter R."

"Ten next," Margaret said.

"Okey. E."

"Six."

"A."

"Fifteen again."

"R," Tracy snapped. Strength flooded back into him for an instant. "R-E-A-R. *Rear.* It's behind the statue. Under the path. Buried below that damned flagstone."

They stared at the path that skirted the base of the pedestal. Directly in the rear of the statue was a broad flagstone of almost the exact width as the pedestal.

"Can you get it up?" Tracy muttered. "See if you can hook your fingers under it."

She kicked earth and grass away from the edge with the pointed toe of her slipper. Tracy helped her as best he could. With straining effort the girl lifted the flat stone slightly, and Tracy shoved his foot under the edge. Together, they managed to upend it and let it fall over backward with a soft bump. The packed earth underneath looked dry and hard as a brick.

"We'll have to dig," Tracy faltered. "I'll have to try and get back over the damned fence again. I saw a broom and a coal shovel in the corner of the other cellar."

"Let me go," Margaret Connor urged. "You'll surely faint if you try to climb over again. I think I can do it in just a—"

Her hand flew to her mouth as she turned. Jerry's fingers groped clumsily towards his coat pocket—and stopped, frozen by the aimed weapon and the harsh menace of the face that peered over the fence-top.

The moonlight was clear on Marty Danker's murderous face. His gun—the same one that had already smashed Tracy's wrist—kept the columnist and the girl rooted in silence. Danker's left hand appeared above the fence and dropped a short-handled shovel to the grass. In another instant he had vaulted easily downward.

He approached with the springy softness of a cat.

"Thanks for the brain work," he jeered. "You did the figgering; I do the digging. Fair enough!"

His voice hardened.

"Back up—the two of you—over near that bench. Lay down with your faces on the grass.... No—wait a minute, Tracy! I'll take that gun you got in your pocket!"

The absolute hopelessness of Margaret Connor's white face sent something fierce and primeval surging through the pain-ridden body of the columnist. For the first time in his careful life, he didn't give a damn whether he lived or died. His legs spread suddenly. He swung his left fist with every atom of his strength at Danker's grinning mouth.

Danker sprang aside and Tracy's blow caught him awkwardly on the ear and skidded off. He fired instantly at the columnist. The bullet ripped through Tracy's dangling arm and spun him helplessly to the trampled grass.

He heard through a deep abyss of raw pain the scream of the girl and the sharp continued explosions of pistol fire. They seemed to roar endlessly. Danker was killing her—tunneling her soft body with lead…. Must stop Danker, kill him, tear him apart….

Blindly, Tracy groped to his knees in absolute blackness. He felt himself losing his balance. He was falling headlong down a narrow, gleaming incline like the polished surface of a coal chute. He could see it clearly as he whizzed, mile after mile, at terrific speed. He felt grimly exhilarated, happy about something, he couldn't remember what….

JERRY TRACY WAS spreadeagled on the grass, a fixed grimace on his unconscious lips, when Inspector Fitzgerald turned him gently over.

"Jeese, he looks dead," Sergeant Killan muttered huskily. "If that swell little guy is dead, I'll—"

"Forget it," Fitz snapped. His face was haggard in the moonlight. Between Tracy and this gray-thatched old man who was getting perilously close to the edge of retirement there was a strong bond of loyalty and affection. Fitz gulped suddenly: "Don't let a little blood scare you, Killan."

Tracy's eyelids were fluttering open. " 'Lo, Fitz. Been trying—dig—buried treasure. Ever hear anything—silly—as that?"

"Silly, hell," Fitz told him grimly. "We found it. It's all there. In a tin box. Two hundred grand."

Remembrance swept across Tracy's blank eyes. "The girl! Where is she, Fitz? Is she all right?"

He felt the soft pressure of lips against his cheek. He could smell the faint scent of lilac perfume.

"I'm safe—thanks to you, Jerry."

Fitz interrupted huskily. "Killan and I got here just as Danker fired at you. Danker is dead. Killan shot him. We were delayed when we stopped off at Dover Street. You see, I didn't know that Danker had escaped from you down there."

"Danker killed the blonde," Tracy said weakly.

"I know it. He came through with a confession when he saw he was done for. I'm holding his gun for the ballistics people."

Tracy's head rolled. Margaret Connor was on her knees in the grass beside him.

"Did you explain to Fitz the financial jam your father is in?" Jerry mumbled. "Fitz—listen—You gotta cut through the red tape and let her get that dough back to her father in a hurry. He's in a bad spot—depression bankruptcy—pay debts—give him chance to face—future—clean reputation...."

Jerry's voice trailed indistinctly.

"Don't worry about it," Fitz replied. "It's okey. Everything will be taken care of."

"Where's the—girl? Can't seem to—see her?"

"I—I'm right here, Jerry. Please don't try to talk—you mustn't talk."

"You're a grand, swell kid, Lilac," he breathed.

"Lilac? I—I don't understand."

"He's delirious," Fitz said huskily. "Let him rest a minute till that damned ambulance gets here."

But Jerry Tracy wasn't delirious. He was slipping into a delicious void, grinning faintly with egotistical pride. He had tabbed Lilac as a decent number right from the start. Old Man Accurate!... Never missed a hunch in his life.... Lilac....

Body Snatcher

Jerry Tracy tries to switch a murder tag

THE SHABBY SUBURBAN bus jolted to a teeth-jarring halt and the driver growled with patient boredom: "Locust Avenue!"

Jerry Tracy fell over a couple of legs and swung off the bus, conscious that his lips were wreathed in a faint, somewhat silly grin. If the boys at Times Square could see the *Daily Planet's* famous little columnist out here in the sticks, could guess what was inside the two paper-wrapped parcels he was carrying, a jeering laugh would go up that would stop the hands on the Paramount clock! Wise guy Jerry, the lad with the case-hardened front—pulling a sentimental pilgrimage to a has-been, because no one else in roaring Manhattan would remember that today was her birthday.

Ordinarily, on a trip out of town, Jerry traveled in his very dodgy Lincoln, with Butch behind the wheel making delighted horn sounds like the *Normandie* going down the bay. But today the *Daily Planet's* columnist had dived inconspicuously into the subway, ridden out to the end of the line and taken a bus the rest of the way. The big package under his left arm was a birthday cake with a pink, gooey trail on top from a baker's cornucopia that said: "Hey, hey, Sweetie!" The flat, oblong package had come from a five-and-dime; fluted pink candles with tin shields to catch the grease and pins to stick 'em in the cake.

Sweetie Malloy had once been a name to adorn the most famous of the Victor Herbert operettas! Beauty, brains and a

velvet soprano voice gone at last—turned out to a forgotten pasturage in a punk suburb. It angered Jerry to think that a woman like Sweetie Malloy should be permitted by fate to settle down in a one-horse, out-of-the-way dump like this.

Chilly raindrops spattered on Jerry's face. He stared at the gray sky and knew with a wry dismay that it was going to be one of those sullen all-night soakers. By the time he had rung Sweetie's bell, the dark pavement of the walk was a dull, glistening black.

The sight of Sweetie's face in the half-open door made Tracy's throat catch, as it always would at each new sight of her. The singer was gone but the woman remained. The pale yellow entry light fluffed her soft hair, was kind to the threads of gray. Time had padded the once taut line of her throat, had put wrinkles around the clear, amber eyes without disturbing their serenity or their fine courage.

"Jerry!" she gasped, with a quick, frightened inflection.

"How about letting a little guy in out of the rain?"

"Why—yes... Of course! Come—come in...."

There was something in the manner with which she closed the door that put Tracy instantly on the alert, made him study the woman. She was scared to a sickish gray pallor. Stealth! That's what the careful click of the closing door had meant.

"Anything wrong, Sweetie?" he asked her, with a level stare.

"Wrong? Why, what a question! With you here?" Her voice steadied. "Everything is right, my friend. Come, let me take your coat and—and bundles. Gracious, what huge packages! Don't tell me they're for—for me?"

"Happy birthday," Tracy said gravely. "We'll open 'em later." He put his hands on both her shoulders as she turned tremulously. "Listen, keed. Do we have to put on an act—you and me? I'm not Ole Olesen or Jake Kazinsky. I'm Jerry Tracy. I came all the way out here tonight because—well, just because... I'm asking you as an old friend, is anything wrong?"

Rain, drumming at the closed window, made a softly sinister sound.

"Everything is very, very right, my friend!" Her laugh quivered. "As—as right as rain."

He let the subject drop for the moment. "The big package is a cake," he said. "Biggest damn' cake in the local cakery. Candles in the smaller bundle. Later on we're gonna let you inflate the lovely bosom—and Lord help you if you don't blow 'em all out with one big foooof! I thought that after dinner—"

"Dinner? Of—of course."

"Corned beef." Tracy grinned. "Same as it's always been, same as it always will be. Cooked à la Sweetie Malloy, with gobs of hot English mustard—"

"And—and chopped cabbage with plenty of salt and pepper, lots of b-butter—"

Her voice stopped quite suddenly. Her mouth twisted, began making queer, choking sounds. She turned away towards the couch. Tracy didn't move an inch from where he stood. The sound of her harsh weeping made his heart ache, but he let her alone, let her have the thing out by herself. After a while her fingers stopped bunching the covering on the couch's arm.

"Jerry, will you do something for me—if I beg you as an old friend?"

The look in her eyes made him wary at once. He didn't reply.

"I want you to leave this house immediately and go back to New York."

"No."

"You don't understand. For your own sake, Jerry, you've got to go! Just forget that you were here."

"No."

He winced at the sound of her tragic laugh. "In that case, you will have to be convinced. You see, you're not the only one with a surprise this evening. I—I have one for you."

Her cold fingers touched his and held on. She walked silently towards the stairs, and Tracy with her. Upstairs in silence, past the bathroom, down a short, incredibly ugly hallway to a closed door which, being opened, disclosed a curtained bedroom where twin boudoir lamps burned softly atop a dresser.

Tracy stared at the room's quiet charm, doubly quiet by reason of the lash of the rain against the shade-drawn windows.

"So what?" he said in a puzzled voice. "Where's the surprise come in?"

"It's—on the other side of the bed."

"It better be a good one, because— Oh!"

He stopped short. His voice sounded like dried peas rattling in a tin pan. "How did this happen?"

"It—it happened."

"Who killed him?"

"I did."

Tracy said very softly: "I knew a guy once who used to lie the same way you do. The more he lied, the more truthful he looked. He never could fool me worth a damn."

JERRY TRACY BENT downward above the sprawled body and surveyed it with narrowed eyes. The man had taken a small-calibered bullet almost exactly through the navel. The corpse was on his back, with his legs together, one arm trailing stiffly towards the dresser. The sleeve of the extended arm, Tracy noted, was quite rumpled. Black, silky hair, a little thin on top; a small black mustache that accented the curve of petulant lips. Eyelids shut tightly. Ears without lobes.

Tracy straightened. "You killed this fellow, Sweetie?"

"Yes."

"Right here?"

"Yes."

"Why?"

"For—for reasons I'd rather not discuss, Jerry."

"We'll skip the reasons. You killed him about a half hour ago, eh?"

"No," Sweetie Malloy said calmly. "I killed him early this afternoon."

Tracy's chuckle held no amusement. "Smart woman refuses to be tripped by cunning columnist." He shook his head. "It's no use lying, Sweetie. Too many other things to explain away. Corpse bled like a pig when he took the slug in the belly—but your rug's nice and clean. The gun on the rug could have done it—maybe did do it—but *not here,* Sweetie. And you should never try to bend an arm after *rigor mortis* has set in; it makes a lot too many wrinkles in the sleeve and sets the mind of a bright little guy galloping with the proper answers."

"Nevertheless, I killed him here in my bedroom," she said, stonily.

"What were you planning to do if I hadn't butted in?"

"I was going to call the police and confess."

"Mmmm... Going to, eh? Since this morning?"

Composure fled from her. "My God, Jerry—stop grinning at me like a—a hyena! Did you ever murder anyone—and—and try to decide what to do? Did you ever stare all day at a dead man and think—and think—till you almost went mad with terror and despair? And then, just when you had nerved yourself to take what you deserved—to have the doorbell ring and—and be tortured by a well-meaning friend who—"

Tracy strode grimly forward as her voice mounted shrilly. With deliberate brutality he shook the hysteria from her.

"Stop yelling. Do you want to get me into trouble, too?"

"No, no!" she gasped. "Please go—please, Jerry! I—I brought you up here to show you how dangerous, how suicidal it would be for you to remain until—"

"Save your breath. I won't budge an inch. Who you trying to shield?"

Sweetie didn't reply.

"Who's the lad on the floor?"

"A—a man named Phil Clement. He was a—lover of mine. If you're familiar with the movies we were—living in sin." The hard desperation went out of her voice suddenly. "Jerry, you must believe me! Phil Clement found out something that I couldn't bear to have exposed, and he—he tried to blackmail me."

"I happen to know," Tracy reminded her, "that the income you live on, Sweetie, wouldn't attract a grasshopper."

"For your own sake, leave before I call the police."

"I'm staying here until I find out the truth."

There was a telephone on the low night table and Sweetie sprang towards it. Jerry wrenched the receiver out of her hand before she could utter a word. He slammed it back on the prong and held the sobbing woman motionless for an instant. Something in the wild stare of her eyes gave him a sudden idea.

"If I promise to leave here in ten minutes, will you have one drink with me as a—a substitute for the birthday cake and the—the candles?"

Sweetie Malloy nodded haggardly.

"Where do you keep the liquor?"

"Downstairs. Kitchen. There's a bottle of Scotch in the little closet off the dinette."

She had sunk into a chair, her eyes closed. He closed the bedroom door softly, his mind grimly on the bathroom and the medicine cabinet. A sedative! There must be a sedative there! He was betting shrewdly on the habit that must have been a part of Sweetie Malloy at the height of her Broadway glamour. He had never known a celebrity yet who wasn't an insomniac. Jerry was one himself. Late hours and the constant whirl of excitement made a sedative as familiar as breakfast food. And where would it be but in the medicine cabinet?

He found a bottle of veronal on the lowest shelf. Soundlessly he tiptoed down the carpeted stairs, hurried to the kitchen. He made two stiff highballs. Into the glass with a slight nick at its edge he put a double dose of veronal. He placed both glasses on a tray and went back upstairs.

Sweetie Malloy reached out listlessly as he touched her shoulder and presented the tray. She took the glass without the nick.

"Whoa!" Tracy said humorously and plucked it from her fingers.

"What's the matter?"

"Ginger ale in the other one. Did you think I wouldn't remember?"

"Oh—thanks."

She took the one with the cracked rim and drank deeply. Finished it with a second long gulp. Tracy emptied his, too.

"Bum Scotch," she said faintly. "It's the best I can afford."

"That's all right, Sweetie."

She sat there holding the empty glass. Gradually the tense lines were smoothing out in her face. "You're the best friend I have in the world," she said dreamily. "I wouldn't drag you into a mess like this for a million dollars. On my birthday—that's funny, isn't it?"

"Pretty funny," Tracy agreed.

Rain drummed with insistent sound on the windowpanes. The overhang of the bedclothes hid the corpse from view. Tracy's lowered gaze watched the relaxing fingers on the empty glass. Sweetie clutched sluggishly as the glass dropped into her lap. It bounced off to the floor and she regarded it for an instant with a blurred grimace. Suddenly her eyes widened, knowledge brightening them.

"Jerry... What—what—"

"Take it easy, keed."

She swayed unsteadily to her feet, her eyes struggling to retain their fleeting look of tragic accusation.

"You've—you've doped—"

"Sure," Tracy said softly.

HE CAUGHT HER weight as she pitched forward. Holding her limp body in his extended arms, the *Daily Planet's* wise little columnist stared down at one of the few really fine women he had known in his life. Sweetie Malloy harboring a blackmailing lover? Sweetie Malloy killing a man—for any reason whatsoever? The idea was preposterous, sheer lunacy.

Sweetie wasn't that kind. She had had no furtive lovers— and only one marriage. It wasn't her fault that Jack Malloy was a rotter and a total loss. He didn't even have dough! But she loved him, married him, stuck with him till the hour he died. She had saved enough from her own savings to purchase this cheap house in the suburbs and provide her with a meager income. Finished with the stage, forgotten by the blatant Broadway crowd, she had moved gallantly into obscurity. And this was the woman who was trying to assume the guilt for a sordid murder, who would have leaped into black, scandalous headlines but for Jerry's providential arrival in the rainy dusk.

He carried her sagging weight across to the bed and dropped her with a soft grunt. He had turned back towards the murdered man when he heard the peculiar sounds Sweetie

Malloy was making. The high-necked dress was cutting into her throat, purpling her unconscious face. For an instant Tracy hunted unsuccessfully for hooks or buttons; then with a sibilant oath he whipped out his penknife and slashed the neck of the dress open.

The tiny gold links of a locket chain were rising and falling with her labored breathing. Tracy frowned, reluctant to pry into her personal possessions. But the thought of the corpse on the rug swept away his sympathetic instincts. He drew the locket gently upward from the white cleft of her bosom.

He snapped the flat case open and stared at the scrap of photograph inside.

Sweetie herself. Taken evidently when she was a child of about fourteen. Self-possessed, mature-looking, very lovely.

He was clicking the locket shut when a peculiar thought stayed his hand. The eyes—they weren't Sweetie's eyes. Even in the child's face, they were harder, clearer, devoid entirely of that shy reticence that had always been Sweetie Malloy's chief charm. He saw now that the hairdressing was too modern; the scrap of dress that showed in the photo was a fairly recent style that was not more than five or six years outmoded. Sweetie's own childhood belonged way back in the early nineties; it couldn't possibly be her. Then who was this clear-eyed, defiant little beauty? Tracy's memory told him he had seen this kid somewhere, was dimly familiar with the contour of the face, especially the reckless flame of the eyes. She'd be about twenty now. A grown woman.

He pried out the picture with the point of his penknife and his breath caught as he read the rounded, childish handwriting on the back of the photo: "To Mother from Lois."

Lois… He knew the face now! His imagination filled out the promise of beauty in the face, matured and hardened the lovely mouth, added a nude body misted to a milky radiance under the glow of diffused lights…. Señorita Lois; she used no other name. Poised in the perfumed darkness of the *Club Español,* dancing like a flitting white moonbeam behind the iridescent translucence of an enormous floating bubble.

Tracy closed the locket, replaced it gently around the neck of Sweetie Malloy. Poor, desperate, gray-haired Sweetie! Pleading guilty to murder, secretly conveying a dead body to her own home and bedroom—to save this same reckless-eyed child? It was only a guess, but to Tracy it seemed a guess perilously close to certainty.

A grim hatred for the charming Señorita Lois grew in Jerry's mind. Without Lois there was no need at all for Sweetie's desperate sacrifice. A childless Sweetie had no sane reason for attempting to frame herself to burn in the electric chair. But if she had a daughter… If her daughter had killed a man, had begged Sweetie in hysterical terror to save her—save her….

Jerry's lean jaw hardened. All Lois had to do, apparently, was to lock her damned crimsoned lips and let her unsuspecting mother take the rap. Sweetie would never disclose the secret. Tracy himself, friend of years as he was, had never once dreamed that Sweetie's marriage with drunken Jack Malloy had produced this pampered and sinuous darling of the *Club Español.* A damned, cowardly murderess, if his hunch was correct. A gal whom Jerry Tracy was going to pay a grim visit before this tragic night was over.

He reexamined the corpse on the floor. Except for tailor marks the clothes were empty of clues. But Tracy was patient with his searching and his patience was rewarded by a stiff, oblong pressure in the lining of the man's coat. He found the hole in the inner pocket, ripped it wide with his forefinger, felt down through the lining and drew up the pasteboard. There were only two lines of print:

Phil Clement

Representing Señorita Lois

Rain still slogged viciously behind the drawn shades on the window. Tracy shuddered slightly at the sound; he knew what he had to do tonight before he called on Sweetie's unnatural and cowardly daughter. He'd get rid of the body, plant it somewhere else for the police to find. With the police short of all clues that might show where and under what circumstances the man had been murdered, Tracy himself would be free for at least one night to go to work on Lois, uncover the whole slimy truth. Sweetie would keep quiet as long as Lois' name remained a secret. Besides, if she stepped forward now and tried to re-assume the guilt, it would drag Tracy himself into a criminal mess—and Sweetie, God bless her, wasn't built that way!

TRACY STRODE TO the telephone on the night table and called his penthouse. To his disgust McNulty, his ancient Chinese butler, answered the call instead of Butch. In a steady voice Jerry assured the Chink that he was perfectly dry and in the best of health, that he wouldn't be home for dinner—and please put Butch on, like a first-class and intelligent Chinaman!

"You got him laincoat an' lubbers?"

"Sure, sure. I'm all right, keed. Honest!"

Then Butch's adenoidal bellow came over the wire. "Hello, Boss. Jeeze, what a night, huh?"

"Where's the Chink?"

"Gone back in the kitchen."

"Swell. I want you to phone my garage and get the car. The Chrysler, not the Lincoln. Don't tell the Chink where you're going."

"How kin I?" Butch asked in a puzzled voice, "When I dunno meself?"

Tracy gave him the address. "Drive out here right away. You can't miss the cottage. It's three from the corner of Locust. Pull into the drive and park at the back of the cottage. Keep your mug covered up as much as you can. I don't want anyone recognizing you on the drive through Manhattan."

"Oke."

"And tell Felix over at the garage to keep his trap shut about the Chrysler going out. If anyone asks later on, both my cars were there all night."

"Oke."

Tracy hung up with a nervous click. He prowled swiftly about the shaded bedroom, pocketed the gun from the rug, tidied the grim evidence of struggle that Sweetie had so pathetically counterfeited, made the room normal and neat except for the huddled corpse. Sweetie was still breathing with drugged regularity; she'd be asleep for hours yet.

The *Daily Planet's* pint-sized columnist went downstairs to the kitchen and made himself a hasty sandwich with some Swiss and rye he found. He was as hungry as hell; and besides, it gave him something to do while he waited for Butch. Inaction always got on his nerves, made them raw and jumpy.

He had finished the sandwich and was hunting for a bottle of beer when the bell rang at the rear door.

Jerry Tracy stiffened. He knew that the prompt caller at the kitchen couldn't possibly be Butch. Then who was it? And should he answer the ring or let the guy get tired and go away? Again the bell rang. The guy outside knew that the lights were on in the cottage, that someone was at home. Jerry would have to answer or arouse suspicion that something was wrong.

A plan formed instantly in his mind. He sprang noiselessly towards the gas range, turned on one of the burners. He grabbed an empty kettle from the table, filled it with water, stood it over the blue flame. Then he walked noisily towards the rear door, flung it open.

To his surprise the caller was a woman. Rain slanted against the columnist's bare head. He stared at the woman, trying to get a glimpse of her dripping face.

"Mrs. Malloy is quite ill," he said curtly. "What did you want?"

"Ill? I'm—I'm sorry."

Her beady eyes stared suspiciously, peered past him through the half-opened door. "I'm—I'm Mrs. Malloy's next-door neighbor. I came to borrow a cup of sugar. You see, we're having a little party and—"

Tracy leaned forward, glanced alternately to right and left. Both adjoining houses were dark from cellar to garret.

"I'm Doctor Rolfe," he told the woman with a cool smile. "We mustn't disturb Mrs. Malloy—but come in, by all means! And—er—get your cup of sugar."

His firm hand drew her unwillingly across the threshold. He took a good look at her in the light. She was fully dressed for the street: hat, coat, high-heeled shoes, gloves. Soaked with rain. Obviously out in the storm longer than it would take to run from an adjoining doorway. Pale angular face. Might be a Swede. Watching the suave stranger that she had not expected to run into with a puzzled, scared expression in her bovine eyes. That lump in the sagging pocket of her long coat was a gun bulge, or Jerry was crazy!

He lifted the lid of his kettle and peered professionally.

"Mrs. Malloy had a bad heart attack this afternoon. She's upstairs in bed, barely conscious. I'm heating hot water now for a—ahem—parallelogram treatment."

He smiled faintly.

"You no doubt know where she keeps the sugar. Help yourself."

The woman's eyes swept the cupboard helplessly. "I—I guess I won't bother, Doctor. Thank you; I—I won't stay."

"Shall I tell Mrs. Malloy who called?"

"No, no. Don't annoy her."

She backed towards the kitchen door, swung it open and ducked out into the drumming rain. The minute the door closed Tracy ran noiselessly into the front room. With his eye carefully glued to a corner of the shifted shade, he saw the woman hurrying from the driveway to the sidewalk. She melted into the darkness towards Locust Avenue. A liar and a faker. As bad an egg as Tracy had ever smelled. Who was she? Did she know about the corpse upstairs? Could she be—his jaw tightened—an emissary of Señorita Lois?

He went back to the kitchen and turned out the gas flame under the kettle. He heard the pulsing hum of a motorcar with a thrill of satisfaction. The car turned slowly into the driveway from the street. It braked behind the cottage and a moment later the bell rang briefly. It was Butch.

Tracy yanked the startled big fellow into the kitchen and snapped an eager question at him. "See any sign of a woman walking along Locust Avenue?"

"Naw." Butch snorted with derision. "On a night like this they ain't nobody walkin'. Street's as empty as a—a motorman's glove. I mean," he added hastily, with a silly grin, "a motorman without no hand."

"Did you see a car parked anywhere along Locust?"

"Oh, sure. About four blocks down. Parked without lights. You tol' me not to show me mug much, so I didn't give it no gander." He grinned. "Jeeze, let 'em park—I was young meself once!"

Jerry wiped the romantic grin off Butch's thick lips with a curt sentence or two.

"Huh?" Butch gasped. "Moider? Right here? An'—an' we're gonna snatch the body?"

"Right. And I don't want any mistakes."

LESS THAN TEN minutes after Butch had arrived, the body of Phil Clement was carried discreetly out the back door of the cottage and stowed away in the rumble of the Chrysler. He made a tight fit—but he fitted. The adjoining houses were still dark. Tracy smeared the license plates with a handful of wet earth. He was climbing in alongside of Butch when he suddenly remembered his two bundles—the birthday cake and the candles! Swearing grimly, he hurried back into the cottage and got them.

Butch swung the car through the driveway and out to the rain-pelted street.

As they turned into Locust Avenue, Jerry's eyes peered ahead through the slanting sliver of headlight-illuminated rain.

"Is that the parked car you saw?"

"Yeah."

"Slow down a trifle when we go by. Don't let 'em see your face. Cut in close and go right by 'em."

"Okey."

Butch ducked his head low over the wheel. Tracy, hunched beside him, gave the stalled car a lightning scrutiny from under the wet brim of his hat. Two of 'em—a man and a woman. The man's back was turned; all Tracy could see was a very sporty, extremely gray topcoat—almost a white-gray. The woman was the dame who had called at Sweetie Malloy's kitchen to borrow a cup of sugar.

Butch, who had glanced casually into the rear-vision mirror, gave a faint yelp. "Hey! They're follerin' us, Boss!"

"I know. Show 'em how fast you can go with a special engine job that cost me plenty of jack."

Butch crooned with delight. "Fast as I like?"

"Sure. Lose 'em."

Butch lost them in a straightaway mile of hair-raising speed along water-slippery concrete. He made doubly sure by two sneaking turns through the bumping darkness that brought the Chrysler to a parallel highway.

"We're going to Brooklyn," Tracy said. "We're going to dump the body in a vacant lot at the corner of Pike and Pacific."

The place registered instantly with Butch. "I getcha. The spot where the cops found Snipe Moretto last week." His smile bathed Tracy with fond admiration. "Jeeze, you sure got brains in that little nut o' yours. The cops'll think it's a gang killin'. They'll think Snipe Moretto's boys got hunk with the Peewee gang."

The flitting Chrysler roared smoothly through the Bronx, crossed into Manhattan, went all the way down to Canal and across the Manhattan bridge into Brooklyn. It was barely nine o'clock, but the steady torrential rain had swept the streets clear of all but a driblet of traffic. No signs of pedestrians at all.

At Pike and Pacific, Butch braked the car to a stop and got out with a hand-jack. Unmindful of the soaking rain he jacked up the rear axle and pretended to go to work on a tire. Tracy drifted unobtrusively to a gap in the rickety fence and peered into the vacant lot. He came back and rested one hand negligently on the closed rumble. An occasional automobile rocketed by, throwing water flying in a soggy splash.

"When I say ready—out with him!" Jerry whispered.

More cars. Tracy straightened nervously as the last one swerved out of sight around a corner. As far as he could see, the street was empty for the moment except for the sullen hiss of the October rain.

"Ready!"

Up went the lid of the rumble. Arms plunged and caught at the wedged-in corpse. In a moment Tracy and Butch had staggered across the deserted sidewalk and vanished through the gap in the fence. They were gone less than sixty seconds. Butch let down the jack and tossed it into the open rumble. Jerry closed the lid with a bang.

The Chrysler was in motion almost before the columnist could close his door. Butch's hands, he noticed, were shaking on the circumference of the wheel. His own were tremulous, too. The car took an erratic slide and straightened out.

"That's that, Boss."

"Yeah. That's that."

A vivid picture was still uppermost in both their minds: a dead man lying in a grotesque huddle in the rainy darkness of a vacant lot. Cold and inanimate, in a sordid welter of tin cans, mud and busted bed-springs... Tracy felt a little sick at the necessity of heaving even a dead man to a rest like that.

Jerry had a grim hunch that if he didn't make a quick job of this case, the gal who asked for a cup of sugar and the guy in the gray-white topcoat might do something damned nasty to a pint-sized columnist who had developed such an uncanny habit of minding other people's business—when they broke the law. Whoever they were, those two were in the thing up to their ears, along with the bubble dancer.

"Drop me off at Nevins Street," he told Butch in a low tone. "I'll grab the subway back. Remember to tell Felix that the car wasn't out of the garage tonight. Get rid of those two packages of mine somewhere. Be sure no one sees you do it. Better smash 'em both up and stick 'em in one of the garage trash cans."

He watched the crimson tail-light of the Chrysler vanish in the rain and descended frowningly into the Nevins Street station. He rode a Seventh Avenue express to Times Square, caught a cab, rode quietly with set jaw to the *Club Español.*

TRACY WAS SOAKED and soggy, a bit squishy at the heels, but the *Español's* doorman recognized him with a respectful grin.

"Bad night, Mr. Tracy."

Jerry said, "Yeah," and made quick puddles towards the cloak room. Suddenly he stopped short in the center of the foyer.

He was staring at a familiar white-gray topcoat. The coat was being handed across to Nita, the checkroom girl, by a thickset, muscular man of medium height, with bushy black hair and a neck almost as big as Butch's.

Tracy began backing quietly towards a convenient Spanish arch, but Nita's face had lifted and her pert red lips were smiling at the columnist.

"Hey, hey, Jerry *mío!* Lousy night, no?"

The muscular man whirled like a cat. His dark eyes focused on Tracy. Jerry advanced smilingly, fumbling casually for his cigarette case, taking in the guy's details with one slant-eyed flash. Didn't know the mug from Adam. The fleshy cheeks, blunt nose, shaggy black eyebrows made a brand-new tintype for Tracy's mental rogues' gallery. But the topcoat was an old friend!

The stranger grabbed the coat from Nita with a brusque snatch. "Forgot something," he muttered, and with his face averted from Tracy, barged through the lobby and butted out into the rain.

Tracy waited for ten hesitant seconds. The hard-boiled bubble dancer could wait, he decided. This was a guy to check on in a hurry.

There was no sign of him on the gleaming black lacquer of the rain-drenched sidewalk. A taxi was moving from the curb and Jerry said swiftly to the doorman: "A guy just came out. Did he take that cab?"

"Was he a sorta short, heavy mug in a light coat?"

"Yeah."

"He walked. Pretty fast, too. Went around the corner."

"Thanks."

Jerry caromed off a bobbing umbrella and made it to the corner without delay. His eyes narrowed with elation. That car parked at the curb down the street looked a hell of a lot like Light Coat's tin wheelbarrow. Might swish by and give it a look.

A hand clutched him as he passed a pitch-dark doorway. The clutch lifted Jerry off his feet, yanked him headlong into the narrow entry.

His fist swung instinctively and skidded off a wet ear. The force of his hasty blow threw him off balance but it saved him a fractured skull. A pistol butt hit Jerry's falling shoulder and laced it with numbing pain. Before it could hit again Jerry's left hand closed desperately on a thick ankle and toppled his antagonist.

Neither of them made a sound. The hiss of the rain on the black sidewalk and the scuffling of their entangled legs on the tiled pavement of the doorway was the only noise audible.

The clubbed gun swung backward for a bone-smashing blow.

Jerry butted his head against the man's nose. He bit his way through the hand that crushed his mouth and chin. The killer yelped shrilly and they rolled apart for an instant. Tracy staggered to his feet, slipped, went down jarringly on hands and knees. He managed to throw one arm upward and he took the savage gun smash on the wincing tendons of his forearm.

His assailant turned, chin and mouth crimson from his butted nose, and ran head-downward through the rain. He darted along the sidewalk and slammed headlong into his parked car. As the gears meshed Jerry leaped to the running-board, clutched at the wheel, tried to throw the automobile towards the sidewalk.

A straight-arm blow to the mouth tore him loose and sent him reeling backward. The pavement came up dizzily and socked the back of his skull with a force that bounced his teeth together. It took him a dazed minute to remember where he was and to sway dizzily upward from the cold puddle he was blotting with his aching back.

The car was in high, roaring towards Sixth Avenue. Its stop light flared crimson; the car skidded around the corner and vanished.

Tracy sat down on the uncomfortable spiked top of a hydrant and tried to pull himself together. His head still felt like an overstuffed chair. A man with a dripping umbrella came down from Seventh, stopped hesitantly.

"S'matter, buddy? Sick?"

"Nope. I'm all right."

Except for an arm that felt like boiled spaghetti and a lump on the back of his head where he had kissed the sidewalk, Jerry was beginning to feel normal. The man with the umbrella handed the columnist his hat and walked off. Didn't even look back.

"If I'd been jumped like this in Peoria," Tracy reflected grimly, "there'd have been six cops with notebooks, a hook and ladder company, and a thousand nosy gazabos. Get half killed in Manhattan and a lone guy with an umbrella hands you back your hat—and goes right on to the drug-store to buy his aspirin!"

The thought made him grin cheerfully. He went back to the *Club Español* with almost a jaunty stride.

He asked for an inconspicuous table and got it. Garcia, the swarthy and affable headwaiter, bubbled with friendliness for the *Daily Planet's* expensive little hireling. Tracy had helped many a good show, had rescued many a lousy one, by a good-humored boost salted away in a pert paragraph.

Garcia rubbed swarthy hands together. "Señorita Lois goes on in about wan hour. You weel like her, I'm sure."

"I can't wait an hour. I want to see her now."

Garcia's chuckle seemed a bit strained. "Ah, no, no... Why not wait, have a few dreenks—see for yourself thees glorious dance she makes with thees glorious body, no?"

"You mean she doesn't want to talk to me?"

"Tonight she is a leetle bit upset."

"Sick, eh?" Tracy's tone was sharp.

"No, no. Worried, per'aps. Maybe a leetle temperament. Ha, ha! She snarl and she snap. She weel talk weeth no one."

"Tell her Jerry Tracy wants to see her."

Garcia shrugged, scowled, departed. When he returned his message was brief.

"She say—" He gulped. "She say how you lak to go to hell in a tin bucket?"

"I see. Got an envelope and a small hunk of paper?"

"But surely."

Tracy cupped the paper behind his left hand, scrawled a brief sentence, sealed the envelope. "Take her this."

In three minutes Garcia was back. There was incredulity in his black eyes, a faint overlay of perspiration on his olive forehead.

"You are indeed a magician, *Señor* Tracy. She see you. Come weeth me."

Tracy threaded his way past crowded tables, paid no attention to the whispered buzz of comment his presence excited.

He crossed a shining expanse of open floor, ducked under a curtain of heavy brocaded material and climbed a flight of wooden stairs to a closed door.

"Beat it," he told Garcia.

He opened the door without knocking, clicked it shut behind him.

"Hello, Toots."

HIS NOTE WAS still in her hand. She had thrown a light robe over her shoulders but the thing gaped candidly and Tracy, in spite of the hard anger that gripped him, was forced to admit to himself that this kid was strictly the goods.

It was hard to say which was uppermost in her swimming dark eyes: rage, or a bright, overmastering fear.

"Listen, you wise little newspaper heel! If you're trying one of your celebrated snoop acts, pulling a cheap bluff—"

"Shut up!" He was not an awful lot taller than the dancer, but he seemed to loom a foot higher as he tramped slowly towards her. "As far as I'm concerned, Toots, you're a two-bit strip act— and I'm doing you a favor to sneeze at you. I never fool and I never bluff. I asked you how you'd like to push a bubble around in a death cell. Think it over, *Miss Malloy.*"

"You—damn you... Who said my name's Malloy?"

She sprang at him without warning, caught both his shoulders in a nail-digging frenzy. Her flimsy robe trailed but neither of them was aware of anything but their locked double glare. Tracy kept his lips compressed, gave no indication whatever that the pointed nails of the dancer were hurting him like hell.

He flung her backward a step.

"If you don't talk—and talk plenty, Toots!—I'm gonna nail

that kalsomined shape of yours to the cross. I'm calling you Malloy because you're Sweetie Malloy's daughter."

He heard the sharp hissing of her breath. There was a moment of utter silence in the room.

"Well? So what if I am?"

"I want to know why you're so damned scared tonight. Are you waiting to hear the newspaper extras that your mother has been pinched for murder?"

Her rouged face was as white as the notepaper that fluttered to the floor at her bare feet. "You're nuts. You're absolutely insane."

"Am I?" He stopped and placed the paper in his pocket. "If I'm insane, let out a scream and have me pinched for annoying you. I'd love to tell the cops why Sweetie Malloy *could not* have killed Phil Clement, your manager."

"Is Phil—dead?"

"You know damn' well he is.... You're the one that killed him. How about going straight back to your apartment and talking this over?" His glance was like the flick of a whip. "Well?"

"Let's go," she gasped.

She clutched at his hand, wrenched the door open. Barefooted, panting, she sprang down the wooden staircase, her left hand dragging the startled columnist. A chorus girl, ascending the narrow stairs, flattened herself against the banister as the almost nude dancer and the columnist swept on past her.

"Well, for Gawd's sake...."

"Hey, wait a minute!" Tracy growled. He pulled the fluttering robe tight, knotted the silken cord securely. "Where's your shoes? You can't go out barefooted, dope!"

There was almost an insane blaze in Lois' eyes. She jerked him forward, pattered through a darkened corridor, swung open a door. There was a paved alley outside and a parked limousine.

"Yours?" Tracy snapped.

"Yes."

"Swell." He swung her up in his arms with a sudden heave and carried her through the rain. A sleepy chauffeur in a plum-colored uniform flung open the automobile's door, gaping stupidly.

Tracy bounced Lois in on the cushioned seat, crawled in beside her. "Tell this lad it's okey. Tell him home, James."

The chauffeur had recovered his scattered wits. He had the door open again, a wrench hefted menacingly in his gauntleted hand.

"It's—it's all right, Peter," Lois whispered fiercely. "I'm—I'm not feeling well. Drive us home."

"And toss that overcoat of yours back here!" Tracy snapped at him.

Lois Malloy jerked the speaking tube to her tremulous lips. "I won't need you any more tonight after we get there, Peter. You can put up the car and go home."

"Yes, Miss."

The apartment building was a swanky stone hive that went up and up through the rain like the side of a terra-cotta cliff. It had a canopy, a doorman, a rubber carpet to the curb and an umbrella ready to be snicked open for milady.

Tracy shoved all the hubbub away with a sweep of his arm. He grinned at the startled doorman. He was just beginning to realize that he was bareheaded and coatless himself. And the bubble dancer's appearance was enough to make any respectable doorman gulp.

Jerry carried Lois Malloy to the silver and onyx elevator. She wriggled loose and slid to her feet as the car ascended. Jerry didn't mind that a bit; it had been quite a trick to carry her with that numb left arm of his. Her eyes, he saw, were free of terror; they were colder now, wary, self-possessed.

"I haven't my key with me," she told the stolid elevator man. "Will you get a duplicate, please?"

"Yes, Miss."

She padded barefooted to her penthouse door and waited with Tracy while the elevator man descended.

"Maid out tonight?" Tracy suggested.

"Yes."

"What's her name?"

"Does it matter?"

"I think so."

"Her name's Selma."

"Selma what?"

She whirled at him suddenly. "How the hell do I know? Just plain Selma!"

The doorman appeared, inserted a key, opened the door, vanished. They went into a gorgeous living-room and Tracy said mildly: "Nice dump you've got."

Lois' bare feet made quick, meaty sounds on the floor. She jerked out a cabinet drawer, slammed viciously about with a gun in her hand.

"Listen, you! Stand right where you are. What do you know about my—my mother? And what do you know about Phil Clement?"

"I know why Clement was killed—and where," Tracy bluffed.

"Yes?" Her voice grated. "He was killed because my mother was dumb enough to take him on as a lover. And if you think you can drag me into her mess, you've got another think coming."

Tracy nodded a little. "I've seen and touched a lot of lice in New York," he said in a slow whisper, "but you're the first dame I've run into who tried to dodge a murder rap by jamming her own mother into the electric chair."

The gun in the dancer's hand was as steady as a rock. Her crimson lips jeered. "Sweetie Malloy gunned Clement in her own house. The body's on her own bedroom floor. She's surrendering to the cops—if she hasn't done so already."

"How do you know all this?"

"Because she phoned me and confessed."

"And you're letting her take the rap?"

"Why not? She killed the guy, didn't she?"

Jerry stared contemptuously until the hard eyes flickered and turned away. He said, quietly: "Your mother was here in this penthouse today."

"What of it? I had some sewing stuff for her. She—she sews things for me."

"I see. Sews things for you. And won't tell the cops she's your mother. But you don't mind if she burns for murder.... God, you get better all the time."

"What you think about me doesn't worry me," Lois said sullenly.

"Is your maid coming back here tonight?"

"I don't know."

"Where does this Selma live?"

"I don't know."

"What does she look like?"

Lois' lovely lips curled contemptuously. "What does any Swede look like?"

"A Swede, eh? Thanks."

He leaned towards her, smiling, and with a sudden gesture wrenched the gun from her hand and shoved her into a chair. She landed with a force that made her bounce.

"I'm taking a quick look about this arty dump, just for the fun of it," Tracy growled.

He disappeared into another room. She could hear him moving about, but her rigid pose never changed. She was still sitting there, barefooted, creamy-bosomed where the coat gaped, when Tracy returned.

He snapped her eyes awake with a sharp question:

"Do you happen to know a guy who likes to wear very sporty gray topcoats?"

He could see the dancer freeze up inside.

"Well? Do you?" he repeated.

"Get out!"

"Sure," Tracy said unevenly. He threw her gun into her lap. "Do me a favor, Toots. Empty that thing into your rotten little skull. I'd do it myself if I had an exterminator's license."

"What's your angle on this thing, Tracy?"

He eyed her steadily. "I'm working for the lad in the gray topcoat."

Lois' breath sizzled briefly. "Do—do you know anything about architecture, Mr. Tracy?"

"Not a thing."

"This apartment is completely soundproof."

"So what?" he asked.

"So—this!" The gun he had tossed contemptuously into her lap streaked upward like a flash of light. Her finger pressed the trigger six times.

The six harmless clicks sounded almost like one. It was nearly twenty seconds before the knowledge that the gun was empty seeped into her rigid eyes.

Tracy gave her a scornful, sandpaper chuckle. "I emptied that toy while I was strolling through the apartment. Wanted to see what you'd do. Here—take 'em back! They stink in my pocket."

He threw the handful of loose cartridges at her. They bounded off her body, rolled helter-skelter across the rug. Lois didn't utter a sound. She was sitting there, watching him like a stone carving, when he slammed the apartment door.

He shivered a little while he waited for the elevator, blinked once or twice to get rid of the image of that baleful face.

THE OPENING DOOR of the elevator found him debonair and cheerful.

"Were any of you boys on duty this afternoon?" he asked on the way down.

"No, sir… That is, come to think of it—Roy was." This little bareheaded guy had eyes that seemed to dig right into a fella. "Roy was—was home sick one day this week, so he hadda take a double stretch to make up for it."

"I get it." The elevator stopped and the doors slid apart. "Which one is Roy? Call him over."

Roy was a tall, gangling youth with pale, good-natured eyes in a weak, taffy-colored face. The shrewd *Daily Planet* columnist tabbed his type instantly: a two-dollar racehorse sport, a policy ticket sucker, a sweepstake boob, an eager patron of small craps games. There were a dozen kids just like him in the *Daily Planet* building. A cinch for a bribe.

"Come here, son. I wanna talk to you."

He went with Roy down a short corridor off the lobby and halted in front of the service elevator. His fingers opened and left a crumpled ten-dollar bill in Roy's moist palm.

"All you've got to do is answer a couple of harmless questions."

Tracy's grin had never been more warmly appealing. His wink was a humorous, good-natured, man-to-man affair. Roy grinned back.

Once the kid had started, he spilled like a broken faucet. Tracy's respectful nods were subtle flattery to egg him on.

The señorita had gone out a little before two o'clock that same afternoon. Said she couldn't wait for the sewing woman, and to send her up for the stuff when she came. The old dame came a little after two. Went up. About a half hour later the service buzzer rang. The sewing woman and the maid met Roy in the kitchen doorway. They both looked scared and sorta funny, he thought. He didn't pay no particular attention; people were always looking funny in a big house like this.

"What did they want?" Tracy asked.

Well, they wanted a trunk up out of the storage room in the cellar. He brought it up. After a while—must have been around three o'clock then—he got another buzz. Went up. Took the sewing woman down and the trunk, too. Got it out to a cab and the old lady drove off with it.

"Did she say what was in it?"

"Yeah. She did. I didn't ask her, but she told me anyway. Old dresses of the señorita's. Felt as heavy as hell." He grinned weakly. "Maybe that was because the old sewing woman forgot to gimme a tip."

"Let's fix that right now." Tracy shot him another ten-spot. "What about the maid?"

Well, Roy thought, that was sorta funny, too. Selma, the maid, came down in the passenger elevator about twenty minutes later. With a heavy suitcase. Gave up her apartment key. Said she was called away suddenly and to give it to the señorita when she came back. The señorita got back around four or so, Roy thought. He gave her Selma's key and she looked pretty angry and pretty puzzled.

"Not scared?"

"No, sir. Just wonderin', sorta. She said okey and rode upstairs. And I guess that's all."

"Do you know Mr. Clement?"

"Oh, sure. Her manager, you mean?"

"Yes. Did he call on her any time today?"

"No, sir."

"How about a short, heavy-set man in a light gray topcoat?"

"Dunno him. There wasn't any visitors except the old sewing woman."

"Thanks, Roy. You've been a big help."

His pale eyes goggled. "You a detective, mister?"

Tracy grinned, leaned closer. "Say, ever hear of a guy named Jerry Tracy?"

"Jeeze, yes...."

Jerry tapped his chest briefly. "Me."

"No kiddin'. I—I always thought you was a much bigger guy. I'll be darned."

"Keep your eyes and ears open—and your mouth shut. Any

time you run across a hot bit of dirt, gimme a ring at the *Planet* office."

"I sure will, Mister Tracy. Jeeze, thanks...."

Tracy went back to the lobby and out to the street. The rain had stopped but the gutter still raced with water. The doorman's shrill whistle brought a cab splashing east from the dark avenue.

Tracy murmured his own address, relaxed with a tired grunt—and immediately leaned forward again. "Change that! Take me to the *Club Español.*"

No sense riding home like a shivering, bareheaded dope! His topcoat and hat were still in the checkroom; Nita would be wondering what the hell was wrong.

The *Club Español* was still wide-open. Nita grinned perkily at Tracy. "Hey, hey, *muchacho!* Where *you* been?"

He saw that she was looking at him with a peculiar stare.

"You sure gummed the works here tonight," she said tonelessly. "Garcia's still tearing his hair. I hear you pulled the señorita out in her B.V.D.s—and damned little of them. The customers raised Cain when they heard her late show was off. I dunno what Garcia told 'em." Nita grinned cynically. "Maybe he told 'em the señorita busted her bubble. Anyhow, there was a lot of arguing, one drunken brawl that was a honey; and half the customers scrammed out to the opposish down the avenoo. First time I ever saw Garcia cry. Tears like big round hunks of putty. I'm not foolin'."

"Yeah?" Tracy said inattentively and turned away. Nita's hand on his wrist pulled him around, restrained him.

"Remember when you first came in tonight, Jerry? There was a mug in a very light-gray topcoat. He scrammed the minute he saw you—and you ups and outs right after him. I wondered."

"Don't tell me you tabbed him!" Tracy's glare was so intent that she pulled back a little, her hand still on his.

"I didn't tab him the first time—but I did later."

"He came back here?"

"Yowsuh. I mean, *por supuesto, ciertamente,*" Nita kidded nervously. "Brought a dame along."

"A Swede?" Jerry whispered. "A big horse-faced number? Sorta pale and angular?"

"Right. She had on a street coat over a very punkerino and secondhandish evening rag. They both checked their coats. Didn't stay long; beat it the moment they heard the señorita wasn't gonna bounce through that 'Me and My Bubble' number."

"Did you dip their pockets, honey?"

"Sure did. Nothing in the dame's coat but a soiled handkerchief and a few hairpins. In the guy's pocket—this."

The slip of paper switched hands with deft invisibility. Tracy cupped it for an instant, read the penciled memo. Two lines: *Selma Borquist, 932 West 10th.*

Something in the way he crawled into his coat and popped the snap-brim hat askew on his rumpled hair brought a solicitous frown to Nita's dark eyes.

"You're not going down there tonight, for Gawd's sake?"

"I dunno yet."

"Listen, Jerry. You're dead on your feet right now. There's a lump on the back of your dome like a hen's egg, and that left arm of yours looks like it might hurt like hell. G'wan home to bed. The Swede'll keep till tomorrow."

"You're a sweet kid, Nita."

"It's the mother in me." She grinned, and wondered why the words should make Tracy look so suddenly queer, as though she had said the wrong thing.

"I feel all in," he admitted. "I think I'll head straight for home, a stiff drink and a swan dive into the hay. S'long...."

He lurched out to the street and Nita, watching the tired drag of his feet, thought angrily: "He'll kill himself one of these days with his damned running around. About as big as a bag of popcorn—and more pep to him than a Mack truck... Crazy little runt...."

WHEN JERRY AWOKE the sun was shining. He picked up his fresh copy of the *Daily Planet* and saw the expected headline on the front page. There was a photograph of the body, with a squat white arrow above it to help dumb tabloid readers pick it out from the tin cans and debris. No identification yet. Jerry, having carefully cut out all the labels from Clement's clothing, wasn't surprised. Twenty-four hours, he thought grimly. After that—Inspector Fitzgerald and the cops.

Butch was behind the wheel of the Lincoln when Jerry appeared on the sidewalk. Off like oiled lightning, down to Times Square.

Butch tossed his plaid cap at a peg and squatted in the outer office with a copy of *Variety* and the *Daily Planet* funnies. Jerry sat down at his desk and hooked the dictating machine closer with a tug of his patent-leather toe.

But before he dived into the column he reached for the phone and called Garbo, the very snooty chief operator on the *Daily Planet* switchboard. He gave her Sweetie Malloy's suburban number.

"When you get it, say anything you like. I want to know how the woman sounds when she answers. Keep my line in. *Verstehen Sie?*"

"If you mean do I understand," Garbo said icily, "the answer is yes, Mr. Tracy, I do."

He hung on and listened with narrowed eyes to the brief two-way misunderstanding between Garbo and Sweetie Malloy. Garbo lingered a second after she broke the connection. "Satisfactory, Mr. Tracy?"

"Quite." He grinned. "Hey, Garbo—listen. Why don'tcha like me, keed? You mad because I call you Garbo?"

She sniffed audibly and clicked off. But Tracy was satisfied. The sleeping draught he had slipped Sweetie hadn't done her any harm. She sounded tired and listless—but she was out of the shadow of the electric chair, and there wasn't a way she could frame herself again. Call in the cops now, and they'd laugh at her!

He tackled the column with vim. At noon Butch appeared with a mound of Swiss cheese on rye and a pitcher of draught ale. Tracy took the stuff in his stride. When he got busy on an overdue column he was like the Twentieth Century singing along steel rails. At four-thirty a messenger arrived and took the cylinders away. Tracy stretched gratefully. He was done. McCurdy always edited the stuff and trimmed the edges. Nice guy, McCurdy. His youngest brat was named Jerry. On purpose.

Tracy went down to the sidewalk and thought things over, while a steady stream of pedestrians buzzed and bumped past him. Sam, his favorite hackman, was parked at the curb. He gave the *Daily Planet's* columnist a wrinkled grin and gestured briefly towards his tin flag; but Jerry shook his head. The subway seemed a better bet for a well-known little guy on an anonymous mission. The small-calibered gun that he had picked up from the bedroom floor in Sweetie Malloy's suburban cottage was a sagging weight in his pocket.

The dump Jerry was hunting was west, between the gaunt Ninth Avenue El and the river. A mean, red-brick hovel, tucked away in a welter of dust and decay. An incredibly filthy fish store on one side, a secondhand plumbing shop on the other.

Tracy hesitated, rubbed his chin uneasily. "Whoa!" he thought. "You're galloping too fast, keed!" After all, he was a Broadway columnist, not a policeman. If he didn't tip the cops—and tip 'em right now—he might get his wise little nose so deep into trouble that it would take him eleven years to convince Headquarters that he was acting not to cover up crime but to expose it!

He stepped into a telephone booth in a cigar store near the corner and called Police Headquarters in a low voice. After a short wait he heard the welcome sound of Inspector Fitzgerald's deep voice.

"Fitz? Listen—"

"Jerry?" Fitz' heavy rumble exploded into a pleasant chuckle. "Haven't seen you in ages. Where have you been keeping yourself, you little bozo?"

"Don't talk!" Jerry snapped. "Listen!" He uttered a sentence or two with curt speed.

Fitz' voice changed instantly. "Right! I getcha." A smart cop, Fitz. Never wasted a second asking how or why. He knew Jerry Tracy well enough from past experience to wait until later for complete explanations. Jerry had a habit of handing him a crisis and a solution all in the same breath.

"You and Sergeant Killan get down here as soon as you can," Tracy said. "In the meantime I'm gonna have a try at the Swedish maid. She might beat it if I waited for you."

"Watch your step, Jerry!"

"You sound like a subway guard," Jerry kidded lightly; but there was a hard line to his lips as he hung up. He was aware that he had reached the point where a single misstep might lower his dapper little body into a graveyard for keeps. He had never thought much about the next world, but he knew he liked Broadway!

He went back to the red-brick tenement and sauntered inconspicuously into the shabby, dirt-littered vestibule.

Jerry glanced at the scraps of paper stuck askew under a row of bell buttons. Most of the name-plates were empty. Borquist was under the last button. Top floor.

He climbed the stairs through pitch darkness, except for the faint flicker of light on the first and third landings. He could barely see the gun in his hand when he rang the bell, after a long, careful listen.

There was no answer to his ring. He waited for thirty seconds, then banged noisily on the wood with a clenched fist.

"Gas man! Gas man, lady!"

The door opened a mere crack, but Jerry was all set. He recognized the scared face of Selma. His foot blocked the door; his shoulder sent it flying open.

Selma backed into the frowsy living-room and Jerry closed the door and held the woman motionless with his gun.

"Up with the pretty arms, keed!"

"What—what's the idea?"

"I came to borrow a cup of sugar," he told her pleasantly.

There was no sound except the rickety roar of an El train slogging past in the growing darkness. Tracy forced the woman ahead of him. He searched every inch of the apartment—bedroom, kitchen, closets. There was no sign of any lurking boy friend. Smiling coldly, Jerry marched Lois Malloy's ex-maid back to the living-room. Selma's knees were knocking with fright.

"Why did you kill Phil Clement?"

"I didn't. I swear I didn't!"

"Who did?"

"Lois killed him. All I did, Mister, was to try and help that little devil of a dancer cover up. Her old lady butted in and gummed the works. She said she'd smear me with the murder if I didn't help her. So we packed the stiff in a trunk and the old dame took it out. That's all I did, I swear!"

"How much blackmail did you ask when you called up the dancer yesterday afternoon?"

No answer.

"Who suggested putting the bee on Lois? Your boy friend?"

"I—I got no boy friend."

"What's the use of lying to me?" Tracy snapped. "The guy was in the car with you out on Locust Avenue. You both beat it out there to stop Sweetie Malloy from crabbing your blackmail act. But you were late getting there—and I got there first. Good old Doctor Rolfe!"

"I dunno what you're talking about." She faltered.

"No?" Tracy's smile was knife-like. "I gave you a break by stealing the corpse myself. You tried to hijack me and get hold of the stiff again, but my Chrysler was too fast for that lousy can you were driving. So the boyfriend hunts me up at the *Club Español* and does his best to rub me out of the racket. He brought you back to the club later to proposition Lois for quick dough, but I foxed him again by kidnaping her in her cellophane panties…. For a virgin with no male acquaintances, you sure manage to get around, Selma."

Her bony face got suddenly triumphant.

"Drop that rod!" a voice rasped behind the columnist.

Tracy became very still. He let the gun fall to the floor.

"Take it easy, Emil!" Selma croaked, her eyes glassy with fear. "Don't shoot the guy in my flat, for God's sake!"

"Turn around, stupid," the voice ordered.

Tracy turned. Death was shining at him out of Emil's fishy eyes. Greed, ruthlessness, murder… No mistaking the gloating satisfaction in those eyes.

"You killed Phil Clement," Jerry breathed. "Not Selma. Not Lois. You."

"Sure I killed him. So what?"

"Shut up, you damn' fool!" Selma hissed.

Emil's chuckle was not pleasant. "This guy is so close to bein' dead that it don't matter much what I say. I killed Clement, and I'm gonna kill you. How d'yuh like that, Mr. Jerry Tracy? The smart guy! The wise little cluck from Broadway! Too smart to look in the dumbwaiter shaft before shootin' off his rat mouth!"

Tracy forced himself to smile. "I guess you're a pretty smart guy at that, Emil," he said in a slow, persuasive voice.

"You're damned right I am."

"How did you work the murder job? You sure made a monkey out of me. Fooled me completely."

Emil kept the gun steadily aimed, but he smirked with pleased vanity.

"A cinch," he sneered. "Brains done it. Selma fixed up a fake love note that got Clement into the dancer's apartment. He fell for it like a sap. He was nuts about the señorita."

"Be careful, Emil," the maid said faintly. "This guy is smart. He's trying to pump you."

"This guy is gonna be dead in about two minutes." His grin widened. "All right, smart guy. I was in the apartment and fixed him and got out again. What more do you want?"

"Yeah—but why kill the guy?"

"Plenty reasons to do it, kid," Emil said cockily, "and if you want more, the stunt was for Selma to accuse this dizzy dancer of the murder the minute she saw the body in her bedroom and yell for the cops."

"But the old lady gummed that scheme," Tracy suggested tonelessly.

"Yeah. The old lady was too tough for Selma to handle. She stuck the body in a trunk and scrammed with it. Can you imagine that?"

"I can't imagine it," Tracy said faintly. He eyed the killer and allowed his tensed muscles to relax. A leap forward to wrest the gun from the watchful Emil would be sheer suicide. His own gun was on the floor. Sweat gathered in tiny beads on Tracy's pale forehead. He knew Fitz could never make it in time. He felt a sick horror at the pit of his stomach.

Emil's smile hardened. He gestured briefly towards his pale girlfriend. "C'mere, Selma."

She moved stiffly. She looked uneasy, frightened.

"Take this rod and—" His hand swung suddenly sidewise and the weapon crashed with horrible impact against Selma's skull. She crumpled to the floor without a sound.

"What's the idea of that?" Jerry whispered thickly.

"The idea, stupid, is to git rid of people I don't need no more. You first and then Selma. Nice?"

"You can't get away with it."

"No? Git moving! Through that hall. Into the kitchen… Right! Now git over by the window. Sit down on the sill."

The window sash was already raised. Tracy, obeying the menace of the leveled gun, sat down. He snaked his eyes outward and downward for an instant—and knew he was doomed. The window faced a narrow, five-story airshaft. There was a blank brick wall opposite. There were windows all the way down below the kitchen; but Tracy, remembering the empty name-plates in the vestibule, felt a sick shudder.

"Tough, ain't it?" Emil said. "We gotta wait for an El train to settle you—but Selma'll be easy. She'll go down like a bag of laundry." He grinned with ghastly humor. "You kin hold on to the window-sill if you like, while you're waitin'."

THE DUSK OUTSIDE had deepened to chilly darkness. Away off in the darkness Jerry could hear a faint rumbling. It grew rapidly to the metallic clatter of a speeding El train.

"So long, stupid," Emil said.

As the roar of the passing train became a clamor that shook the ancient tenement, the killer's fingers tightened.

A woman screamed shrilly. A bullet whizzed past Emil and shattered the glass above Tracy's bent head.

A wave of hot, incredulous joy swept through the columnist's body as he recognized the face of the woman with the gun. He dived headlong from the sill as the startled murderer whirled. For an instant all three of them were inextricably tangled on the kitchen floor: Tracy, Emil—and Lois Malloy.

A kick from Emil sent Lois bouncing against the wall in a moaning huddle. The man whirled to fire into Tracy's face, but the columnist's fist was already whizzing. It caught Emil on the Adam's apple and paralyzed his throat with pain. He dropped his gun, sprang frantically to recover it. Tracy's foot kicked it spinning towards the wall, where it rebounded towards Lois.

The dancer was hurt and badly rattled. Swaying there on her knees, she scooped up the gun with her left hand, but to Tracy's horror, instead of firing at the plunging Emil, she threw the weapon out the open window—and her own after it!

The two men tripped over her and went down in a flailing fury of fists and feet. Tracy fought like a silent, tight-lipped demon, his mind ablaze with a single thought: his own gun! Lying on the living-room floor where he had dropped it!

A smash on the jaw rocked him groggily, but he managed to dig his face desperately against Emil's neck and get the hold he wanted. He let Emil's own weight do the trick. A slight bend of the knees, the sudden instant of leverage he had learned on the gym mat from Artie McGovern himself—and the snarling murderer flew over Jerry's head and landed on the floor with a jarring impact.

Jerry dived out of the kitchen like a lean arrow, but Emil beat him to it.

Emil had ducked back, picked up Tracy's gun. He fired as Jerry appeared. A long sliver of wood jerked outward from the casing of the doorway. The panting columnist tripped over the unconscious body of Selma and fell in an awkward heap on his hands and knees. He was up in an instant, rigid with fear, his heart pounding inside his dry throat.

He saw Emil leering at him.

Emil was standing quite still, legs planted apart, barely five feet away. Tracy could see the black muzzle of the gun, the tautness of Emil's knuckles, the pressure of his bent forefinger on the trigger.

In that split second of eternity all fear whipped away from the mind of the doomed columnist. He thought with a kind of hypnotized clarity: "I'm gonna die.... He's gonna kill me...." There was no horror in the thought; only a puzzled incredulity. Not someone else! Jerry Tracy!

The gun exploded. Tracy heard the racketing roar. He was still standing there, glassy-eyed—and unhurt! Maybe it didn't hurt when you got killed.... Then he realized that Emil's bullet had slanted astonishingly upward, not straight into his own stiffened flesh. There was a ragged hole in the plaster ceiling and Emil was falling limply forward. He landed on his face and lay there, full length on the floor.

Tracy could see the blood gushing sluggishly from Emil's back. A pair of legs seemed to be walking towards the columnist out of a dream. They were queer legs—blue serge pants that seemed to end in fuzzy nothingness at the hips—until a brisk palm slapped Tracy's face with stinging emphasis and brought him back to sanity.

He was gaping stupidly at Inspector Fitzgerald. There was a big blue gun in Fitz' paw and a faint haze of smoke at the muzzle.

"Hey—wake up!" Fitz barked. "You all right?"

"Yeah... I—I guess so."

"I shot him right through the kidney. Another second, Jerry, and you'd have been cold meat. Why didn't you duck when I yelled?"

"I didn't hear you."

Fitz grinned shakily. "Lord, I let out a yelp like a steamboat whistle! And you just stood there!"

"How—how did you get in?"

"Fire escape. Same way the girl did. We were right behind her, the sergeant and myself. Afraid she'd spoil the whole business. Killan tried to grab her, but she's as quick as an antelope. Up and in before we could do a thing. Damned glad it worked out that way. Otherwise you'd be deader than hell. I'm not kidding."

Tracy drew a long, shuddering breath. He still felt very woozy as he turned his head. Lois Malloy was in the living-room doorway, white-lipped, rigid. He saw her gazing fearfully at the body of Emil and the senseless huddle of Selma. The sight of this slim, courageous girl brought reason back to the fuddled columnist. Lois had saved his life! She wasn't a rotten little coward! He'd been completely wrong about her from the very start!

He walked slowly towards her, laid a hand on her smooth arm.

"Beat it, babe," he told her gently. "You can't afford to show in this mess. Leave it for me to handle."

She shook her head. Her dark eyes never left his for an instant. They were deep, unsmiling, very lovely. "How about you, Jerry? You're in this thing yourself."

"I'm okey. Fitz knows about most of it already. Thank God it was Fitz' bullet that finished Emil. I'm in the clear. So are you, if you beat it right away—before a lot of reporters come smelling around like a pack of hungry hyenas."

"There's a fire escape in the rear," Inspector Fitzgerald

suggested dryly. "If you both want to do a quick fade, it's all right with me. I can use all the credit this case is worth. I'll tell the news-hounds I broke this case on an anonymous tip.... You've got about two minutes if you two want to dodge headlines."

"Thanks, Fitz," Tracy muttered. "You're a prince."

He seized the dancer's arm, hurried her to the rear of the apartment. The window was still open. He swung her slim weight up in his arms and helped her to the fire-escape platform. In the darkness there was nothing visible except the blank brick wall opposite and the shadowy dimness of a back-yard far below.

They stood there for an instant in the darkness—a couple of clear-eyed square shooters. Human to the core, both of them.

"Why did you pretend to be such a rotten little tramp, Lois? You deliberately made me think you were out to frame your own mother."

She nodded ruefully. "The mule in me, Jerry. I was playing it close for a showdown; letting whoever was in it think it was running all their way. I was trying desperately for a lead, but I was almost ready to call a copper when you barged in. You made me damned mad for one thing. You called me dirt right off the bat. Remember? I won't take that from anyone.

"For another thing, what you did gave me more time. And I was hurt enough and stubborn enough to want to go on playing it my way without you. Of course I was wrong and rotten. I knew it all the time. Well, that's me."

Lois Malloy drew a deep breath.

"It was really Sweetie's own idea for me to live alone. She wanted me to prove myself—alone. She was always ready to step in, if I—I seemed to be failing."

"Failing?" Jerry whispered huskily. "I never want to meet anyone finer than you, Lois. You and Sweetie make a grand pair of thoroughbreds."

He swung her impulsively towards him. His voice was suddenly eager, boyish. "How would you like to drive out to the suburbs—right now? Is it a go? We'll pick up a birthday cake—"

"And some birthday candles—"

"And we'll give Sweetie the best damned—"

"Oh, Jerry… Come on—hurry!"

Storm Signal

Jerry Tracy is featured for a murder and suicide set

TOMMY FLEETER FEINTED with his right; his left hand moved so fast that the glove seemed almost invisible. Yet Jerry Tracy ducked and the jab missed his face and slid across his shoulder. He countered instantly, but Fleeter took it without effort on his elbow.

They were off in a corner of the big barn-like structure, and nobody was paying much attention to them. Jerry was dressed in full length woolen tights and soft-soled gym shoes.

Ordinarily it was fun to try to lay a glove on the lean and phantom-like bald head of the ex-lightweight champ; but today the *Daily Planet's* little columnist was panting and puzzled. Fleeter's face wore a faintly vicious scowl. He was putting steam into his jabs, stinging Tracy. Acting as though he was sore about something.

Jerry noticed him peering across the gym and his own face turned briefly. His eyes widened as he caught a glimpse of the girl. Instantly Fleeter's left banged against his face and filled his brain with sheet lightning. His heels went up in the air and he flew off the edge of the heavy wrestling mat and banged the polished floor with the back of his head.

Fleeter bent over him, helped him up with an impassive face. "You left yourself wide open, kid."

He didn't apologize as he usually did. He grinned mechanically and motioned to a handler. The man unlaced the columnist's soggy gloves.

"You sore at me, Tommy?" the columnist asked quietly.

"Nope."

"Worried about something?"

"Nope."

The gymnasium owner tightened his lips and avoided Tracy's eyes. He picked up a medicine ball that someone had left carelessly out on the floor and replaced it alongside the wall.

The girl who had been the unconscious cause of Tracy's black  eye was still lounging over near the rowing machine. She saw Tracy coming towards her and she turned her back, pretended to watch a guy lifting weights. She was rather a flamboyant little dame, full bosomed, dark-eyed, sullenly beautiful. Broadway knew her as Tess Roland, the creamiest torch singer that ever raised prickles on a male spine. Jerry always called her Storm Signal. She was nineteen and had been married twice. Her first husband had been shot by gangsters, her second was supposed to have committed suicide.

There were few dames tough enough to give Tracy goose pimples. Tess was one of 'em. She was bad luck for a lot of guys—and she'd been staring in a funny, fixed way at the back of Fleeter's bald head, her face like a thundercloud. Jerry had a grim feeling that Tess wasn't in the gym for fun. Her nasty tongue and her quick temper were usually to be found in hotcha parlors or in the ornate penthouses of the more successful of the gun gentry.

He tapped her lightly on the backbone with his forefinger. She turned leisurely and her red lips curled with a sneer of cold contempt.

"Hello, Snipe. Where did you get the shiner?"

"You gave it to me."

"Huh?"

"Skip it, Storm Signal."

"Listen, I'll crown you if you keep calling me that."

Tracy's glance was just as hard as hers. "You don't look natural in a gym. You've never been here before. Wherever you show, it's tough luck for somebody. You've got Tommy sore—or scared. I'm not sure yet."

"So what?"

"Lay off him, Storm Signal. He's a friend of mine. I like his wife, his three kids—but most of all, I like Tommy. I thought I'd tell you."

"Thanks. Any friend of yours is tops with me." Her lovely voice grated with rage, "How about keeping your nose outa my business, you cheap little keyhole peeker? Any time I want to talk to Fleeter, you don't stop me, see? If you try, I'll make good on a promise and slide you into a cemetery."

Tracy shrugged, smiled. There was anger in his eyes, hate in hers. She turned with an insolent writhe of her hips and walked straight across to where Fleeter was standing.

TRACY HESITATED. HE didn't want to butt in on a pal's private affairs, but Tommy had acted damned queer all through their friendly bout. His gloves had lashed out at Tracy with punishing force. Jerry knew Fleeter's quick temper and had wondered what was the matter. Now he was sure he knew. The Storm Signal was up to something dirty.

Paul Yager had been in the gym earlier, giving Fleeter a quiet little buzz in a corner. He had looked worried and had beat it when Tracy had walked up with a grin and a handshake. Yager was tops with both Tracy and Fleeter. He had only one weakness—he was nuts about Tess. Had he been warning Tommy about this unexpected visit of the glamorous Storm Signal, or was the torch singer cooking up something dirty that involved both Fleeter and Yager? She had never made any bones about the fact that she regarded Yager as an amorous pest in her life.

Jerry Tracy tightened his lips. He walked coolly over to where Tess Roland was whispering at the ear of the rigid faced gym owner. She stopped whispering the moment she saw him, but Tracy's sharp ears caught the last sentence or two. "I tell you, you're in a spot, Mister! Don't pay a damned bit of attention to anything Tracy tells you!"

She gave the columnist a triumphant, malicious smile and her heels clacked down the length of the gym floor with Fleeter pacing beside her. Fleeter's face was absolutely wooden.

Shivering, Tracy descended cold iron steps to the locker room and peeled off his soaked tights. "Want a rubdown, Mr. Tracy?" Otto called from his smelly cubby as the columnist padded naked and pink towards the showers.

"Not today, Otto. I'm in a hurry."

Twenty minutes later he crossed the gymnasium like a brisk little fashion-plate and entered Tommy Fleeter's private office. Clancy was the only one around.

"Hello, Mike. Where's Tommy?"

"I dunno. He breezed."

"That's funny. I wanted to see him." Jerry added sharply. "What's the matter with you?"

Clancy was staring curiously at him. "Tommy said he wanted to see you—to ask you something. And he was sore as hell. He went downstairs to look for you and when he came back he said you'd gone, slammed into your clothes without a shower and taken a runout. I never seen him so worked up. I know he couldn't a meant it, Mr. Tracy, but he said you were afraid to talk to him."

"What—the hell! He must've run down and right up again. Didn't even look in the showers where I was. What was the matter with him anyway?"

"Search me. He chased me out then while he made a phone call. When I came back he was white as a sheet. He'd got into his street clothes and started for the door. I ask him what's eatin' him. He don't say a word. I try to touch him on the arm and then he swings at me and slams the door behind him. He don't come back."

"Forget it," Tracy said smilingly. "He's probably up at the Dutchman's waiting for me. We always knock over a light beer after I work out. The last one there pays the check."

"Yeah, but he swung at me! Him, the most good-natured guy on earth!"

"Forget it," Tracy said. The moment he got outside his stride lengthened. He thought of Tess Roland's dark, sullen eyes, and of Fleeter's tremulous hand rubbing at his bald head. Storm Signal! What in hell had she told Fleeter to upset him so?

TRACY WALKED MECHANICALLY onward to the Dutchman's. He discovered that Tommy Fleeter had already been there, had barely left. And the manner of his coming and going was even more disturbing than his behavior with Clancy.

"He comes in," the Dutchman said, "like he's sick. He valks straight up to der bar and he orders—vot do you t'ink?—viskey!"

"Whiskey?" Tracy said. "You're crazy. He hates booze."

"Straight viskey," the Dutchman said stolidly. "He gulps it down. Bing! Orders another. Bing! Two straight viskeys. Und not a vord—und out der door."

"Did you watch where he went?"

"Uptown he goes, not down. I'm so surprised I come out from the bar und go by der door und vatch. Straight viskey. Bing! Und then he gulps und—"

"Yeah, I know," Tracy snapped. "He went bing twice. Okey.... Thanks."

He walked to the corner and stood there for a moment in deep puzzlement, He was actually starting to walk aimlessly north, when he chuckled wryly and snapped back to reality. He had a column to turn out and he had already used up the whole morning. Tommy's sudden fade was queer, but what of it? Jerry himself had done screwier things than that, and for no other reason except a perfectly normal urgency to get something important done in a hurry. The only funny thing about Fleeter's sudden runout was the whiskey—and the sinister visit of Tess Roland. Tracy stood irresolutely on the sidewalk, cursing the dark-eyed torch singer in a low whisper.

A rolling cab slowed near the curb and Jerry nodded and got in. He squeezed the puzzle of Tommy Fleeter out of his busy mind. He'd call up the gym later on and find out if Tommy was okey. He had a hasty bite in a Times Square caféteria and plunged into his delayed column. It was getting dark when he sighed and quit.

His door opened. A heavy voice said urgently: "Jerry! Hey, Jerry!"

Butch was staring at him. "Hey, did yuh hear about Tommy Fleeter?"

Tracy's eyes narrowed. He'd forgotten to call the gym; the thing had completely slipped his mind under the rush of business.

"What about him?"

"He's disappeared. Walked out at noon and never came back. I dropped in to say hello to Clancy, an' boy, he was sure noivous."

"Tommy probably had an appointment somewhere and then went on home."

"Nix. Clancy said he called Mrs. Fleeter an' she didn't know nothin' about it. Clancy said she sounded scared. It's the first time in his life Tommy ever pulled a funny sneak like that. And besides, he was supposed to be at the gym this afternoon to fix up some papers about a mortgage or somethin'. Clancy said to keep me trap shut, but he looked plenty worried."

"Mmmm… I'll take a run up and see what's the matter."

"Better make it fast," Butch muttered. "They close the place at five, yuh know. How 'bout me comin' along?"

Tracy shook his head. "You g'wan back to the penthouse. Tell the Chink to hold dinner for a while. I'll phone."

"Gee whiz, don't I ever git no breaks?"

But Tracy, after a quick glance at the clock, had slid into his coat and plunked on his derby, and was out the door. He'd be lucky if he made it in time!

He didn't. When he stepped out of the cab he saw that the ramshackle building Fleeter owned was dark from cellar to roof. It annoyed him to discover that his heart was pumping with excitement. What the devil was there to get excited about? Tommy was the last guy in the world to get himself into a mess.

He turned on his heel, went down to the corner drug-store and looked up Mrs. Fleeter's phone number. He was about to lift the receiver when he changed his mind and came out of the booth. Once more he leafed through the book. Storm Signal! The torch singer's sullen face was like a bright, sneering photograph in his brain.

He called the doorman of the *Albion Theatre*. The show Tess had been in had folded two weeks before; not even her glorious voice could save the badly produced musical. But there were rehearsals for a new piece going on right now and Dinty would be on the rear door. He got Dinty after a brief wait, identified himself, and found out where Tess Roland lived. It was a swanky hive on Central Park West. He wrote the address down in his notebook and called Mrs. Fleeter.

Belle sounded scared. Clancy had called her twice that afternoon about Tommy's mysterious disappearance. She had telephoned the gym a few moments ago and discovered that Clancy had closed up the place as usual and had gone home.

She didn't know where he lived. She didn't know what to do. Should she call the police?

"No," Tracy said. "I'll be down to see you later."

Belle's voice shook. "Come right away, will you? It ain't like Tommy to pull a trick like this. He's the most considerate man alive. And there's a special reason why he should have come home this afternoon. Maybe he's in danger. He's had more than one argument with tough guys that tried to use the gym for a hangout."

"I'll be right down."

He dropped another nickel in the box, bracing himself to meet McNulty's displeasure over the spoiled meal. To his surprise the Chink didn't answer the call. Butch's gruff voice came on the wire. He spluttered with profane excitement when he recognized Tracy's brisk tones.

"Hey—Jerry—it's cockeyed—it's nutty, but...."

"What's the matter?"

"He was here!"

"Who?"

"Fleeter. Tommy Fleeter."

"Good. Did he leave any message for me?"

"Good, nothin'!" Butch growled. "He made a wreck outa the place. Damned near scared McNulty to death. I found the Chink tied up like a mummy—and Fleeter has vanished again. Will you tell me what the hell—"

"You say Fleeter *searched* the place?"

"Yeah. The minute McNulty opened the door Fleeter socked him and tied him up. Never opened his trap once. The Chink says he looked like a crazy nut, smelt like he'd been drinkin' likker. Went through every room and closet, read all your letters. Told McNulty he'd kill him if he breathed a word who was here—and scrammed…. You better git home, Boss, and find out what this thing is about."

"Stop yelling at me and listen. Are you scared of Fleeter's punch?"

"Not if I got a chair-leg or somepin in one hand."

"All right. Bust a chair and make yourself a club. I got other places to go. I don't know what it's all about, but there's a chance Fleeter may come back to find what he was looking for. He didn't take anything away, did he?"

"Nothing McNulty could see."

"If he comes back, nail him. I'll be through as soon as I can."

"Okey."

Tracy hung up and walked towards the deserted gymnasium. His jaw tightened as he recalled Mrs. Fleeter's nervous words on the wire. Tommy had never played gentle with the gunners and racketeers that buzzed like blue-jowled flies at the edges of the fight game. The Family Man, fight writers called him. He had retired undefeated with a comfortable fortune. The crash in Wall Street had wiped him clean. He could have come back and picked up plenty from fixed fights—but he didn't. He had dough enough left to start his legitimate gymnasium and to keep it swept clean of rats. That part was okey, Jerry thought; but why should his old friend be searching the penthouse and scaring the life out of McNulty?

Tracy stared at the deserted façade of the squat two-story gymnasium. He hated to leave the neighborhood. He had an uneasy feeling that inside the gym might be the key to the riddle of Tommy's disappearance. He grinned wanly at the thought. Should he go peeking into lockers, prying around the caged handball courts on the roof, dragging the swimming pool, for a guy who was apparently ducking all over town?

DISGUSTED, HE TURNED away. Suddenly he gave a quick, incredulous exclamation. There was a public garage across the street where portable gasoline tanks cluttered the dark sidewalk and a dim light burned over the arched entrance.

Tracy reached the garage doorway on the jump. He was starting towards the rear when the door of a small side office opened and a man in greasy gray overalls came out. He stared at Tracy's excited face.

" 'Smatter, Mister? Lookin' for someone?"

"Yeah. A bum. He ducked in here just a second ago."

"He musta come in damned quiet. What about him?"

"He gypped me," Jerry said hesitantly. "He asked me for a dime for coffee and I slipped him a buck. I just discovered that I gave him a five by mistake. He beat it in here when he saw me coming back."

"Yeah? Maybe he's in the men's room. Over behind that big truck in the back." The garage man chuckled. "A fin for a cup of coffee, huh? Boy, that was a neat panhandle!"

Tracy was already around the end of the truck. He opened the door of the small men's room. It was empty. He stared at another door, a sheet-metal affair, further along the rear wall of the garage.

"Where's that lead to?"

"To the back," the garageman said. "It's locked. Key's on the nail alongside."

But it wasn't locked. The key was in the keyhole. It opened when Jerry whirled the knob. He found himself in the darkness of a small paved courtyard enclosed by a ten-foot board fence.

"You sure you saw the bum come in?" the garageman said. "That's a high fence. He must have been some jumper."

"Gimme a hand up," Tracy said.

The garageman frowned at his persistence, but he heaved Tracy aloft and the little newspaper columnist peered briefly. He sucked in his breath with disappointment. He was staring at a deserted sidewalk and a dark street.

He dropped back into the courtyard and gave the man in overalls a dollar. "Sorry to trouble you," he said. "I hated to lose the fin, that's all."

"What's the bum look like?"

"Dunno," Tracy lied. "I didn't get much of a look at his face."

He walked back through the garage and out to the street. Bum, hell! It was Tommy Fleeter! He had seen his pale face clearly as Fleeter had whirled and run into the garage. That ten-foot fence in the rear was pie for the ex-champ. But what the devil was he hanging around the gym for? And why did he run like a scared rabbit when a man stopped and looked at the gym? Jerry was pretty certain Fleeter hadn't recognized him. He had been standing in the shadows, a dim figure from across the street.

He walked a block or two uptown until he spotted an empty roller. He hailed it and drove in moody silence to Fleeter's home.

It was a neat but unpretentious walk-up on the better edge of Yorkville. Belle Fleeter opened the door herself. Her eyes were red. She looked thoroughly scared. She was a stout little woman, grayish hair, with a nice mouth and clear, pink skin. She gestured towards the closed door of the living-room with a tremulous hand.

"I don't want Bobbie to know there's anything wrong. He's inside doing his homework… Jerry—what has happened?"

"Take it easy, Belle."

"Do you think I ought to call the police?"

"Not till we know more about this thing. Why are you so worried? Was Tommy in trouble of any kind?"

Belle shook her head dully. "He's been as straight as a string all his life. That's what scares me. We've been married twenty years and today was our wedding anniversary. Tommy always comes home early with flowers, and we have dinner out, and—and celebrate." She smiled wanly, "This is the first time we—we haven't celebrated. It's not like him, Jerry, He's been hurt or—or kidnaped."

Tracy could hear the slow click of typing in the adjoining room.

"Bobby's doing his homework." Belle said. "I—I bought him a little portable typewriter and he does all his lessons on it." The fear vanished momentarily from her red eyes. "A smart little fella. We're hoping to send him to college."

"That's swell. How's Freddie doing?"

"Better than he was. He's up at Fishkill in a military academy. Ethel's in Pittsburgh—you knew that, I s'pose?"

"Yeah. How's the show doing?"

"I had a letter from her yesterday. She's out of the chorus—she says Klemmer gave her a specialty dance. She—" Mrs. Fleeter whimpered suddenly and caught Jerry's arm. "Do you think I ought to send her a wire about—her father?"

"Why worry her? What good can she do here?"

"You don't understand. Ethel has always been Tommy's favorite. They're—they're crazy about each other. When she wanted to go on the stage I put my foot down, but Tommy let her go. She's only nineteen, but Tommy said the stage couldn't hurt anyone as smart and decent as Ethel. She adores him. If he's in trouble and I don't wire her, she'll never forgive me."

"Let her stay where she is," Tracy said.

He patted Belle's shoulder, "Look. Tommy may show up any minute and chase all this scared look out of your eyes with a reasonable explanation. In that case we don't want any cops and we don't want any fuss. And suppose he is in a jam? We still don't want cops—not till we find out whether police and newspaper publicity are going to hurt him."

The faint clicking of the portable typewriter in the next room was the only sound for a moment.

"Clancy said something about a mortgage that Tommy had to attend to this afternoon. Was it important?"

"No. It was just an interest payment Tommy had to make. Just a small payment, a few hundred dollars. He has the money in the bank, plenty to cover it."

Tracy nodded, picked up his hat. "I'll move on, see what I can find out, I'll call you back later, in case you hear anything in the meantime." He paused in the doorway. He was about to ask her if she knew anything about Tess Roland, the torch singer; but he decided not to add to Belle's fright by suggesting that there might be a woman back of the unaccountable flight of Tommy Fleeter.

HE HAD LEFT his cab waiting at the curb for him. He gave the driver Tess Roland's address. Storm Signal! She had started the whole screwy business. A bad egg with a singing voice like an angel. He had never understood why Paul Yager had made such a play for her. Paul was a good guy, but he sure was a sucker for dames. Anyone with sense would have given the Storm Signal a wide berth.

The taxi hummed along the transverse road through Central Park and stopped in the Elegant Eighties. Tracy's impeccable appearance got him a respectful nod from the doorman and a quiet-voiced, "Chilly night, sir."

He didn't answer. He was putting on his well-bred act. He had no intention of sending his name up to the Storm Signal and being told over the house phone in a throaty, million-dollar voice, to go roll his hoop. He clicked past the desk and paid no attention to the desk man's hesitant "Ahem!" The elevator was open and he stepped in.

"Eight, please,"

"Who did you say you wished to see, sir?"

"I said, eight, please!"

The operator gazed at the flinty visage of his passenger, at the imported derby and the faultlessly correct overcoat. He stuck his head out irresolutely and passed the buck to the man at the desk.

"Dammit all!" Tracy said with quiet fury, "What are we waiting here for?"

"Okey, Charles," the desk man murmured.

The car ascended in a silence as soft as down. Tracy got off at eight, walked leisurely down the hall, drawing off his gloves with slow deliberation. The moment the car sank he turned on his heel and went back to the stairs. He ascended to the twelfth floor, blessing the doorman of the *Albion Theatre* for his foresight in telling him the apartment number. Smiling, Jerry made a mental note to send Dinty a case of the punkest brand of gin Butch could locate; Dinty didn't like good gin, said it had no body to it.

Tess Roland opened the door. She gasped and tried to slam it when she recognized her caller. But Jerry hadn't expected to be welcomed with palms and hosannas. He was all set. He slid in like an agile moonbeam and clicked the door shut behind him.

Tess's dark eyes flared. "Where do you get that push-in stuff? Out!"

He kept right on until he had entered the living-room.

"Merely a conference, babe. A small intimate powwow."

He couldn't tell whether she was angry or scared. Both, probably; that was why she was standing there like a dope, goggling at him. More than one emotion at a time was too much for her. Had it been plain rage, her nails would have been into him by this time. He sniffed the air of the room suddenly. His own voice got coldly menacing.

"Listen, Storm Signal—"

"I told you not to call me by that name!"

"A certain gentleman has disappeared. A guy with a bald head, a decent wife, and three sweet kids."

"Nuts to you, Mister."

"Where did your friend duck who was in this room a minute ago?"

"You *would* think there was a man here, you evil-minded little rat! Out, before I get tough!"

"I didn't say a man, Storm Signal. And I'm rat enough to know strange perfume when I smell it. Who's the dame? And why did she scram when the bell rang?"

Tess Roland laughed stridently. She had backed against a low mahogany chest across the room. She jerked out a pistol and pointed it at Tracy with almost a single motion. "Beat it—and keep your nose clear of something that doesn't concern you."

Tracy laughed harshly. "You're not scaring me with that rod, baby. You're bluffing. What are you trying to hide from me?"

"Out!"

"What have you got against Fleeter?"

"I'm trying to help him, you sap."

"You sure have funny ways of—" His hand shot towards the gun with the speed of light. There was a single crashing report and a bullet drilled into the floor. Tracy wrenched the gun loose.

Tess' eyes were burning bright. "You fool," she gasped.

"Maybe. I'm gonna take a look around this joint right now. One funny move out of you and I'll bounce a lump on that skull of yours."

She tried to struggle but his fingers were twisted on her left shoulder like bands of steel. There was a closet in an L-shaped recess across the room with a brass key in the lock.

"In you go, Storm Signal!"

He was tensing his left hand to clutch at the knob, when the door was suddenly thrown open.

A girl sprang out of the closet, white-faced, staring. Tracy took one look at her and the gun in Tess' back wavered.

"Ethel!" he whispered in incredulous wonder. "Ethel Fleeter!"

Tommy Fleeter's daughter was trembling. She tried to speak but her throat gagged wordlessly. Tess Roland swung furiously about and tried to wrench the pistol from Tracy. Her desperate attack galvanized him into motion. With a swift heave he flung her head foremost into the open closet and locked the door.

The key dropped into his pocket. He could hear Tess pounding and yelling and the furious sounds made him smile grimly.

He stared at Fleeter's daughter. "When did you get in from Pittsburgh, Ethel?"

"This—this morning."

"Are you a prisoner? What hold has this tough dame got on you?"

"Jerry, you're making a big mistake. Tess is my friend. She's dad's friend."

"Oh, yeah? Did you know that your father has disappeared?"

"My God—no!" Her face became the color of chalk. "Then they've got him. They're taken him for a ride!"

"Who?"

"I don't know." Her voice became hysterically accusing. "My God, why did you butt in? Did you speak to Dad? Did you advise him to stay and fight?"

"I don't know what you're talking about. Why did you sneak here from Pittsburgh? And why are you hiding in the apartment of a mugg like Tess?"

"I'm not hiding."

He stared at her suspiciously. She looked very frightened and very stubborn. But there was no crookedness in those clear brown eyes. The same sweet little kid he had always known. It was impossible to think she could be ganging up on her own father.

He flung eager questions at her but she locked her lovely red lips.

"All right," he said grimly. "Get your hat and coat. We're going places."

"Where?"

"Back to your own home. To your mother's."

"No. For God's sake, don't do that! You'll frighten her to death, spoil everything."

From the locked closet came the faint sound of furious banging, Tracy's eyes jerked towards the closed door. "Who brought you here from Pittsburgh? Tess?"

"I came of my own free will. She's a good—good friend. She's trying to save Dad's life."

Ethel saw the grim doubt in Tracy's eyes and made a sudden helpless gesture.

"I've got a brief case full of—of papers that made it imperative for me to see Dad. His life is in deadly danger. I—I beg you to do what Tess asked you—keep yourself out of this. You'll only make matters worse."

"Where are the papers?"

She pointed tremulously, "In the bedroom. In a brief case on the dresser."

She had slumped into a chair, her hands over her face. Tracy whirled on his heel and hurried through the bedroom door. He was staring at the empty top of the dresser, looking for the brief case, when he heard a swift rush of feet in the adjoining room.

Ethel Fleeter was racing towards the open door. She beat Tracy's quick clutch for the knob and slammed the door. The bolt shot home. Raging with chagrin, Tracy knew that he had been neatly trapped. The yarn about the brief case was a phoney. Fleeter's daughter had pulled a fast one on him.

Grimly he hurled himself against the locked barrier. It wouldn't budge. His eyes glanced upward and he saw the transom. It was a small one, but not too small for a determined little guy like Tracy. He found a chair and climbed atop it like a nimble monkey. The transom swung wide. He could see into the room where he had left Ethel. It was empty.

It was no cinch to wriggle past the narrow opening of the transom, but he managed to pry himself through. He dropped awkwardly to the floor on the other side, ran to the apartment door and peered out. The corridor was empty. The arrow of the elevator was motionless on the figure one. Ethel already had time to reach the street level and vanish.

But she had gone alone! A muffled sound from the apartment brought Tracy back. The dim thumping of Tess' fists on the inside of the closet door filled the columnist's blood with savage satisfaction. The Storm Signal would talk now, by God, if he had to club the truth out of her!

HE UNLOCKED THE door and hauled her out. Her eyes glared around the empty room. "Where's the kid? Gone?"

"You damned well know she's gone." He sunk his fingers into her slack arm. "Talk—and talk fast!"

The torch singer made no effort to struggle. She glared at Tracy with listless terror.

"You fool!" she breathed.

"Old stuff. Make it sensible."

"Okey. I wired Ethel to come here from Pittsburgh. She came of her own free will because she trusts me. The finger is out for Tommy Fleeter. I've been trying to persuade him to leave town. That's why I sent for Ethel. You think I'm a louse, but that doesn't bother me. I hate your little wiseguy guts. But I happen to like Tommy Fleeter and I'm not going to let you talk him into being killed."

"All very nice and all very noble. Who's supposed to be trying to kill Tommy? And why did you tell him to pay no attention to anything I said? It seems damned funny that right after you got to him, he took a runout."

"That's something I don't understand," Tess admitted slowly, "It's been puzzling me like the devil. I—I don't like that vanishing act."

She was glaring at the columnist. She looked as nasty as ever, but there was a ring to her voice that sounded queerly like the truth. Still, she had tried to stick him up with a gun, and she *did* hate his guts!

"Where did Ethel go?" he asked abruptly.

"I don't know. Probably rushed out to try and find her father before it's too late." She drew a deep breath. "Believe it or not, wise guy, as you damn' please. I got the tip from Paul Yager."

"Yager, eh? You trying to frame him, too?"

"You want to know the truth, don't you? Then why don't you close that monkey trap of yours and listen?"

Tracy listened to the terse, sullen words of the torch singer. Yager had come to her the day before with the news that Tommy Fleeter had got himself in dutch and was marked for slaughter. Yager didn't know who was back of the planned kill, but he had good enough underworld connections to know that the rumor he had picked up was true. He came to Tess and they talked it over. He and Tess both like Fleeter and they decided to try and persuade him to leave town until the thing blew over, or until Yager could find out who was back of the plot. He knew that Tess and Ethel Fleeter were good friends; Tess had done a big favor for Ethel when the kid had first broken into theatrical business, and Ethel had never forgotten it.

Yager had already been to see Fleeter but the gym owner

laughed at the warning and refused to budge. So Tess played her ace. She wired to Pittsburgh, telling Ethel what was brewing and the kid grabbed the first train to New York. She came secretly to Tess' place. She planned to meet her father there and persuade him to leave town for a few days. She didn't want her mother to know anything was wrong. That was why she had kept under cover.

"You're lying," Tracy said flatly. "Ethel knows I'm Tommy's friend. Why did she trick me and duck out the way she did?"

"Because neither of us want you to gum up this thing," Tess said sullenly. "What would you have advised Tommy to do if you had known this morning what was afoot?"

"I'd have told him to stay and fight—not to run away like a dope."

"Exactly. That's what Ethel and I were afraid of. So I went to see him at the gym this morning and—"

"You told him the situation was desperate and not to pay any attention to anything that Jerry Tracy might say. I heard that much."

"Right," Tess snapped. "I never liked you and I never will. I wasn't going to have you call in your dumb police-inspector pal and get poor old Tommy a bullet in the back. Listen, stupid, do you really think I'd frame Fleeter? Do you think Paul Yager would?"

"Paul's on the level," Tracy said, "You're the one I'm leery about. What else did you tell Fleeter?"

"I told him Ethel was in town and I'd get in touch with him later. You butted in then, so I breezed. When I called up the gym, Clancy said Tommy was gone."

"Yeah. And he took a gun. Why? And he turned up later at

my penthouse—"

"Huh?" Tess gasped. "I didn't know that."

"Well, you know it now. He tied up my Chink and scared him half to death. He searched the whole apartment, ripped everything upside down and disappeared again. Why is he hiding? What the hell is he up to? Why is he ducking away from me, his best friend?"

"I don't know," Tess muttered. "It sounds screwy, that's a fact." Then she caught his arm suddenly, held it taut in her strong fingers. "Listen, mugg. We don't trust each other, but we got one thing in common. We both like Tommy and want to keep him from getting hurt. Right?"

Tracy looked at her suspiciously. "So what?"

"Let's team up and find out what's wrong?"

"You're crazy."

"It's you that's crazy," Tess snarled. "Here's three people, all trying to help Tommy, and all tearing at one another's throats. Four, by God, if you count Paul Yager. Lemme call Paul and tell him what's happened. Or do you think he's a heel, too?"

"Call Yager," Tracy growled.

Tess darted across to the telephone stand. She waited a few minutes, her face frowning. Then she slammed down the instrument with a muttered oath. "Can't get him. He's not in." There was fear in her face. "Do you think someone got wise to the fact that Paul was trying to tip Fleeter to his danger? Do you s'pose someone has taken him for a ride?"

"Who?" Tracy snapped irritably.

"I don't know. I've told you all I do know. For —— sake, why don't you wipe that foxy look off your pan—and *do* something!"

"Okey." The little columnist ran back into the bedroom

where he had squirmed out of his overcoat. He donned it and picked up his natty derby.

"I'm going to have to trust you."

She laughed bitterly. "Forget about yourself for once. Who cares whether you trust me or not? Find Fleeter! Find his daughter! Find out what's happened to Yager."

"Thanks. That's just what I intend to do. And don't go hunting for your hat and coat. You're staying right here."

"Why?"

"For phone calls. There's a chance that Ethel may call back."

"Where'll you be?"

"I don't know yet. I'm going to try and trace Ethel. Call my penthouse if anything turns up. Butch and the Chink are there."

He caught her suddenly by one shoulder and shoved her chin up so that his gaze went deep into her dark eyes.

"What's *that* mean?" Tess sneered. She threw off his hand with a force that spun him away. But Tracy had seen enough to make his lips curve in a mirthless grimace. "If it was me that was in trouble, be damned if I still don't think you'd stick a knife into me, you hellion."

"It must be tough to have to depend on me," she jeered.

"It is, Storm Signal."

She swung an angry fist at his jaw, but he ducked away.

THE ELEVATOR MAN gazed at him queerly, remembering that he had let him out, not on the 12th, but on the 8th floor. In a heavily elegant silence Tracy descended to the street level and hurried out to the sidewalk.

He caught the doorman by a limp hand and left a crumpled

five dollar bill in the man's cold palm.

"A girl left this building about ten minutes ago." He described Ethel Fleeter. "Which way did she walk?"

"She didn't," the doorman said.

"Huh?"

"She took a car."

"Taxi?"

"No. A sedan. It was parked near the entrance here. The moment she came out of the house, the guy in the car waves his arm and calls her over. I couldn't hear what he said, but she went over to the curb, talked with him. She didn't seem to want to get in. Finally, she does. They drove downtown."

Tracy nodded. His mind was buzzing with a queer surmise. Was it Paul Yager, returning unexpectedly to Tess' apartment? He described Yager to the doorman but the latter shook his head.

"That wasn't the guy. Smaller and fatter. A round, moon face and a double chin. Looked like an Irishman. I couldn't help noticing him because the girl seemed sorta scared when she got in."

"Okey. Thanks."

Tracy nodded and walked off. From the doorman's description he was certain of the identity of the man who had enticed Ethel Fleeter into the sedan. It was the last person on earth he would have thought of.

Mike Clancy! Fleeter's own trusted associate in the gym.

The *Daily Planet's* columnist raced a half block and caught an empty cab at a red light. He gave the address of the gymnasium and asked for speed. Clancy! Why in the name of common sense hadn't he thought of that before? Tommy Fleeter's friendship for the Irishman had been a sort of guarantee that Clancy had reformed and was on the level. Yet his past had been damned unsavory. A crooked fight manager, an associate of yeggs and gunmen, Mike Clancy had found himself ruled out of the sport, blacklisted and busted. He was in the gutter, down and out, when he appealed to the soft-hearted ex-champ.

Fleeter took Clancy in and had a heart to heart talk with him. The result was that Clancy wept, promised to be decent—and was given a job. He had been in the gym ever since and had turned out to be an invaluable assistant to Fleeter. At least, so the sport world thought; and Tracy too. Now he wasn't so sure. He remembered that queer, challenging look that the Irishman had given him when he had told Jerry about Fleeter's inexplicable runout.

The gym seemed to be the logical place to pick up Clancy's trail. The while mixup seemed to center there.

It was across the avenue from the darkened gym that Tracy had caught his brief glimpse of the vanished Fleeter, Jerry had had a peculiar feeling at the time *that Fleeter was trailing him,* had followed him there from his office on Broadway. But Clancy's sudden pickup of Fleeter's daughter gave Tracy a more logical and less fantastic picture. Maybe Fleeter was tailing Clancy. Maybe that was why he had been hanging around the gym! His queer visit to Tracy's penthouse was still a mystery, but Tracy put that aside for the moment. One thing at a time, or he'd go nuts.

Jerry paid off his cab-driver a block away from the shambling two-story gymnasium. His eyes gave the darkened building a quick once over as he walked past. This time it wasn't completely dark. There was a light burning behind a drawn shade in a room on the second floor. Tracy's heart expanded with excitement as he recognized the location of that room. It was Fleeter's office.

Jerry Tracy continued around the block. There were a row of tenements in the back and he went through the lower hallway of the one that abutted on the gym. The back door was locked on the inside. He opened it and went through a dark concrete backyard towards a high board fence.

A quick swing upward and he was over the fence in the rear of the gym.

He tried the ground glass windows of the basement. Behind them, he knew, was the darkness of the swimming pool. To his disgust he couldn't budge a single window. His roving eyes surveyed the yard. There was the usual scattering of broken bottles and tin cans hurled out the rear windows of the tenement dwellers—and a rotted hunk of timber where one of the fence posts had been recently repaired.

Tracy picked it up and hefted it. He hesitated. If Clancy and Fleeter's daughter were inside, Jerry wasn't anxious to advertise his presence by the noisy jingle of broken glass.

The racket of a fire engine somewhere down the invisible avenue gave Tracy the break he was waiting for. He gripped the chunk of timber. As the fire engine roared past the silent tenement behind him, it gave an ear splitting blast of its siren. Tracy swung the club and scattered the heavy pane of opaque glass.

It was pitch dark inside. He waited at the jagged opening for five long minutes, listening intently. He could hear nothing.

He dropped to the tiled walk surrounding the pool and made his quiet way to the locker room. He knew the layout of the place accurately from the hundreds of pleasant visits he had made there. He climbed the iron steps from the locker room as soundlessly as a cat. The gym floor was in profound darkness, but he could see a reflection of yellow light from the corridor where Fleeter's office was located.

Tracy drew his gun and crept quietly through the darkness. He tripped over one edge of an unseen wrestling mat, and for a startled moment or two he stood like a rigid statue. But nothing happened.

The door of Fleeter's office was closed. The light reflection came from the transom. Tracy listened but there was no sound whatever from within. His left hand turned the knob slowly. The gun in his right was like part of his body.

Suddenly he threw the door wide, For a bare second he was motionless. Then he cried out faintly and sprang forward.

Mike Clancy was seated at Fleeter's battered old desk. There was blood on the chair, blood on the floor; his bent head was soaked with crimson. No need to wonder how he had met his end. The room was a shambles; furniture overturned, articles from the desk scattered all over the floor. The implement that had crushed Clancy's skull was a heavy bronze statue of a crouched boxer. It lay near the dead man's feet, stained with a dark smear of blood.

Clancy's head lay forward on the desk.

The body was still warm. Whoever had killed Clancy had done it damned recently. There was no trace of Ethel Fleeter. Yet Tracy, sniffing the air of the room, detected at once the same elusive scent he had smelled in the apartment of Tess Roland. Ethel had been in this musty office not many minutes earlier. She had seen Clancy killed and had been kidnaped—or had gone off willingly with the murderer!

A sudden icy thought made Jerry's heart jerk. Had Fleeter done this thing? Had he been trailing Clancy ever since he had left the gym at noon? The murder had all the ear-marks of Fleeter's explosive hot temper. Clancy evidently had known more about this thing than Jerry had suspected—and had paid for his knowledge with his life. A vivid picture of Fleeter's lovely daughter swam suddenly before the columnist's eyes, but he shook his head stubbornly at the monstrous notion. He still believed Tess Roland's explanation of the girl's mysterious undercover trip from Pittsburgh. Tess and Ethel were pawns in this thing. Paul Yager, too. They were being used by someone playing a deep game.

Tracy's eyes narrowed. The dead man's right hand lay clenched on the dingy surface of the desk. There was something gripped in his closed fingers. Jerry forced the fingers apart and the stub of a pencil rolled across the green blotter.

The columnist stared at the blotter. He could see multifarious ink smears but no sign of any warning scrawl.

He lifted Clancy's head gently and the motion upset the dead body's equilibrium and slid him from the chair. Tracy caught him, laid him quietly on the floor. He stepped back to the desk and examined the surface of the blotter where Clancy's head had rested.

There were bloodstains where he had sagged forward. Evidently he had dragged himself from that ugly pool on the floor towards the desk. He had fallen weakly into the chair, had forced himself to seize the pencil stub and write. Tracy could see part of the wavering pencil scrawl. His breath sucked in as he recognized his last name. The rest was merged indistinctly with the smear of blood on the blotter.

Jerry tore the blotter loose and held it closer to the light. Held thus, the sheen of the graphite marks was faintly distinct in the blood smear. Clancy had died before he could complete what he was writing. The message or warning, or whatever it was, ended in a meaningless curlicue. But part of it was unmistakably clear:

Tracy pen +

The face of the *Daily Planet's* columnist was haggard under the rays of the desk lamp. Not a sound stirred in the deserted gymnasium building. What the devil had Clancy been trying to write. Tracy…. Pen…. Plus…. He repeated the words under his breath and suddenly he gave a whispered cry of understanding. It wasn't a plus sign! The poor devil had been trying to make a T when he died. Tracy pent—Tracy penthouse!

AGAIN THIS WHOLE dizzy case was pointing straight to Tracy himself. Tommy Fleeter's first act, following his queer disappearance, had been that unexplained visit to Tracy's penthouse where he had nearly scared the Chink to death. It was Tracy's own home that was the center of this murder web, not the gymnasium. Fleeter himself was back of it! That was why Ethel had locked her lips when Tracy had tried to question her. That was why she had tricked Tracy and given him the slip. They were all pawns—Paul Yager and the Storm Signal and poor dead Clancy. And back of it all, Tommy Fleeter and his daughter from Pittsburgh!

Abruptly Tracy reached for the telephone on the long metal bracket alongside the desk. This was murder. Time for the cops! Friend or no friend, Tommy would have to come forward and face things. For a friend, Jerry was willing to go to lengths that few men in Manhattan would dare, but he had never once in his life condoned a murder or tried to impede justice.

He started from force of habit to call Police Headquarters. Then he remembered that Inspector Fitzgerald wouldn't be there at this time of night. He hung up and called Fitz' home. He'd give Fleeter that much of a break. Fitz was a personal friend of the ex-champ. He'd hold off the newspaper boys until both he and Jerry were convinced that Fleeter was responsible for the murder. After that—Jerry closed his lips and tried not to think of that part.

He got Fitz on the wire and spilled him the gruesome news.

"Everything points to Fleeter and his daughter," Jerry said in a low voice, "but I want to be sure. Do me a favor and don't call Headquarters yet. I'll be down at my penthouse. There's a bare chance that Fleeter may be there. If he is, Butch will have him sewed up for you. I left orders for Butch to jump him if he showed, and to hold him for me."

"I never liked that mugg, Mike Clancy," Fitz' gruff voice barked over the wire. "That reform stuff of his was the bunk. He must have put the finger on Fleeter and the old boy let him have it. You know Tommy's temper when he's monkeyed with."

"Yeah," Tracy said listlessly. "But I don't think Clancy was crooked. I've got a queer feeling that his skull was battered in *because he was on the level* and because he had found out something that the killer couldn't let be known."

There was a sputter at the other end of the wire, and Tracy added with a jerk of nervous anger. "How can I tell? No reason at all. I just think so.... Get down here in a hurry and look things over. Then burn it up to my penthouse. I'll be waiting for you—maybe with Fleeter."

He hung up, stared for a second or two at the crumpled figure of Clancy. His eyes were veiled and expressionless. He turned and walked silently from the room.

There were plenty of nighthawk automobiles flitting north and south along the dimly lit avenue outside, but the sidewalk was empty of pedestrians. Tracy fixed the bolt of the spring lock so that the gymnasium door closed without locking. He wanted things to be as easy and quiet for Fitz as possible.

He went down the steps to the sidewalk in no particular hurry. A block southward was a subway kiosk and a dozing cab-driver. Tracy drove to the corner nearest his swanky penthouse and walked the rest of the way.

The hallman was someone that Tracy had never seen before. He had a uniform cap but no uniform. He asked the columnist what floor he wanted.

"I live here, dope," Jerry snapped.

"Oh, I—I beg your pardon, Mr. Tracy." The man's eyes blinked. "I'm just filling in for Roy."

"So I see. What's the matter with Roy?"

"He's sick. His stummick ain't so good."

"Drunk again, eh?"

The hallman grinned faintly.

"Anybody call to see me?" Tracy asked.

"No, sir."

"No phone calls?"

"No, sir."

"Okey. Up!" He stepped into the car, frowning. "I expect a visitor. When he comes, bring him up."

"Yes, sir."

The operator closed the doors and dropped the car out of

sight almost before Tracy had stepped into the stone corridor on the penthouse level. A sudden suspicious thought made Tracy frown. Maybe Fleeter and his daughter were already hidden inside the apartment. A tip to that guy in the uniform cap would close his mouth as tight as a clam. He looked as shifty as hell. Abruptly Tracy thought of Butch's huge head and heavy fist. If Fleeter had bribed his way into the penthouse, Butch, forewarned by Tracy's own orders, would have stuck a rod in him the minute he showed his face.

Jerry rang the bell. A full minute passed and there was no answer. No Butch. No Chinaman. He didn't ring the bell again. Instead, he fished for his key, inserted it noiselessly in the lock and opened the door very quietly.

The foyer lamp was burning brightly as usual, but there was no sign of either Butch or the Chinaman. The pantry was empty and so was McNulty's bedroom adjoining. Tracy tiptoed onward, his gun steady in his hand. He peered into the little cubby where Butch slept. Empty. So was the living-room and the dining-room. The door of Tracy's bedroom was shut.

The moment he opened the door, the reek of whiskey hit him like an acrid fume. He took one look and walked slowly, dazedly towards the bed.

A girl was lying there in a huddled ball, one arm trailing limply over the edge of the counterpane. Ethel Fleeter! Her head had fallen back and her eyes were closed. There was a half-filled whiskey bottle on Tracy's night table, but the reek came from the girl's parted lips. She smelled like a distillery. She was dressed in blue satin lounging pajamas; the rest of her clothing was scattered aimlessly all over the room.

He caught her roughly by the shoulder, shook her till her

sluggish eyelids fluttered open. "G'way," she mumbled drowsily. Her eyes were moist and glazed.

Tracy dropped her with a sibilant oath and ran towards the bathroom. He found a bottle of smelling salts and jammed it under the drunken girl's nose. Again the eyes opened. She began to whimper, to roll her tousled head away from the fumes of ammonia.

"Wake up!" Tracy snapped. He slapped her flushed face. "Come out of it! I want to talk to you!"

He heaved her upward, got one arm under hers. She struggled dazedly, knocked the ammonia bottle out of his hand. She began to laugh suddenly in a high pitched, ridiculous giggle. He couldn't make her stop. In an effort to close off that senseless sound he clapped his left hand over her mouth. Her limp body toppled and pulled him off balance. He fell tangled with her on the soft mattress.

A voice said with slow, terrible softness: "God Almighty!"

TOMMY FLEETER WAS standing rigidly in the doorway like a dead man. He watched Tracy roll awkwardly away from Ethel and bound to his feet. Fleeter's eyes glared at Tracy, at his drunken pajama-clad daughter, at her clothing scattered all over the room. His throat made a thick, sobbing sound.

Tracy cried swiftly: "Listen, Tommy—"

Ethel had raised herself unsteadily on one elbow. She was staring fixedly at her father but there was no recognition in her drunken grimace.

"God!" Fleeter whispered, "It's true."

He began walking slowly towards the columnist. Tracy saw madness in the man's eyes and he backed step by step towards the night table where his gun lay. He was afraid to move too fast. Words bubbled softly from his lips, low-toned, persuasive words. He knew Tommy wasn't listening.

Fleeter sprang suddenly. Tracy whirled, scooped the gun from the table. Fleeter's rush knocked columnist and table to the floor. In an instant ice-cold fingers were clamped on Tracy's wrist. The gun was wrenched from his grasp and went clattering across the bedroom.

Tracy struck at the white face and managed to roll free. He sprang to his feet and Fleeter went after him like a steel spring. What followed was one of the strangest, most insane perversions of reality in Tracy's whole career. He was fighting for his life, cool-headed, pale as a ghost, trying to box with one of the greatest boxing champions that ever stepped into a ring. And getting away with it!

Fleeter had forgotten that he was a boxer. He was a cave man, whimpering, flailing blindly with fists like awkward stone hammers. His eyes were drained of everything but the lust to kill this man who had betrayed his friendship. Blood streamed from his nose where Tracy had jabbed desperately. He followed the retreating columnist with no attempt at footwork or science. Jerry couldn't elude him. A terrific swing caught Tracy on the jaw and staggered him. The hooked fingers clawed for Tracy's throat.

Ethel Fleeter's strangled scream gave the columnist a second's dazed respite. Her father lifted his face, peered dully at her. Tracy tore his gasping throat free and threw up a protecting arm.

"Father!" Ethel moaned. "Don't—don't!"

The blank drunken look was gone from her eyes. There was

fear in them, horror, a terrified pleading more potent than the sound of her scream.

She tried to rise from the bed and fell dizzily. Fleeter staggered across, threw an arm about her.

"Listen, Tommy!" Tracy begged. "You don't understand. This is a fake, a frame-up. I'm your friend."

"Friend?" Fleeter gasped hoarsely. "You call this—friendship?"

Ethel was trying to talk. She couldn't articulate; her words were without meaning.

"You brought her from Pittsburgh," Fleeter mumbled. "You hid her here. Did you think I didn't know it? Do you think I didn't trail you?"

"Tommy, I swear to God, I had nothing to do with this. Someone is trying to frame all three of us. Someone who killed Mike Clancy."

"You killed him! I followed you."

Jerry groaned. "He was dead when I got there. Who told you that your daughter was in New York?"

"Tess Roland. She warned me. And then Clancy told me more—after I had telephoned to Pittsburgh and found out that Tess was telling the truth."

"Tommy, she lied like hell."

"I followed you to the gym," Fleeter said thickly. "You went through a tenement in the back and busted a window. I saw Clancy's body with his skull battered in. I didn't care about that; I wanted to save Ethel. I knew that you'd lead me to her if I kept after you. I trailed you out the front door of the gym and down to a taxicab. I took another. And right here in your own home—I find the two of you—my friend and my daughter—stinking with liquor—"

"No!" Ethel cried. "Dad, you're wrong. Tracy had nothing to do with this. He didn't kill Clancy. Clancy's murderer brought me here. He forced me to drink that liquor at the point of a gun. It wasn't Jerry, Dad. It was—was—"

Her voice choked off in a scream. She stared frozenly past her father's back.

"GOOD EVENING, FOLKS," a sneering voice said.

Tracy whirled.

The man in the bedroom doorway was Paul Yager. There was a gun in his hand and it menaced the three in the room with murderous impartiality. He looked as natty and neat as a clothing ad. A taut grin curled his thick lips. Only his muddy eyes betrayed him; they were unsteady, blinking, haunted by a grim urgency. Tracy read ruthless murder in those blinking eyes.

"It was you," he gasped. "Not Tess."

"Tess, hell," Yager grinned. "I fooled her the same as I fooled you. She thought she was helping Fleeter and his boob daughter. I told her the finger was out for Fleeter—but I didn't tell her *it was my finger*. And I didn't tell her it was a double-barreled stunt to get Fleeter and wise Jerry Tracy at one crack."

"But, Paul," Fleeter faltered. "I—I don't understand. You're a good guy. You're my friend."

"That's what you think," Yager snarled. "You're gonna make me two hundred grand. I've got Paddy Elkins fixed to lose his title bout next Thursday. I had to make sure of the referee—and you're just too damned honest to live!"

Tracy cut in with a tremulous whisper. "But why drag in me and an innocent kid like Ethel? I don't get it."

"Oh, yes you do! I can see it in your eyes. Tracy, the dirt

slinger! Caught at last in his own dirt." Yager chuckled horribly. "Betrayed father finds daughter and famous Broadway columnist in latter's million-dollar bedroom. Kills both and commits suicide. How close do you think the boxing commission will come to the truth?"

In the back of Tracy's brain was a single, numb thought. Inspector Fitzgerald! He must already have left the gym. Tracy had cautioned him to beat it straight down to the penthouse. There was a bare, life-and-death chance.

"I gotta hand it to you, Paul," he said dully. "But can't you protect your dough without murder? Can't you—"

"Nuts," Yager growled. "You think you can stall me that easy, you little punk?"

"You croaked Clancy, didn't you?" Jerry added persistently.

"The hell I did! Fleeter himself did that little job—didn't you, Tommy?"

"He's a liar. He killed Clancy. I was there. I saw him do it!" Ethel's voice shrilled hysterically from the bed. Her face was dead white and there was no trace of drunkenness in her eyes.

Yager watched her over the barrel of his gun. "Tell 'em some more, kid," he said blandly. "Maybe you know more about it than me. Let's hear how much you really *do* know."

"Keep quiet, Ethel," Tracy warned. "Don't open your mouth."

But Fleeter's daughter was beyond all fear. Her face was pale with loathing as she stared at the smiling killer. Her voice was a scornful whiplash. "I heard everything Clancy said before you murdered him," she breathed. "Clancy accused you to your face—and you killed him. You had the whole thing figured."

"For instance?" Yager said in a silken murmur.

"You spilled a few vague hints to my father and got him

worried. Then Tess told father the lies you had fed her and she warned him to pay no attention to anything Tracy might say. In the meantime you looked up Clancy and told him that Tracy and—and I were living secretly together in Tracy's penthouse. It was a clever scheme, because you could pretend you were afraid to say anything directly to Tommy Fleeter, for fear he wouldn't believe you, being Tracy's friend, Clancy fell for the trick; he did exactly what you figured he'd do—he disclosed the fake seduction news to my father. And father phoned promptly to Pittsburgh, learned I had come to New York, and went haywire with rage. He grabbed a gun and tried to trail Tracy secretly, after he had become convinced that Tracy was trying to elude him. You made him think that Tracy was not a pal, but a rat."

"Nice beanwork," Yager grinned. "Very smart. Clancy got his for the same kind of smartness." His eyes became coldly opaque. "I think I'll hand it to you and Tracy first. Tommy will get his last—in the temple—to make it look like a nice suicide. You appreciate a joke, Tracy; why don't you laugh?"

Tracy's glance remained steadily on the opposite side of the room. He tried to fight down the sudden flick that came into his harrowed eyes.

Yager's gun muzzle shifted towards the girl like a flash of light. Tracy didn't move, although he saw the trigger finger of the murderer tighten.

There were two shots, spaced barely a second apart.

Inspector Fitzgerald had fired first from the doorway. His bullet ripped through Yager's arm and deflected the murderer's slug six inches to the left of its target. It went through the pillow and the headboard of the bed and missed Ethel Fleeter completely. She toppled sidewise in a dead faint.

In an instant the bedroom was a turmoil of action. Inspector Fitzgerald sprang from the doorway followed by the resolute figure of Tess Roland. Yager ran full-tilt into the two of them. He butted Fitz in the pit of the stomach and knocked him against Tess.

Yager dived at the floor like a flash. His uninjured left hand clutched at his fallen weapon and he swung the barrel upward with a crashing spurt of flame. Tracy was on the floor too, trying desperately to hold the killer's hand. He felt the hot recoil of the barrel and saw Tommy Fleeter stagger. Fitz couldn't shoot; Jerry's body was in the way. Again the hot barrel under Tracy's fingers jerked with flame and Fitz threw himself sidewise. He tripped over a chair and fell headlong, his gun arm twisted under his body.

Tracy tried to kick at Yager with stiffly outflung feet. He could see in a queer hazy flash, the figure of Tess Roland tiptoeing forward with a gun in her hand. Her face was like a clay mask. She had picked up Tracy's gun, the one that Fleeter had hurled across the room in their first insane encounter.

Yager was on his feet, glaring at the fallen Fitz. He fired, and the sleeve of Fritz' arm jerked. Tess Roland swung her clubbed gun at the back of Yager's skull. There was a sound like a bat meeting a baseball. Yager's teeth crunched together. He fell forward and his nose dug into the trampled rug. He lay there, queerly poised on face and knees like a Mussulman at prayer.

"Okey," Tess gasped.

Fitz was on the fallen killer like a staghound. He kicked him over on his back. There was a flash of handcuffs and a curt click.

TRACY PAID NO attention to either cop or killer. His

arm was about Tess' jerking body. He couldn't shake the spasmodic hysteria out of her. He shoved her to the bed and held her grimly horizontal. His voice beat through her hysterical moaning like a silken whip.

"It's all right, Tess. It's all over. Quit it, quit it, quit it...."

By degrees he got her out of it. Fitz touched the columnist's rigid back. "She all right now?"

"Yeah. Get her a glass of water."

"I'm—I'm all right," Tess whispered jerkily.

"Lay still. You're shaking like a tambourine." He took the glass from Fitz. Her teeth made clicking sounds on the rim. On the other side of the bed Ethel Fleeter was moaning. Her father dropped to his knees beside her.

He saw Tracy staring at him, and he got up and shuffled towards the columnist. His face was a deep, unhappy red.

"Jerry, I—I don't know what to say. If I'd had any sense at all, I'd have guessed that this thing was a frame. But I—I was mad with grief and rage. If only I'd been able to talk to you—"

"Why didn't you?" Tracy said somberly. "My God, Tommy, you know I am your best friend. Yet you rushed out of the gym without giving me a chance to—"

"I didn't," Fleeter contradicted. "I tried to talk with you but you were gone—you ran out the minute I turned my back—and I naturally thought that you had rushed off to your penthouse to try and hide my—my daughter before I could—"

Tracy said sharply: "Wait a minute! Did you go down to the locker room?"

"Yes. Not five minutes after you did."

"And I was gone?"

"Yes."

"Who said so?"

"Otto. He stopped me at the door of the rubbing room and told me. He said that you'd climbed into your clothes in a hell of a hurry, asked him for the key to the side door, and ran out like a streak through the bowling alley. He said you looked scared and white."

"He did, eh?" Tracy's tone was grim. "That, of course, was a damned lie, I was in the shower. I wonder how much Yager paid Otto to lie to you…. Don't you see, Tommy? They didn't want you to talk to me. It would have spoiled the whole plot. They had to keep us apart, make each of us suspect the other."

Fleeter nodded haggardly. His hand groped out in a dazed gesture and Tracy gripped it. "Forget it, Tommy. I'd have done the same in your place. It was a cleverly stage-managed nightmare—thank God it's over."

He turned to Inspector Fitzgerald. "How did you and Tess team up so neatly, Fitz?"

"I met Tess rushing into the lobby downstairs. She'd got leery and tried to phone you. Operator told her your phone was off the hook, so she piled down here in a hurry. Some gal! Sergeant Killan is holding that doorman downstairs. He's a phoney. Yager substituted him for the regular attendant. That's how he got the girl in here so easy and fixed up the plant."

"How did you get in?"

"Fleeter left the door open when he followed *you*."

Ethel Fleeter was wide awake, whimpering. Fitz glowered at her. "Did you see Yager kill Clancy?"

"Yes. Yes…. Clancy thought something was wrong. He was suspicious of Tess and went up to see her. He—he saw me come out. He picked me up in his car and brought me to the gym to talk over what he ought to do. Yager came in, killed him and—and—"

"You saw Yager bat Clancy to death with that bronze statue?"

"Yes…. Clancy accused him of trying to frame Fleeter and Tracy. They fought all over the room. I—I tried to run, but Yager caught me…. It—was horrible."

"Eyewitness," Fitz said and nodded. "That's nice."

A rumbling voice filled the room with sudden echoes.

Butch's massive body was recoiling with amazement on the threshold of the bedroom. Behind him was the seamed face of McNulty, Tracy's Chinese servant. For the first time in his slant-eyed imperturbable life, McNulty looked dazed.

"Where have you damned fools been?" Tracy snapped.

Butch shook his big head and made gagging sounds. He was beyond talk. But McNulty wasn't. The fear went out of his slant eyes and was replaced instantly with righteous anger.

"Why you tell lies over telephone?" he hissed. "You say Bootch come quick, bring McNulty. You say big spot, tough jam, come like hell Mount Vernon. You theenk that very funny, huh? You theenk McNulty is boy scout, make runaround like fool. I feenesh, Mister Tlacy. I quit. Confucius say—"

"Shut up!" Tracy roared. "Get into your kitchen and stay there. By the lord, I'll take you by the neck and kick the Confucius out of—"

McNulty grinned. "You velly stlong man when you angly, Mister Tlacy. Me like. Me stay."

Tracy turned towards Tess Roland. Her face was set in the old sullen lines. Once more she was the Storm Signal, the gal who hated his guts.

"You sure don't like me, do you?"

"I sure don't. I hate to be made a sap of by a guy like Yager. But if it was just you, Boy Friend, you'd have been croaked and be damned to you before I'd have lifted a finger. It's Tommy Fleeter I like and that sweet kid of his. Where's my hat? I want to get out of this lousy dump of yours."

"Why?" Tracy asked her huskily.

"You know damned well, you dirt slinging little heel!"

"Why?" Jerry repeated. There was a humbleness about him, a slow flush in his face that made her look at him with tight lips.

"You want to know? Okey. You did me dirt with that rotten column of yours. Something that only a cheap snipe like you would pull. You put me out of a job, damned near got me killed by hinting at something that was filthy, dirty—and a lie from beginning to end! I got out of the jam you caused, because I'm a gal who can take care of myself. But I've hated that wizened little pan of yours ever since—and that was two years ago. Last September."

"Wait a minute!" Tracy's eyes were suddenly wide. "September, you say? Two years ago?"

"September the twenty-third. And I swore then that if I ever got half a chance to bump you—"

She grinned haggardly. "And then Tommy and Ethel Fleeter get mixed in the thing and I have *to save your dammed life*. That's a laugh on me."

"It's a laugh on me, too," Tracy said quietly. "I didn't write that squib, Storm Signal. I wasn't in town. I was down in Florida covering the races and the racketeers. A hurricane roared into Miami and blew down all the wires. I wrote no column for three days. Those three columns were banged out in a hurry by a sub of mine in New York."

"You're lying," Tess snapped.

"Look it up. Check on me." His voice was as bitter as hers. "If you'd have opened your trap and told me what was biting you—"

"Who wrote it? Who was the guy who subbed for you?"

"That," Tracy said dryly, "is something you'll never learn from papa. I don't want to encourage homicide."

His feeble grin drew a wry smile from her lips. "Okey, Jerry. Let it lay that way. For a couple of wise birds, we don't seem to be doing so well by each other. Is there a drink in this joint? I could do right now with a big one."

"If there's anything in this house that you want, Storm Sig—"

Tracy stopped short, his face red as he realized he was calling her by the sardonic nickname that she loathed.

"Go get me that drink," Tess Roland told him in a funny kind of voice. "And Storm Signal is all right by me, you—you heel. I guess you kinda got me used to the damned monicker!"

Murder Maze

Murder has Jerry Tracy on the run

BUTCH, WATCHING JERRY TRACY moving leisurely about the ornate living-room of the penthouse, scowled and made urgent snapping sounds with his big fingers. "For the luvva mud, Jerry, why don't you git started? You're gonna miss that show! You make me noivous, hoppin' around like one o' them premeer bally—bally—"

"Bally who? Trying to go British on me, keed?"

He swerved towards the ringing telephone, cupped it at his ear. "Oh, hello, Ned.... Sure thing; swell. How come you're up my way? I thought you never left Times Square without dog teams and dried reindeer meat.... Thanks for the lift. Be right down."

He banged the phone and headed for the door.

"That was Ned Wortman. Calm the furrowed brow, Butch. Ned's driving me over to the *Garfield.*"

Downstairs Wortman grinned and started the car promptly. He was one of the town's lesser theatrical producers. A big man, definitely on the fatty side, he was perspiring freely. The evening was hot and sticky. He glanced at the *Daily Planet's* famous little columnist and there was envy in his grunt.

"Kid Kool himself! You look like an ad for an icebox."

"Why get sweated over a first night, Ned? I've seen a thousand. So have you."

His boyish chuckle belied his words. He knew everyone, went everywhere. He liked cops, newsboys, letter carriers, taxi-drivers—the people closest to the pavements of Manhat-

tan. You could argue with Jerry, but you couldn't get sore at
him. One of Tracy's envious rivals—and there were a few of
those, too—summed it up one night at *Lindy's:* "I wish I could
hate the mugg. He makes my own column look as stale as last
year's almanac. The guy is Broadway, damn him! Kick him in
the pants and he'd honk like a Checker Cab; slice him open
and you'd find a tintype of Times Square."

Ned Wortman drove southward with deft speed and turned
into the noisy hullaballoo of West 44th. A whistle shrilled
and he swung his sedan in towards the curb. All of New York
seemed to be packed in front of the *Garfield Theatre.* Over the

marquee amber lights were a hot dazzle: *Summer Scandals.* Movie lights flared as celebrities rubbed elbows with a packed mob of hero gawkers wriggling like ants behind stolid-faced cops.

Tracy beamed at the uproar. "Come on, Ned. You shove and I'll push!"

Wortman shook his head, smiling faintly. "Don't wait for me. I'll park the car."

"Okey."

A hand swung the door open and Tracy alighted. He stepped right into what appeared to be a rather one-sided wrestling match. The *Garfield's* starter was tussling angrily with a sharp-eyed eager-faced boy. The kid had darted from the crowd and swung Tracy's door open in the expectation of a tip and a quick scram. The doorman tried to boot him away but he hung on.

"Leggo, you big chiseler," he piped shrilly. "It's my dime! I opened the door didn't I?"

His eyes swung towards Tracy. There was appeal in them, and a tense urgency that Tracy instantly understood. He knew this kid. Eddie Frayne. One of a small group of ragged, city-wise kids who picked up news nuggets for the column in places where grown-up stooges couldn't get. Tracy had spotted Eddie's old man in a decent job, had plucked the kid away from petty thieves and saved him from a reform school. Eddie adored the grinning Tracy and had given him a few hot tips for the *Daily Planet* column that every editor in town had missed.

"Let him alone, Mike," Jerry told the starter sharply.

"Okey, Mr. Tracy, if you want to encourage the little rat."

"What'll it be, kid? A dime and beat it—or will you match me for a quarter, pay if you lose?"

"Match you for the quarter!"

A cop, who had walked across, grinned and drifted away. That was exactly what Tracy wanted. He bent closer to the kid, took his time handing him a buck. His smiling lips barely moved.

"Something, Eddie?"

"Yeah. I seen something that looked kinda screwy. I beat it over here because I knew you'd—"

"Make it fast. People are watching us."

"You know that guy Ala Dhinn? The dago with the turban that the papers say ain't allowed to talk to no women? On account of he's a swummy or somethin'?"

"A swami, Eddie. What about him?"

"I seen him with a dame about an hour ago. In his big limousine. They pulled down the curtain when they seen me watchin', but it was this Ala Dhinn guy all right—and the dame was Peggy Arlen. I wouldn't have beat it here so fast, only I knew you like the girl."

There was a sudden anxious look in the eyes of the *Daily Planet's* columnist.

"Where did you see all this?"

"Over on Fifty-fourt', near Eighth."

"You're certain it was Peggy Arlen?"

"Yeah. I took a good look to make sure. The guy in the turban seen me and he yanked down the shade and the car breezed away in a hurry. An' that ain't all. I—"

A HAND TOUCHED Tracy's arm. He turned and the tension went out of his eyes as he saw Ned Wortman grinning at him.

"Still giving the public a free look at you, Jerry? Who was the kid with the dirty face?"

Tracy's head whirled. Eddie was gone, lost somewhere in the packed crowd. "He opened the car door and I gave him a buck."

"Pretty good pay—a buck."

"Not for that kid," Tracy said quietly.

He followed the producer into the theater. The lights were beginning to dim.

"See you after the show," Wortman whispered, and Jerry nodded to his friend and hurried up the aisle to his free seat in the fourth row center.

The opening number was magnificent but Tracy found himself unable to concentrate on the stage. He was thinking of the turban-swathed head of Ala Dhinn; his olive face, the black, inscrutable eyes. Tracy had wondered lately what the guy's real racket was. Plenty of money, apparently, and no visible means of support. A couple of Oriental servants, a brownstone house in the elegant Eighties and no graft discernible to the naked eye. Set-ups like that always interested the canny columnist. To him the "swami" stuff was just so much baloney.

Eddie's tip gave Tracy a sharp sense of worry. Why should this smooth Ala, who so ostentatiously fled the society of women as degrading, be riding in his limousine with a sweet little blonde like Peggy Arlen? Lightweight, Jerry called her, because she was like a drifting feather when she danced in the spotlight of the *Club Onyx,* and because she was as scatterbrained and impulsive as a monkey. A slim, satin-skinned little girl with clear blue eyes. The daughter of Peter Arlen; left in Tracy's care by a grand old actor whom Jerry had reason to love with affectionate gratitude.

Pete had been Jerry's first friend in New York—when he

had arrived broke and hungry. It was something Jerry never talked about. But he had never forgotten the one man out of six million who had fed and sheltered a small, thin-faced kid named Tracy. Arlen had noticed him hunched and shivering on a chilly corner, had stopped and talked to him. Arlen could have handed him a dime and walked off, but that wasn't Pete's way of doing things. He staked Jerry to a meal and a room, found out he was a cub reporter from a country paper, and pestered his newspaper friends until he'd landed a small job for Tracy. Jerry had long since paid back the money—but not the debt. The debt would last as long as Arlen lived.

Now he was out in Arizona, dying with gentle dignity from tuberculosis. Jerry's money was tactfully paying the bills. But the money was nothing—it was Lightweight herself that mattered. "A good girl," Pete Arlen had whispered weakly. "Jerry, will you—for the sake of old times—" Jerry had. She was a graceful dancer, beginning to attract a little attention. Pretty as a tea rose, and as level and straight as a ruler. Jerry enjoyed the duty of dropping in regularly to see her. He did it deftly, so that she was unaware of his friendly surveillance. His army of stooges had strict orders to keep an eye on the girl and report the presence of grifters or phoney guys. Eddie's whispered tip was the first hint of trouble that Tracy had received.

He thought, uneasily: "I'll call her up at the *Onyx Club* during the intermission."

Eddie had seen the swami and Lightweight at Fifty-fourth and Eighth.... That was where Lightweight had her hotel apartment.... What was she doing there instead of dancing for the dinner show at the *Onyx?* And how did she happen to know this swami well enough to pop into his luxurious limousine? It must have been damned important, or Ala Dhinn wouldn't be risking this publicity gag of his concerning women....

TRACY REACHED SUDDENLY under the seat for his hat and tiptoed down the dark aisle to the rear. The doorman gave him a puzzled glance, said softly: "Not running out on a hit, are you, Mr. Tracy?"

"Nope. Be right back, Mike."

He walked with long strides to the drug-store on the corner. He squeezed into a phone booth and called the *Onyx Club*. Purdy, the dance director, sounded as sore as hell.

"No, she ain't here and didn't send no excuse," Purdy snapped. "If you see her, tell her she's fired!"

"Any idea where she is or who she's with?"

"No. I phoned her apartment a couple of times and got nothing. I'm sorry, Jerry. I know she's a friend of yours—but she's through, and I'm not kidding. She's gummed up my whole floor show."

Tracy soothed him with a good-humored gag.

He stepped out into the electric-lit clamor of Broadway. It was hard to thumb a cab at this hour, but he got one finally. He was a peaceable guy and he didn't like the idea of tangling with a queer number like the swami—but maybe the whole thing wasn't as nasty as it looked. Lightweight trusted Tracy; she'd pay attention to any advice he gave her. It was a nuisance to have to run out on a good musical, but what else could a decent guy do?

The hotel where Lightweight lived was a dingy old building with a wheezy elevator operated by a rheumatic looking negro. Tracy rang Lightweight's bell with a nervous pressure of his finger.

"Who is it?" It was her voice—and not hers. Shrill, frightened.

"Jerry Tracy."

"Oh."

The door opened. Frightened? She was terrified! Her blue eyes bulged; her face was chalk white. She was wearing a cute apple-green evening gown and green high heeled slippers. Even frightened she looked sweet, babyish and appealing.

"What's wrong, sweetheart?" Tracy asked her sharply.

"Not—not a thing, Jerry."

"How come you're not at the *Onyx Club?*"

"I was delayed."

Tracy's worried glance went past her. A dim light was lit in the bedroom, but the door was partly closed. "You're sure there's nothing wrong? I don't want to pry into your personal affairs. I'm here because I'm your father's friend and yours, too. If I wasn't, I'd be off minding my own business."

"I know that, Jerry." Her face got paler. "I'm perfectly all right," she said, but her honest voice couldn't make the lie sound convincing.

She stepped between Tracy and the bedroom doorway but he moved her gently aside. Her hand on his was like a dab of ice. Tracy didn't like the idea of opening that door, but he did so gingerly. He felt relieved and a little foolish when he saw that the room was empty.

"Beat it, Jerry," Lightweight pleaded. "I—I'm waiting for somebody."

Her wan smile made Tracy feel helplessly angry.

"Who? That fake swami with the turban and the smooth line of gab?"

"What do you mean?" Her voice trembled. "What do you know about Ala Dhinn?"

"I know you were riding in his swanky limousine an hour or so ago."

"Jerry, will you—please—leave? I can't talk to you now. I'll meet you in—in a few minutes at the *Onyx Club*."

"Nothing doing. We'll both go—right now. Where's your wrap?"

She screamed as he stepped to the closet door. Her scream and his casual twist of the knob came almost simultaneously. Over his startled shoulder Tracy saw Lightweight rushing from the room, her face contorted with terror. Then from the open closet a man came plunging silently at the little columnist, knocking him headlong to the floor.

Tracy let out an instinctive yelp of fright. He punched desperately at the staring face above his. With a quick twist he squirmed from under his assailant, sprang catlike to his feet. The man, like Tracy, was in evening clothes. He lay limply on his face where Tracy's heave had thrown him. He didn't move. With a feeling of sick horror the columnist knelt and turned him on his back.

The starched shirt front was dappled with crimson and the ugly smudge of burned powder. He was stone dead.

Tracy's eyes jerked dazedly towards the man's blank face. Stuart Parker! A goodlooking, rather vapid playboy who had been, for the last few weeks, making a romantic rush for Lightweight. Dead—and the girl gone!

Tracy forgot his own safety. He darted arrowlike to the

living-room intent only on the girl. The hall door was wide open. He ran towards the elevator shaft, his eye flicking the indicator. The pointer showed that the car was motionless at the ground floor. It was barely thirty seconds since Jerry had so innocently jerked the closet door open. The elevator couldn't possibly have ascended and taken the fleeing girl down in that short space of time.

He turned and ran towards the stairs. One flight down told him the answer. The window at the dimly lit landing was raised from the bottom. He stuck his head out and saw rusted fire-escape steps and a narrow alley that led to Eighth Avenue. There was no sign of Lightweight; terror must have given her the speed of an antelope.

Tracy mopped his pale face. The thought of Lightweight—a sweet little kid in an apple-green evening gown—trying to cover up murder made Tracy gulp sickishly. If she'd only waited, told him the truth... She wasn't a murderess—not Pete Arlen's kid!

He turned and ran swiftly back up the stairs. Her door was still open and he closed it, his heart beating. He leaned against the inner panel, wondering what in God's name to do now. Police? He'd have to. And yet....

His jaw tightened as he remembered something about the living-room that he had overlooked in his quick anxiety to get at the root of the girl's terror. Her evening wrap hadn't been in the closet at all. It had been lying across that arm chair over in the corner. She must have snatched it up as she fled. She had thought faster than he had. Wrapped in the cloak, all she had to do was to grab the nearest cab and vanish like any other fugitive killer....

It was a tough situation to cope with, but the *Daily Planet's* columnist didn't hesitate. He walked straight to the phone in the living-room and asked for Police Headquarters in a steady voice. He asked to be connected with Inspector Fitzgerald.

"Can you keep something under the hat, Fitz, until you rush up here and have a talk with me?"

"Sure. Where are you, Jerry? I thought you were over at the *Summer Scandals* for the opening tonight."

"No." He gave Fitz the address of the apartment. "It's police stuff, Fitz—but I don't want any homicide men here till I've talked to you."

"Homicide?" Fitz sounded puzzled. "You trying to tell me that you're mixed up in a kill?"

"It's something I was dragged into, Fitz. Something that looks damn' dirty."

"Wait a minute, Jerry! You sound scared. You surely didn't—"

"No. But someone else *did*. I'm asking you as a favor to keep quiet about it till you can hop up here."

"Right."

Jerry's fingers jerked as he hung up. He thought: "I've got to get a grip on myself, if I'm gonna help Lightweight." But he was still jittery when Fitz knocked briefly on the door and walked in.

SERGEANT KILLAN WAS with the inspector. Tracy laughed unevenly as he saw their red, perspiration streaked faces. He'd forgotten it was hot. It seemed funny that his own armpits could be so icy wet on a midsummer night that fairly sizzled with heat.

Killan's black eyes peered suspiciously at the empty living-room. "What is this—a rib, Jerry?" he snapped. "Pulling one of your Broadway gags?"

"Try the bedroom," Tracy said.

The wiry, black-browed sergeant bounded out of sight and gave a sudden curt exclamation. "Uh, uh…. Hey—Fitz!"

Tracy didn't follow Fitz. He was still standing stiffly in the living-room when the gray-haired inspector drifted back and touched his arm.

"Did you do it, Jerry?"

He shook his head.

"Did you see it done?"

"No."

"Any idea who gunned him?"

"I—I'm not sure."

Fitz eyed his friend for a slow, probing instant. Then he pushed the *Daily Planet's* columnist gently into a chair. "Sit down, Jerry. Pull yourself together for a minute till I take another look."

After a while Tracy got up and went into the bedroom. Sergeant Killan was over in a corner of the room, holding back a long chintz curtain with his gloved hand. There were hooks in the angle of the wall from which hung a couple of Lightweight's house dresses. Jerry recognized an old hat of hers on a shelf. The curtain, hanging straight down to the floor, could easily have hidden a crouched man. Had Lightweight tried to protect the real killer, drawn Tracy after her to permit a murderer time to escape down the fire-escape that showed dimly outside the opened window?

Inspector Fitzgerald lifted an expressionless face from the sprawled body. "So what, Jerry? How about some facts?"

"The apartment belongs to Lightweight—you know—Peggy Arlen. The corpse is Stuart Parker."

"Yeah. So I see. I've been looking through his pockets.... How come you're in on this mess, Jerry? Did Lightweight telephone you at the theater and tell you she'd just croaked a boyfriend?"

"No. I—I just had a funny hunch that something was damned wrong.... Did you ever know me to lie to you, Fitz?"

"Nope."

"Well, I'm not starting now. Here's exactly what happened—and I'm not holding back a single thing."

He told Fitzgerald how he had stepped out of Ned Wortman's car in front of the *Garfield Theatre,* and he repeated the scrap of information he had received from Eddie, the street gamin, about Ala Dhinn and Peggy Arlen. He detailed his every thought and action up to the moment when he had lifted the telephone in Lightweight's living-room and called police headquarters.

Fitz frowned. Sergeant Killan looked skeptical.

"You really figure that fake swami is back of all this?" Killan said. "Where's the logical connection? Where's Parker fit in?"

"I happen to know that Parker was a nut for Oriental cults. Maybe he was backing this Ala Dhinn, got hep to something phoney and was killed because he threatened to squeal to the police."

"It just don't wash, Jerry," Killan growled. Heat always bothered him and he was in one of his irritable moods. "You think we can take the word of a dirty-faced little sidewalk kid who—"

"You'll take Eddie's word and like it before you're done," Tracy said.

"Wait a minute, both of you," Fitzgerald said. He stepped to the phone, identified himself curtly and asked for Ala Dhinn's number. He talked for a moment and then hung up.

"The swami's secretary says Ala hasn't been out of his house since sundown last night. Today is his holy day; he spent his entire time in prayer and meditation."

"He's lying," Tracy said quietly. "That guy's a phoney."

"On the kid Eddie's word?"

"Why not?"

Sergeant Killan snorted and Fitzgerald shook his head. "It's no use, Jerry. Even if we could bust the swami's alibi—which I doubt—there's not a single thing to connect him with this mess. You can't walk in and grill a guy whose been lecturing to some of the wealthiest people in town. Not on the vague sayso of a kid who's probably a petty thief from an underworld tenement."

"And besides," Killan cut in impatiently, "what's the fact that the swami was ridin' with the dame got to do with this killing? You admit the girl was here! She tried to get rid of you, you find the dead guy propped in her closet—and she promptly beats it. If she was innocent, why didn't she tell you what it was all about?"

"Because she didn't dare." He knew from their faces it sounded foolish, and added quietly, "The swami was hiding back of that curtain in the corner. He had a gun on her. She was thinking of my safety, not hers."

"Nuts," Killan muttered. His hot face darkened. "What you trying to do—cover this dancin' dame's runout?"

"We'll have to send out an alarm and pick the girl up," Fitz said. He dropped a restraining hand on Killan's shoulder. He saw that Tracy and the sergeant, ordinarily the best of friends, were at dagger points. He felt pretty hot and irritable himself. Damn the weather!

"You asked me to keep something under the hat, Jerry. What?"

The anger faded from Tracy's eyes. He knew Fitz's intense loyalty to him and he spoke softly, pleadingly. "I don't want to appear in this, Fitz. I've got a show to review and a column to write." He grinned a little and shoved on the old cynical look. "Tracy meets girl. Tracy forgets job. Tracy remembers job. No kidding, there's a nude number in the last act I've got to catch for the column customers."

"Okey, Jerry," Fitz said.

Killan chuckled faintly, and stuck out his red paw. "The heat's got me down," he muttered. "Sorry I lost my temper, kid."

"Forget it, Sarge. My underwear itches, too."

JERRY TRACY WIPED the grin off his face in the elevator. He walked back toward the *Garfield*. But he didn't get any further than the *Apex Theatre* just east of Broadway. The intermission had filled the sidewalk outside the *Apex* with a languid, cigarette smoking crowd. The crowd didn't interest Tracy but the three tap dancing kids in the adjoining alley did. He recognized them instantly as pals of the vanished Eddie. They were putting on a shrewd little amateur act, ducking with sweaty grins for the occasional dimes and nickels that people in the crowd tossed.

Tracy watched the ragged trio for a moment and then walked hastily back to the drug-store on the corner. He called the *Garfield* box office and left a message for Ned Wortman, the theatrical producer who had driven him to the *Summer Scandals*. Wortman was a good guy. He could depend on him to take a few notes about the opening night celebrities and their escorts, and to shoot the stuff by messenger to the *Daily Planet* office. Maybe Tracy could pep it up later.

He sauntered back to where the three kids were still energetically doing their tap dance, and waited until the crowd drifted back into the *Apex Theatre* for the last act. The kids recognized him, but their grins hardened when he asked casually about the whereabouts of Eddie. They hadn't seen Eddie in a week, didn't know nothin' about him!

Tracy, who knew plenty about gutter loyalty, instantly smelled a rat. Eddie had pulled a fast one of some kind; the kids were trying to protect him.

"Okey," Tracy shrugged. "You're doing him out of five bucks. If you guys want to be smart about it and gyp a pal, it's okey with me."

Three pairs of shrewd eyes stared at him. They were weakening.

"Tell him."

"Naw. Eddie'd be sore."

"Not at Mr. Tracy! You dope, he works for him."

Jerry handed the nearest kid a dollar bill. "Split it three ways and don't act dumb." He grinned. "What'd Eddie do, scram with somebody's change?"

They grinned back, awed respect in their glances. You just couldn't kid Mr. Tracy. A wise guy!

They told him with suppressed grins what had happened. A sap had given Eddie five bucks and asked him to buy a pack of Egyptian cigarettes in a little shop around the corner. Told him when he came back he'd get a quarter for his trouble. Eddie said sure—and never came back. They figured he had taken a smart runout.

Tracy, who knew Eddie better than that, chuckled with just the right note of amusement. "What did the man look like?"

"It wasn't a man. It was a loony lookin' dame. She drove up to the curb in a big automobile. When Eddie didn't come back she didn't get sore at all—just drove away."

"What do you mean, a loony dame?" Tracy asked quietly. "Was she a blonde? A cute looking dame in a green evening wrap?"

"Naw. She looked like a gypsy, only not so dirty. A funny red mark right in the middle of her forehead about as big as a dime. The guy in the car with her looked like a dago. Had a white towel wrapped around his nut. He peeked out after Eddie left."

"I see," Jerry said.

The swami was again unexpectedly sticking his phiz into Tracy's. The "loony dame" was a front, obviously primed by this suave Mr. Ala to scoop up Eddie with a transparent trick.

The whole thing stunk in the nostrils of the *Daily Planet's* worried little columnist with the unmistakable odor of a snatch job. This Ala guy wanted Eddie! Obviously because the street gamin was a witness to something the swami was desperately anxious to keep under cover. And the "loony dame" with the funny red mark on her forehead about the size of a dime? It might or might not be a legitimate caste mark. Where in the name of common sense did Eddie—and Lightweight fit into this screwy puzzle? Tracy's head ached with the desire to go home like a sensible man and leave the whole thing to the cops. There was a double reason why he couldn't. Eddie—and

Lightweight! Tracy had been hauled into something of which he couldn't let go. He'd have to ask a couple of questions before he let down a kid who trusted him, and the daughter of his old friend.

"Where's this Egyptian cigarette joint?"

"Around the corner. A block up Broadway. Coupla doors east."

"Okey."

HE WALKED CASUALLY away. On the crowded sidewalk of noisy Broadway he increased his pace. It was hard to hurry because the sidewalk was roofed over with timbers to protect pedestrians from a building that was being torn down by wreckers. The timbered tunnel continued around the corner into the side street for thirty feet or so.

The cigarette shop was just beyond. A dusty, dogeared sort of shop with a cardboard cigarette cutout in the window and not much visible inside. A bell tinkled as Tracy opened the door, and a fat, olive-faced man behind a small counter glanced up with a greasy smile.

"Goot evenin', sair. You weesh tobock—cigarette, no?"

"I'm looking for a boy I sent around here a little while ago. I gave him a five spot to buy me some cigarettes. Was he here?"

The greasy smile vanished from the face of the man behind the counter. He looked more like a Greek than an Egyptian. His eyes were suddenly scowling, his fat lips pressed together like sullen red cushions.

"No leetle boy come here, Mister."

"He had five dollars."

"No!"

"You sure he wasn't here?"

"No! No boy come!" The words were spat out with explosive ugliness.

"Okey," Jerry shrugged. "Have it your way, pal. I guess I was wrong. Gimme a pack of cigarettes to show there's no hard feelings."

Smilingly, he closed the door of the shop behind him. His face got serious. There was a narrow alley alongside the building, its entrance cluttered with dented ashcans. Tracy idled closer, glanced keenly east and west, and melted out of sight. He wanted to have a quiet look at the back of that shop. He didn't like anything about that guy behind the counter—his looks and his talk had been sullen and nasty. There was a bare chance that Eddie might be lying roped and gagged in a small dusty bundle somewhere in the rear.

The alley widened into a small unpaved parking area that served the rear of the tobacco shop and a restaurant that faced on the street beyond. A man in a cook's white hat was emptying garbage into a pail outside the restaurant. He stared indifferently at the columnist, yawned, and went back to his pots and pans.

Tracy saw tire marks on the ground, deep-treaded marks where a car had recently stood behind the tobacco shop. There was a grated rear window beyond the closed door and he stepped closer and applied a wary eye to the edge of the dust-encrusted pane. His finger made a small clear patch near the edge and he peered inside.

It was just as he had thought. If the guy inside was a snatch artist, he was too wise to keep the captured kid on the premises. There was no sign of Eddie and no place where he could have been stuck out of sight. No living quarters in the back of the shop. The face of the swarthy dealer was vaguely visible as he leaned on the counter, staring straight out towards the sidewalk where Tracy had breezed with smiling apologies. The man looked sullen, suspicious. He walked to the front door and stood there looking out at the swift flow of traffic.

Tracy backed away from the window and bent over the tire marks. They confirmed his uneasy hunch that Eddie had gone through that shop like greased lightning. In—a hand over his mouth, maybe a sock over the skull—then out, into a sedan with a long wheelbase. The latter was an easy deduction for Jerry's quick-witted intelligence. The car had had to back up to make the turn. Its length and weight were clearly evident in the broad tread marks. Tracy's lips tightened as he thought of the loyal kid, baited with five bucks and snatched by a dark-skinned dame and a so-called swami. He walked through to the rear street and turned thoughtfully west. Eddie and Light-weight, two swell people he didn't want hurt, vanished into thin air because they obviously knew something about a dead man propped in a hotel closet.

On the way to the corner of Broadway the face of another dead man flashed into the suddenly alert memory of the *Daily Planet's* columnist. The name of the man was Sol Davis. Murdered very thoroughly by a killer who had left no trace except the method of murder, which was disturbingly Orien-tal. Sol's body had been found in a West Side doorway of the Low Fifties barely three weeks before—strangled to death by a thin cord that had been twisted deep in the flesh of his throat.

The only connection between Davis and young Stuart Parker was show business. Davis, a bald, prosperous and rather secretive old bozo, was one of the town's lesser theatrical impresarios. He owned a small chain of theaters. Stuart Parker would have owned considerably more than that, if he had lived to see the estate of his father finally settled. His father had been Sam Parker and his holdings in theatrical real estate were large. Was there a motive for murder in that? What possible connection could there be between two murdered theatrical men and a fake swami in a brownstone house?

FROWNING, TRACY STEPPED into a phone booth and rang up Lightweight's suite. He was answered by a voice he recognized—Masterson, a friendly enough dick from headquarters. Masterson reported that neither Fitz nor Sergeant Killan were there. They had buzzed off somewhere else. How come Jerry knew there was trouble in the dancer's apartment?

"I guess 'em before they happen," Tracy rejoined with a dry chuckle, and hung up.

The chuckle was phoney. It was tough when you were a little guy with a column to write—and murder kept clutching you by the back of the pants! The chance to slip information to the inspector was out for the present. He'd give Fitz a buzz later on, he decided.

The familiar prosaic noise of Broadway hit him with reassuring clamor when he emerged from the drug-store. Lights like fuzzy yellow balloons, honks of taxis, guys and their dames slogging north and south through the hot night like a packed outpouring of ants.

This was not Bagdad—this was Manhattan! The place where well-dressed pals slapped you on the back and tried to borrow money. Where showgirls and debs, anxious for a line or two in the *Daily Planet* column, put on the old honeyed smile and told their escorts: "You know Jerry, of course! The grandest little guy in town!"

But Tracy couldn't shake off the worried feeling that he was marked for trouble like a hot-cross bun. Every move he had made tonight was wrong. The hell of it was, the mess had been wished on him through no fault of his own.

He decided to hop back to his penthouse and have a tall snort of bonded Bourbon. He'd snap out of his shivers by watching Butch, his oversize hoofs cocked up on a console table, spelling out the latest Broadway chatter from *Variety* with twitchings of his thick, good-natured lips. Butch, bless him, had never heard of Bagdad. If you asked him about it, he'd probably tell you it was a town near Bridgeport.

Butch's big feet were, as usual, propped up on the console table. But he wasn't poring over *Variety*. He was reading—of all things imaginable—a book!

Butch grinned at his pint-sized employer. "Hi-yuh, boss. Hey, why didn't yuh tell a guy yuh had books like this? Boy, I'm tellin' yuh this one's a knockout. All about a smart little kid that had a magic wop to wait on him."

"What the devil are you talking about?"

"The kid had a trick lamp. Every time he rubbed it— out jumped a Guinney slave to wait on him. Boy, he was a hard-working wop!"

Tracy said slowly: "Not Guinney, Butch—Genie."

A look of awed disbelief jerked into Tracy's wide eyes. He shook his head suddenly, like a man who's just seen a ghost eating a hot dog and swilling orangeade in broad daylight.

"Hey!" Butch yelled in sudden alarm. "Cut it out, Boss! You'll tear de pictures!"

"Where did this come from?" Tracy asked. He was eying with grim wonder the book he had just snatched. It was a single volume edition of the *Arabian Nights*.

Butch, who realized by now that something was wrong, said defensively: "Keep your shoit on, Jerry. I got it from the Chink."

"From McNulty?"

"Yeah."

"Where did McNulty get it?"

"Search me."

Tracy's sharp summons brought his bland-eyed Chinese cook padding cheerfully from the distant confines of the kitchen.

"Where did you get this thing?" Track asked.

"Leetle while ago. Bell ring at door. Lady bling book."

"What lady?"

McNulty sighed. His almond eyes were calm, filled with a gentle rebuke. "Allatime you squeal like toy balloon, Mister Tlacy. How can McNulty think? Confucius say—"

"The hell with Confucius! Tell me about this book."

It had arrived as McNulty had said. A youngish, dark eyed woman had left it and promptly departed before McNulty could question her. The Chinaman had thought nothing of it; people were always sending gifts to Tracy.

Tracy leafed through the volume with puzzled eyes. He had come home to mind his own business—and now this! His first surmise was that the book contained a message of some sort. Otherwise, why the mysterious gift; and why, of all fantastic coincidences, the *Arabian Nights?* He was so jittery that he leafed through the volume twice before he saw that on two successive pages a sentence had been underlined.

The first sentence read as follows: *He was in the habit of going out early in the morning, and would stay out all day, playing in the streets with idle children of his own age.*

Tracy frowned, turned over the page and read the other underlined sentence: *In this situation, as he was one day playing with his vagabond associates, a stranger passing by stood to observe him.*

The message was obviously a reference to the vanished Eddie. Tracy glanced at the top of the page and uttered instantly a low cry of comprehension. The chapter was headed in bold type. *The Story of Aladdin.*

Alladin—nerts! Ala Dhinn—and Eddie! That's what it meant. But why the warning? Was this so-called "loony dame" trying to help Tracy—or frame him with a new come-on?

McNULTY BROUGHT HIM a tall Bourbon, but it didn't help a bit. The puzzle seemed almost mathematical. Jerry drew with the nervous point of his pencil a triangle and two parallel lines. The triangle was Lightweight, a street gamin named Eddie—and a thoroughly scared Broadway columnist named Jerry Tracy. The parallel lines were two dead men; Sol Davis, strangled to death with a garrot cord three weeks earlier and Stuart Parker, shot dead tonight and crammed into a cabaret dancer's closet. The death lines were parallel because both Davis and young Parker had something to do with show business; they both owned strings of theaters.

A sudden practical idea came to Tracy. He thought of his friend, Ned Wortman. He'd give Ned a ring and kill two birds with one stone. He had to make sure that the obliging Ned had phoned into the *Daily Planet* office the opening night chit-chat he had so obligingly promised. Besides, Ned was himself a producer. He might have some slant on Davis or Parker, that Jerry could relay to Inspector Fitzgerald.

Tracy was reaching for the phone to call Wortman when the bell suddenly rang.

"Hello?" he said.

"Jerry? *Is that you*, Jerry?"

The voice was a woman's. Thin, high-pitched, yet barely audible. Tracy recognized it instantly.

"Lightweight?"

"Y-yes.... Jerry—quick—for God's sake, hurry!"

"What's wrong? Where are you?"

"He followed me! I'm—I'm sure of it. Jerry, he means to kill me!"

"Where are you?" Tracy cried, his thin face drawn with anxiety.

"In the *Garfield Theatre*," Lightweight whispered.

"But the show's finished. The joint's closed up. How did you get in?"

Her frightened words spurted over the wire. "First alley exit on the left. I'm hiding in the manager's office in the rear of the orchestra. Jerry—quick—"

"Wait a minute! Who's after you? Who are you talking about?"

A soft click sounded in Tracy's ears. The line was dead.

He banged his own receiver down.

"McNulty! Where are you?"

The Chinaman came pattering in as calm as a summer breeze. He looked cool and unflurried in his dark trousers and smock of thin silk.

"I may need you to identify that woman who brought the book here. Come on!"

Butch was heaving out of his comfortable chair, his big face angry, his thick lips pouting like a child's.

"Hey! Wait a minute! Ain't I goin'? You passin' me up for a dopey Chink?"

Tracy's voice cut short Butch's outraged snort. "Stay here and keep an eye on things. There may be a tough guy dropping in here to take a crack at me. If he does—rough him up!"

Butch grinned shakily. "Dat's different. Whyn't yuh say so in the foist place? I thought yuh was givin' the Chink the play over me."

In a moment the columnist and McNulty were outside the apartment, dropping swiftly in the elevator to the distant street. A whistle of the doorman brought a parked taxi from the corner. At Tracy's curt order the cab shot through the warm darkness towards Times Square. Speed! Grab the terrified Lightweight and hustle her back to the penthouse—then the cops, and a thankful bow-out for a peaceful columnist!

McNulty's almond eyes were blandly inquisitive. "You want catchum someone, Boss?"

"Yeah," Tracy snapped.

They alighted from the cab a block away from the *Garfield Theatre*. It was late, but Broadway was still sluggishly alive with the remnants of after-show parties. Around the doorways of restaurants mildly cockeyed parties waddled with alcoholic gravity towards sweating taxi-drivers parked at the curb. The sidewalks were still baking with heat absorbed during the sizzling afternoon.

Down the side street the *Garfield Theatre* was a squat pyramid of blackness. Tracy approached the place at a gait that was not too hurried. He didn't want to draw attention to himself or the Chink. There was no swanky limousine parked outside the deserted theater, no sign of the suave Ala Dhinn. That made Tracy feel better. The two investigators ducked silently into the paved exit alley on the left side of the theater, and Tracy tried the handle of the first door. It was unlocked, as Lightweight had said.

He admired the kid's smartness. Of all places in New York for a gal on the dodge to hide, an empty theater was a natural. Fitz and Killan were undoubtedly turning the town upside-down at this very instant, and Lightweight was hidden right under their noses, a few blocks from the spot where Stuart Parker had tumbled stone-dead out of her hotel closet.

The theater was pitch dark inside. Tracy whispered into McNulty's inclined ear and the Chink stood guard just within the exit door. Tracy padded noiselessly along the black aisle to the rear.

He knew where the manager's office was. No light was visible through the ground-glass panel of the closed door. Gently he turned the knob and the door pushed open easily.

He whispered cautiously: "Lightweight! Are you okey? It's Jerry!"

No answer. He struck a match, shielding the faint yellow glow with his cupped palm. The office was empty.

His faint whistle brought McNulty materializing like a yellow ghost in the darkness of the doorway. Tracy shut the door and lit another match. Suddenly he gave a low exclamation.

His finger was pointing towards a desk in the dim corner of

the room. He advanced until the small object atop the desk became clearly outlined in the light of his match. Tracy recognized it; it was a plaster bust of Napoleon. Like so many showmen of his type, the pudgy little manager of the *Garfield Theatre* rather fancied his pot-bellied resemblance to Napoleon. He always kept the concession to his vanity on the desk.

But it wasn't the bust itself at which the eager finger of the columnist pointed. It was a girl's handkerchief, wrapped around Napoleon's plastered brow and tied loosely with a hastily made knot. In one corner were embroidered initials—P. A. Peggy Arlen—Lightweight!

Neither the handkerchief nor the initials, however, were the tip-off. It was the way the handkerchief was fastened to the bust. It had been knotted in a crude semblance of a wrapped turban! Lightweight, trapped in the middle of her desperate telephone appeal to Jerry, had had a warning of the approach of Ala Dhinn—and the wit to leave this hasty clue.

Tracy's reaction was swift. He scooped up the telephone on the desk and called Police Headquarters in an eager whisper. He was doomed to disappointment. Neither Inspector Fitzgerald nor Sergeant Killan were in the building.

"Out on a case," a bored voice growled sleepily. "Who are you, and what do you want the inspector about?"

Tracy hung up without replying.

With a gesture he felt for the small calibered gun on his hip. He had grabbed it before he left the penthouse.

"Come on, keed," he told McNulty.

IT WAS STICKY and hot outside. Big wet drops of rain were beginning to splash on the dark pavement of the deserted sidewalk. Tracy considered the idea of a cab and then dropped it. His own car was in a garage not two blocks away, over near Sixth Avenue. He heeled it along through the increasing rain, the noiseless feet of McNulty pattering swiftly beside him.

Ten minutes later Tracy's car turned from Central Park West into one of the Eighties. There wasn't a single pedestrian visible in the long block. The rain had become a sullen torrent and the sidewalks and gutter streamed with splashing water. A sudden flare of lightning and the long roll of thunder seemed to cool the air miraculously. Tracy kept his mind on Lightweight and it helped to brace him. He pulled in at the curb and braked.

The swami's residence was a brownstone, high-stooped affair in a neighborhood that was still untouched by the ever-expanding inroads of furnished room joints. Either Ala Dhinn had dough or he was a front for somebody who had!

Tracy walked up the stoop and rang the bell. The moment the door opened, he and McNulty slipped inside. The turbaned servant made an angry gesture of protest.

"What's the idea?" he snarled.

"If you're an Oriental, I'm an airedale," Tracy said huskily. "That Brooklyn accent doesn't go with the walnut stain and the trick pajamas. Where's the swami?"

"He's busy," the servant sneered. "If you are on the same business as that dick ahead of you, you're barking up the wrong tree."

"What dick ahead of me?" Jerry asked quickly. His eyes narrowed. From a closed door down the hallway he heard a surprisingly familiar voice. He nodded to McNulty. The Chinaman stuck a stiff forefinger against the servant's back and shoved his captive ahead of him. Tracy flung open the door.

A curt voice from within said sharply: "Stick 'em up!"

Tracy grinned with shaky relief. "Hello, Fitz. What you doing here?"

Inspector Fitzgerald lowered his weapon. He looked grimly puzzled.

"I took your tip," Fitz admitted slowly, "and dropped in for a chat with this swami bird. He's phoney, all right. No more of a Hindoo than I am. He claims his act is none of my business and strictly on the level. Got any dope on him?"

"Maybe," Tracy said quietly.

He was staring straight at the swami, reassured by the presence of Fitzgerald. In a close-up the swarthy face looked more like a smart Italian's than anything else.

A light, rustling sound jerked Tracy's gaze around. A man had risen from a chair in a corner and was disappearing quietly through an inner door. Tracy got a quick look at the fat averted face, and took a swift forward step. He changed his mind instantly and remained where he was. The door closed.

"Who was that guy?" Tracy asked Fitz.

"The swami's secretary. I had him in here for questioning. I told him he could go. Want him back?"

"Nope," Tracy said. "The secretary, eh?" He swung towards McNulty. "Walk this other bird out in the hall and keep your gun on him. Don't let him move."

"This is an outrage," the swami protested nervously. "I'm a respectable, law-abiding person. I demand—"

"Shut up!" Fitz growled. "What do you know, Jerry?"

"I know that this specimen here is a crook and a kidnaper. Where are you from, Ala—Delancey Street or Coney Island? And who taught your secretary how to use a strangle cord?"

"I don't know what you mean," the swami said.

"Ever hear of a cute little dancer named Peggy Arlen?"

"No."

"Or an unfortunate little street Arab named Eddie?"

"Certainly not."

"Been anywhere near the *Garfield Theatre* tonight?"

"No." His voice got silky. "As I have just explained to this police gentleman, I have not been outside my home today. Today is my time for rest and meditation."

He was glaring at the dapper little columnist, his lips taut with repressed fury, when the telephone on the desk in the corner of the room rang suddenly.

Fitz' arm blocked off the swami's forward movement. "You answer it, Jerry."

Tracy was already at the phone, his eyes alert. He said in a deliberately blurred murmur: " 'Allo?"

Words came over the wire with an excited rush. "Sorry, swami, but we had to croak Ned Wortman. We snatched him okey, but he tried a fast one just a minute ago and we had to hand it to him. He's as dead as a mackerel."

"That ees well," Tracy said calmly and replaced the phone. He stared at Fitzgerald. "Is it true that Wortman was kidnapped tonight?" Fitz nodded, a little bewildered by the curt question.

"He was grabbed right after he left the show at the *Garfield Theatre*. There's a confidential alarm out for him now. How did you know?"

From the hall doorway came a gentle cough in the tones of McNulty. The Chinaman's yellow eyelid dropped in an unmistakable wink.

Tracy said: "Wait a second, Fitz. I'll be right back."

He shut the door behind him. McNulty's eyes were motioning down the hall towards a tall chair alongside a shadowy hatstand.

"Look-see," McNulty whispered.

The chair was straightbacked, with a knob on either side. One of the knobs was covered with a pale green scarf. The scarf had been hurriedly wrapped around the knob in a loosely draped, turban-like effect. It was almost invisible in the shadow.

"Some more of the same," Tracy said gently. He untangled the scarf and stuffed it into his pocket.

He was turning back towards the room where he had left Fitz and the swami, when he heard the sound of light footfalls approaching from the rear of the long hallway. He stood quite still as he saw the woman advance.

She was dressed in flowing robes. On her forehead was a circular red caste mark. The dark-skinned effect was undoubtedly make-up. If this was the so-called "looney dame," it was a cinch that she was no Hindoo, but a white woman. She walked straight towards the foot of the stairs. She paid no attention whatever to Tracy or McNulty or the servant. McNulty eyed her carefully and nodded to Tracy. But his identification of her was not necessary.

She was carrying a book. As she turned to ascend the stairs she lifted the book with a negligent gesture so that Tracy could see the name on the cover. It was a copy of *The Arabian Nights*. An exactly similar edition to the one that had so mysteriously turned up at Tracy's penthouse. Without a sound, without even a glance, the woman in the long robe walked quietly up the dimly lit stairs and disappeared.

Tracy felt his heart quicken. In danger herself, perhaps, and trying to warn Jerry. The book stunt must have been the only way she could work the game without alarming the swami. Coupled with the turban on the chair in the hall, it meant that Lightweight was a prisoner in this house. And Eddie, too! The dame in the robes and the walnut makeup was trying to snitch on what was evidently a criminal racket without risking her neck as a traitress.

Tracy paused for a moment to consider one other angle. Ned Wortman! A third victim—and a theatrical man like the other two, Davis and Parker. According to Inspector Fitzgerald, Wortman had been kidnaped. According to the voice on the telephone, Wortman had been not only kidnaped, *but killed.* The *Daily Planet's* shrewd little columnist was now absolutely certain that Wortman had been kidnaped but was *not dead.* The voice on the wire had been too eager to pour out the hooey.

But the real reason for Tracy's puzzled frown lay in something more substantial. He had recognized that breathless voice on the wire. It was the same fat guy who had said "no" to Jerry's queries in the Egyptian tobacco shop. The same guy who had sneaked so quietly from the swami's room the moment Jerry had walked in. He had obviously called up on another phone from somewhere in the house and spilled his message about a murder, knowing that Tracy or the inspector would answer the phone at the first warning tinkle of the bell. It looked like a clever stunt to draw them away from the house while the swami and his fake "secretary" got rid of Lightweight and the kid.

TRACY DECIDED TO do a little smooth faking himself. He opened the door of the parlor and gave Fitzgerald a good imitation of a crestfallen grin.

"Sorry, Fitz. I'm afraid I've pulled a boner. We owe Mr. Ala an apology."

"Huh?" Fitz growled.

Tracy saw that the inner door was opened a trifle. He suspected that the ear of the wily "secretary" was not far from that infinitesimal crack.

"Ned Wortman's been killed. We'll have to race uptown in a hurry if we're going to nab the real murderer."

"Uptown where? And who says Wortman is dead?" Fitz was watching the columnist keenly.

"I got it from Inspector *Malarkey*." Tracy said, with a faint emphasis on the name.

"Malarkey? But there isn't any—"

Suddenly Fitz got it. Jerry was trying to kid the swami. He didn't dare say hooey or baloney. Malarkey was as close as he could get.

"Come on," Tracy urged. "I've got my car outside at the curb. We can make it uptown in a hurry." He grinned at the suspicious eyes of Ala. "Sorry, swami, that we busted in on you this way. I made a bum guess. If you're sore about it—sue the *Daily Planet*. Okey, McNulty; come on!"

The three hurried through the hall. The front door closed behind them. In the pouring rain that danced with a drumming sound on the stone stoop, Tracy clutched Fitz' arm. The silly look was gone from his face. He was Jerry Tracy again—smart, eager, the little guy that Broadway respected and loved. He whispered urgently in the old man's ear.

"Lightweight and Eddie are hidden in that house," he concluded. "That dame with the book cinches it. She's on our side, Fitz, trying to tip us to the truth."

Fitzgerald, who had seen no one but the swami and his two henchmen, started to spurt questions but Jerry shook his head.

"No time for talk now. Hop to a booth and shoot in a call for a couple of squad cars. You've got to surround this joint and search it in a hurry, or there'll be two more murders in tomorrow's headlines. The Chink and I will stick around in my parked car in case the kidnapers try a fast sneak with Lightweight and the kid."

Fitz' red face looked worried. "Are you sure about all this, Jerry? I can't afford to make a dumb play."

"You're making a dumb play by wasting time."

"Okey. You've never let me down yet."

They started to descend to the sidewalk.

"Hold it, you muggs!" a hard voice said.

The door of the vestibule had opened without sound. Two men with automatics were grinning at the departing guests. The fellow who had snarled the command was the fat-faced secretary. The other gunman was the lad whom McNulty had cornered in the hall.

There was death in the grim faces in the vestibule opening. And the slanting rain, spattering into the eyes of the broad-shouldered cop and the little columnist, made any attempt at movement a suicidal proposition. McNulty muttered something in Chinese, and stood quietly watching Tracy.

"Take the door, Andy," Fat Face growled at his pal.

"Right. Can you ease 'em in, Nick?"

"Just like hot grease." Nick chuckled. "Forward march, gents!"

Under the watchful glare of the secretary's beady eyes, the three prisoners passed quietly back inside the house.

The party was herded along the dim hallway and into the room of the swami. Ala looked more frightened than triumphant.

"You're making a foolish mistake, Nick," he said faintly. "Why didn't you let them go? We could have arranged things much better."

"Nuts to that. We got dynamite to get rid of before it busts in our faces. Three hunks of it right here—and two more upstairs." Nick's fat face looked hot and sweaty. "All we gotta do is pull the fuses on these guys, and then we're sittin' pretty."

Ala's face got whiter. He had lost all of his fake suavity. For the first time, Tracy received a strong impression that the secretary, Nick, was the real boss of this gang. Andy, the other gunman, paid scant attention to Ala. He kept watching Nick. Both these yeggs were either running the racket themselves, or working for someone else.

"You're not going to kill these people, are you?" Ala gasped.

"Sure."

"You're crazy. We can't get away with it."

"No? Watch!"

His gun barrel swung toward Fitz' belly. Tracy, helpless under the weapon of Andy, sucked in a frightened breath.

"Don't!" he begged. "For God's sake boys—you can't—"

McNulty was shivering. He began to wail in Chinese. Suddenly his hand jerked towards his flowing sleeve as though drawing a knife. It drew Nick's gaze and created diversion enough for Tracy to dive headlong at the thug. His plunging body struck Nick in the shins and sent him forward. There was a crash as he fell. His bullet plowed into the floor.

Fitzgerald fired almost simultaneously. His slug ripped

into Nick's body. Andy fired at Fitz, missed—and Tracy's fist caught him in the mouth. The flame of Andy's pistol almost blinded him, but the deflected bullet missed his neck by a hair's-breadth. McNulty, who had wriggled across the floor, yanked the gunman's ankles out from under him. As he fell, he dropped the gun and Tracy struck him over the skull with the butt.

As he whirled, he saw the swami leap away from an open drawer of his desk with an automatic. Ala fired wildly— twice—before Fitz' spurt of flame cut him down. It was neat shooting, too. The swami hit the floor with a sodden smack and didn't move. Fitz leaped over his body and snapped cuffs on Andy, the thug Tracy had slugged.

THE ONLY SOUNDS in a suddenly quiet room were the faint groans of the wounded Nick and the mouselike rustle that McNulty made as he regained his slippered feet. Nick's eyes were glaring. His hands were pressed tightly over the wound in his side. Blood welled between his clutching fingers.

"Confucius say," McNulty remarked breathlessly, "it velly bad to hurt human man. He say nothing about rats."

Tracy whirled towards the open doorway behind them. He had heard the patter of light footsteps, the sound of a sobbing breath. An instant later a girl was swaying in the doorway. A girl in Oriental robes, with a vivid caste mark on her forehead.

She was gasping, trying to talk. The fake Hindoo pose was gone. Her words were nasal New Yorkese, shrill with terror and excitement.

"Quick! Upstairs—prisoners! A dame and a kid!"

Tracy's voice crackled. "Any more gunmen?"

"No. Just Nick and Andy—and Morello."

"Morello?" Fitz barked. "Who's he?"

She pointed with a quivering finger at the dead body of the swami. She began to weep hysterically. Tracy shook her out of it, hurried her to the staircase outside.

"Nobody's going to hurt you," he said gently. "Show us where to go."

Up one carpeted flight. Down a narrow hall. Up another.... On the top floor the girl pointed towards a locked door. Fitz rattled the knob without result and sprang back a few steps. He threw himself fiercely at the barrier. It ripped on the fourth try and fell inward with a crash.

Tracy uttered a clipped exclamation of despair as he hurdled the prone body of the inspector. The room was empty. There were faint marks on the bed and a few loose cords. A window had been raised from the bottom and rain was driving in on the soaked carpet. Lightweight was gone! It looked as though she had managed to squirm out of her bonds and scram in terror via the window route.

An instant later Tracy was sure of it. With his head poked outward into the driving downpour, he saw the blur of fire-escape ladders and an alley below. He saw something closer at hand and, leaning swiftly, picked the thing up. It was a fragment of cloth, ripped from a woman's gown. A bit of satin material. Apple-green!

Fitz was yelling grimly at the girl in the Oriental make-up, but Tracy intervened. "Don't holler at her, Fitz. You'll scare her dumb—and she's trying to help us."

He smiled at her, patted her quivering shoulder. There was reassurance in his voice, friendliness in his smile. "Where's the boy? Where did they hide Eddie?"

They found him in a front room, face down on a bed, tied up like a miniature mummy. Jerry's pocket knife slashed the cords away.

Eddie was bleary-eyed, almost senseless, but a faint grin wavered on his wizened, dirty little face as he recognized the *Daily Planet's* columnist.

"Jeeze, Mister Tracy, I knew you'd show up.... You're—you're tops, no kiddin'."

He flopped forward, out cold. There were ugly smudges of red on his face and neck where he'd been slapped around by someone.

"Dig up some water, McNulty," Tracy said. He whirled towards the girl behind him. "What's your name—your real one?"

"Dot Hagen."

"Who's Morello—is that the swami?"

"Yes. I—I swear I had nothing to do with this. Morello forced me into the racket. I pulled a fast one out at Coney Island last year and Morello put the heat on me to play ball."

"Coney Island, eh? Is that where he figured out his swami stunt?"

"He was a mind-reader. He used it as a cover for blackmail. He used to kid customers along, squeeze scandal out of them—and then make 'em pay plenty to keep it quiet."

Fitz glared at her. "You trying for an out on this? You claiming that Morello and his two gunmen forced you into murder and kidnaping?"

"Easy, Fitz," Jerry cautioned. "I think she's on the level."

"I swear it," she whimpered. "You can ask Mr. Tracy. I

snatched Eddie because Morello was right next to me in the car with a gun. But I tried to warn you, Mr. Tracy. I—I sent you a marked book, figuring you'd tumble and come with cops. The book was the only chance I had. Morello had his eye on me all the time. I figured you'd see the hookup between Alladin and Ala Dhinn. I—"

A groan from the bed brought Tracy swinging around. Eddie had recovered consciousness under the ministrations of McNulty. The Chinaman lifted the limp kid in his arms and frowned reprovingly at his two companions.

"Boy hurt. Allatime talk, talk, talk…. You talk—boy die. Velly fine!"

Fitzgerald clutched Dot Hagen's shoulder. "You don't know where Lightweight is now?"

"No, no…. Morello had her tied up here ever since he snatched her from the theater. She—she must have—"

"Let's get downstairs," Tracy said.

Nick was still lying on his side, with one hand clutching his wound, the other doubled weakly beneath his body. He was obviously dying. His glazed eyes glared at the girl. She shrank back.

"Don't worry about him," Jerry said gently. "He can't hurt you. Nick and Andy did the killing for Morello. Right?"

Dot Hagen shook her head. "No. They were here to watch Morello and me. They didn't kill Sol Davis. They didn't kill Stuart Parker."

"Huh?" Inspector Fitzgerald stared at her. "Who did? Morello himself?"

"No. Morello was just a front, a fall guy. So was I. Except that Morello didn't get wise to it in time—but I did."

"Who's the undercover boss?"

"This kid knows," she said faintly, pointing to the dazed Eddie who hung limply in McNulty's arms. "That's why he was snatched—to shut his mouth."

"Who *did* it?" Fitz repeated impatiently. "Talk up. Nobody's gonna hurt you."

"A slimy, rotten hypocrite!" Dot Hagen flashed, her terror whipped away by hate. "A big shot. A wise guy by the name of—"

SHE SCREAMED AND her hand clutched at her breast. Nick had whipped his hidden gun from under his wounded body, and had fired upward from the floor where he lay. Dot Hagen's mouth was still open soundlessly as she fell.

The dying killer's gun roared as it jerked towards Fitz and Tracy. But both of them had leaped aside at the first explosion. The inspector's gun swung downward. Nick's body bounced as police slugs ripped into him. This time he really was dead! Breathing hard, Fitz stood over him like a frozen marionette, smoke curling thinly from the barrel of his .38.

Tracy had dropped to his knees beside the unconscious girl. To his relief he saw that she was not badly wounded.

"Forget her," Fitz barked. "She's as bad as the rest."

"Not much. She's been trying to help me right from the start. This kid's going to a private room in a hospital. At my expense. And I'm spotting her to a decent job when she gets well—and don't you forget it!"

Fitz nodded. "All right. Have it your way, Jerry."

"Wait a minute," Tracy interrupted. His own voice was barely audible. There was a queer look on his wizened little face—a flash of quick comprehension. He was staring straight at the semi-conscious street urchin in the arms of McNulty. "Of course! Unless he were a witness, there'd have been no reason for snatching Eddie."

"Huh?" Fitzgerald gaped at the columnist.

"Outside! My car's still there. We've got to get Eddie out of his doze in a hurry. He's got the key to this puzzle without realizing it."

The rain was still pouring hard. Fitzgerald slid in past the wheel of the car. Jerry threw open the rear door and motioned for McNulty to get in with Eddie. The Chinaman was bending forward when he gave a little yelp.

A tumbled rug was rising from the floor of the car. It fell sideways and revealed the stark face of a girl. It was Lightweight, her wrap gone, the apple-green evening gown torn and bedraggled.

"Jerry!" she moaned. "Thank God, it's you. I was afraid that—"

The crisp sound of automobile brakes whirled Tracy around. Two cars were slithering in towards the curb. Squad cars! Out of them tumbled cops with drawn guns.

A tall bluecoat sprang at Tracy and began to frisk him. The cop gasped as Fitzgerald's gray head poked belligerently out of the suspected car.

"Murphy! Reardon! What the hell are you fools trying to do?"

"Huh? Are—are you in on this, Inspector? Somebody phoned Headquarters and said there was a gunfight going on in that brownstone. I—we—"

"Get inside and take charge," Fitz snapped. "You'll find three men and a girl in there. Get an ambulance here quick. Hang on till I get back."

"Yes, sir." Reardon saluted, gazed bug-eyed for an instant at the Chinaman, the limp and dirty-faced Eddie, and the pale-green wreck of Lightweight's evening gown. Then he turned and sprang up the front stoop after the other cops.

Jerry Tracy's foot was on the gas pedal, but he didn't press it.

"Do you know who killed Parker in your apartment?" he asked Lightweight.

"Yes. I didn't dare tell you when you butted in. It was Ala! He was in my room, behind a curtain, while you were talking to me. He had a gun on your back."

"Ala?" Fitz asked, but Tracy shut him up with a quick glance.

"Any idea of the reason behind all this killing?" Jerry continued.

"Yes. The whole thing is a—a theatrical racket. Ala and his two henchmen are trying to get control of every theater in New York. They've already got most of the houses right now. They're planning to shake down managers, producers, actors— tie up every legitimate playhouse in Manhattan. They killed Sol Davis and Stuart Parker. They're after Ned Wortman next."

"Ned's been kidnaped," Tracy said.

"Kidnaped? My God, you've got to find him! They'll kill him! He knew they were after him. That's why I was spying on the swami, to help Ned. He signed over all his theatrical properties to me, in case they got him. Oh, Jerry—you've got to find Ned before he's killed. Find him!"

"Ned signed over his whole string of theaters to you? He trusted you that much?"

"We're—engaged to be married," Lightweight whispered.

Fitz said: "Uh, uh, I see," in a tone that was still puzzled.

Tracy's eyes widened with surprise. This was something he

had been utterly unaware of in spite of the trouble he had gone to keep a watchful eye on the girl. He had seen Wortman plenty of times in the last month. Ned and Lightweight had certainly put one over on him! Jerry's patent-leather foot pressed the gas pedal and the car shot away.

"Where are the transfer papers Ned signed over to you?" he asked as the automobile streaked downtown through the rain.

"They're in Ned's safe. In his apartment."

Fitz nodded at that. "Whoever is behind the kills may be searching the place right now!"

"Yeah," Tracy said.

At the desk of Wortman's apartment house Fitzgerald did all the talking. He showed his badge and asked for a pass key— and got it.

"Has Mr. Wortman come in since I phoned earlier this evening to ask about him?"

"No, sir. He left just before dinner and he hasn't returned."

"Any visitors for him? Anybody stop by to ask if he was home?"

"No, sir. Not a soul."

"Okey."

The clerk's eyes stared at the queerly assorted group. Eddie had stirred, grunted weakly and slid out of the Chinaman's embrace. He was on his feet now, pretty rocky, the Chinaman's arm supporting him.

"I'm all right," he whispered faintly to Tracy. "I—I kin take it."

"Swell, Eddie. You've got more guts than all of us. Let's go."

The elevator deposited them at the twelfth floor. Fitz, at a nod from Jerry, inserted the master key and opened the door very gently. The front of the apartment was dark, but there was a light showing above the transom of a rear door, and through the closed barrier came the indistinguishable buzz of voices. Two men, whispering quietly together.

Fitz threw the door open and Jerry followed him.

THE INSPECTOR'S GUN wavered for an instant with surprise and then stayed steady in his big hand.

"Hello, Ned," the *Daily Planet's* columnist said quietly.

Wortman and his companion had whirled about as the door was flung open. The man with Wortman was bald, heavy-set, very obviously flustered.

"Hello, Jerry," Wortman said. "Hello, Inspector—Fitzgerald, isn't it?" He sounded puzzled, yet polite. There was faint amazement in his low-toned laugh. "What is this—a raid of some sort?"

"You're supposed to be kidnaped, Ned," Jerry told him evenly.

"Oh, by gosh, right you are." He started forward and Fitz barked suddenly. "Stick, Mister! Right where you are. What's the idea of the fake alarm on a snatch?"

"No fake at all. I was grabbed by a clever rogue who calls himself Ala Dhinn. Lightweight telephoned me tonight, and told me this Ala had killed Stuart Parker in her apartment. He'd threatened to kill me if I didn't turn over to him—certain things. I was ready for trouble and I got away. I let the kidnap alarm go through to scare off that damned swami."

"Was that why you sneaked into your apartment by the back stairs—to dodge this Ala?"

"Of course." He laughed shakily. "Wouldn't *you?*"

"Were those certain things that Ala was after, the deeds to your chain of theaters?" Tracy asked.

"Sure…. Say, how in the world did you know that, Jerry?"

"In!" Jerry called quietly and Lightweight walked slowly through the doorway.

Wortman's face lighted with instant relief. "Darling! Thank God you've surrendered! I told you it was foolish to run away. Gentlemen, this is my fiancée. She'll tell you that for weeks I've been threatened with death. She'll confirm my statement that I signed over all my properties to her in an effort to protect myself against racketeers."

"How about showing us those papers?" Fitz said heavily.

"Why not?"

He walked to a safe in the corner, twirled the knob and produced a sheaf of legal transfers. They were, as he had said, indisputable evidence that Lightweight was sole owner of his chain of theaters.

The baldheaded little man beside Wortman continued to say nothing, Tracy smiled at him suddenly.

"You're name is Merkert, isn't it? John J. Merkert?"

"That's right."

"You're a lawyer—Ned's lawyer?"

"Yes."

"You're also the lawyer—" Tracy's voice hardened, "—for the estate of the late Sam Parker, and the very, very recently deceased Stuart Parker?"

"Why—why—what do you mean?" Merkert backed up a step, his face suddenly frightened.

"I'm talking about a very clever rat we both know. The rat killed Sol Davis. He killed Sam Parker. And tonight, he finished up with Stuart Parker. Which gives the rat Davis' holdings, and Parker's holdings—together with his own…."

His glance jerked grimly from the lawyer to the other man. "Where's the *other* safe, Wortman?"

"Eh?" Wortman took a step forward and recoiled before the gun in Fitzgerald's hand. "Jerry! Have you gone mad? Are you accusing me of conspiracy—of murder?"

"You're damned right. You kidded Morello into playing the swami act for you. You kidded Lightweight into believing and trusting you. But you can't kid me...." His cold whisper got louder: "In, Eddie!"

The little street Arab came in. His eyes were bright with excitement, but he cringed as he saw Wortman glaring at him.

"Listen, Eddie," Tracy said to him gently. "You remember the tip you gave me when you opened the car door for me tonight in front of the *Garfield Theatre?*"

"Sure." Eddie's voice was thin, reedy. "I told you I seen Lightweight and the swummy together in the swummy's car."

"Right. And you started to tell me something else. You said: *And that ain't all. I—*' Then there was an interruption, and when I looked around you were gone. Why did you scram? Were you scared?"

"I'll say!" He pointed at Wortman. "I was scared o' that guy."

"Why?" Tracy's voice was soft, encouraging.

"Because he's the guy I was gonna tip yuh about. As soon as the swummy and the dame drives off in the car, up comes this guy with another feller. The other feller is pretty drunk. He don't wanta go in the hotel. But Wortman says Lightweight's expectin' 'em. I knew that was queer because Lightweight wasn't upstairs. She was in the car with the swummy. And the quick way Wortman forces this drunk down the hotel alley and in a side door looked sorta dirty to me."

"Did you recognize the drunk with Wortman?"

"Sure. He was Stuart Parker. That's what I started to tell yuh when—"

There was a stab of flame. Wortman had whipped a gun from a shoulder-holster. He fired at Tracy. But the columnist had seen the quick glint in his eye that preceded the gesture, and had leaped nimbly aside. The bullet ploughed into the wall.

Fitz was close enough to nail Wortman without a shot. His gun butt hit the producer's skull with a sound that seemed almost gentle; but Wortman dropped with a meaty thud and Fitz clipped steel cuffs on him with neither haste nor excitement.

Merkert, the lawyer, gave a shrill scream. His pudgy arms were stiffly in the air above his head. "Don't shoot! I'll talk—I swear I will."

Tracy smiled. "There is another safe?" he suggested.

"Yes, yes!"

"Find it. Open it."

THE STARK SUDDENNESS of events had unnerved Merkert. He saw himself caught, convicted, faced with the grisly, legacy of the electric chair. His trembling hand ripped an oil landscape from the wall. There was a small circular safe set into the surface behind the painting. Merkert fiddled tremulously with the dial and the door swung open after three or four nerve-racking tries on his part.

The safe was crammed with real estate deeds to nearly every legitimate playhouse in Manhattan. All of Davis' holdings. All of Parker's. And all of Wortman's! He had, as Tracy suspected, fooled Lightweight into signing duplicate papers, transferring his holdings *back* to him.

"He made me sign two sets," she replied dazedly to Tracy's question. "He said it was customary."

"It was a death warrant," Jerry told her. "It was his ace in the hole. If anything went wrong, he could always point to his original transfers to you to support his persecution story and give him a smooth alibi. If his scheme had worked—and it would have worked without discovery, if Eddie hadn't stopped me at the door of the theater—he'd have framed you and Morello for his last two kills and destroyed the papers. He didn't really need those others tucked away in the wall safe. Yours were not recorded. But Wortman was such a damned sure-thing crook that he couldn't help coppering his bet. And that gave me the handle to scare him into gunplay."

Tracy patted the shaking shoulders of Lightweight.

"Tell me," he said gently, "did you actually *see* the fake swami when he was holding the gun on my back in your room?"

"I saw only the gun in the fold of the curtain. I—thought—"

"It was Wortman. After he killed Parker he drove to my penthouse and picked me up to help his alibi. Had the gall to drive me to the theater. A smart guy."

"Why did he use the swami for a front?" Fitzgerald asked.

"Because young Parker was a nut on Oriental cults. I told you so right at the start. Wortman knew it; that's why he cut in the swami. He planted Nick and the other gunman to keep an eye on Ala. If you'll remember, Sol Davis was garroted with an Oriental cord. That was the first plant to frame the swami. Parker's death was a natural follow-up. The police, finding out Parker's interest in Oriental cults, would connect the two murders. After Wortman had pinned the killings on the swami, he would have bumped him and Lightweight and buried 'em in some cellar. Wortman would be in the clear—with most of the important theaters in Manhattan in his pocket."

Lightweight didn't say anything, but there was something in her level glance that made Jerry think of a grand old actor in Arizona to whom he had made a promise.

He did something very unusual for him. The girl flushed as he released her, tried to cover the tears in her eyes with a shaky smile.

"Guys have gotten married for less than that, boy friend," she faltered.

"Not me. I'm too homely to make the grade."

She laughed; but there was something in Lightweight's laughter that was faintly wistful.

Little Guy

Jerry Tracy rides a murder wave

THE FLOOR SHOW was very good and Jerry Tracy was watching it with more than usual attention, because the doll-like girl in the leopard-skin number was a square-shooting little kid in hard luck whom he had placed in the show over the angry objections of Morrie Green. She was getting more than a lot of applause and that pleased Jerry. It meant that the kid had made good in spite of a mean and grafting dance director. It meant that the next time Tracy came around to place a hoofer, Morrie Green would be afraid to complain to Wertheim about wise Broadway "buttinskis" who were trying to queer the show by shoving in phoney talent on him for personal reasons.

Wertheim himself was watching the number with a broad grin. Morrie Green was grinning, too, all over his mean little face. In the morning, Tracy knew, the dance director would be telling everyone on Broadway how he had personally discovered this little blond bombshell with the twinkling toes.

A waiter bent over the table where Jerry Tracy sat drinking alone. Jerry frowned and set down his big, globular snifter of Napoleon brandy.

"Who?"

The waiter repeated the name.

"Huh? I'll be darned. Sure thing! Tell him to come on in."

He grinned with quick pleasure as he saw the enormous, fat figure of Phil Halliday away off in the shadow that surrounded the outer rim of tables. He liked Phil as well as any man he knew. A swell, good-natured guy with a mountainous stomach and a deep, jolly laugh. Phil had been down in Florida with his sleek, Diesel-powered ketch. Jerry had been on the boat plenty of times at City Island and zippy, cockeyed times they had been, too.

Suddenly the smile went out of Tracy's eyes. Good God, he thought, is that Phil? The man looked sick, shrunken. And he wasn't in evening clothes either, which was unlike Phil. He came forward through the narrow aisle that separated the tables and his rumpled sack suit hung on him like wet-wash on a clothes-line. People in evening dress glanced up curiously. A few nodded, as people will to any wealthy man; and to the nodders Phil Halliday gave a fixed, glassy smile.

He ploughed straight to Tracy's table and the two men clasped hands. Phil's palm was moist, sweaty. He dropped heavily into a chair.

"God, Jerry, it's good to see you. I've been chasing you all over this infernal town tonight. Missed you at Billy's Tavern. Tried a dozen other places. You get around fast, don't you?"

"I thought you were still in Florida."

"Got back this morning." He brushed the small talk aside with a nervous gesture. "Listen, Jerry, I've got to talk to you."

"Anything wrong?"

"God, yes. I'm up against something that's taken the guts right out of me." He smiled feebly. "That's something in a man of my size, eh?"

"Bourbon," Jerry told the hovering waiter. "The best bonded stuff you've got in the house. Make it a double jolt."

He studied his friend sharply. Phil Halliday was staring at

the table-cloth with a fixed, smiling grimace. His heavy face was tanned a deep brown; that, Jerry knew, came from lazy, nude hours spent tarpon fishing on the deck of the ketch under the blazing Florida sun. But the gray pallor under the tan, the tremble of his thick fingers on the table-cloth were utterly unlike him.

Phil was not the ordinary fat man; he had an enormous frame, most of it hard beef. Still in his early forties, he could outwork and outplay men half his age and his weight. A good-natured, steam-roller of a man, ordinarily without a nerve in his big barn-door body. But not now....

Tracy said quietly, "It's not woman trouble. I know you well enough for that. And I can't think of anybody who'd have a gun in pickle for you."

Halliday's eyes lifted with a jerk. "Jerry, it's fantastic, it's—it's idiotic. Someone is trying to kill me by slowly driving me mad. I'm convinced that's the ultimate object of this hellish series of—accidents."

"Accidents?"

"If you want to call them that. At first, I wasn't sure. After the cat and the dog episode, I began to worry. Then when my captain—you know Nick Devlin—after he fell twenty feet from a dry-dock platform and damned near broke his neck, I—"

"What the hell are you talking about?" Jerry asked in a swift undertone.

He was leaning forward, tense, interested, when the liquor came. He shoved the waiter a bill and got rid of him. Halliday downed the Bourbon with a long gulp. A faint patch of red came into his cheeks.

"First the dog and then the cat," Tracy said. "You mean Scotty and The Barnacle?"

"Yes."

"An accident?"

"Killed." Halliday said. "I found the dog with his head crushed in on the pier at Biscayne Bay. He'd apparently been playing with the rope of an insecurely placed anchor and the anchor had fallen and smashed his skull in."

"Mmm.... What about Barney?"

"Barney was drowned. Whoever killed him was aware of the cat's habit of sleeping, curled up under one of the thwarts in the dinghy. The dinghy lost its plug during a rainy, stormy night and Barney drowned."

"But why?" Tracy asked, his lean face alert. "What the devil's the sense—"

"Let's get out of this damn place," Halliday cut in abruptly. "My car's outside at the curb. I want to ask you a favor." His eyes burned. "Will you?"

"Sure thing, Phil. You ought to know that."

They skirted the dance floor where couples were now whirling to the dizzy hotcha of Dink Morgan's orchestra, and Tracy grabbed his Chesterfield and his derby from a dark, beautiful Jewess made up as a Russian gypsy. Halliday wrapped himself in a belted raincoat and slapped on a fuzzy fedora. His big body made a joke of tailors' irons. Jerry Tracy had once described him in his *Daily Planet* column as "a large bag of clothes, fresh from his tailor."

There was a long sedan at the curb and Halliday squeezed in behind the wheel and stepped on the starter.

"Are we going places, Phil? I thought we came out to talk."

Halliday's face turned. "I want you to drive out to my house in Scarsdale. Will you?"

"Why, sure, Phil. If you think—"

"I think it's damned urgent or I wouldn't ask you. I'm worried sick about Cora. I'm afraid she—"

"Cora?"

"I'm married again, Jerry. I've kept it quiet."

Tracy whistled, gave Halliday a surprised stare. "I'll say you've kept it quiet. Congratulations! Must have been pretty sudden. Do I know her?"

"No. She's a Florida girl. A—bit younger than I am." His voice thickened. "One of the sweetest, grandest women that ever walked. Jerry, I—I don't want to slop over, but I can tell you that if ever a man—" His knuckles on the steering wheel whitened. "I gave her a gun before I left the house. I made her lock every door and window. I'm afraid she may be the next to be—harmed."

Tracy said sharply, "I've never seen you crack up like this before. Snap out of it, keed!"

"Will you drive out with me and talk this thing over with both of us?"

"Mmm.…Just accidents, eh?"

"Just accidents. Scotty—Barney—Nick Devlin, the captain of my boat. The thing keeps creeping closer and closer. I tell you, when it attacked Molly Clarkson—"

"Wait a minute!" Tracy said. "You mean your secretary—the manager of your brokerage office downtown?"

"Yes."

"I didn't know she was in Florida."

"She wasn't. She had a—mishap right here in New York today."

"You mean the accidents jumped from Florida to New York as soon as you came North?"

"Exactly," Halliday said.

"Have you said anything to the cops?"

"What the hell is there to say, Jerry?"

"Not much, I guess. O.K., Phil, let's shove off for Scarsdale!"

PHIL'S LONG SEDAN shot away from the curb. A heavy hand reached tremulously across and vised for an instant on the thin arm of the *Daily Planet's* little columnist. "I knew I could depend on you."

"Nuts. I'm a sucker for puzzles, that's all." Tracy was silent for an instant, then his gloved fingers tightened into a fist and punched Halliday gently in the ribs. "I'm also a damned liar," he added. "I'm not forgetting a certain favor you did for me once or the chance you took when you did."

The sedan was boring swiftly along the Concourse before Tracy asked any more questions.

"Let me get the facts straight," he said finally. "First Scotty, the dog, got hit with an anchor. Then the cat, Barney, drowned. Then Nick Devlin, the captain of your boat, had his accident. He was third in the series?"

"That's right."

"Did Devlin think it was an attempt at murder?"

"He doesn't know. The boat was laid up temporarily in dry dock at the time. He'd had a few drinks and he can't stand many. He's not sure whether he was shoved off the platform or not. He thinks he was. Anyhow, he was picked up almost immediately—with a broken collar-bone and a couple of fractured ribs, and a nasty gash on his scalp. I was right on the job, suspicious as hell by that time, and you can bet I searched about pretty carefully. Not a sign of any assailant or any shred of a clue."

"No notes? Queer messages of any sort?"

"None. I thought of that, too. I figured that anyone trying to break down my nerve by such a roundabout method of intimidation must be a crank, a nut. But I've never at any time received a single gloating message."

He shivered and the racing sedan swung past a slower moving car. They were on the Bronx River Parkway now, humming smoothly along in the darkness. Halliday sent the needle of the speedometer climbing steadily.

"Tell me about your secretary," Tracy said. "Miss Clarkson was the fourth victim?"

"Yes."

"When? And how?"

"This afternoon. Not more than three hours after I had called up my brokerage office to tell her that I'd come unexpectedly back to New York. She was pushed off the subway station on her way home. Went headlong to the tracks. Train coming into the station damned near ran over her. Motorman threw on his brakes and stopped barely twenty feet away. There was quite a mob on the station and she said she thought it was an accident. She called me up at my home in Scarsdale and—and joked about it." Phil Halliday's big body shuddered. "She said I shouldn't have cut short my vacation in Florida, that I was hard luck."

"Did she know about these other queer happenings?" Tracy shot at him.

"Of course not. How the hell could she? She sent me a daily

letter about office affairs and wires when they were necessary, but I certainly don't discuss my personal affairs with her, if that's what you mean."

"Did she know that you were married again?"

The sedan curved from the Parkway and hummed along a dark, tree-bordered road that lay cold under the frosty stars.

"No," Halliday said. "Miss Clarkson has no knowledge whatever of my recent marriage in Florida, or for that matter, of the existence of Cora."

"By the way, what is your wife's maiden name?"

"Cora Barfield." He turned the wheel suddenly and drove into a chipped-stone driveway. "Here we are now—and thank God, there's Cora! I've been scared every second I've been away."

A woman was standing framed in the yellow light of the opened door of the house. The strong light silhouetted her figure and face, made it impossible for Tracy to see what she looked like. Halliday slowed the car as a clear, rather sweet voice called out vibrantly: "Is that you, Phil? Is everything all right?"

"Yes, dear. Go indoors; you'll catch cold."

"Did Mr. Tracy come with you?"

"Yes. We'll both be right in as soon as I put the car up."

The woman's voice seemed to catch with a kind of clipped sob. "Thank God!" Jerry heard her whisper. He watched her as she turned away. She seemed to be tall, graceful, with a pale, lovely face under a heavy swirl of dark hair. The car rolled onward toward the garage.

"I like her voice," Tracy said quietly.

"I love her, Jerry," Halliday whispered. "More than I've ever known it was possible to love a woman." He had stepped out of the car. His huge, bulking figure in the doorway of the garage was suddenly touched with dignity. "We're going to have a child. We—we weren't certain until just before we left Florida."

"That's nice. That'll be good for you, Phil. I'm damned glad to hear of it. You always did want a kid."

"Yes. I—" His hand clutched the sleeve of the columnist. Tracy winced; Phil's big fingers bit like steel pliers. "It's not myself I'm frightened about, Jerry. They can kill me—if they can—and be damned to them. But they won't; don't you see?"

"Come on, Phil. We'll talk the whole thing over with your wife."

"Wait! I've got to make you see what this means to me. Can you see how they've been striking deliberately closer and closer to the few things I really love in this world? My dog and my cat—then Devlin, my captain, as grand a little man as ever walked. And now, by God, Miss Clarkson! My secretary—as loyal and faithful as they come. I think enough of her to cut her in for a sizable share of my money when and if I kick off.

"The thought that sent me scouring the town for you tonight is—who's next? Can't you see that it can be no one but Cora? If I only knew what was back of it all—what they want—"

"Who do you mean by 'they,' Phil?"

"I don't know."

Tracy shoved a hand through the big man's dangling arm. "Let's go inside. I've got a hunch on this thing already."

He had, of course, nothing of the kind; it was merely a device to snap Phil out of his talkative spree and get him into the house. Jerry had seen enough terrified people in his career to know that fear sometimes made people drunkenly garrulous, sent even normally tight-lipped men off on a wordy jag of repetition and reiteration.

They crunched up the stone pathway toward the house. It was a two-story stone structure, built in the Norman style, covered with dark ivy, very lovely under the silver of an almost circular moon.

CORA WAS WAITING in the chilly doorway, her face white. Phil Halliday swept his wife into a taut, murmuring embrace. Tracy, a cynical expert in such matters, was convinced instantly that both these frightened people loved each other. He followed them into the living-room and Tracy noticed that Halliday locked the door.

He introduced the *Daily Planet's* columnist to his wife with a blurred smile. "Jerry Tracy, dear. A friend when you need him. That's why he's here."

She held out her hand and Jerry held it for an instant. It was cold as ice, but very steady. The columnist found himself liking this Cora Barfield who had married his good friend, Phil. Very lovely. A soft, pleasant voice, with just the barest slur of the South in it. Clear, dark eyes, very bright, and dark hair, thick and vital looking.

The only jarring note was her mouth; it was tight, small, thin-lipped; he couldn't decide offhand whether it was the type of cruel little rosebud that went with a quick, selfish temper, or whether it was an added note of determination to match her lovely dark eyes. At all events, he was certain at once that Phil's wife was neither a child nor a clinging vine.

He glanced about him. "No servants, Phil?"

"Just us two. I've been afraid to—"

"Naturally. You want my advice?"

"Of course," Cora said instantly.

"All right. I'm advising you both to leave this house tonight. Just in case there's anything really serious behind the facts you've already told me. I'll drive you both back to town and you can take a suite at a good first-class hotel, where you'll have a better measure of protection than in an empty house here in Scarsdale. I'd suggest the Albermarle. Agreed?"

Phil nodded. Cora said, "Yes."

Tracy asked Phil's wife a few routine questions and was answered with a sure steadiness—almost too steady, he thought, with a quick awareness of her tension. She was just as frightened as Phil, but a different kind of fright; a sort of inner desperation that stiffened her tall, slender body. He marked the swift rise and fall of her bosom under the stretched material of her moss-crepe gown.

Cora Barfield. Twenty-five. That made her exactly twenty years younger than Phil. A native Floridian. An orphan. No relatives on earth.

"None?" Tracy asked her incredulously.

She nodded instead of answering. Afraid to trust her voice, Tracy decided. His eyes and his ears told him she was lying. And not used to lying, either. Tracy let the matter drop and turned the subject to the last series of "accidents," the attempt on the life of Halliday's secretary.

"How did the woman sound when she called up, Mrs. Halliday? Was she frightened? Did she think it was an attempt at murder?"

"I don't know," Cora said. She added, quietly, "Phil took the phone call."

"I see. How about it, Phil? She kidded you about being a hoodoo, didn't she?"

"Miss Clarkson was inclined to think it was pure accident," Phil Halliday nodded slowly. "Although afterwards, when Cora got home and we talked it over—"

"Oh, you weren't home at the time?" Jerry asked Mrs. Halliday.

Her hesitation was like the flirt of a bird's wing, so hastily did she cover it with her smile and her soft voice. "No. I'd been shopping. I—I needed a few things to wear."

"Naturally," Tracy said. To himself he thought, "Oh, yeah? Scared to death, convinced that your husband's life and your own are in deadly danger, and off you go shopping, all by yourself? Nuts, lady; that doesn't wash."

Cora was watching the smiling little newspaper columnist with an unfathomable expression. She blinked suddenly and swayed. Her big husband sprang forward with a solicitous murmur.

"I'm all right," Cora said. "I'm a little tired. If you don't mind, I think I'll lie down until we're ready to leave."

She turned toward the small console table against the wall and picked up her handbag. Jerry, alert to small things, wondered why she wanted the bag. It looked stuffed; there was a ridge in the cloth as though a square of stiff cardboard might be jammed inside. A mounted photograph? Jerry wondered. She flushed as she saw him staring at the bag, and walked rapidly upstairs.

Phil, staring anxiously up the staircase, said gently, "Lock the door of your bedroom, dear. I'll call you when Jerry and I are ready to leave for town. And take a look at the windows, too."

They heard the door shut and the lock-click. Halliday made a brief, embarrassed gesture. "Sounds silly, all this precaution, but, frankly, I'm jumpy."

"Your wife have any enemies?"

"None."

"And you don't want the police in on this thing, you say?"

"No."

"Any special reason?"

"I just don't want 'em, that's all. What is there to tell 'em?"

"Not a damned thing," Tracy said cheerfully. "How about yourself, Phil? You're a broker, a man of affairs, independently wealthy. Any enemies?"

The clock on the mantel ticked monotonously.

"I've thought of a possible two," Phil said slowly.

"Men or women?"

"Men."

"Let's hear about them."

"Well, the first one seems a bit silly. I wouldn't have thought of him at all, except for the fact of my recent marriage. A man named David Cullop. A malicious little devil. We once had a kind of ridiculous set-to. It all dates back to the time I married my first wife, You see, Cullop and I—"

Jerry's upflung hand stopped him. "Wait!" the columnist cried. He was on tiptoe, listening with a queer rigidity.

"What the devil!" Halliday cried.

Tracy pivoted, ran swiftly toward the window, jerked the heavy curtains aside. He hadn't been mistaken! The faint sound he had heard was the slur of tires on packed gravel. He was just in time to see the red tail-light of an automobile whirling out of the driveway into the road. It was gone in a flash. A second later he heard the unmistakable sound of a motor accelerating to racing speed down the road.

Halliday's face, behind Tracy's hunched shoulder, was white. "My car!" he gasped. "It's gone. Someone has stolen it!"

"Quick!" Tracy cried. "Upstairs! The bedroom!"

Fast as the little columnist was, Phil's pounding feet left him behind. Phil was rattling the knob of the locked door as Tracy reached the top of the stairs.

"Cora! Are you all right? Cora!"

No answer. He shouted, pounded on the panel with his fist. But there was no reply.

HALLIDAY WHIRLED FRANTICALLY toward the stairs but Jerry's hand stopped him.

"No sense in that, Phil. The car's gone. Break down the door!"

Halliday sent his big body plunging against the frail wood. It shivered and groaned as he bounced off the barrier.

"Any way she could have been taken out the window?" Jerry shot at him.

"Yes. There's a shed roof right under—"

This time the lock snapped and the door burst inward with a rending crash. Halliday fell flat on his face and Tracy leaped over his prostrate body. The bedroom window was wide open, the curtains fluttering in the icy draught. There was no trace of Cora Halliday.

Tracy stuck his head briefly out the window and jerked it back again. He dashed about the room like an excited little terrier, peering, searching.

"What are you looking for?" Phil asked him thickly. He seemed dazed, utterly bereft of motion in the center of the room.

The handbag that Cora had brought upstairs with her was gone. Had she really been kidnaped, Tracy wondered grimly, or had she…. He motioned to Halliday and the two men raced downstairs and out to the garage. The doors were wide open. Jerry remembered now that Phil hadn't locked the garage when they had driven in. They had been in too much of a hurry. But Phil had locked the ignition. Jerry remembered that distinctly.

The floor of the garage was painted white, with a soft, flaky substance like whitewash. There were footprints visible in the narrow space alongside the wall where two people had squeezed in past the parked car. Two! The mark of a woman's high-heeled slippers and the broader imprints of a man's shoes. A little man. Tracy laid his shoe over one of the marks. It was almost an exact fit.

"My God," Halliday moaned. "Someone kidnaped her. Took her out the bedroom window, lowered her from the shed roof, forced her into the car—"

"How? The car was locked. You've got the ignition key, haven't you?"

"Cora had a duplicate key in her handbag. Whoever meant to kill her found it in her bag and decided to kidnap her instead."

Jerry shook his head. "Your wife walked," he asserted in a level voice. "There's the marks of her feet, right alongside the man's. Could she have gone willingly, do you think?"

"You're crazy," Halliday shouted. "Look there—what's that?"

He pointed with a shaking finger and Tracy got down on his haunches and studied the dark drops on the concrete floor. He touched one of the smears with a finger-tip and his lips tightened. It wasn't oil as he had surmised at the first glance, but blood. Fresh, smeary blood that made his finger-tip ruddy.

The sight of the bright, sinister stain left Tracy completely fuddled for a moment. His whole cocksure judgment of the thing underwent a rapid change. Cora had gone upstairs, frightened to death at his searching questions. She had deliberately taken with her the handbag containing the duplicate ignition key, but she hadn't meant to go away in the car. Someone had slugged her. A little man with footprints no bigger than Tracy's. Not a cunning runaway by a Southern girl with dark, resolute eyes, but an assault and a kidnap job.

"O.K.," Jerry said. "Back to the house. I want to make a phone call."

"We've got to get a car right away. We've got to try and follow—"

"Nuts," Tracy rejoined harshly. "It's going to take brains to find your wife, Phil; not gasoline. First thing is to notify the police."

"No!" Halliday said. His jaw was squared, grim.

"Why not?" Tracy stared at him.

"No cops," Halliday growled.

They entered the back door of the house and Tracy strode through to the living-room. He studied the big man's drawn face. Was Halliday merely in a craze of fear or was there some deeper reason behind his aversion for a police investigation? Calmly, the little columnist decided to find out.

He picked up the telephone instrument, his finger carefully holding the bar down behind the shield of his half-turned body.

"Let me have police headquarters, please."

He was watching Halliday out of the corner of his eye, but he was unprepared for the grim, bearlike rush of his friend. A fist swung glancingly off Tracy's jaw, a furious hand snatched the instrument from him and banged it down on its cradle.

"Damn you!" Halliday said thickly.

He wrestled fiercely with the dodging columnist, his face red with wrath. Jerry slipped nimbly out of his clutch. For a second or two the two men confronted each other warily, like enemies.

"What kind of a crooked set-up are you letting me in on?" Tracy said coldly. "You've lied to me. You've both lied to me."

"Listen, Jerry—"

"The hell with you. I'm quitting right now. I'm out." Thoroughly angry, he walked over toward where he had left his hat and overcoat. A hand spun around and he threw up a defensive forearm. But Phil was no longer threatening him. There were tears in the man's blinking eyes. He was trying to smile and making a botch of it.

"Jerry, I'm sorry. Don't let me down, please... For God's sake—we're *friends!*" He laid a trembling hand on the columnist's shoulder. "Stick with me, will you?"

"But no cops, eh?"

"Call 'em in, if you insist. But I'm asking you not to."

There was a long silence. "O.K.," Tracy said finally. His gnome-like face was creased in a pinched grimace. "I've been in screwier messes than this for guys who haven't half the pull on me that you have, Phil. The cops are out for the present. Are you willing to string along with my judgment?"

"I'll do anything you say, Jerry. Anything!"

"All right. I'm gonna call up the Scarsdale Station and order a taxi. You're going back to town with me as soon as you pack a few things in a bag. I want you to do what I asked you and your wife to do when I first got here. I want you to register at a good hotel and stay there under cover, until you get orders from me."

"I don't give a damn about myself," Halliday muttered. "Find my wife and get her back safely."

"Go pack your bag. We're wasting time."

Halliday halted irresolutely. "Don't you think we ought to examine Cora's room a bit more carefully?"

"The answer we're looking for," Tracy told him steadily, "is not in this house, Phil."

JERRY UNHOOKED THE phone and called the Scarsdale Station. By the time he had the number from Information and had hired a cab, Halliday was descending the staircase, a suit-case in his big, bronzed hand.

"You mentioned two men you thought might be enemies of yours," Tracy reminded him. "One of 'em was a man named David Cullop, you said, but you don't think of him seriously in the role of criminal or murderer?"

"That's right. The last time I saw Cullop was fifteen years ago. Our quarrel then was idiotic, childish, rather than—"

"Killing a dog and a cat is childish, too," Tracy said. "There's a pettiness about it that suggests your malicious little friend, Cullop. Or perhaps—" His eyes glinted for an instant and he shut his mouth suddenly.

"Or what, Jerry?"

"Nothing. Who's the other guy?"

"His name is Wilbur Genung. Of the two I'd say he's a more likely bet. He hates my guts. If he could wipe me out without danger to himself I'm sure that he'd try. He's a colder proposition than Cullop."

"What did Cullop do?"

Phil Halliday's broad face creased into a grim smile. "He tried to brain me with a Chinese battle ax. It was emotion with poor Cullop; not the greed and cold nastiness of Genung. I knocked him stiffer than a herring on the floor of his apartment. The poor little guy was half mad with grief. He didn't really know what he was doing."

"And this other guy—Genung? A big, tall guy? With broad shoulders?"

"No. A little fella about your size, Jerry. A shrimp." Halliday's moon face flushed as Jerry grinned; then he gasped.

"Oh—I see what you're getting at. You mean that either Cullop or Genung might conceivably have left that small man's footprint in the garage."

"Well?" Jerry said. "Could they?"

Halliday's mouth tightened. "Yes," he said. "Either of them."

There was a sudden, blasting ring at the front door that made Halliday jump nervously. Tracy calmly picked up his overcoat and slid it over his evening clothes. "That's our taxi. Let's go."

He clicked out the lights in the living-room that Halliday had forgotten and made sure that the front door was securely locked.

Tracy's eyes sparkled as the cab got swiftly under way in the chilly darkness. His hand dropped reassuringly on his friend's. "I've got a hunch about this disappearance of your wife, Phil. That's why I'm not trying to jump on a horse and gallop in all directions. You can take my word for it, every snatch job that was ever pulled fits into a pretty general picture. This one doesn't. It's way out of focus. A girl doesn't bother taking her handbag under circumstances the blood on the garage floor indicate." They swerved together in the corner of the seat as the speeding taxi swung into the smooth blackness of the Bronx River Parkway.

"Huh?" Halliday whispered. "Blood—handbag? What in God's name are you jabbering about?"

"I mean that your wife is either dead right now—hold on, Phil! I give you my honest word, I don't think she is dead. If she isn't, then there hasn't been any kidnaping at all. Unless you might call it a partial kidnaping, in which event, I think I've got a vague glimmering of something that makes sense."

Halliday groaned. "Man, you sound crazy mad!"

"Maybe. Tell me why you suspect the emotional and childish Mr. Cullop and the much more dangerous Mr. Genung."

The big man steadied. He gritted his teeth and gave Tracy the facts.

DAVID CULLOP'S ENMITY dated back to Phil's first marriage. He and Halliday had been rivals. Phil had won. Cullop took his disappointment rather badly. Phil, who was big and good natured and hated the thought of unpleasantness, had gone to see Cullop in an effort to smooth things over and keep the friendship of the man. Cullop had acted like a maniac. With tears streaming down his face he had accused Halliday of double-crossing him by spreading a pack of lies. With a scream of rage he had ripped a decorative Chinese battle-ax from the wall and had attempted to brain the startled Phil. Phil ducked the murderous blow and dropped the little man cold with a hard left to the jaw.

"Ever seen him since?" Tracy asked.

"Not once. That was fifteen years ago." Halliday laughed

harshly. "A nasty little devil. He told me he'd get me sooner or later, that he'd wring my heart the way his had been wrung. Maybe that's why I can't get him out of my mind. That meticulous woman-like method of attacking everything that's near and dear to me sounds exactly like Dave Cullop. He's still in New York. Has an importing business down in Water Street somewhere. I'd like to know whether he's been in Florida during the last few weeks."

"So would I," Tracy murmured. "How about the other guy?"

Halliday told him. Wilbur Genung. A little man like Cullop. But a tougher breed. A hard-bitten realist, interested only in money and the things that money bought. Originally a friend of Halliday's. A hard and desperate market plunger. He had made tremendous profits in the boom years, basing his speculative plunges on the advice of Phil, who was his broker. When the bottom fell out of stocks, Genung was cleaned to the lining of his socks. He blamed Halliday. Called him a thief. Accused him of coppering his own bets at the expense of his clients. Made no threats but walked quietly into Phil's office one afternoon and tried to shoot Phil to death. Phil kicked him in the stomach and wrested the gun from him. There was no publicity because Phil refused to prosecute. Genung hobbled out, looking sick and white.

The taxi hummed swiftly along the smooth Parkway. There was little traffic and the driver kept stepping up his speed.

"Ever seen Genung since?" Tracy asked.

"Plenty of times. Never exchanged a word, though. Every time we've met since then, Genung always stops short, grins, and passes on. Cullop is a babe alongside of *that* specimen."

"Is he still broke?"

"Lord, no! He's in the money again. His kind always is. As rich now as he ever was. He's one guy that can make me shiver." Halliday's huge shoulders twitched. "I keep remembering what he told me when he shuffled out of my office, all bent over and cringing with pain from the kick in the belly I handed him."

"What did he say?"

"He said," Halliday muttered, "that he wanted to apologize for coming after me with a gun. Did you ever hear a man curse so that it sounds like he's praying? Well, that was Genung, as he swayed there in the doorway of my office, all bent over, holding his belly. He said, 'We're both long livers, Phil. There'll be plenty of time for me later on. The next time I won't use a gun. I'll use brains.'"

"That makes two little guys with feminine habits of thought," Tracy said slowly. "It'll be interesting to check up on Mr. Genung's recent travel notes, if any. What line is he in?"

"No business except the market trends. He lives somewhere on Central Park West. You can find his address in the directory, if that's what you mean."

Tracy gave him a sudden glance. "Ever been bothered particularly before you married Cora?"

"No."

"Was Cora ever bothered before she married you?"

"No."

"No acquaintances?" Jerry persisted. "No relatives?"

"You heard what she told you tonight," Phil said stiffly. "She's alone in the world. An orphan."

"I forgot," Jerry said. His eyes narrowed as he thought of Cora Halliday and her handbag. He remembered the ridge against the taut cloth. The more he thought of it, the more he was convinced that the ridge came from a mounted photograph crammed into the bag. What else—unless she made a hobby of carrying around calendars? And why should she hide a photograph from her husband's knowledge? Had her "shopping" expedition been an effort to locate someone she feared—or loved? And why had she taken the bag upstairs with her? She wanted that bag either for the key to the car or to hide a photograph that she didn't wish her husband to see. Tracy remembered Cora's hard little rosebud mouth and he decided not to get too excited over Cullop and Genung unless he could prove that either or both had recently been in Florida.

He left Phil at the very swanky desk of the Albermarle Hotel.

"Stay here as if you were glued," Jerry told him in a low voice. "I'll call you tomorrow morning. Keep your chin up."

He shook hands and grabbed a cab home. He rode straight up to the dizzy level of his expensive penthouse and went quietly to bed. There wasn't a damned thing he could do at this hour of the night; and like most small men he liked to conserve his nervous energies by getting as much sleep as he could. He'd been whirling like a busy little comet ever since noon and he was dead tired. Five minutes after he slid naked between the sheets he was completely asleep.

JERRY TRACY ROSE earlier than usual the next morning and dawdled through a long, heavy breakfast; after which he got dynamically busy. He called Halliday at the Albermarle ostensibly to report a vague overnight progress in his search for Cora, but in reality to make sure that Phil was still safely in his hotel room and not ranging the streets in an aimless hunt for his vanished wife. He repeated his warning to the big man to continue to lie low and he promised to call him back later in the day.

He located the address of David Cullop's importing firm in the directory and at five minutes past nine he called up and asked for Cullop's secretary.

"This is Mr. Tracy," he said blandly. "An old friend of Mr. Cullop. Has he returned from his trip yet?"

"Not yet, sir," the girl's voice replied.

Jerry's heart leaped. "I'm very anxious to get in touch with him. Do you happen to have his Florida address?"

"Florida?" The voice sounded puzzled. "You must be mistaken. Mr. Cullop is in Canada. He left over two weeks ago on a shooting trip."

Tracy laughed as though at a great joke. "Oh, did Dave change his mind? I told him he would! Do you happen to have his Canadian address?"

"Just a minute.... It's at Moose Gap, Ontario. Care of Seeger's Camp."

"Thank you." Tracy pronged the receiver, lifted it and called Western Union. He dictated a carefully worded telegram to Seeger's Camp and again pronged and lifted the busy phone. This time he called the Biddle Detective Agency and to his delight got Fred Biddie himself on the wire.

"I want a little quiet sleuth work, Fred," he said. "Put the best man you've got on the job. The name of the party is Wilbur Genung. He lives at 10425 Central Park West. I want to find out if he's been out of town during the last two or three weeks—and if so, when he returned. Don't go near Genung himself. Get all the details you can without letting him know he's the object of surveillance."

"Right. How will I get in touch with you?"

"I'll call you back myself later on."

Five minutes later Jerry Tracy was in a taxicab, riding leisurely down to Broad Street. He went straight to the brokerage office of Phil Halliday. Tracy gave the switchboard girl his name and asked for Miss Clarkson. A moment later the door of an inner office opened and Halliday's secretary emerged with a friendly, questioning smile.

"Mr. Tracy? I'm afraid you won't find Mr. Halliday here today. As a matter of fact, he's been away since—"

"It's you I wished to see, Miss Clarkson."

"Me?" She looked briefly puzzled and then laughed. "You're not trying to sell me insurance, I hope?"

She was, Tracy thought, one of the most unassumingly attractive women he had ever met. Doubly pretty because of the contrast between her young, unlined face and her frosty gray hair. Tracy's admiring guess was that she wasn't a day over thirty. There was a large square of adhesive tape on her forehead and she flushed as she saw Tracy looking at it.

"I fell off a subway platform yesterday," she said with a faint shudder. "Perhaps that's why my mind is on insurance. What was it you wished to see me about?"

Tracy lowered his voice. "I'm a private detective, Miss Clarkson. Mr. Halliday hired me to investigate your accident. He doesn't think it was an accident. He hired me after you called his home at Scarsdale to report what had happened to you. Suppose we go into your private office."

"Why—yes. Come in."

She seemed suddenly ill at ease. The smile left her lips as Tracy closed the door behind them. "You frighten me. Does

Mr. Halliday think that someone *pushed* me off that station?"

"Where did it happen?"

"The Fulton Street platform."

"I think," Tracy said slowly, "that you were meant to be killed, Miss Clarkson."

"But why? In heaven's name why?" The terror in her eyes was growing. "Who could possibly want to harm me?"

Tracy picked up a pencil, played with it for a moment. "You see, a peculiar series of accidents have been happening to Mr. Halliday down in Florida. He returned to New York yesterday morning. And the moment he gets back—the accidents begin up here."

"But, why me?" she whispered. Tracy was amazed at the swift manner in which her composure had fled. There was horror in her eyes, but it was an inward horror as though she were contemplating a sudden sickening idea.

"Did Halliday mention to you over the wire yesterday anything that happened in Florida?"

"No. He—joked. Said I must have got dizzy from drinking too many co—cocktails."

"His dog died first. Then his cat. Then the captain of his boat narrowly escaped death. And the very day he returns to New York, you miss a tragic accident by pure luck. In other words, everyone that Mr. Halliday depends on, is fond of..." Tracy's voice got careless. "And now his wife has disappeared."

"What!" The horror ebbed from Miss Clarkson's eyes, leaving her dully incredulous. "It *wasn't* she, then! It must have been the brother!"

Tracy's lean hand vised instantly on Miss Clarkson's wrist. "What are you talking about? Whose brother?"

"Mrs. Halliday's," she gasped. "I—I suspected it was she who pushed me from the platform. I was afraid to say anything."

"You knew then that Halliday was married again?"

"Yes."

"That's funny. He told me he hadn't mentioned his marriage to you at all."

"He didn't."

"Then how the devil—" Tracy began.

"She was here yesterday. In this office. Showed me a photograph of her brother. Threatened me with—with harm if I breathed a single word to Mr. Halliday of her visit."

Tracy sighed. It was tough on Phil, but he'd suspected something like this right from the start. He took out a cigarette, lit it, inhaled deeply. "Tell me about her," he said.

THE VISITOR WAS Cora, all right. Miss Clarkson described the dark-eyed Southern gal to a T. She had come in calmly, quietly, and identified herself to Halliday's flustered secretary in the privacy of the inner office. Had even brought her marriage certificate with her to prove her identity, and a photograph in her handbag of a man that she said was her brother.

"What did he look like?" Tracy asked.

"Well, it was a small picture; a photo mounted on cardboard. A sandy-haired man, rather young, with a long, straight nose and rather heavy blond eyebrows. Not too tall, about your size—"

"By God, another *little* man," Tracy growled. "That makes three of 'em!"

"What?"

"Don't mind me. Go ahead. What did Mrs. Halliday want?"

Miss Clarkson's voice was tense, very low. Cora wanted to know if her brother—Jim Barfield she called him—had been in the office recently to see Halliday. Miss Clarkson had said no. Cora's dark eyes had seemed to burn right through the flustered secretary; she had been so intense, so grim, that Miss Clarkson had become instantly afraid of her. Had Jim by any chance called at Miss Clarkson's home? Had he sent her any messages? Had she seen him anywhere?

"I finally convinced her," the gray-haired secretary told Tracy with a shudder, "that I knew nothing whatever of her mysterious brother—if that's what he was. She smiled at me then; and if ever I saw murder in a woman's eyes, I saw it in hers. She told me quite calmly that if I breathed a word, the merest hint, to Mr. Halliday of her visit to me or her conversation that she'd kill me without hesitation. She said her brother was a blackmailing crook, an ex-convict intent on breaking up their marriage if she didn't keep paying him tribute. Said she had lied to her husband and told him she was an orphan. Said that if Mr. Halliday ever found out the truth about her brother and the rest of her family, she'd know where to look and what to— to do. She took a knife out of her handbag—"

"A knife, eh?"

"Yes, sir. A small one with a pearl handle. She showed it to me for a minute, and then walked out of the office as calmly as she had come in."

"You didn't see her on the subway station later, by any chance?"

"No."

"Or her brother?"

"No. At the time I was too upset to—"

"I can well imagine," Tracy said grimly. "Thanks for your information. It will help a lot if you keep quiet about all this."

He made her repeat her description of the sandy little man with the long straight nose and the heavy, blond eyebrows. He thought about Cora's determined red lips and those small male footprints in Phil's garage all the way back to his penthouse. Cullop and Genung seemed to recede into a harmless background.

Tracy's first telephone call, however, made him swear with sharp surprise. The Biddle detective agency's report yanked Mr. Wilbur Genung right back into the screwy line-up. He had had an accident, it seemed. Had been away from home for two weeks. In the hospital with a sprained ankle.

Fred Biddle's operative, posing as a postal investigator on a lost letter follow-up, had dug the story out of the hallman of the apartment house. Had gone to the hospital and verified the fact that Genung had been there, all right. But he had been there only *two days*. His whereabouts for the rest of the fortnight were completely unknown.

The wily Mr. Genung had obviously had time to fly to Florida and back, with plenty of chance for dog-and-cat killing in between. And he had returned, according to the hallman, the day before yesterday.

He was not overly surprised when the phone rang presently and an answer arrived to the telegram he had dispatched to Canada. The message was as follows:

MR. DAVID CULLOP HAS NOT BEEN A GUEST AT
SEEGER'S CAMP THIS YEAR STOP MADE ALL PRELIM-

INARY ARRANGEMENTS AND THEN CANCELED
BERT SEEGER

Jerry Tracy bounded to his feet and slid into his overcoat. He started for the door and then hesitated. For an instant he played with the irresolute idea of taking Butch with him— Butch, his oversized, very faithful and very dumb body-guard. He decided not to.

Both these lads—Cullop and Genung—were by Halliday's own admission tough little monkeys and Jerry was not anxious to stop a Chinese battle-ax or a swift right hand to the jaw. But he was afraid that Butch might queer the whole thing by some stupid mistake and throw the whole case into the lap of the newspapers. And Phil Halliday didn't want publicity. Besides, you couldn't call copper because of a drowned cat and a smashed dog in Florida—and the rest was merely a haze of suspicion. For instance, Jerry was still a long way from believing that Cora had really been kidnaped. And a mustache could turn either Cullop or Genung into her "brother." The whole set-up smelled funny.

DAVID CULLOP WAS a little guy, no bigger than Tracy, with a vindictive lower lip that pouted unpleasantly and red-rimmed eyes. The eyes narrowed when Jerry introduced himself as a friend of Halliday's. Talking very quietly, the *Daily Planet's* columnist sketched the peculiar chain of events that had happened in Florida and New York. Cullop stared at him silently, his lower lip jutting, until Tracy got to the subject of the Chinese battle-ax and the threat that had been uttered.

Instantly Cullop threw back his head and laughed. Roared with shrill merriment.

"Oh, that? Of all the idiotic nonsense! Man, it happened a full fifteen years ago! As a matter of fact, Halliday did me a favor when he acted as he did; although, naturally, you can imagine I didn't think so at the time." Again his laughter bubbled, but it was mean, nasty. "I didn't know that dear old Phil was married again. I didn't even know he was in Florida. If you think that I drowned his damned cat, you're completely haywire, my friend. I'd have had to have a long arm indeed to reach all the way down from Canada, from the camp where I went to do some winter shooting."

Tracy eyed the man's face with a meaning smile. Cullop's face and the back of his sinewy little hands were tanned a deep tropical brown.

"Pretty strong winter sun up in; Canada."

"Eh? What the infernal hell are you getting at?"

"I'd like to know why you took the trouble to make a sneaky visit to Florida, Mr. Cullop. I had a wire from Seeger's Camp which definitely proves that you're a liar."

"All right. You're a gentleman and I'm a liar. So what?"

"What brought you to Florida?"

"None of your damned business." Cullop's fingers were clenched, his red eyes were blinking.

"That's what you think. How would you like me to go to police headquarters and—"

He was utterly unprepared for the savage fury of Cullop's rush. The little importer sprang forward, with a yelp of rage. Tracy's upflung arm was not fast enough to ward off the furious blow of the hairy, sun-tanned fist. It landed on Tracy's jaw and sent him staggering backward against a table.

His right countered awkwardly and sent Cullop spinning

away. It was a push, rather than a punch. Instantly the little importer came charging back. Tracy's left hand, however, had seized a heavy cut-glass urn and he swung it upward like a glittering club.

"O.K., Mister Cullop!" he panted. "Come on and take it!"

Cullop skipped nimbly backward as Jerry advanced. The murderous rage spilled out of his ugly red eyes as quickly as it had appeared. He darted behind a table and threw up a pleading hand. He began to laugh a little. Jerry stared at him, white with rage.

"What's so funny about all this, you little rat?"

"I'm sorry," Cullop croaked. "It really is funny, you know. I had no intention of— We've both been behaving like children. Put down your cut-glass bludgeon, my friend, and let's talk this thing over sensibly."

Cullop became very bland, almost jovial. Jerry stood there, the heavy vase in his hand, trying to chisel a little truth out of him. It was a hopeless task. For five minutes the smiling Mr. Cullop parried, punned, uttered his mean, barking laugh—and Tracy got nowhere.

The angrier he got, the more silken and suave Mr. Cullop became. In the end, Jerry gave up and walked out.

"Give my best to dear old Phil," Cullop said sneeringly. His eyelids blinked.

"Tell him I grieve at the untimely demise of his cat and his dog. If he'll let me know where the unfortunate little beasts are buried, I'd love to send a floral remembrance to mark the hallowed spot."

"Nuts," Tracy growled fiercely and slammed the door.

On the sidewalk downstairs he rubbed his jaw and thought

of Butch. That sly little devil upstairs had socked like a pile-driver! And, according to Halliday, Genung was even tougher; he was the lad who had pulled a gun! Suddenly Tracy grinned stubbornly and thumbed a cab to the curb. Lightning, he thought, never strikes twice in the same place. He gave the driver the address on Central Park West.

MR. WILBUR GENUNG was a more surly, gruffer proposition. Gray hair with a faint sprinkle of blond. None of Cullop's febrile rage or suave palaver. A little guy, with a foot no bigger than Tracy's. In a husky voice he came straight to the point, wanted to know who the hell Tracy was and what the hell Mr. Halliday meant by sending a private detective to his home.

"You don't like Mr. Halliday very much, eh?"

"I think he's a dirty, double-crossing louse."

"Is that why you kidnaped his wife?"

Genung stared, "Wait a minute! I've seen you before some-where, haven't I?"

"Maybe. I just came back from Florida."

Genung looked puzzled and then chuckled as he saw Tracy's glance. "Oh, you mean the tan I've got? Bum guess, Mr. Gumshoe." He threw a casual gesture toward the sun-lamp in the corner of his study. "Try it some time, my friend. It'll do wonders with that pale little puss of yours. Fifteen minutes a day—and damned fools will come around and tell you you've been in Florida."

"When all the time you've really been in the hospital?"

"Right." His face flushed. "Oh, you've found that out, eh?"

"I've found out," Tracy said quietly, "that you spent only two days there. Where were you the rest of the fortnight. Miami?"

Genung was peering steadily at the columnist. "By God," he whispered, "now I know you! You're no detective. Jerry Tracy—the snooper, the newspaper buttinski, the cheap little dirt peddler! Get out before I throw you out!"

"Yeah?" Jerry's eyes gleamed. "You tried that once on Phil Halliday, didn't you? You got kicked in the belly, if you'll remember. Were you thinking of that kick in the belly when you arranged a sprained ankle and a phoney hospital alibi?"

This time Jerry landed first. His fist beat Genung's by a scant second and drove him back on his heels. Genung came charging forward with a roar of rage. For a minute or two they tussled and again Jerry felt a numbing smack on the jaw. But Tracy was cooler than the raging little stock speculator and he managed to hold him off and tie him up with a straight left.

Jerry's right crossed like a streak of light and landed with all of his strength in the pit of Genung's belly. The man's mouth flew open with the sharp agony of paralyzed diaphragm muscles. He went down in a tight writhing ball on the floor and his opened mouth made quick, gasping sounds. His eyes were bulging with the fierce agony of trying to breathe.

"You'll always be a sucker for the belly," Tracy told him in a harsh monotone.

He walked over to the sun lamp and examined it. There was no bulb in the thing. Genung swayed to his knees, both hands still clutching at his solar plexus. He couldn't talk but the look in his eyes was unmistakable as he glanced toward the top drawer of a carved cabinet. Tracy opened the drawer with a quick jerk and took out a shining .32. It was fully loaded. He shoved it into his pocket and walked out. Genung tried to rush at him as he reached the door. There was an opened pocket-knife in his hand. Jerry hit him briefly with the butt of the gun.

"Try *that* on your piano, Mr. Genung," he said and slammed the door.

He hadn't found out a thing to compensate him for the two cracks on the jaw. But he did know that both Genung and Cullop were still very much in the puzzle. He decided to give Fred Biddie's detective agency another ring, put their Florida office to work.

IN THE MEANTIME, poor Phil Halliday was probably sweating blood in the Albermarle Hotel, wondering what Tracy was up to. If Tracy told him the truth he'd have to report honestly that he'd been blundering around like a fat-head. No news whatever of Cora's whereabouts. Nothing but a whirligig of suspicious little men. Three of them so far. He was convinced that the key to the whole puzzle lay in those footprints on the whitewashed floor of Halliday's Westchester garage.

He took a cab to his Times Square office and picked up Butch.

"What's the matter with your jaw?" Butch asked him with a slow grin.

"I've been using it instead of my brains. Come on, big boy; we've got to see a man about his dog and his ship's captain and his wife and three little guys from school."

The afternoon was getting much colder and darker; beginning to look a lot like snow. People walked head down, their coat-tails lashing in the stiff gale. Jerry chose to walk instead of grabbing the inevitable cab. It was not more than six or seven blocks to the Albermarle Hotel, and besides, there was something in the cold smack of the wind that matched his feeling of savage disgust. He hadn't gained an inch in this queer run-around.

Light snow began to fall. Jerry pulled his muffler higher on his throat and turned up his coat collar. He had just passed the glass and steel maw of a subway kiosk when he heard the rapid click of heels behind him. The sound filled him with a queer premonition of peril. But before he could whirl he felt the sudden searing agony of a sharp blade in the flesh of his neck.

Blood gushed from a ragged slash in his muffler and coat collar. It stained his clutching hand crimson. Weakly he stumbled forward and fell to the pavement. Butch, who was several feet ahead, turned as he heard Jerry's cry. He sprang to him with a frightened yelp as he saw Jerry lying on the pavement, his neck and throat red.

The sidewalk, the falling snow seemed to reel dizzily before the fallen columnist's glaring eyes. He could hear the roaring yell of Butch's voice, feel the excited fumble of the big hands on his prone body.

"The subway!" he gasped faintly. "Don't mind me. Down the subway. Go get him!"

He was dimly conscious of the shuffling of many feet, the stare of countless eyes, the shrill bleat of a police whistle. He saw the bent head of Butch reappear, huge and red like a bloated balloon, felt himself lifted in Butch's paws....

He dreamed that he was on the swaying back of a camel moving mile after mile over a perfectly level and incredibly hot desert....

A SLIGHTLY JEWISH voice said calmly, "You've a very lucky gent, Mister," and Tracy opened his eyes and saw the face of an ambulance surgeon. He was flat on his back across a couple of chairs in the back of a drug-store. The place reeked with steam heat. His coat and muffler were gone and there was a white, lumpy bandage around his throat.

"Very lucky," the ambulance doctor repeated. "If it had been the other side of your neck—zippo!—that knife would have sliced right through your jugular."

"Did they catch the guy?" Jerry whispered weakly.

"Nope. He got away. Who was he? Did you know him?"

Butch, who was bending close toward his employer, seemed to be making urgent little gestures with his big head. One of his eyes closed in a brief, heavy wink. Instantly Jerry's brain cleared. He remembered how Butch had gone helter-skelter down the subway steps after the fugitive. He must have discovered something and was uncertain whether to spill it or not.

Tracy got quietly stubborn with these fussy people who were trying to rush him off to a hospital. He told the cop his name and refused hospital treatment. He forced the shrugging ambulance doctor to admit that the wound itself was not dangerous; a shallow scoop, more bloody than serious. The muffler and coat collar had turned the blade of the assailant's weapon and inflicted a gouge rather than a gash in the flesh of his neck.

Tracy mentioned the name of his own personal physician, the most famous and highest priced surgeon in New York. The ambulance man shrugged and said dryly, "O.K.—if you want to go home. It's your neck, Mister Tracy."

The slow *ding-etty-ding* of the ambulance vanished and the

cop made a passage for Tracy and Butch through the lingering crowd outside the drug-store. Butch helped his pale-faced employer into a taxi and Jerry whispered to the driver, "Albermarle Hotel. Make it nice and slow." He had crammed the bloody muffler into his pocket and his slashed overcoat collar was turned up high over the bandage on his neck.

"Did you get a look at the guy that sliced me?" He asked Butch.

"It wasn't a guy," Butch stuttered. "It was a dame."

"Huh? A woman? What she look like?"

To his disgust Butch couldn't tell him a thing, except that she wore a black hat and looked like a dame. "Oh, yeah, she had silk stockings," Butch added, with the air of a man imparting valuable information.

The time spent bending over his bleeding employer had given the desperate woman too long a start. She was past the turnstiles and the door of a train was closing behind her by the time that the heavy-footed Butch had reached the change booth downstairs.

"I found this on the steps," he said huskily.

"Ah," Tracy said.

The object that Butch had laid in his palm was a knife. An ugly little thing with a pearl handle. He snapped it gently open and the blade was drenched with fresh blood.

"I didn't know whether you wanted me to show it to the cop or not," Butch mumbled.

"You're a smart pal. I didn't."

His eyes closed. He recalled Miss Clarkson's vivid description of Cora's visit to the brokerage office. The dark-eyed, red-lipped Mrs. Halliday had taken a pearl-handled knife out of her handbag and warned her husband's gray-haired secretary to keep her mouth shut—or else. The kidnaping job was a phoney. Cora was behind this whole case.

Knowing Tracy's tenacious habits of investigation she had come out of hiding, trailed him and handed him the old "or else." Hadn't even tried to make this one look like an accident. And had taken a hell of a desperate chance to cut him loose from Phil. Phil! What in hell could he tell Phil?

"Step on it," he said to the taxi-driver. "Make it fast as you can to the Albermarle."

HE AND BUTCH were walking down the soft-carpeted corridor toward the door of Halliday's suite, when the door opened and Halliday himself came striding out. He was wearing his hat and overcoat and was obviously taken back by the sight of Tracy and his companion.

"Hello! What happened? Did you change your plans?"

"Plans?" Jerry echoed sharply. "What plans? What are you talking about? Where are you going?"

Halliday's glance had jerked toward the columnist's bandaged throat. Tracy had loosened his coat collar and Phil's eyes widened as he saw the faint staining of blood on the bandage.

"For God's sake, Jerry!"

"A little accident," Tracy said softly. "What's that envelope in your hand?"

"Your telegram. I just got it a few minutes ago."

"Telegram? I sent you no telegram."

"You didn't ask me to meet you out in Brooklyn?"

"Hell, no. Let's see that thing!" He was reaching for the

yellow envelope when he heard soft footsteps and saw a bell-boy approaching.

"Inside, Phil," he grunted curtly and followed the big man back into his room. Butch closed the door with a discreet little click.

Tracy ripped the sheet of yellow flimsy from its envelope and read it with frowning eyes:

IMPORTANT DEVELOPMENTS STOP HAVE LOCATED CORA STOP UNHARMED AND IN GOOD HEALTH STOP MEET ME ONE HOUR AFTER YOU RECEIVE THIS AT TWO NINE-FOUR LAYDEN ROAD BROOKLYN

JERRY

"You say you didn't send that message to me?" Halliday asked in a puzzled voice.

"No."

"What's it mean?"

"It means," Jerry said quietly, "that we're getting darned close to a murderer. The person who sent you that telegram did so in the belief that I'd be dead when you got it. I forgot to tell you, this bloody initial on my neck is a souvenir from a killer's knife. Your number is up at last, Phil, and that's why you got this phoney telegram."

Halliday's big face got slowly chalklike. "You—you think that Cora is dead?"

Tracy was silent for a moment. How in God's name could he tell this big, decent guy that the woman he loved and trusted was a rat? He laid a steady hand on Phil's massive shoulder.

"Cora is alive," he said slowly. "I'll take my oath on that. It's the only thing that I'm certain of. You sure you don't want the police in on this?"

"No, I'd rather not, Jerry. Not till, I find Cora—talk to her."

"O.K. Butch, I want you to grab a cab and hustle back to my office." He tossed the big fellow a key. "You'll find half a dozen guns in the bottom drawer of the steel cabinet. Pick out three. Make sure they're loaded. There's a diamond cutter there; get that, too. Then call up my garage and have my car delivered at the curb. Tell 'em not the Lincoln; the Buick. We'll be along later and you can pick us up outside my office. Got all that?"

"Yeah."

"Scram!"

He smiled with pinched approval as Butch left the room without a word. Guys like that were worth their weight in gold. Butch had never been in the army as far as Tracy knew, but if ever a guy knew how to obey without a lot of useless gaff, it was that damned lop-eared, fat-bellied ex-pug, whose loyalty to Jerry was so ingrained that it made Jerry swallow fiercely to cover the lump that came galloping into his throat.

"If that place at Layden Road is a trap," Halliday said curtly, "how are we going to get in without tipping the person behind this plot?"

"That's what I'm trying to figure now. Wait! I've got it."

Into Tracy's mind came the picture of a girl. Daisy Furlong—the cute little dancer whom he had helped to a place in Wertheim's chorus over the nasty objections of Morrie Green. This was a spot where a smart, muscular little gal like Daisy might fit in nicely as a scout. The kid had brains and courage; a match for Cora or any other woman!

He unhooked the phone and called Daisy's cheap hotel room

in the West Forties.

"I'm in a jam," he told her quietly. "Can you give me a hand?"

"I sure can, boy friend. Where are you?"

"I said *jam*, Daisy. Something that may get you a bullet in the gut. Are you game?"

He could hear the crisp sound of her oath. It sounded velvety, impatient and sort of nice. "Where are you?"

"Albermarle Hotel. Suite 1124."

"You woke me up out of a sound sleep, you little bum," Daisy said. "I'll be over as soon as I can toss something over the Woolworth lace panties. Hey, Jerry!"

"What?"

Her voice got softer. "Did I ever tell you that your old man had a swell idea when he thought of you?"

Jerry said, "Nuts," and hung up with a smile.

He was still smiling when the phone rang again. The sound of the bell faded his grin, the voice on the wire wiped it away altogether. Tracy listened more than he talked, said a few non-committal words and hung up.

"Who was it?" Halliday asked uneasily.

"Your friend, Mr. Cullop. Apparently he trailed me after I left his place, witnessed my knife accident and trailed me here. Must've tried your name on the switchboard dame. I'm still trying to figure whether he sounded scared or triumphant."

"What did he want?"

"He wants me to come back and see him. Admits he was in Florida. Says he phonied up that Canadian excuse so he could cover up a two weeks' sneak South with one of his neighbor's wives. Offered to squeal on her to prove his point. Nice little guy, eh?"

"Do you think he's lying?"

Tracy shook his head. "I don't know. I wouldn't trust that little red-eyed monkey with a rubber dime. Or Genung either, for that matter. Either one of 'em could very well be the guy who is helping—"

"Helping whom?" Halliday growled.

"I don't know."

He turned nervously away from Phil's rigid stare. Phil would have to take his answer the hard way—the only way—from the cornered Cora herself. It was a situation that Tracy was trying grimly not to think about.

DAISY FURLONG ARRIVED presently, very small and slim under her shabby coat. Eying the thread-bare appearance of it, Tracy made a mental note to stake the kid to a decent fur bennie. She could pay him back later from the new dance job. That stuff about Woolworth panties was no joke. She'd been out of work for a long time and she hadn't sold out either.... Jerry gave a warm, approving glance at her thin, decent little face. Like Butch, she listened, nodded, and asked no questions.

They took a cab downstairs at the hotel canopy and drove to Times Square. It was snowing harder and harder; small flakes filled the air like milky fog and covered sidewalks and pavements with a rapidly growing skim of white.

Jerry's neck was beginning to hurt like the devil, but he clenched his teeth and tried not to think about it. He paid off the driver of the taxi and they walked the half-block to where Butch waited like a stolid statue behind the wheel of Tracy's own car.

None of them had the faintest idea where Layden Road was,

but Butch asked a traffic cop on the other side of Williamsburg Bridge and wrote down a flock of directions on the back of an envelope.

The address proved to be in Flatbush, in a neighborhood of fairly decent looking private houses with lawns, hedges and individual garages. Number 294 was midway down a tree-lined block, and Jerry, thankful for the flying snow, made Butch roll slowly past while he gave the joint a steady scrutiny. The shades were all drawn; no lights in the place except a dim yellow reflection behind the shades on the ground floor. Garage door closed in the back; a sort of furtive weediness to the whole place.

Butch made a slow right turn at the next corner and the car came to an abrupt stop when Tracy touched the big fellow's arm.

"All set?" he asked the bright-eyed little dancer.

"All set, Jerry."

He got out of the car with her.

"Go ahead and tell 'em your piece about the ad for a nurse maid. Look dumb and tell 'em 249 instead of 294." He lowered his voice so that Phil couldn't hear. "And for gosh sake, watch your step. You're up against a smart woman."

She smiled jerkily. "I'm not afraid of any dame on earth. It's the men that give me all my headaches."

She wasn't gone more than five minutes. Her eyes were shining with excitement when she returned. Tracy kept her back out of Halliday's ear-shot.

It wasn't a woman, Daisy told the *Daily Planet's* columnist. A man—a little guy with sandy hair and a scrubby blond mustache. He had crowded the doorway and eyed her suspiciously, but apparently fell for her yarn about a want ad. Told her she had the wrong house, that 249 was a block further up. Daisy had managed to get a good look past him and was positive that the house didn't contain a stick of furniture. No sign of a chair or a carpet—nothing. There was an oil lamp standing on the floor, just inside the entry. The little man had muttered something about being the caretaker and had slammed the door in her face.

"Any sign of a gun on him?"

"No. All he had was a fountain pen in his hand. At least it looked like a fountain pen."

Tracy uttered a crisp little grunt. "Tear gas—I'll bet apples on that! I've seen pens like that before. I was wondering how they'd tackle a big man like Halliday! Get back in the car, babe, and stay there. And thanks a million; you took a hell of a chance and I won't forget it."

A moment or two later Tracy and Halliday walked inconspicuously through the flying snow to the corner of the next avenue. They ploughed through the storm, eying the houses that backed on Layden Road. Halliday wore Butch's shiny derby and his skimpy blue pea-jacket.

Butch himself had donned the broker's belted raincoat and his fuzzy gray fedora. He waited in the parked car, a watch in his big red palm, calmly watching the flight of ten minutes. He was under orders at the end of that time to stride rapidly down Layden Road with the air of a man in a desperate hurry, to break into a trot as he turned into 294, and to ring the bell loudly and long. Not to shoot if he could help it when the door opened, but to watch out for a snootful of tear gas.

The swirl of the storm masked Phil Halliday's big body as he and Tracy hurried down a snow-covered driveway and ducked behind a frame garage. He ripped a passage through a privet hedge and helped Tracy through. There was a six-foot board fence dividing the property from the place on Layden Road, and Phil chinned it and took a rapid look.

"O.K.?" Tracy whispered.

"Yeah. Looks quiet enough to me. Every shade drawn in the back. Seems to be a dim light in the kitchen. How about that neck of yours, Jerry?"

"The hell with it! Up on the fence, Phil, and gimme a hand over. Don't make any more noise than you can help."

There was an evergreen bush on the other side, already frosted thickly with snow. The two men ducked silently behind it. Tracy's arm-pits had taken the full strain of that swift swing over the fence; but it was his neck that hurt. It hurt so that it was hard for him to keep from groaning. He could feel the slow trickle of blood under the bandage. The sifting snow flakes felt cold and good, and he was tempted to pull down his coat collar; but he was afraid that the sight of the bright stain of blood on the bandage might scare Phil and make him want to tackle the show-down alone.

Eight minutes... nine minutes.... With a cautious glance toward the dark garage the two friends slipped shadowlike through the gloom. They waited outside the shade-drawn window of the kitchen. The wind made soft, blubbery moanings around the corner of the house. Tracy took a diamond cutter from his pocket and listened tensely.

BUTCH'S GRIM RING at the front doorbell came exactly on the dot and was clearly audible over the howl of the wind.

The pane of glass was cut deftly out while the bell was still ringing. Tracy whirled and pitched it into the soft snow. By the time he had turned, Halliday had let the shade softly up on its roller and was inside the kitchen. He drew his gun as Tracy followed him over the window-sill.

The kitchen was absolutely bare except for an oil lamp on an old tub cover.

Through the closed door the columnist could hear the distant rumble of Butch's fog-horn voice. "I'm Mister Halliday. I gotta telegram from Mister Tracy tellin' me he was—"

A door slammed with a force that shook the floor. Butch's voice ended in a shrill, strangled cry. There was no further sound. The house dissolved into quiet.

Tracy was out of the kitchen before Halliday's cramped muscles could move. He darted like a noiseless arrow through a narrow hallway and into the front room. One side of the room was heavy with thick tendrils of greenish, curling vapor. Butch was on the floor, flat on his face. A little sandy-haired man was backing away from Butch's fallen body with a handkerchief before his face and a clubbed gun in his hand.

He whirled with a breathless snarl as he heard the patter of Tracy's onrushing feet, and Tracy clipped him accurately on the temple. The fellow went down with a rush, and stayed down. Tracy kicked the gun out of his quivering hand with one grim swing of his snow-caked toe. Halliday, half-hidden by the cloud of tear gas, was trying to lift Butch in his big arms. He began to cough and so did Tracy.

"Drag him out to the kitchen, Phil! We'll be blinded in a second if we don't. I'll take the little guy."

"O.K. Slam the door after you. Got to keep this damned

stuff in here." He picked up Butch and staggered back to the kitchen. Tracy tried to drag the little guy out, but it was too much for his waning strength. His head felt as though it were held on to his body by a wavering silken thread. Halliday came running back and picked up the fallen thug, and Tracy slammed the door weakly.

On the kitchen floor the two slumped figures of Butch and his assailant were still dead to the world. There was an ugly contusion on Butch's forehead; his nose and left cheek were smeared with blood.

Halliday was staring with perplexity at the smaller man. "Who in God's name is he, Jerry?"

"He's your jailbird brother-in-law, Phil," a feminine voice said very quietly.

Both men whirled. They stiffened helplessly under the menace of the woman's gun. Halliday uttered a choked cry of amazement. "Why what— Is this a joke?"

"Drop the guns," she said. "Drop them—or die right now!"

There was a double thump as the weapons fell to the bare floor. The smiling woman advanced two very cautious steps and kicked the guns toward the dusty base-board.

"I was sure I had killed you," she told Tracy with a fixed, bloodless smile. "I can see now that the knife didn't quite work. That was an error and a bad one."

"My compliments to you, Miss Clarkson," Tracy said huskily. "You fooled me completely."

Her young face under the premature gray hair was softly attractive; she looked almost pleasant. Only the baleful glitter of her eyes betrayed the hate lurking within her. Halliday's choked cry made his secretary's lips writhe with cruel enjoyment.

"Your wife," she said, biting out the words from behind even white teeth, "is dead. I killed her. The same as I'm going to kill you and your snooping friend, Tracy—and that overgrown body-guard of his on the floor. You're all going to march out to the garage presently to be painlessly asphyxiated; then you're going for a ride along the north shore of Long Island—and over the edge of a convenient cliff."

Halliday groaned and his muscles twitched as he gathered himself for a forward spring.

Tracy caught Phil's sleeve. "Don't!" he whispered. "She's lying about your wife. Cora's still alive."

Time.... Play for time, a warning voice whispered in Tracy's brain. Halliday's murderous secretary was gloating visibly, crazily-proud of her cunning.

"Nobody really pushed you off the subway platform," Jerry said in a flat murmur.

"Correct," she chuckled. "If you'd lifted the adhesive tape on my forehead, you'd have found the skin unbroken."

"You flew down to Florida, of course?"

"Of course. You see, Mr. Halliday was foolish enough to write a letter about his marriage to his brother in California at the same time he was writing to me about office affairs. He put the wrong letter in my envelope and I got the news of the marriage. I turned over the office here to a friend and took the first plane south. I determined to kill you, Phil, but to torture you first as you've tortured me."

Her eyes became shiny and menacing. Tracy, staring at her, felt a shudder of comprehension.

"How—how did I ever harm you?" Halliday faltered.

"Fifteen years of drudgery—the best years of my life.... For what? A salary? A bonus at Christmas? Don't make me laugh! It was marriage I wanted. I'd have worked it, too, if it hadn't been for that sly slut in Florida."

"You're crazy, raving mad," Halliday breathed.

"Am I? You took me to shows, dinners, put me in your will—"

"I liked you, of course. I felt sorry for—"

"Just a part of the office furniture, eh?" Her laughter was chilling, horrible. "You don't know the half of it. I'm in a bad spot, my friend. For years I've been systematically robbing you. I'd have had it all after I'd married you. But now I'll have to be satisfied with what I've already chiseled out of you—and it's plenty. There'll be no new will and no Mrs. Halliday. And I'm not going to jail, either."

"Put up your gun," Halliday begged thickly. "I—I give you my word I won't prosecute, if you haven't killed Cora."

"Too late," Miss Clarkson jeered. Her gun was very steady. She laughed a little as the blond thug on the floor groaned and swayed to his knees.

"That's Jim Barfield—didn't know you had an ex-convict brother-in-law, did you, Phil? I showed him how he could cut in on bigger profits than by blackmailing his damned sister. Get those guns, Jim. We're all going out to the garage."

Barfield grinned and staggered across to the weapons. He shoved one in his pocket. The other two guns were bright with menace as he kicked Butch lightly, steadily, in the face; little bruising impacts, until Butch groaned, gulped, stirred. He backed Butch across toward the others and Miss Clarkson's left hand unlocked the back door and threw it open.

FLYING SNOW COVERED them like a white shroud.

They stumbled backward in it, hands helplessly aloft, unable to make the slightest move to leap at the shining guns that drove them so relentlessly toward the garage.

Halliday's secretary held them at bay in the dim light of a lantern on a rusted hook. Jim Barfield tied them up. Halliday's own sedan was there, the one in which Cora had been kidnaped. Miss Clarkson stepped on the starter, awoke the engine to a slow, rhythmic purring.

"Yell all you like," the pale-faced murderess laughed with vindictive fury as she went to the door. "I've already tested the acoustics of this little lethal chamber."

The heavy garage door rolled shut and locked behind her.

Halliday's voice said tremulously, "We've got to try and—"

"Don't talk—work!" Tracy snapped.

Neither of the three trussed men could reach one another. They were securely tied to three of the wheels of the car, the ropes passing tightly between the spokes. They struggled grimly, writhing and twisting at their bonds, their faces pale in the light of the lantern. The sound of the running motor of the sedan was like a steady croon of death in the air-tight garage, a creeping death that was odorless, tasteless, deadly. Carbon monoxide....

Jerry's slashed neck didn't pain any more. He had a queer feeling of drowsy well-being. He knew what it meant, fought against it. If he could only rip himself loose, reach up to that tiny window high up in the rear wall of the garage.... He thought he saw a white face glimmering outside the window and bit his lips savagely to fight off the hallucination. It was only when the glass of the window smashed into fragments and a small bleeding fist protruded that he snapped back to dizzy reality.

It was Daisy Furlong, the little dancer whom he had ordered to stay in the parked automobile around the block. He had completely forgotten the nervy little kid!

"Gas!" he cried to her thickly. "Hurry!"

She writhed head-first through the narrow aperture like a snake. Hung for an instant—and deliberately let herself fall, head downward. As she fell, her supple dancer's body twisted in the air and her head snapped forward toward her chest. She took the jarring crash on her back and shoulders with the dexterous grace of a circus tumbler. She was up in an instant, panting, slashing at Tracy's bonds with a knife she had snatched up from a grindstone table over near the cobwebbed wall.

The three men were free in almost an instant. Jerry ran weakly toward the sedan and shut off the pulse of the motor. Butch and Halliday began to hurl their big bodies grimly against the locked garage door. It was immovable.

"No use," Daisy cried fiercely. "Those two rats have the key. We'll have to climb out that damned little peanut of a window!"

Phil Halliday's lips curved with a blurred, impotent smile.

"Guess you're elected, Jerry. Butch and I are too big to get through."

"Yeah," Jerry said. "Come on. Gimme a lift!"

"Me first," Daisy cried. "We'll need two of us! Besides, Jerry's hurt. He'd kill himself trying to get down outside." She lunged forward between the two big men. "Come on, damn you! Toss me up!"

They tossed her upward like a bird. Hanging outside the tiny window-frame in the flying snow, her feet poised on the crazy contraption she had built out of a broken chair and a couple of rusty pails, the dancer pried Tracy through the tight opening of the window and managed to lower him by the arm-pits before her sagging perch fell apart.

As they ran toward the house Daisy thrust something into Tracy's cold hand. It was the knife with which she had cut his bonds.

"I got a hunch you'll need it, boy friend," Daisy whispered. She looked elfin, sprite-like in the flying snow, as pretty as hell. But her grim hand on Tracy's arm was as steady as a steel hinge.

Miss Clarkson had left the kitchen door of the house unlocked. They opened and closed it without a sound. The lamp still burned desolately on the bare boards of the floor. Upstairs they could hear the slow shuffle of feet. A sinister, dragging sound that echoed through the thin plaster of the ceiling.

It was dark in the lower hallway and they ducked out of sight behind the curve of the staircase. Tracy crouched alertly, his knife swung stiffly backward like a machete. *Bump, bump,* came the slow sound of descending feet on the stairs. The feet reached the bottom step and turned.

Tracy saw the little blond guy first. His back was toward the columnist. He and Miss Clarkson were panting breathlessly, carrying the limp body of Cora Halliday between them.

Cora's body dropped with a thump as Tracy leaped forward. The man and the woman sprang apart. Jerry dived straight at the man; Daisy took care of the woman.

The dancer dived headlong at Miss Clarkson as the blond guy yelled and drew his gun. His draw was fast, but Tracy's swing of the long-bladed knife was even faster. It chopped downward in a whizzing arc and hacked into the flesh of the extended arm. The gun dropped and the little guy screamed and staggered backward, blood spurting from his gashed flesh.

Tracy kicked him savagely in the shins and brought him down in a crashing huddle. Both men clutched for the fallen gun and Tracy won. The columnist was like a streak of light. His bandaged throat ducked away from the clutching fingers of his foe and he brought the butt of the gun down on the man's skull—hard. Again and again he struck, until the desperate squirming underneath him ceased.

He got up, staring drunkenly at Daisy. "Little guys are my meat," he said thickly.

"That's the way I feel about tough dames," Daisy said.

The dancer's face was gouged and furrowed from Miss Clarkson's nails. A split lip didn't help her smile any. One hand was twisted deep in a pocket of the murderous secretary's dress, the other was a steel band on the woman's gasping throat.

She drew her hand out and tossed Jerry a key. "Scram! Get those boys out of the garage. I'll take care of this crazy buzzard. The other guy is out like a light."

EIGHT MINUTES LATER Cora Halliday, roused from her drugged stupor, was in her husband's big arms. He sat with her on the dusty staircase and haltingly, dazedly, she told some of the horror she had undergone. Miss Clarkson, fettered and helpless, glared like a gray cat. She had become suddenly old, wrinkled, stringy looking. She kept mumbling to herself in a quiet undertone, but no one paid any attention to her.

In the yellow light of an oil lamp Cora Halliday's lovely face was still stark with remembered terror. Her brother had been blackmailing her, Cora told the attentively listening men. She had been paying him money to keep his mouth shut about his prison record. She had cut loose from her shiftless and criminal family years earlier and had gone to Miami. It was there that Phil met and married her. She loved him desperately. She was afraid she'd lose him if he ever found out about her jailbird family. Phil wanted a child and so did she—and it made her afraid, afraid....

"Is that why you didn't want the police in?" Tracy asked Halliday in a low voice. "Did Cora ask you not to?"

"Yes. I loved her, believed in her. I always will." He bent and kissed his wife's lips with a proud, deliberate gesture. "My God, Cora, I *love* you. Didn't you know that?"

"It was your brother who kidnaped you?" Tracy asked Cora.

"Yes. I was certain he'd followed us to New York and I went to Phil's office and showed his photo to that—that she-devil. I made no threats. That was a lie on her part. She was already in cahoots with my brother, Jim. He had told me and I went to see her—to beg her—

"When I looked out my bedroom window last night, I—I saw my brother beckoning to me. I climbed out the window to beg him not to disclose his identity to my husband. He struck me over the head—drove me to this horrible house."

She began to weep. Phil Halliday smoothed her hair with awkward tenderness, looked at Jerry. "Does this mess put you in a bad spot, Jerry?"

"Not when the cops get here," Jerry said. "Inspector Fitzgerald has had dealings with me before. He'll have a complete confession out of this blond monkey on the floor before you can shake a lamb's tail. But it's got to be cops now, Phil—and newspapers, I'm afraid."

"Right." Halliday's big jaw clenched. "Call in the cops, Jerry.

My wife and I have nothing to hide from anyone, thank God."

A timid hand plucked at Tracy's sleeve. Daisy Furlong's smile was wan, humorously exasperated. She touched her blood-streaked face.

"Well, there goes a swell dancing job. I wouldn't mind losing it so much if it weren't for the thought of Morrie Green. Boy, how that slimy little punk will grin when he fires me!"

"You leave Morrie Green to me," Jerry said huskily. "You're going back to that job on a wave of publicity that'll lift you right out of those dime Woolworth panties that you've been buying of late. A year from now you'll have silk ones with gold lace. I'll see that you're tops, with everything you want."

"Yeah," she said. "Everything I want." Her voice sounded suddenly flat. She saw Jerry was puzzled at her lack of enthusiasm. She rumpled his hair with a fierce little pat.

"You're a swell guy, Jerry. They don't come any better."

Tracy couldn't match up her smile with her eyes. They made him think of kids he had seen staring at cakes in a bakery window. He had a funny feeling there were tears back of Daisy's pert eyes.

He couldn't figure it at all.

Manhattan Whirligig

Jerry Tracy decides blackmailers aren't worth killing

BUTCH CAME INTO the penthouse bathroom without knocking. He always did. The fact that Jerry Tracy was taking his pre-evening bath meant nothing to Butch. He told his pint-sized employer with simple dignity:

"Dere's a screwy guy outside with a full-time grouch. He wouldn't gimme his name. Says either you come out, or he'll come in and yank you out. Do you wanna see the guy or shall I brush him off?"

Jerry grinned, rubbed lather out of his ear. A small man, he looked pink and microscopic in the enormous tub.

It was probably the biggest tub on the island of Manhattan.

"What's he burned up about?"

"He says he wants to talk to you about a duck."

Jerry laughed at that, a brief chuckle without warmth or amusement. Stony triumph swam for an instant into his eyes. "I wondered how long it would take the harpoon to start hurting. Is he a tall gent with iron gray hair, ditto on the mustache, a gray goatee tucked under his lower lip?"

"Kayo. You know him?"

"Yeah." The *Daily Planet's* famous scandal columnist heaved upward out of soapy water. He stepped onto a thick white rug and began to towel his lean, hard-packed body with vicious pleasure. "Take yourself a walk, Butch, or eat a sandwich or something. I'll see the guy alone."

"Do you think you can handle him?"

"What do you think?"

Butch took a look at the compact nakedness of his employer. His grin widened, became fond, almost parental. "If you'd only cut out cigs, you little punk, you wouldn't make a bad featherweight." His big palm made a smacking sound below Tracy's spine. He lumbered cheerfully away.

Jerry drew on his silk robe, kicked into flat slippers. He had looked forward to this interview with cold pleasure. Like a

man who waits for a snake to glide from under a stone so that he can mash it with one clean stroke of a club.

"How do you do, Doctor?"

His visitor bounced upward from a living-room chair. Tense with rage, he came striding toward the columnist, a crumpled copy of the *Daily Planet* gripped in his clenched hand. His knuckles were white. He shook the rolled tabloid under Tracy's nose.

"You slimy little rat! You can't get away with this, do you understand? If you think for one minute that I'm going to sit idly by and allow a cheap newspaper jack to make a laughing stock of my daughter and ruin my professional standing in the community—" His words stuttered passionately. Tracy didn't move an inch backward. He was utterly calm, his eyes hard with dislike.

"Let's cut out the yelling and get down to brass tacks. You're Dr. Andrew Stoner, a gentleman, a scholar, and Park Avenue's swankiest psychoanalyst. I'm Jerry Tracy, a rat from a Broadway sewer. So what do you want?"

"You know damn well what I want! An apology printed in tomorrow's column, or I promise you that you'll wish you'd never—"

"Oh, you mean the duck squib? You mean this?"

Deliberately he read the paragraph aloud, clipping the words out with slow, nasal amusement:

RAISED EYEBROWS DEPARTMENT

Seen yesterday on Park Avenue. Over-rich, over-dressed deb, creating Gloria-sensation by public stroll with pet duck.... Deb is daughter of prominent dream-book doc. Can it be that the duck stroll is a tie-up with papa's biz slogan? Quack! Quack!

Dr. Stoner's face was purplish. He said, menacingly, "Are you going to retract?"

"No. I'm going to print one twice as amusing tomorrow—and every day after that—until I've run you out of town on a wave of ridicule. If you don't like it, sue! The *Daily Planet* keeps a smart lawyer on a yearly retainer just to take care of crooks like you."

"Crook? What do you mean?"

"Don't you call a blackmailer a crook, Doctor?"

The red faded from Stoner's aristocratic face, leaving it white and pinched. Tracy shoved past him, strode toward a desk in the corner, his silken robe fluttering backward from his naked legs. There was a portable typewriter on the desk and the columnist slid a blank sheet around the cylinder. He made the keys rattle like a machine-gun. Then he spun about, his voice as metallic as the machine.

"Here's tomorrow's squib. How do you like it?"

It was Jerry who was angry now. Stoner had regained his self-control. The typed sheet was steady in his hand. He read the paragraph with lidded attention:

> What wealthy Park Avenue psychoanalyst is the town's smoothest magician? He has only one trick—but one is all he needs.... He turns a breakdown into a shake-down. Duck that one, Doctor!

Stoner's teeth showed like nicks in a razor blade. "How much am I supposed to pay you, Mr. Tracy?"

"Not a dime. If you've got the sense I think you have, you'll link arms with that snooty blond daughter of yours and take a well bred sneak for Penn Station. Try Kansas. I haven't any friends there for you to bleed."

"Do you mind telling me what particular friend of yours I've bled?"

Tracy's throat raided impatiently. "The name doesn't matter. If you think I'm bluffing, get this! I know all about the appointment for tonight at nine-thirty. I know the street and the brownstone house where the dough is to be passed. It's only a grand tonight, because my friend is a minor victim and has to be squeezed with caution to make the gravy last."

"I think you're insane."

"Out! I've just taken a bath and I want to stay clean. Is that plain?"

"Let's both be plain," Stoner said slowly. His words seemed to crawl up out of his throat from a long way down.

"I don't know what your game is, Tracy, but I know danger when I see it. I have no intention of going to the police. I'm perfectly able to protect myself and my daughter Gloria from scandal. I'll be watching the *Daily Planet* to see if that second squib appears. If it does, it will be the last paragraph you ever write. I mean that literally and exactly, Mr. Jerry Tracy. Good evening."

His face veered menacingly over his shoulder from the foyer, then the penthouse door clicked.

Tracy said, "Nuts!" in a hard, angry murmur. He was uncomfortably aware that he had said too much. He should have kept his mouth shut about the brownstone and the appointment for nine-thirty, but the clever Stoner had stung him into foolish verbosity. Well, it couldn't be helped now. He rubbed damp palms against his silken robe and yelled grimly for Butch.

He gave him the typewritten paragraph that Stoner had tossed contemptuously on the rug. "Take this down to the *Daily Planet* office and hand it to McCurdy—no one else. Tell him I want it run at the top of the column. Scram."

Butch hesitated. "You goin' out tonight, Boss?"

"Yeah."

"Me, too?"

"No."

"O.K., pal. You needn't bite me head off." He clumped off, worried but obedient. Whenever Tracy was in that curt, monosyllabic mood, Butch knew better than to argue.

HALF AN HOUR later Jerry Tracy was in a taxicab, riding swiftly through windy darkness toward the modest east side apartment of Al Redman. The thought of Al and his wife made Jerry's jaw harden. Al and Florence! Two of the swellest humans a guy could know. Florence was completely unaware of the mess in which her husband was tangled.

At this hour she was probably preparing dinner in the huge kitchen of their old-fashioned, comfortable flat. Al would be in the living-room pretending to read the paper. Tracy had already phoned Florence that he and Al were going to a hockey game that night. It was an easy out. Florence had an amused indifference for any kind of competitive sport.

It was hard to couple Al and Florence with the suave Park Avenue racket of Dr. Andrew Stoner. Geographically and socially they lived on different planets.

Al Redman was cashier of the Times Square branch of the Mercantile Bank. He walked to work every morning from the East Forties, had an apple and a glass of milk at noon, and walked home again every night with his evening paper. He was a tall, gangling man with placid brown eyes and a shy, friendly smile. Nothing of the hard Broadway glaze about Al.

Perhaps for this very reason friendship had grown between the quiet cashier and his dapper columnist customer. Not that Jerry saw Al often; that was impossible for a feverish little comet like Tracy. But they did go to fights and hockey matches occasionally, and after Jerry had met Florence, he got in the habit of spending a pleasant evening in their cosy walk-up apartment over near the East River.

After a hectic day rubbing elbows with the phonies, the snides and smoothies along the Main Stem, an evening with the Redmans was like a vacation along a leafy trout stream. No wisecracks; ale instead of daiquiris; good solid talk about things remote from the headlines.

Al's noon-hour visit to the Tracy penthouse had been utterly unexpected. His voice over the telephone wire had sounded high-pitched, strident. The moment he walked in, Tracy knew that something was desperately wrong with the man. Not from his appearance, although his smile seemed taut and twisted. It was the way Al's feet tripped over the edge of the rug with unseeing awkwardness, the manner in which his bony fingers vised around Tracy's extended hand.

"Jerry, I've got to talk to you. God knows I don't want to drag you into anything unpleasant, but I don't know where else to turn."

"Trouble?"

"Yes."

"Florence know about it?"

"No."

Tracy grinned. "Let's tackle it. What sort of trouble, Al?"

Redman said faintly, "This sort: I debated for nearly an hour in my cage at the bank, whether I'd use my lunch time today to come to you for advice, or to go to a certain doctor's office on Park Avenue and kill him."

There was silence for a moment.

"Sit down, Al," Tracy said gently. "I'll mix you a drink and then we'll—"

"No drink. I've got to hand a thousand dollars in hundred-dollar bills to a blackmailer at nine-thirty tonight. He's already taken every penny of my personal savings. Now he wants me to get it from the bank. Do you understand? From the bank!"

Tracy nodded. "I'll do the worrying about the dough, Al. You give me the facts, as straight as you can talk. Take a deep breath. O.K. Shoot!"

He listened, watched the rug. Years of listening to the troubles of frightened people had taught Tracy the value of the averted face, the inclined ear, the impersonal silence of the confessional.

Al Redman blurted it out, relief in his racing words. The crook was Dr. Andrew Stoner. Al had gone to him for treatment following a breakdown from overwork in the bank during the hectic days and nights that had followed the market crash. Stoner had cured him—and trapped him. How thoroughly he had been trapped, Al didn't realize until months later, when he had received a curt telephone summons to a brownstone house on the lower west side. The nature of that summons filled him with sick dismay.

Al had given Florence a fake excuse and gone. He was met at the brownstone door by a masked man with a gun, conducted to a room, handed a sheaf of typewritten pages and told to read. He found it to be a photostatic copy of every word he had uttered months earlier in the secluded quiet of Dr. Stoner's study on Park Avenue.

Included in the pages was a secret that Redman was unaware he had divulged, lulled to hypnotic peace by the polished discs that always rotated during the psychoanalyst's treatment. It was a confession that Redman had falsified the books of the bank where he was employed and had borrowed two thousand dollars.

"Borrowed, I said—not stolen!" Al gasped.

Technically, it had been theft; actually, it was not. Redman had needed two thousand dollars for an emergency operation on his wife. He took it, knowing he could replace every penny of it within ten days from savings that were temporarily frozen in an investment. The money was replaced, the books adjusted.

The masked man with the gun had demanded three hundred dollars as the price of his silence. He had pointed out deftly that the sum demanded was not large; that blackmail was cheaper than ruin. The bank officials might sympathize with the motives of a trusted employee, but they could scarcely keep him any longer. Nor would they recommend him to any other bank. Redman would not only lose the only livelihood for which he was fitted; he would be blacklisted for life.

Tremulously he had agreed to pay and was conducted from the house by the masked blackmailer with the gun. From that moment he had paid again and again at intervals nicely calculated to keep him from growing desperate.

Tonight he was expected to pay a thousand dollars which he didn't have. His tremulous plea that he was broke amused the masked man who always interviewed him. He suggested with a chuckle that Redman repeat his knowledge of bank procedure and hide the theft with a dummy transaction on the books. Nine-thirty tonight or else....

Tracy's voice was very steady in the high-ceilinged penthouse room. "You're certain the guy with the gun was Dr. Stoner?"

"I'm sure of it. Same height, same build. His voice was disguised—metallic, like a damned cricket—but I knew him. And there's a small, crescent shaped scar on Stoner's hand—an acid burn. I've seen that same crescent on the black-mailer's hand every time I've kept an appointment. I tell you, it's Stoner himself, shuttling like a damned Jekyll and Hyde between Park Avenue and a musty old brownstone on the fringe of Greenwich Village. God knows how many fools like me he has—"

"We'll let the rest take care of themselves." Tracy said curtly.

"I'm a columnist, not a cop. I've got enough when he tries to put the heat on a pal of mine."

The rasp went out of his voice. Smiling, he rose. "You've got just about time enough to make it back to the bank. Scram, or the vice-president in charge of time clocks will be giving you a look. Forget about blackmail. I'll take care of the doc."

"But—"

"I'll call Florence and tell her I've got you dated for a hockey game. What time do you generally eat?"

"Six-thirty."

"I'll drop in while Florence is busy in the kitchen. I'll give you final instructions then."

He got rid of the dazed cashier by using what he called, the Vaudeville Push. It consisted of loud, jovial, reassuring while the victim was propelled to the door and out. He knew that Al's ragged nerves were close to a break. But once he reached the street he'd get a grip on himself. Having spilled his secret to Tracy, there was no immediate danger of his going haywire with a gun. The grooves of habit would slide him swiftly back to his cage at the bank.

THE TAXI IN which Jerry Tracy had ridden eastward through windy darkness halted in front of the modest apartment building in which Al and Florence Redman modestly lived.

"Stick around," Jerry said. "I'll be down in about five minutes."

The hackman eyed the expensive derby, the imported Chesterfield, the flash of dinner clothes exposed by the V of the silken muffler. When guys said stick around, it meant either extra business or a gyp sneak. This guy was O.K. With a grunt the chauffeur unfolded a tabloid, swore when he found it was too dark to read, and went into a doze.

Al Redman opened the door upstairs. He said in a quick whisper, "She's in the kitchen."

"Swell."

They moved quietly into the living-room and Tracy closed the door. He handed Al a sealed envelope. "Stick it in your pocket. Quick."

"What is it?"

"A thousand bucks. Ten centuries. Keep that date at nine-thirty. Let the doc think you stole it from the bank. I'll get in touch with you later tonight or tomorrow morning."

Al's face went white. He said slowly, "I can't let you throw a thousand dollars away like that, Jerry."

"Nuts. I spend a grand every year buying my hat back in restaurants—and think of the fun I'm getting.... You do exactly what I told you and leave the rest to me. So long, keed."

He squeezed Al's cold hand briefly and left the apartment as quietly as he had entered it.

Tracy climbed back in the cab, feeling a little edgy. He wanted to dine alone and do a little thinking before he attempted to crash the brownstone. He hadn't told Al, but he had decided that was the only thing to do. He wanted to be hidden inside the dump and see the money passed. It might lead to gunplay, but it seem the only logical way to crimp Stoner's racket. Tracy was confident he could talk the smooth doc out of trouble, once the cards were laid on the table. Stoner was just as vulnerable to police publicity as his frightened victim.

Smiling faintly, the *Daily Planet's* little columnist drove to Raoul's. The swanky Park Avenue atmosphere of Raoul's would keep his mind on business. It amused him to see the doorman touch his hat respectfully, to see the headwaiter skim toward him with a fawning smile. Even at Raoul's publicity in Tracy's famous newspaper column was not to be sneezed at.

He was conducted to his usual table and his favorite cocktail was brought—even to the added dash of gin—without Tracy having to utter a word.

He was sipping meditatively, his back toward the other diners, when he happened to glance at an exquisite mirror on the draped wall. He stiffened, remained staring.

Two more customers had just come in. A tall, serious-faced young man was ordering drinks at a nearby table, his eyes frowning intently at the wine list. The girl opposite him was Gloria Stoner. In spite of himself Jerry had to admit that Gloria was physically gorgeous, a knockout. Tall, well-bred, coolly sure of herself, she sat back against her furred wrap, her shoulders like cream above her silver evening gown. She was watching Tracy.

Tracy sipped some more, set down his cocktail glass. Gloria's deft glance in the mirror had conveyed very accurately to the columnist the sense that she considered him a small bug in a black Tuxedo—though possibly an interesting bug. He could tell from the tightening of her lips that she knew who he was.

The man with her was Hadley Brown, her fiancé. Except for rather sullen eyes, he looked boyish in dinner clothes. A bit like a Harvard tackle with a grouch, Tracy thought. Actually he was a broker who did most of his business at polo fields and golf clubs.

Hadley Brown's frown deepened as Gloria spoke to him in a low voice. He shook his head, turned to stare at Tracy's back.

Tracy's interest quickened as he realized what was happening. The girl was getting rid of her companion. She did it so deftly, so competently that it was a pleasure to watch it.

Hadley Brown stood up. He shrugged at the girl, his face politely blank. He started toward the cloak room, then abruptly changed his mind. Veering, he came toward the table where Jerry sat amused and a bit mystified by the whole peculiar procedure.

Brown leaned close over Tracy's shoulder, so that the columnist had to turn slightly to look up at him.

"Listen, you."

"Yes?"

"I don't know what your game is—"

"I like solitaire, if you don't mind."

They both spoke in undertones. It was impossible for anyone else to overhear the conversation. Tracy kept smiling. Brown's face was taut, hostile.

"This isn't the time or the place to create a scene, Tracy. I just want to tell you that I know you're trying to cause trouble of some kind for my fiancée, and I'm warning you to watch your step! If you don't, I'm ready to go the limit to make you stop. Is that clear?"

"Sorry I can't offer you a drink, Mr. Brown," Tracy murmured. "I would, only I don't care either for you or your manners."

"Remember, if you bother Gloria—"

"Good evening, Mr. Brown."

For an instant the watchful columnist thought that the angry young man was going to reach out and throttle him where he sat. Instead, Brown straightened, continued his quiet way toward the cloak room. Except for Gloria no one could possibly have guessed the savage tension that underlay Brown's momentary pause at Tracy's table. He was gone with a light, springy step. It was as though he had merely halted to exchange a polite, low-voiced greeting with an acquaintance.

The only queer note was the blaze in his narrowed eyes. Tracy knew danger when he saw it. This very swanky guy wasn't bluffing when he said he'd go the limit. Not by a damned sight!

Tracy thought with cold excitement: "Mr. Hadley Brown, eh? Where the devil does he fit into this little affair of the doc, the duck and the daughter?"

He had a hunch the daughter was going to make the next play.

A few moments later he saw without surprise that Gloria's waiter was drifting discreetly across the room toward the table where Jerry sat toying with his empty glass.

The waiter said, "Miss Stoner presents her compliments to Mr. Jerry Tracy, and asks if he won't bring his drink to her table and join her at dinner."

Tracy grinned. This was stuff he liked. When he spoke his voice was nasal, very clear. "Why not? But tell her the pleasure is all hers."

GLORIA AND JERRY Tracy had a cocktail together. He found he wasn't as calm as he thought he was. He knew it when Gloria canceled her dinner order, her blue eyes cold with mockery.

"I see by the papers, Mr. Tracy, that duck seems to be in fashion at the moment. Perhaps you'd better bring me roast duck, Henri."

"A swell idea," Tracy said harshly. "Eventually your duck will be cooked. Now's as good as any time."

But he couldn't get a rise out of Gloria. He wondered why the hell she had sent for him. She looked wary, tense, but he couldn't lead the conversation to her father. Perhaps she was nervous because of the decorous silence in the restaurant, the presence of so many other diners.

Jerry got angrier at himself as the meal progressed. There was smiling chit-chat between them, the crisp crackle of nastiness sugared over with amusement. Tracy let his barbed tongue go to work, but Gloria was as clever as he was. It was only after the liqueur glasses had been drained that Jerry got his chance to grin. It came when Gloria asked regally for the check.

"One always pays for entertainment," she said with cool impudence. "I'll sign for both of us, Henri."

To Jerry's delight, Henri shrugged, dropped his voice to a confidential whisper. "But, Madame, there ees no check. Dinner at Raoul's, eet ees always complimentary for guests of Mr. Tracy."

Grinning, Tracy helped Gloria with her furred wrap. She waited while he got his coat and hat at the check room. There was no sign of Hadley Brown. Tracy was still puzzled by this whole apparently senseless interview. Was it chance or a carefully designed maneuver?

Tracy got his answer when the two passed through the revolving door to the starlit chill of Park Avenue. The doorman's husky whisper to Gloria made things crystal clear.

"Well, I see you found him, Miss Stoner."

"Yes. I seem to be lucky tonight."

They moved toward the cab at the canopied curb. Tracy gave the girl an edged smile. "I get it now, sister. A deliberate pick-up, eh?"

"Of course. How else would one meet a Broadway columnist?"

"O.K. You win. If you'll excuse me, I'll be getting back to the good old gutter."

He stepped over the curb, got into the taxi. Before he could slam the door, Gloria slipped in beside him. Sat down with a cold little smile he didn't quite like.

"Over to Fifty-ninth," she said clearly to the driver. "Then up through Central Park."

Tracy looked at his wrist watch. The time was not quite eight-thirty. He had a little more than an hour before he was due at the brownstone house on the fringe of Greenwich Village.

He said abruptly, "I don't know what the gag is, babe, but I'm busy. I'll give you to Fifty-ninth to get down to brass tacks. What do you want?"

"I want to talk sense to you."

"Shoot."

She turned slightly and he saw that her silver evening bag was open. The furred edge of her wrap hid the snout of a tiny automatic pistol. It was squat, steady—but no steadier than the sound of Gloria's whisper.

"One move out of you and I'll put lead through that cheap shirt front of yours."

"It's not half as cheap as a gun bluff, sister."

The taxi whirled through the plaza at Fifty-ninth, turned into the park. There were not many cars on the dimly lit road. Gloria kept her eyes and the gun on Tracy.

"I'd like to know just what you've got against my father."

"Why don't you ask him?"

"I'm asking you."

"How do you want it? On a plate with mayonnaise, or straight?"

"As straight as you can talk."

"O.K. Your old man is a crook. The rottenest kind. He's been putting his dirty finger on a personal friend of mine—and holding it there till it hurts. So I'm running him out of town, and you with him, babe, because I think you're a crooked chip off the same block of ice. And you might as well shove that rod back in your bag because I've been gunned by blondes a hell of a lot tougher than you."

He still didn't like the look in her eyes. They were slitted counterparts of her father's. Her voice made him think of Stoner, too.

"Have you any proof of all this?"

"I don't need proof, sweetheart. I'm not a cop. I told you once, I'm just a pal of the victim."

"I think you're a liar. There isn't any victim, except Dad. So get this! If my father can't protect himself, I will. You print one more of those slimy squibs about us in your moron newspaper, and—"

"Sure. I know. You'll kill me."

"Not at all," Gloria Stoner said. "I'll see that you're killed, Mr. Tracy. A slight difference in method. Get your hand away from that window!"

But Tracy continued calmly to revolve the handle of the taxi's window. The cab had stopped at a red intersection light. A park cop was leaning against the metal traffic pole, kicking his cold shoes together. Tracy stuck his grinning face out the opened window.

"Hello, Mike! How's tricks?"

"Oh, hello, Jerry. For gosh sake! What are you doin' way up here?"

He ambled across the road, his heavy patrolman's brogans making a slow slap-slap on the frozen pavement. The girl beside Tracy slid her automatic back into her expensive evening bag. It was like a pleasant family reunion. Gloria smiled, Jerry smiled, the cop smiled.

Jerry got out of the cab and closed the door. The traffic light changed to green, but Jerry didn't get back. The cop looked puzzled. So did the driver of the taxi.

Gloria bit her lip, said harshly, "Good-by, Mr. Tracy. It was so nice to meet you. Go ahead, driver! What are you waiting for?"

Her face, framed in the open window, was stiffly menacing. "Remember that slight difference I spoke of, Mr. Tracy," he called. "I'll see you later—or perhaps someone else will."

Tracy shrugged imperceptibly. He watched the crimson tail-light dwindle around a curve like a blood-red will o' the wisp.

"Flag me the first empty cab that comes along, Mike."

"Boy, that was an expensive blonde! She looked sore. How come you're leavin' her?"

Jerry chuckled suddenly. "She lured me into a cab and tried to get fresh. I wouldn't mind if it was Spring, but—"

"She could get fresh with me any time she liked," Mike said, his eyes thoughtful he held up his gloved hand presently and halted another cab. "So long, Jerry."

At Tracy's order the cab left the park, turned into Fifth Avenue and headed swiftly south. Tracy glanced at his watch, saw that he had plenty of time to get down to Greenwich Village. He felt better. Still, that gun of Gloria's was no phoney! She certainly had meant business.

THE BROWNSTONE HOUSE was on Brixton Street, a quiet cul-de-sac where the village plays crooked tag with Varick Street. Jerry Tracy covered the last two blocks on foot, walked past the joint on the opposite side. He thought of it as a joint purely through habit. To him, any edifice from the St. Regis to the Automat was either a joint or a dump.

Actually, the brownstone looked respectable enough; a high front stoop and area-way, neat blue shades drawn half-way down on the windows; a couple of empty ash cans at the entrance to a clean paved alley that went down six steps behind a grilled sidewalk gate.

There weren't any lights on in the house, nor any enameled name plate in the parlor window. That was the only difference from its somber neighbors. Most of the others showed doctor or dentist signs. If this quiet dump with the side alley was really a blackmail spot, the canny Doctor Stoner had picked his number with a shrewd eye for conservative privacy.

Tracy continued to the corner, braced himself against the sweep of the circling wind. Nine-ten. Twenty minutes leeway before Al Redman was due to spend Jerry's grand. The *Daily Planet's* shivering columnist crossed the street, came back on the proper side. What a sap he was to be wearing a Chesterfield! The thing felt like cold tin against his ribs.

He tried the grilled alley gate, found it unlocked, went through and down the steps. He was old enough at the skulking racket to know that witnesses never noticed a casual pedestrian. The muggs who hesitated and peered and tiptoed were all long since in the can—or acting thug roles for the movies.

There was a small yard in the back hemmed in by a high board fence. The cellar door was locked. Windows all dark;

shades half drawn, same as the front. But there was a light shining from one of the side windows.

Tracy found a wooden tub filled with empty bottles. He laid the bottles on the ground and carried the tub back to the alley. By standing on it and stretching, he was able to hook his fingers over a stone sill. The window at the head of the alley was built dormer style, and its massive bulge screened him from the view of any chance passerby on the sidewalk.

He chinned slowly, peered through the dusty lower pane. Dark velour curtains left a vertical three inch gap. Through it Tracy could see nothing but a brightly lit unfurnished room and the white blur of a knob on a closed door.

Gingerly, Tracy drew up one knee and anchored himself on the cold stone of the outer sill. He still had about fifteen minutes before Al Redman arrived with the ransom money. If Jerry could get inside, witness the transaction from conceal-ment, he'd have no qualms about showing himself to the wise Doc Stoner.

Pistol fire would make things just as tough for the sleek psychoanalyst as it would for Tracy. There'd be a dangerous moment or two; then Jerry and Stoner would get down to brass tacks and talk business. Jerry was no white knight for the general public. He'd offer Stoner an even swap: You lay off Al Redman, and I'll lay off you!

He put even pressure on the lower window, and to his delight it moved slightly. Unlocked! He lifted it steadily, inch by inch. Eagerly intent on masking any betraying squeak from the warped frame, he forgot completely about the possibility of an alarm.

The staccato clamor of a bell froze him into startled rigidity.

Instantly, he lowered his body, hung like a taut pendulum. But inside the brownstone dwelling things were happening with startling speed.

The door of the lighted rear parlor burst open. A tall figure was visible, bounding toward the opened window. A black mask where the man's face should have been. A gun in his hand. And on the clenched hand—Tracy saw the thing with instinctive, photographic clarity—the bluish outline of a small crescent-shaped scar. The acid burn that Al Redman had sworn was on the back of Dr. Stoner's aristocratic hand!

Tracy's dropping feet hit the wooden tub and he bounced, crouching, to the pavement of the alley.

Stoner was leaning out the window, his gun a dull glitter. Tracy felt his back crawl as he raced pell-mell for the alley steps that led upward to the sidewalk. But Stoner fired no shot. Instead, Tracy heard the short, bubbling bleat of a whistle.

He was half way up the steps when he heard it. It brought sanity back to his panting body. A signal! An ambush!

The thought halted Tracy's flying legs.

Peering through the grilled gate, he saw a figure rising noise-lessly from behind the newel post of a stone stoop. The head was bent queerly askew like the pose of a violinist. Its cheek cradled the stock of a rifle. The rifle was short-barreled, with an ugly protuberance clamped to its muzzle.

As Tracy threw himself backward, flame spat in a thin streak from the silenced rifle. There was a muffled *plop-plop plop-plop* like a series of wheezing coughs. Bullets whizzed through the bars of the alley gate and chipped stone from the wall of the house.

Tracy gave a strangled yell as he plunged backward down

the alley steps. The sound was involuntary, ripped out of him by fear. But he had sense enough to realize that his yell might make that possum dive of his look like a natural.

He pitched limply down the steps, rolling over and over like a dead man. Spread-eagled at the bottom, he held his breath, his body slack against the freezing pavement.

He knew that the killer was at the gate, staring down at him. He could hear quick, eager breathing. Then there was a soft patter of retreating feet, followed by the faint slam of a car door.

A motor roared. Gears clashed with rattling urgency.

Tracy bellied cautiously up the alley steps. His eyes, level with the sidewalk, caught a swift glimpse of a vanishing coupé and the man behind the wheel. A plump, dough-like face on hunched, heavy-set shoulders.

Car and gunman were gone in the shrill whine of an accelerating motor. The whole affair had happened with extraordinary precision. Except for the ugly chipped spots where bullets had drilled the alley wall, there was no evidence to show that murder had missed a very frightened little newspaper guy by a margin so narrow that Tracy's heart seemed to be beating way up near his tonsils.

He glanced backward along the alley. The window was closed. Stoner had evidently vanished the moment he had blown his signal whistle. Tracy had recognized the dough-faced gunman with a gasp of wonder. He was a man whose bullets Tracy had never dreamed he would ever he called upon to dodge.

Yet, thinking about it as he lay crouched against the alley steps, Tracy could see how logically a guy like Tick Anderson fitted into the picture. A little business deal, that was all. "Strictly business," was Tick's favorite motto.

Tracy's derby was still lying upside down on its crown where it had wobbled. He scooped it up, jammed it tremulously on his head, made a quick sneak for the sidewalk. No pedestrians in sight.

Wind nipped eastward at him from the Hudson like an iron claw. He hurried to the corner, his eyes peeled to snare a rolling cab. A belated pat at his hip pocket told him that he had lost his .32 somewhere back in the alley, but he was damned if he was going back to get it!

He was waiting there breathlessly, his shoes scuffed, his Chesterfield rumpled and dusty, when he caught sight of the crimson neon light of a shoe shine parlor. It reminded him that he looked like a bum. He went in grimly, had himself shined up and brushed off.

The Greek attendant looked curiously at this pint-sized little dude who had all the ear-marks of a booze spill in the gutter, except that he was obviously a long way from being drunk. Sorta angry looking, too, the Greek decided. He made no comments and was rewarded with a tip that made him bow low at the waist.

FOUR MINUTES LATER Jerry Tracy was in a cab rolling north.

"Blue Grotto," he told the driver. Tick was probably back there by this time, sipping a very dry Martini at his favorite table. His car garaged, his rifle parked, and an alibi handy in case he needed one.

Try as he would Jerry couldn't summon up any vicious anger against the guy. It was like hating a paper-hanger because he hung paper. Rub-outs were Tick Anderson's business. Everybody in town knew it, including Tracy.

Outside of that, the guy was as cheerful and friendly a mugg as you'd want to meet in a week of Sundays. The fact that he and Tracy were casual pals, bumping into each other at prize fights and hockey matches, had nothing to do with the main idea.

Tick would have bumped the Mayor of New York if the proposition was right and the dough was laid on the line. His code of ethics was simple: If suckers got themselves lined up for a kill, that wasn't Tick's fault. He considered himself a high-class merchant same as Rogers Peet. Only Rogers Peet sold pants and vests.

The Blue Grotto was a bright glitter just north of Times Square, where Broadway cuts a slashing chunk out of Seventh Avenue.

Tracy said "Hello, Andy!" to Manhattan's toothiest doorman and got a delighted, "Hi, Jerry, howth tricth?" Andy's uppers and lowers were brilliant to look at, but they made his speech a little disconcerting. An ex-pug, he'd had most of his real teeth extracted by leather. Drunks sometimes amused themselves by paying Andy to hiss. Tracy had immortalized him in the column as "the sthpittin' image of an admiral."

"Tick Anderson around?" Tracy asked.

"Yeah. Inthide thomewhere."

Within the blue-glass front of the joint, noise hit Tracy like a hot, pulsing wave. Manny Bloom and his Tooting Troubadours. Clatter of dishes, clink of knives and forks. Fat, gravy voices. Lean, querulous voices. "… so I sez, sure I'll take thirteen weeks on a network program. But I ain't woikin' for apples…." Broadway with a napkin under its chin. "Hello, Jerry. What's the rush? Who d'you like in the third tomorrow at Hialeah Park? Sheik?"

Tracy plodded past them with his glazed celebrity grin. Some were tramps; some were the real McCoy, good guys; but he didn't have time for any of 'em tonight. He had a little business with Tick Anderson. He could see Tick already, exactly as he had expected to find him—large as life at his regular table in the corner, his doughy face staring quietly at the dry Martini in his hand.

"Hi yuh, Tick."

The face jerked upward at Jerry's breezy salutation. For a second the merest flick of a frown darkened his eyes. Like a cloud blowing across a blue lake. It was gone instantly and he was up on his feet, his beefy hand extended in welcome.

"Jerry, you little bozo, it's good to see yuh. You don't know how damn good it is, pal."

"Maybe I do, Tick. How's for a Martini?"

"Sure thing. Sit down, pal. Hey, waiter! Hey, you with the tray! Double Martinis here. Dry, or you kin take 'em back!"

Tick Anderson beamed. He was like a host in a tavern. Twinkling, cheerful, genuinely pleased with himself and with Tracy. The only flaw in the picture was a certain embarrassed reticence in the back of his blue eyes. The drinks came and they touched rims and sipped.

Smilingly, Tracy pinned him down to the murder attack. Smilingly, Tick admitted it.

"How come, Tick? Any special reason?"

"How the hell would I know?"

"How much did I bring?"

"Five grand."

"It's nice to know that I rate a top price," Jerry said quietly. "I hope it wasn't C.O.D."

Tick said reproachfully, "Now, Jerry! You know me better than that. I get it in advance, rain or shine." His pudgy hand reached out, patted the fingers of the columnist that were twined loosely about his glass stem. "I'm damned glad, pal, that it didn't rain tonight. Listen, kid, why don't yuh gimme a friendly break? Why don't you blow town for a few days?"

"You think there'll be more rain?"

"I dunno, pal. If there is, I hope to geez you'll show a little sense and duck."

"It wouldn't be ethical, I suppose, to ask you who the paymaster is?"

Tick said again, with the same embarrassed inflection, "Now, Jerry!" He played with his empty cocktail glass.

Tracy changed the subject abruptly. "How's Jane?"

"Swell. Gimbel's gave her a raise last week. She's got three dames under her now. That kid's got clever ideas, Jerry. She oughta be runnin' a high-class—you know, snooty—little dress shop of her own. She could clean up in no time."

"She looked a little thin the last time I saw her, Tick." Tracy's voice became casual. "It's a damn shame she won't let you—"

"Yeah." The enthusiasm faded from Tick's eyes, leaving them pinched and morose.

Jane's eyes were a lot like her brother's, Jerry remembered. Same shade of blue. So bright and alert that they were startlingly like blue enamel when they flashed on you in a smile. But there was no doughy flesh in Jane's countenance. She was thinner, taller than her gunman brother, with high cheek bones and a kind of delicate tension around the lips that had missed her brother altogether.

Tracy was one of the few people on Broadway who knew that Jane existed. She lived in a cheap walk-up flat in the Seventies, adjoining the El on Columbus Avenue. Worked in Gimbels and made twenty-three-fifty a week. She was the only thing on earth that Tick Anderson really cared about. Tick cared enough, Jerry noted, for his jaws to go ridgy like iron at his helpless inability to do for her the things he wanted to do.

"Yank her out of Gimbels!" his jaw said. "Get her out of that —— tenement flat!"

But Jerry knew that while life ran in either of them there'd be no dress shop, no cosy apartment, no neat little Packard for Jane Anderson—not unless she bought 'em out of twenty-three-fifty a week at Gimbels.

Even Tick knew that now. They each had their blind spot and it was no use arguing. Over two Martinis Tick could prove logically that his occupation, while illegal, was as fundamentally honest and necessary as that of a garbage man. Furniture and clothes wore out their usefulness and guys were paid to lug it away. Saps got in bad with big timers. Ditto.

For the life of him Tick couldn't see a hell of an inch of difference. He'd been complimented by cops for some of his jobs. On vague hearsay, of course. But Tick could never make Jane see his point.

Jane's code of ethics was as peculiar as his. She'd have rotted in jail before she'd have tipped the police to any phase of Tick's methods of livelihood, but she wouldn't take a dime from any of his earnings. From the time that Tick had swung into the big money, Jane had resolutely stuck to Gimbels and her walk-up flat on Columbus Avenue. They saw each other often, loved each other devotedly, but—well, no use arguing....

A waiter came by, caught Jerry's nod and the two had another drink. Smilingly Jerry reached for his Chesterfield and derby which he had parked on an unoccupied chair against the wall.

He said in a low voice, "I'll try to remember to duck in case it rains later on. But I still think you're silly, Tick, to spray at guys that write columns for newspapers. It might some time cause trouble for Jane."

Tick's hand moved like lightning from its cushioned laxity on the table cloth. His fingers clamped on Tracy's wrist, bit until the pressure hurt like hell. The muddy cloud had drifted over the blue lake of Tick's eyes. He didn't raise his voice, but there was ruthless menace in the jut of his head.

"What do you mean by that crack?"

"No crack," Tracy said, his lips compressed a little from the pain in his wrist. "Just advice."

"Listen, mugg. If you're thinkin' of putting the heat on Jane— If you raise a single lousy fingernail to cause that kid any trouble—"

"I'm not. You know me better than that."

"I don't know nobody where my sister's concerned, pal!"

"Let go, sap," Jerry breathed warningly. His head, twisting partly aside, had given him a quick glance at two men who were hurrying toward the alcove table. Tick let go his grip instantly, faked a grin.

"Well, so long. Keep your neck in, pal."

Jerry rose, resisting the impulse to rub his aching wrist. Doctor Stoner and Hadley Brown were standing together, just back of Tracy's chair, glowering at the *Daily Planet's* columnist. Tracy wondered whether either of them had heard those last tense interchanges between himself and the moonfaced gunman.

He saw Stoner's glance and Brown's, too, move past him toward the now placid figure of Tick Anderson. Tick stared at both of them as a subway guard might stare at a couple of passengers on his car platform.

"Take it easy, Hadley," Dr. Stoner said in his suave, perfectly modulated voice. "Remember we want information, not a scene."

"Where's Gloria?" Brown growled.

"You talkin' to me, pal?" Tick replied amiably.

Again Stoner cut in with a bland murmur. His hand lifted to his gray goatee, smoothed it. He smiled patiently.

"We may be mistaken, of course, but Mr. Brown thinks and so do I, that you may be able to cast some light on the rather erratic movements of my daughter tonight."

"What makes you think that?"

Tracy was eying the back of Stoner's lifted hand. On it, clearly distinct, was the bluish outline of a small, crescent-shaped scar.

"Gloria had dinner with me at Raoul's on Park Avenue, if that's what you mean." Tracy's smile glinted mockingly toward the doctor's sullen companion. "Mr. Brown can tell you about that, I think. He was a party to the—dinner arrangement."

"Where did you take her afterwards?" Brown growled.

"She took me. We went riding in Central Park. The conversation became boring and I left her." Tracy's quiet voice got cooler. "What am I supposed to do? Follow the gal all night and turn in a half-hourly report? I think you must have me mixed up, Doctor Stoner, with some other guy. Someone that you've hired, maybe? For five grand?"

Tick Anderson sat playing with the stem of his cocktail glass. He seemed not quite interested, not quite aloof. Stoner frowned as he noted that diners were staring across from near-by tables. The restaurant orchestra blared suddenly into a noisy swing number. Under cover of the brassy din, Stoner leaned toward Gloria's fiancé and whispered an inaudible sentence. Hadley Brown shrugged, nodded. The two walked away.

Jerry Tracy let a waiter help him on with his Chesterfield and adjust the velvet collar above his silk muffler. "So long, Tick. Be seeing you—and I hope I see you first."

His gibe brought no response from Tick. Hadley Brown's sullenness seemed to have transferred itself to the heavy-featured gunman. Tick's blue eyes were sultry. After a brief, unpleasant pause, the *Daily Planet's* dapper little columnist clicked briskly through the noisy warmth of the restaurant and twirled himself out through the revolving sidewalk door.

"TAXTHI, MITHTER TRATHY?" the doorman spluttered cheerfully.

Jerry shook his head. He turned, heeled it northward along the cold sidewalk. The bite of the wind in his face felt good, seemed to wash him clean of tobacco smoke, breaded veal cutlets and jazz. The exhilaration lasted for three blocks, then he began to get cold again. It was ridiculous to think of walking all the way to Jane Anderson's flat. That was where he had decided to go—Tick or no Tick.

This was one of those damned confidential things where Jerry's police connections were of no use whatever. Jane was on the level, a good friend of Tracy's. If she knew that Jerry's life was actually in danger, she might take a hand, tell him things. She'd never betray Tick; but to imagine her sitting idly by and allowing Jerry Tracy to be sprayed into a graveyard with bullets—well, that was unthinkable.

He hailed a cab, climbed into its heated interior with a wriggle of pleasure. The taxi followed Broadway's crooked slant across town. Tracy grinned, thought of a mild little squib for the column: "Broadway—consistently crooked from Bowling Green to 103rd." A punk gag—but what the hell—you can't always be good.

He watched street lights wink past, blurred and blobby outside the frosted window of his cab. At Lincoln Square the driver swerved into Columbus Avenue and racketed expertly north under the gloomy structure of the Elevated.

Tracy paid him off at a windy corner in the Seventies. Jane Anderson lived on the top floor rear of a dismal old barracks. It gave Jerry the creeps just to look at the cheap brown varnish on her apartment door.

There was no immediate answer to his ring and he was about to push the button again, when the door opened on a hesitant crack and Jane was staring at him.

"Oh! Hello, Jerry." Her smile was quick, forced. He could see tension in the thin, sensitive lips. There was a sort of angry hangover in her eyes that he couldn't understand. "I—I never expected to see you tonight. What are you doing so far from Times Square?"

She was trying to be offhand and making a botch of it.

He grinned. "Now that I'm here, sweetheart, don't I get asked in?"

"Listen, Jerry, if you don't mind—some other time...."

A voice said with cold clarity from inside the apartment. "Mr. Jerry Tracy, eh? By all means, have him in!"

It was a cool, high soprano, edged with contempt. The familiar sound of it pulled Tracy's brows together. Gently he shoved the door open in Jane's hand, so that he could step past her and in.

There was no foyer to cross. He found himself standing in a shabby living-room, staring grimly at Gloria Stoner. She had laid aside her furred wrap and had made herself comfortable on the sofa. She was still wearing the silver evening gown, one shapely leg crossed comfortably over the other. A cigarette waved him welcome.

"How do you do?" she said, her voice a nasal mockery of Tracy's. But the cigarette gesture was jerky. Her eyes had the same angry tension as Jane's. Tracy knew that the crossed legs and the cigarette was a build up, a swift pose decided on the moment she had heard his voice outside the apartment.

He turned away as though he hadn't seen her. "I didn't know you went in for blond bims from Park Avenue, Jane. What's she doing here?"

"I sent for her."

"Why?"

Jane didn't answer.

"You're always talking about brass tacks, Mr. Tracy," Gloria said from the sofa. "How about opening a box of them right now, and sit down?"

Tracy's fingers reached out, cupped Jane Anderson's slack hand in his. She flushed under his probing stare. "I think I understand. She's here because you're worried about me. Right?"

"Yes."

"We won't mention any names because it's not necessary. You found out that somebody has hired somebody else to gun me to death. You figured that Gloria is part of the crooked setup. So, knowing how hopeless it would be to argue with—"

"Tick—isn't that his name?" Gloria interrupted spitefully. "We've been through all that before you came. Your girl friend with the blue eyes has just finished threatening my life, if I don't call off a mysterious gunman named Tick who, I gather, is her brother."

"O.K. So what are you gonna do about it?"

"Do?" Gloria rose abruptly to her feet. "I'm going to protect myself and my father. I've heard talk about blackmail and extortion until I'm sick of listening. I knew before I came here that—"

She sprang to her feet, faced Tracy with blazing eyes.

"You think I'm a fool, don't you? You think I'm a pampered, over-soft deb, and that I don't know what it's all about. Well, I do! It's plain enough to me now what I'm up against."

"For instance?"

"A wise, undersized little crook, using your newspaper prestige to hide the fact that you're a criminal racketeer. Pretending to be so damned noble, and in league with a killer and his moll. The Broadway type—a man who would sell out anything or anybody for the dirty dollars it brings. All right! Let's talk business—your kind of business!

Eying her warily, Jerry drew in a quick breath of instinctive admiration. Gloria's rage had stripped away all of her cool poise, all the sophisticated Park Avenue veneer. She was like a sinuous, vital young animal—a damned beautiful one, too.

"What's your price, Mr. Tracy? How much do you want to call off this clever hold-up of yours?"

Tracy smiled. The momentary gleam washed out of his hard, practical eyes.

"No bribes, thank you. Maybe I know about your type, too. The Park Avenue type. Everywhere you go—butlers and footmen and grafters with their palms out! Drop a little perfumed dough in somebody's palm, and no more worries, huh? As far as you're concerned, you think everybody is a butler. Well, I'm not, sweetheart, and you can't square me with a cash register!"

Sobbing, Gloria swung away from the tight-lipped columnist. Jane recoiled as the girl swished fiercely toward her, her bare arm outflung passionately.

"Jane, for God's sake, why don't you stop this—this horrible farce? You know exactly what's going on. Your brother's a gunman. Do you want him used as a stupid catspaw by Tracy? Do you want him hounded by police, arrested for conspiracy, sent to jail?"

"No, no. I—" Jane's face was ashen. She shook her head as though trying to clear it of doubt and dismay. "Jerry, are you sure that—that you—"

"Forget it, Jane. I'll talk to this dame. She's got a swell act, but there's one little question Gloria hasn't answered yet. She's going to, right now!"

With a quick gesture Gloria threw her furred wrap across the satin sheen of her shoulders. She moved regally toward the door. Tracy stepped in front of her, slightly shorter, not so rigid, but immovable nevertheless.

"Wait a second, babe. Why the big rush?"

"I'm leaving, Mr. Tracy!"

"You told me in the park that if I kept bothering you, you wouldn't kill me yourself—you'd have me killed. Remember that 'slight difference' you talked about?"

"Get out of my way!"

"You wouldn't be coming here to try to put the finger on somebody, would you, Miss Stoner?"

She slapped him stingingly across the face.

Jane Anderson cried out breathlessly, sprang toward the other woman. But Tracy, his cheek dead white except for the four red marks where gloved fingers had struck him, fended Jane away. He bowed to Gloria, stepped out of her path.

With her hand on the knob, Gloria turned. Her eyes were startlingly like her father's. The same lidded look. Then the door clicked and she was gone.

The roar of a passing El train made the floor quiver. Jane was looking at Tracy, dull incredulity in her gaze.

"Jerry."

"What?"

"Did Tick really—"

"Yeah. He did."

"My God!"

"Come over here, Jane. Let's sit down. We've got to figure this thing out some way. Did Tick tell you I was lined up?"

"He sort of hinted," Jane whispered.

Tracy nodded. "Queer guy. Funny, the cockeyed slants he has. I was talking to him a little while ago over in the Blue Grotto. He told me how glad he was he missed. And he meant it, too."

"That won't stop him from trying again."

"I know it."

The carpet was faded in front of the sofa. So were the brown curtains that hung in the doorway between the living-room and Jane's bedroom. Spotlessly clean, though, with the proud neatness of poverty. You could see where the nap was worn down from Jane's restless feet. Poor kid, she had plenty to make her restless, even after a long day on her feet at Gimbels.

"Do you think there's any truth in this stuff," she said faintly, "about bones and skull pressure and—" She picked at a loose thread on the sofa cushion.

"You mean a surgical operation? Nuts. Tick's trouble goes deeper than that. It's his way of thinking. The guy's got no imagination. He likes me as well as anyone, but if he popped me tomorrow I'd be just a tin can on a fence to him. He—well, he's just incapable of seeing that when a guy gets killed, he dies. That's as close as I can get to it. Does it make sense to you?" The rumble of an approaching El train drowned out Tracy's hesitant words. He stared dully across the room at the brown curtain in the bedroom doorway. Some wiseacre on the editorial desk had told him once that a kid run over by an ice-wagon in front of his mother was a more poignant tragedy than the end of two million anonymous Chinks in a rice famine. There was a connection with Tick somewhere.

Suddenly Tracy stiffened. He was staring at a small ominous O in the vertical gap where the brown curtains were slightly parted. He saw a gun muzzle, a gloved hand.... The muzzle was swaying infinitesimally sidewise, toward the end of the sofa. Toward Jane's averted profile....

Tracy's body moved like a steel spring. His hand clutched at Jane's arm as flame spat from the curtain fold. The grinding roar of the passing El train masked the sound of the explosion. Jane Anderson fell head-first to the floor with Tracy tangled on top of her. There was a dusty bounce against the back of the sofa as if something had slapped it.

He heard something hit the living-room carpet behind him and he whirled on his knees. The fleeing killer had tossed his weapon into the room. It was lying on the floor, a small automatic with thin grayish vapor rising from its muzzle.

A door slammed somewhere as Tracy dove for the gun. Before he could wrench the brown curtains aside he heard the distant click of a bolt. He went billowing into the bedroom, fighting awkwardly to free himself from the tangling curtain.

The door he had heard slamming was on the opposite side of the bedroom. He tried it fiercely. Locked. He flung himself against the panel a couple of times before he realized he was too small a man to break it down. With the killer's pistol still in his hand, he raced back to where he had left Jane.

She was up on her feet, the sleeve of her house dress ripped from shoulder to elbow where Jerry had clutched at her.

"You hurt, Jane?"

"N-no."

"What's on the other side of that bedroom door?"

"Bathroom and kitchen."

"Is there a fire-escape in the kitchen?"

"Yes. It's the only one there is. Did you—did he—"

"The guy made a getaway, if that's what you mean," Tracy snapped. "He's gone—powdered—on the lam." His glance moved downward to the pistol in his hand. Suddenly he gave a queer bewildered exclamation. "Here's a funny one. It's *my own gun!*"

"Yours?"

"Yeah. I lost it earlier tonight in an alley down in Greenwich

Village." He examined the weapon and found that just one bullet had been exploded. No fingerprints except Jerry's; the killer's hand had been gloved. He had meant Jerry to pick up the discarded gun; the tossing to the floor had been planned, not accidental.

Jerry shivered as his glance moved from the brown curtains to the bullet hole in the sofa. He guessed, instantly, the whole purpose of the attack. Frame-up!

He explained the frame jerkily to Jane. A girl dead; a slug from Jerry's .32 in her body; Jerry's own prints on the weapon. And a brother who loved the girl with fanatical devotion, racing to the apartment on a lying tip that Jerry had gone there to strong-arm her.

"Tick?" she gasped.

"Who else? Tick and I had an argument about you before I left him at the Blue Grotto. Stoner came up in time to hear the tail end of it. He sees his chance for a beautiful double-cross, playing on Tick's one weakness. He thinks that Tick deliberately missed that alley ambush and allowed me to get away. But if he could make Tick hate my guts, what a beautiful out for the doctor! The kill would look like a personal vendetta. Stoner's real motive would never appear—which is to wipe me out and end the threat to his blackmail business."

"But the frame-up didn't work."

"You think so?" Tracy murmured huskily. His face was toward the apartment door. He seemed to be listening while he talked. "Try and make Tick think it's O.K. when he sees my gun and the bullet hole in the sofa, and that ragged rip in your sleeve where I yanked you to the floor."

"He'll never believe me," Jane gasped.

"He's got to believe you. Sssh! Listen!"

Outside the apartment a faint thudding sound became audible; the hurrying rush of feet ascending stairs. It grew swiftly louder, approached the door. There was heavy breathing audible, then the swift rattle of the knob.

"Has Tick got a key?" Tracy breathed in Jane's ear.

"Yes."

STANDING RIGIDLY BESIDE the girl in the center of the room, Jerry waited. He had tossed his gun over to the sofa. He felt icy-cold along the spine as he heard the lock click open.

Tick's muddy-white face appeared in the doorway. The gunman's left hand closed the door gently behind him. He remained rigid, watchful, only his clouded blue eyes moving. They took stock of Tracy and his sister; noted the long jagged rip along her sleeve; swung toward the gun on the sofa and the bullet hole above it.

His own gun lifted. He began to circle sidewise.

Jane threw herself desperately in front of Tracy. "Tick! You've got to listen to me. You've got—"

"Get away from her, Tracy."

"Don't do it, Jerry. Don't move." Jane's voice was shrill, pleading. "I know what you're thinking, Tick, but it isn't true."

"The hell it isn't."

"The hell it is!" Jane retorted. Terror left her as if by sudden magic. Her words became taut, steady. Tick gaped at her, disconcerted a little. He had never seen her so coldly imperious. Not a shrinking line in her whole slender body. Jerry had wisely kept quiet. He saw that with every passing second, Tick's mastery of the situation was slipping. Tick was confused, uncertain.

"Have I ever lied to you?" Jane said. "Do you think I'd double-cross you—for Jerry Tracy or anyone else on earth?"

He said thickly, "I got eyes, ain't I?"

"It's brains you need, Tick, not eyes!" The hardness swept away from her. She made a queer laughing sound, more sob than laughter. There was impatience in it, the half-amused anger of a mother with a stubborn child. "Oh, Tick, Tick! It's so hard to talk sense to you!"

"Tracy came over here to rough you up, didn't he? He fired that gun, or maybe you grabbed it and—"

Jane shook her head. She told him in a level voice exactly what had happened. Tick blinked. When Jane talked like that, looked like that, it was the pay-off. Good enough to cash bets on.

There was a long silence. Tick put his gun away.

He said to Tracy, "Who do you think it was?"

"Are we on the same side, Tick?"

"The guy tried to kill my sister, didn't he? For —— sake, Jerry, how much guarantee do you want?"

"O.K. Who hired you to rub me out?"

"The guy was about Stoner's build. He had a black mask on that covered his whole pan when I talked to him. Spoke damn little. But he sounded a hell of a lot like Stoner. Come to think of it, so did the voice on the phone that told me to come tearin' over here."

"Where was the dough paid?"

"In a brownstone dump down in Greenwich Village. 79 Brixton Street. Same place where I blasted at you in the alley."

There was no embarrassment in his voice and none in Tracy's.

"That's what I thought, Tick. What's your idea of our next move?"

Tick's idea was simplicity itself. He was all for visiting Dr. Stoner's Park Avenue home, enticing him out to a car on some pretext, and dropping his body in a vacant lot somewhere. Queens County would probably make the best cemetery, Tick thought.

Jerry talked him out of that. Jane wasn't much help; she looked sick, forlorn. Jerry had saved her life, she had saved his. The reaction left her spent and weak.

Grimly Jerry Tracy outlined the situation as he saw it. Stoner's attack from behind the bedroom curtain had been made so swiftly that in all probability Stoner was uncertain as to whether his scheme had succeeded. He or some agent of his was undoubtedly down in the street, waiting to see if the duped Tick Anderson hurried out with a pale and terrified Jane. If that happened, it meant that Tracy was cold meat upstairs and the doctor was sitting pretty.

"On the other hand," Tracy said, his smile knifelike, "if Tick and I walk out arm in arm, it's proof positive that the frame-up failed. It means that we're both wise. Worse than that, Stoner will know that he's got to get rid of not only me but Tick. His life won't be worth a nickel from now on. He'll have to make a protecting move, and make one damn fast. And that's how we're going to take him."

Jane said tremulously from the sofa, "Promise me you won't let Tick do any—gun-work."

"Guns are out," Tracy said. "We don't want cops in on this set-up any more than Stoner does. I gave my word to a damn good friend of mine to pull him out of a blackmail hole without publicity. All I'm after is to end the doctor's graft and drive him out of town. What do you say, Tick?"

"Yeah."

They started for the door. Tick paused suddenly. He was staring at Jane, and for the first time Tracy saw fear in the man, a kind of wincing horror back of the hard blue eyes.

"We can't leave the kid here. She might be killed. I'll stick."

Tracy shook his head. "She's safer here alone. The further away we are, the safer Jane is."

"I guess you're right." He walked hesitantly toward the sofa, ran his hand for an instant through Jane's dark brown locks. He said roughly, "Keep that door locked. Get me?"

Jane nodded, didn't reply. When the door had clicked behind them, she sat motionless until the sound of their feet vanished. Then she rose suddenly.

She walked through the connecting doorway to the bedroom. By craning her neck out the window, she could see along a rear yard to the street. Beyond the edge of a fence was the black interlaced blur of the Elevated structure on Columbus Avenue. Under it, where the corner turned, a taxicab was parked.

Watching steadily, her hand braced on the cold stone of the sill, Jane saw Tracy and her brother approach the cab. Tick got in first, Tracy after him. The taxi rolled out of Jane's vision.

She drew back into the bedroom, hurried to her clothes closet. Breathlessly, she slipped out of her torn house-dress, pulled a street dress over her head. She had only one decent coat, a brown sport coat without fur trimming. It was on her in a twinkling, her brown felt hat pulled deftly over forehead and one eyebrow.

An address was as clearly in her hand as though the letters were printed on the inside of her skull. 79 Brixton Street. The place where Tick had said he had been paid his blood money.

Where the criminal father of a well-fed blonde —— Jane didn't finish framing the ugly word or the sentence.

She opened a bureau drawer, took out a small pearl-handled gun. Tick had given it to her once, made her keep it for protection, in spite of her protests that she was afraid of weapons. She slipped it with a steady hand into the pocket of the brown coat.

JERRY TRACY AND Tick Anderson raced along in the taxicab through chilly darkness. Jerry wasn't certain whether their arm-in-arm exit from the tenement had been noticed or not. A man had been buying a newspaper at the corner stand, another loitering aimlessly in the doorway of a cigar store. Just for luck Tracy gave the cab driver his penthouse address before he got inside. Gave it in a loud, clear voice.

If there were any fireworks due to start, they might as well come right now—tonight. He felt elated, wound up, tight as a clam. Beside him Tick seemed dopy, half asleep.

The taxicab swerved presently into a wide side street with a hundred foot clearance from curb to curb. Tracy's penthouse was invisible from the street, perched on a granite set-back that concealed his paved terrace and a palisade fence of split cedar that didn't look like much but had set Tracy back plenty. The roof of the apartment building seemed to scrape the stars. Tracy always felt an inch taller when he looked up at it. Not a bad dump for a little guy!

The night hallman was out at the curb, flicking open the cab's door and bowing with one motion.

"Good evening, Mr. Tracy. I have a message for you."

"When? Who from? Phone call?"

"Just a few minutes ago. From a Mr. Al Redman. A phone

call; yes, sir. I typed a memo report."

Tracy turned to his dough-faced companion, tapped him briefly on the shoulder. "Wait here in the cab, Tick. I'll be out in a minute." To the chauffeur he said with a faint grin, "Maybe I can build up your meter some more."

The switchboard alcove inside was done in marble like a chapel crypt. Tracy ripped open the envelope and read the neatly typed memo:

> Mr. Al Redman states that he is calling from a drug-store on the corner of Brixton and Varick. He would like to meet Mr. Tracy as soon as possible in the cellar of a brownstone house which Mr. Tracy knows about. The rear cellar door is unlocked. Mr. Redman said to make it quiet clear that the matter is urgent.

Tracy smiled, shoved the message in his pocket. "Thanks," he told the hallman and hurried outside to the waiting cab. His crisp order sent the taxi buzzing over to Lexington Avenue where there was an all-night drug-store on the corner.

Knowing Redman's methodical habits and the layout of his apartment, the *Daily Planet's* columnist had no hesitation in calling him at this late hour. Al always went straight to the kitchen for a snack before he retired. If he'd gone to a movie after the brownstone appointment as Jerry had advised him, he'd probably be just about home. The telephone was on a small bracket near the kitchen door. Al's quick grab would choke off the ring of the bell before it could awaken Florence in the bedroom.

Tracy's guess was good. The bell buzzed only once. Then there was a click and Al's voice whispered cautiously, "Hello?"

"Jerry."

"Thank the Lord. I've been waiting in the kitchen to hear from you. Jerry, something darned queer happened tonight. I—"

"Wait a minute. Did you try to get me on the phone a little while ago?"

"Phone? No." He sounded puzzled.

"O.K. Forget it. Did you pay the dough tonight?"

"No. That's what I want to tell you about. I got there right on time and rang the front doorbell, same as usual. Nobody answered. I rang about six or seven times. Then I left—afraid to stand there too long. I went to a movie so's not to get home too early."

"That's swell. You hop to bed now and don't wake up Florence."

Tracy hung up.

Jerry's taxicab sped down Seventh to Greenwich Village. At Sheridan Square, Jerry said "Here." He and Tick walked the five blocks down Varick to Brixton. He explained to Tick in a grim whisper.

"That phone message to the penthouse was the dumbest kind of a fake. Stoner must be pretty jittery to think I'd fall for it. We're going to call on him, but not through his conveniently unlocked cellar door. We'll try the last place he'd think of; the alley window with the burglar alarm."

Tick looked doubtful. "Won't he hear the bell?"

"Don't be a sap."

There were a couple of shivering bums hanging around the Varick Street corner, but Brixton Street was deserted, a crooked tunnel of darkness. The wooden tub on which Tracy had climbed from the alley pavement to the back parlor window was lying upended where he had left it. The window above was closed. He didn't try to raise it.

Propped darkly against the sill by the big hands of Tick, he removed the lower pane very neatly with a diamond cutter which, he told himself savagely, he should have used on his original visit.

He passed the square pane down to Tick, who laid it flat on the alley pavement. A moment later Tick was up on the sill and into the pitch-black room. They stepped cautiously toward the wall and Tracy's lips breathed a low-pitched whisper into the gunman's ear.

"Don't move. You're too heavy. I'm sneaking out that door and down the hall. Stoner's probably down in the cellar, just inside the rear door. I want to see if he's got a light on."

There was no carpet on the parlor floor but Jerry's small, expensively shod feet made no creaks. He passed through the parlor door and into the hall. It was so dark that his extended hand was invisible. He had taken barely three or four steps when he heard a queer sound from the room he had just quitted. It was a quick gasp, like the loud exhaling of air from a man's throat. Almost instantly there came to the startled columnist's ears the dull thump of a falling body.

Tracy whirled, tiptoed noiselessly back to the parlor. The room was wrapped in profound silence. It was too dark to see anything but the outline of the window. Moving with infinite care, Jerry stepped closer to the wall and approached the spot where he'd left Tick.

His foot touched Tick's ribs before he saw him. The gunman was flat on his back, his body rigid. Jerry felt Tick's face. The eyes were wide open. Yet Jerry, bending above him, running his hands over Tick, could feel no blood. Puzzled, he laid a quick palm on Tick's heart and felt it beating faintly.

Without warning something touched Tracy with numbing agony on the flesh of his neck. He fell forward, twisted, paralyzed, every muscle in his body locked with pain. He knew that the breath had sucked out of his lungs, but he was powerless to breathe in again. Too late, he realized what had happened to Tick. Electricity... the numbing shock of high voltage....

The thought burst like a pale rocket in his brain, exploded into streaky blobs of light, then the lights drifted downward, downward into darkness, carrying Tracy with them into oblivion.

BUMPING OF HIS body down a wooden staircase brought Jerry Tracy dazedly back to consciousness. Someone was dragging him callously along as though he were a sack of potatoes. His wrists were bound securely behind his back; his fettered feet went thump-thump down wooden steps to a concrete floor.

Each step hit Tracy soddenly, bruising every inch of his body. His eyes jerked open.

Bright illumination from an electric bulb showed him a low, whitewashed ceiling, wooden bins for coal, the squat pot-bellied shape of a furnace. He was in the cellar of the brownstone, alongside the similarly trussed figure of Tick Anderson.

Laughter rustled behind him. Turning his aching neck, he was able to see the tall figure of his assailant. A hooded black mask covered the man's head and face.

"Intelligence versus stupidity," the blackmailer said slowly, his voice pitched deliberately to a metallic throatiness. "You should never have locked horns with a psychoanalyst, Mr. Tracy."

It was impossible to detect in the voice any trace of the suave Doctor Stoner. But there was so strong a hint of self-satisfaction and conceit that Tracy took the cue immediately. Huskily, he called himself a sap, asked humbly for the details of his capture.

"Simple enough. I knew you had the Broadway mind, which is to say, the mind of a child. A child would check on my telephone message and discover it to be a fake. A child would assume I was waiting in the cellar. A child—or a Broadway columnist, if you prefer—would decide that a burglar-proof window would be the last place I'd think of particularly when a previous attempt had failed so dismally at that same window."

"You used electricity, of course?" Tracy said quietly.

"Naturally. House current stepped up to a paralyzing voltage by a compact device in the parlor closet. There was a chance that even in the darkness you might have noticed that the closet door was slightly ajar, but you were so convinced that I was in the cellar and so anxious to hide *your* presence, that you never thought of *mine*."

Again the slurred laugh chuckled behind the mask. "In short—"

He stopped. Whirling, his masked face jutted intently toward the cellar steps. From the floor above had come a sudden clattering sound, the crash of something overturned.

Before Tracy's opened mouth could yell, the masked man crashed the butt of a pistol against his forehead. As Tick tried to roll away the gun struck again. Both victims were hauled swiftly to the open door of a coal bin and thrown inside. The door closed. There was a faint click of a padlock, followed by a complete and sinister silence.

Lying half across Tick, his forehead warm with a trickle of blood, Tracy knew that the silence was a blanket covering the noiseless ascent of a killer up those cellar steps.

He was about to scream a warning, when again he stopped. This time his action was voluntary. In the dim half-light that trickled through the cracks of the coal bin, he saw a figure rising slowly from behind a pile of empty barrels in the corner. A girl in a brown felt hat and a brown sport coat. Her face deathly pale, a finger laid warningly across her lips. Jane Anderson!

Sobbing, she sprang at the two prisoners. A small penknife slashed desperately across their bonds. Tick waddled bear-like to his feet, caught his sister as she swayed.

"Gawd, kid, what are yuh doin' here? How did you—"

"I was afraid you might—get into trouble. I sneaked in the rear cellar door. The light was lit and there was no one in sight. Then I heard him coming downstairs and I hid in the coal bin—"

Tracy was hurling himself desperately against the padlocked door. The barrier held and bounced him backward. From the floor above came a shrill scream, the horrified cry of a woman. "Father! Help!"

Tick seemed dazed, witless in the emergency. Tracy yanked him away from Jane, snarled at him in high-pitched fury: "Quick! Kick that door down!"

The padlock held but the cast-iron hasp snapped. The door went outward in a rending crash of wood. Tick got up, his body automatically shielding his sister from the empty stairs.

Tracy went past him like a track sprinter. His .32 was a bright glitter in his hand. Over his shoulder he clipped, "Stay here! Stay with Jane!"

"No, no!" Jane cried. "Help him, Tick!"

He took the stairs recklessly, aware that he was risking death. He had recognized that scream from the floor above. The voice, vibrant with terror and horror, was Gloria Stoner's.

There was a light on in the hallway at the top of the stairs. The narrow hall led to the front of the house. As Tracy raced through he heard a faint moan from a front room. Whirling, he sprang through the doorway and threw himself sidewise with almost the same motion.

Gloria Stoner was rising dazedly from the floor in the opposite corner. Her temple and cheek were stained with blood. There was a gun in her up-flung hand and she pointed it at Tracy, her eyes shiny with madness.

The gun flamed as Tracy ducked aside. He caught at the back of a spindly chair. He felt the breeze from a bullet, heard its harsh thwack as it hit the wall above his bent shoulder. Then he sent the chair sailing across the room.

It hit Gloria's legs and buckled her backward. Before she could fire again he was on her like a panther, wrenching the hot weapon from her hand, hauling her roughly to her feet.

"Where's your father? Where is he?"

Her head rolled drunkenly under his grim tug. She was paralyzed, incapable of speech. He could hear Tick's voice, the sound of feet racing along the hall from the cellar stairs.

"Jerry, where are you?"

Jane was there, too. She and her brother stared inward from the threshold of the hall doorway.

"Did you see Stoner?" Tick roared. "Where did he go?"

"I don't know. Keep an eye on both these women. I think—"

He saw Gloria stare suddenly over his shoulder. She fainted, went slack in his arms, toppled to the floor.

Jane Anderson darted forward. "Look out, Jerry! Behind you! The kitchen door!"

It was opening slowly on a crack. Now it flew wide. Too late, Tracy saw the masked face, the level menace of a gun. Jane's arm flew out wildly as the gun flamed. She struck at the wrist, knocked it upward. The bullet smashed into the plastered ceiling.

But in the same instant, Jane Anderson caught in an enveloping clutch, was swung like a helpless shield in front of the masked gunman—and Tick's gun was blazing!

To Jerry's horror Tick's bullet struck the girl. He saw Jane slump sidewise in the blackmailer's grip. Blood stained her throat crimson. Her captor tried to hold her upright, firing from behind the limp protection of her body.

Tracy crouched backward for an instant against the wall, powerless to make a move across the line of gunfire. Tick's heavy gun jerked in his hand as he pumped bullets. He was revealed starkly for what he was, and always would be—a killer. Tracy's yell of horror went unheard in the din.

To Tracy the desperate gun duel seemed to endure for minutes. Actually, barely five seconds had elapsed from the moment the little columnist had crouched against the wall. He gritted his teeth and hurled himself forward.

As he did, the blackmailer pivoted suddenly and fired. The flash was so close to Jerry's face that he could feel the heat of it across his cheek. He caught gun and wrist, bent the smoking weapon upward between the man's shoulder blades.

Across the room Tick Anderson was standing very stiff and straight. There was a round black circle on his forehead as if a fly had suddenly come to rest there. Tick's gun clattered to the floor. As he pitched forward, his left hand started to waver weakly toward his forehead. The blind, dying gesture was never completed. Tick fell flat on his face, lay there without motion.

Tracy began to wrestle desperately for his own life. The masked man tried to twist away from the jiu-jitsu hold of the maddened little columnist. Jerry wouldn't let him. He shoved his foe's bent arm upward behind the straining back, forced it higher, higher, until a scream burst from the blackmailer's tortured lips and his gun dropped from wide-opened fingers.

Tracy clipped him savagely across the skull, sending him sliding to his knees. Again and again Tracy struck at him until the slumped blackmailer lay inert on the floor.

The room was very quiet.

For an instant Tracy remained swaying on his knees, his stomach tied in sick knots. The sight of the motionless bodies of Jane and her gunman brother snapped him out of his nausea.

He sprang hastily toward the girl. Blood from her throat dyed the columnist's handkerchief a bright crimson. His hand shook like a leaf as he dabbed at the wound. But even the hasty swab he made disclosed that the wound itself was shallow, a horizontal rip across the flesh, not a perforation.

He thought numbly: "Thank God for that."

He turned Tick Anderson over. Tick was stone dead. The bullet from the trapped blackmailer's gun had crashed into his brain. Staring at Tick's relaxed face, Tracy recalled with astonishment that last futile brushing gesture of Tick's hand as he fell. Cold-blooded, hard-dying to the last.... Tracy was glad, suddenly, that Tick was dead. He knew him clearly for what he was. Likable, good-natured—but a killer. A hopeless misfit in a world of normal, decent people.

The blackmailer began to groan suddenly. Tracy turned. He saw that Jane, too, was recovering consciousness. Her eyelids were beginning to flutter. He caught Tick by the shoulders, dragged his body out to the hallway where Jane couldn't see him.

Jane's eyes were wide, glassy. She cringed as she saw the masked figure lying close to her.

"Dr. Stoner?" she gasped. "Did he—"

"Not Dr. Stoner," Tracy said. There was certainty in his tone, a grim sureness. "Look, let me show you something."

JERRY TRACY PICKED up the slack wrist of the black-mailer, eyed the bluish scar on the back of the hand. With a sudden gesture he drew his blood-soaked handkerchief across the scar. It made a smear on the flesh, but it did something else. The scar wiped off like a picture.

"My guess," Tracy said slowly, "is that our very wise pal here is a rat named Hadley Brown."

He ripped the black mask away.

"Not a bad guess for a guy with the Broadway mind," he added harshly. His voice was brisk, purposely hard, peremptory. He wanted to keep Jane's fuddled mind from the thought of her brother out in the hall.

"It took me a while to get wise to Gloria's crooked fiancé. The thing that had me fooled at first was that Gloria and her father seemed to—" His head craned and he sprang to his feet. "Where is Gloria? Where did she go?"

There was a slow shuffling sound from the kitchen. Gloria Stoner appeared in the doorway, supporting her father. Dr. Stoner's face was pale; blood from a ragged wound in his scalp made a trickle down his face, touched his gray mustache and goatee with a fleck of crimson. Tracy shoved a chair forward and the psychoanalyst crumpled into it with a groan. But Gloria remained upright, unwinking, pale as marble.

"I found him jammed in the kitchen broom closet, where he was dragged after we were both attacked."

Her voice trembled. She was staring at Hadley Brown, at the ripped mask that lay on the floor beside him. Brown was sitting up, very quiet under the menace of Tracy's gun. His eyes were slitted, watchful.

"I rather guess our marriage is off, eh what, darling?" he jeered with a dreary attempt at jauntiness.

Gloria took the bitter shock like a thoroughbred. Turning, she said in a numb, curiously gentle voice, "Thank you, Mr. Tracy, for—the truth."

"I knew it in the cellar when he began to talk to me—in a disguised voice. It had to be either your father or Hadley Brown, because they were the only two people who knew Tick and I had quarreled about his sister in the restaurant. The blackmailer advertised the fact that he had a scar on the back of his hand. The fact that he disguised his voice to me in the cellar told me instantly he was not your father. Why show the scar and hide the voice? He was not Stoner, but Brown, coolly using his fake scar to incriminate Stoner in case he ran into trouble."

Doctor Stoner said feebly from his chair, "We came here tonight suspecting you and Tick Anderson. Gloria heard enough in Jane's apartment to let us know that the whole conspiracy was centered in this house. We entered by a window, hoping to trap you both; but I was clumsy enough to knock over a chair, and—"

Tracy was staring steadily at Hadley Brown. "I want the photostatic copies of those case histories you stole from Doctor Stoner's study."

"Go to hell," Brown snarled.

Tracy remained unruffled. "None of us wants publicity in this affair, including you. You can hand over those photostats to me or I'll call police headquarters and we'll let cops go to work on you. Think it over for sixty seconds."

Hadley Brown's hesitation was brief. His lips moved sullenly. He pointed jerkily.

Tracy sprang across the room to a sofa, threw it upside down with a quick heave. On the under side of the upholstery was a square section of cloth held in place with snapper fasteners. Tracy ripped the snappers loose and a bulky manila envelope tumbled out. Inside the envelope were the typed case histories photographed from Doctor Stoner's files—nearly two hundred sheets of thin onion-skin paper.

Tracy's voice was savagely low: "I hate like hell to turn a rogue like this loose, but if we prosecute it means agony for decent, respectable people. Tomorrow I intend to visit each one of these victims and return their case histories. If they destroy the evidence with their own hands, they'll know their secrets are safe. That will end Brown's racket forever. In the future, Doctor, I'd advise you to be more careful in your methods of guarding your medical records. You needn't worry about Brown. I'll damn well see to it that he gets out of the country and stays out."

His flinty eyes made the blackmailer quail.

"Try South America. If you ever come back, I'll arrange damn quick to have you electrocuted for murder."

Hadley Brown shrugged. In silence they watched him leave.

Jane asked faintly, "Where's Tick? He—he's all right, isn't he?"

Tracy didn't hesitate. He knew there was only one thing to do—to shock her into merciful oblivion and get her out of the house without delay.

He said curtly, "Tick is dead. He was shot to death."

"Dead?" Jane stared at the white face of the *Daily Planet's* columnist, knew that he was speaking the truth. She moaned, swayed. Tracy caught her as she fainted.

Gloria said swiftly, "We've got to get her out of the house while she's unconscious. If there's any way that we can help you—"

"Have you got a car outside?"

"Yes. It's parked down the street."

"Take Jane home with you. Keep her overnight. Feed her something to make her sleep like hell. I'll come up to your place tomorrow. By that time I'll have some plan worked out to take care of her until she gets over the shock." He blinked sweat out of his haggard eyes. "It's a tough deal for Jane, but I think I can manage her, once I get the police end of this thing straightened out. Jane's name is not going to be printed in murder headlines—or yours or your father's."

"You're pretty swell, Jerry," Gloria said.

"Hurry up. Get your father in the car. Start the motor. I'll take care of Jane."

He watched from the doorway until he heard the muffled clamor of the automobile's engine. It was very late now and Brixton Street was cold and silent, swept clear of any sign of pedestrians. Tracy was panting when he reached the car and slid Jane to the rear seat alongside Gloria.

Gloria propped the girl upright with one circling arm, let the slack head rest against her shoulder. To any prying eyes Jane would pass for a girl who had had one drink too many.

Dr. Stoner sat hunched behind the car's wheel, wiping the streaks of blood from his face with a tremulous hand.

"Are you all right now, Doctor? Can you drive?"

"Yes. Are you coming along with us?"

Tracy's grin was a tired blur. "Can't. I've got a couple of jobs yet. Scram!"

The car purred softly toward the corner, swung around it out of sight. Tracy hurried back to the brownstone house.

With a steady hand he picked up the telephone from a table in the front parlor and called police headquarters. He asked for Inspector Fitzgerald, had the call transferred to the inspector's home. He and Fitz were close friends, veteran collaborators on dozens of tough cases. Tracy said damned little, but what he did say was concise and to the point.

When he hung up he had Fitz's promise that there'd be no tip for the reporters and as little publicity as possible. Fitz knew that Jerry Tracy would drop casually into the inspector's private room at headquarters the next day and spill him the complete truth of the affair, with not a single fact held back. It was the way the two always worked. Fitz, grimly elated by the welcome news of Tick's sudden end, would keep the scandal under wraps as a routine gang feud. The public always took stuff like that for granted.

There was a bulging manila envelope under Tracy's arm as he plodded with tired steps to Varick Street to find a night hawk cab. He drove to the Forties and east to the Redman's apartment.

It was Al Redman who opened the door. It was Florence, his wife, who said quietly, "Come in, Jerry." A robe was thrown loosely over her nightgown. She took one look at the *Daily Planet's* columnist and the shuddering tension left her gaunt face.

"It's all right, Jerry?"

"Of course, it's all right." He swung angrily toward Al. "What the hell did you tell her for?"

"I couldn't hide it."

Tracy stopped glaring, patted Al's shoulder. "Sorry. I'm as edgy as a razor blade. Here, take a look at this."

He handed the bank cashier a packet of sheets from the manila envelope. Al's trembling fingers made the thin pages rustle as he flipped them over. He said thickly, "Jerry," and could say no more.

Tracy's gaze, swinging away in embarrassment, saw a portable typewriter on a desk over near the wall. The sight of it whipped the lines of weariness from Tracy's mouth. He jerked the cover off the typewriter, spun a sheet of paper around the cylinder. He sat watching it for a while and the faces of Doctor Stoner and Gloria were bright in his mind.

He hit the keys with a clattering touch that sent the carriage dinging back and forth.

Readers of this column will remember a couple of squibs I wrote about a Doctor, a Deb and a Duck. I was wrong about the Doctor, the Deb AND the Duck. The Doctor is on the up-and-up. The Deb is a square-shooter. As for the Duck, he's entitled to the last word—and it will serve me right if it's a wise-quack....

Tracy grinned bleakly, stuck the paper in his pocket. He was walking toward the apartment door, his body drooping with fatigue, when a hand turned him gently around.

"Where you going?" Florence said.

"Home, lady. I'm so tired it's not funny."

"You're doing nothing of the kind. What you need is food. I'm going to fix you the best hamburger sandwich you ever ate in your life."

"Darn you, you're a mind reader." Tracy's smile was blurred. "I'll have mine with onion."

About the Author

THEODORE ADRIAN TINSLEY (October 27, 1894–March 3, 1979) was a native New Yorker and a 1916 graduate of the City College of New York, where he edited the college magazine. After serving in Meuse-Argonne, France with the 2nd Anti-aircraft Machine Gun Battery during World War I, Tinsley briefly taught and then worked in the insurance industry. Through his brother, illustrator Frank Tinsley, Ted sold his first pulp story, "Cross Words at the Circle K," a humorous Western with a crossword puzzle theme which appeared in *Action Stories* in 1925. During the 1920s, he wrote in various genres, but started specializing in crime and mystery stories in 1932, after he had returned from an around-the-world ocean trip which included a stop in Bali.

In February, 1935, Tinsley married author and *Breezy Stories* editor Mary Ethel White at the Little Church Around the Corner in New York City. They met at a meeting of the American Fiction Guild, for which Tinsley served as National Treasurer for two years.

After scripting *The Shadow* for CBS, Tinsley was assigned to write four Shadow novels per year, which he did between 1936 and 1942 for a total of 27 stories published under the byline of Maxwell Grant. His first Shadow, *Partners of Peril*, served as the basis for the debut Batman story published in *Detective*

Comics. His second entry, *Foxhound,* was adapted for the 1938 Shadow film, *International Crime.*

His series characters include Major John Lacy in *Black Aces,* Jerry Tracy in *Black Mask,* Martin Breed in *Clues—Detective Stories* and Terry "Bulldog" Black in *Nick Carter, The Whisperer* and *Crime Busters.* Tinsley's most famous creation, Carrie Cashin, of the Cash and Carry Detective Agency, headlined *Crime Busters* and its successor *Mystery Magazine* from 1937 to 1942. His only known personal pseudonym was Reid Sleyton.

Tinsley broke into the slick magazines with a sale to *Liberty* in 1937 and continued selling to that magazine until the end of his fiction-writing days.

During World War II, Tinsley joined the Office of War Information, which led to a post-war position with the Veterans Administration, from which he retired in 1960. While at the VA, he wrote radio scripts for Bob Hope and Bing Crosby, as well as speeches for General Omar Bradley and other notables.

In retirement, Tinsley moved to his wife's hometown of Auburn, Alabama, where he died at the age of 84.

www.ingramcontent.com/pod-product-compliance
Lightning Source LLC
Chambersburg PA
CBHW021957050726
47498CB00001BB/153